CHERIE PRIEST

WINGS TO THE KINGDOM

AN EDEN MOORE STORY

TITAN BOOKS

WINGS TO THE KINGDOM
Print edition ISBN: 9780857687739
E-book edition ISBN: 9780857687883

Published by Titan Books
A division of Titan Publishing Group Ltd
144 Southwark Street, London SE1 0UP

First edition: May 2012
1 3 5 7 9 10 8 6 4 2

This is a work of fiction. All the characters and events portrayed in this novel
are either fictitious or are used fictitiously.

This edition published by arrangement with Tor Books,
an imprint of Tom Doherty Associates, LLC.

A CIP catalogue record for this title is available from the British Library.

Printed and bound in Great Britain by CPI Group Ltd.

What did you think of this book? We love to hear from our readers.
Please email us at: readerfeedback@titanemail.com,
or write to us at the above address.

To receive advance information, news, competitions, and exclusive offers online,
please sign up for the Titan newsletter on our website.

WWW.TITANBOOKS.COM

THIS BOOK IS DEDICATED TO THE TWO GROUPS I'M SURE
TO MISS MOST: MY FORMER COWORKERS AND MANAGERS AT
MARS INTERACTIVE, AND THE RESIDENTS OF THE VILLAINOUS
LAIR—PAST AND PRESENT.

To Mars,
Where I always loved the people I worked with, even when
I didn't love the work. The support, flexibility, and encouragement
have been invaluable, and deeply appreciated.
(And yes, Powell, this means you, too.)

And to the Lairmates,
Many thanks for the parties, the cons, the clothes, the cat traps,
and the company. I am endlessly grateful for the way your home
has always been a soft place to land. You and yours have always
made me feel safe.

ONE

A DARK AND BLOODY GROUND

The first time it happened—the first time anyone admits to it, anyway—was at a Decoration Day picnic being held at the battlefield at Chickamauga, Georgia. Several dozen doddering representatives of the Sons of Confederate Veterans had come together on a fine June afternoon for chicken-salad sandwiches and punch. Some sat in metal folding chairs, with their wives at their elbows, while others shuffled around the buffet table in search of the correct sliced cheese or condiment.

With so many aggravatingly credible witnesses, there was no denying that something strange had happened. People would argue the details for weeks, but this is the version I caught first. I suppose the best thing to do is tell it the local way—which is to say, this is partly how I heard it happened, and partly how I *bet* it happened.

He was confused to find himself in the woods.

Why would he leave us?

The soldier didn't remember falling in the trees, and what he did remember of trees came to him in hazy fragments of gold and red—not this dark-shadowed hollow where he first arose.

Above, the canopy was green; and below, the ground was covered with new, sprouting things. Back when last he'd seen it, this had been a field. He was nearly certain of it. This whole place had been made of fields and farms, or then again, maybe it hadn't. Maybe, if he concentrated, he could capture something else—the pressure of his arm against a tree and a squint that made his forehead ache as he leveled his rifle. How tough it must have been to fire with all those trunks in the way, with all that smoke in his eyes. How difficult to aim with all that noise in the woods around him.

How did he ever send off a single shot?

The harder he thought about it, the farther into the distance the details fled. Holding still meant holding on a few moments more, but all he could keep for sure was a dim memory of sound and smelly haze, and a nagging sense of hunger.

Beyond the trees he could hear people sounds, and they weren't the sort of sounds that warned of trouble. He homed in on the clattering of forks and the papery flutter of napkins. He dragged himself on towards the staccato hum of voices and hoped for the best.

He came up from behind the hill, walking slow and careful. The land looked so different now. Nothing familiar at all. Everything was lush and trim and tidy. He listened again, and considered the noises. They were lunch noises, or the sounds of a nice party. How strange that would be, if this place had become a garden while they slept. The more he considered it, the more likely and likeable he found the idea. It was nice to think of the green-eyed keeper as a gardener, rather than an undertaker.

A rough road headed more or less in the direction of the people, so he stumbled up to the edge and started walking.

Where did he go? Why would he leave us?

As he pulled himself along, foot over foot down the rutted strip of dirt and gravel, he considered how he might deliver his message. He didn't know what he looked like, but it was safe to guess that the years had not been kind. Time was hard enough on the living.

These people might not listen for long. They might run away before he had a chance to tell them how wrong everything had become. He'd better condense as much as possible. But how? And how to begin?

The green-eyed one, he's gone. He left us.

No, may as well leave that part out, for surely the world had noticed that much. The odds were good they were already wondering where he'd gone. For all he knew, they could even be looking for him.

Two men made a bargain.

No. Unnecessary backstory. Skip that bit. They might even figure that part out on their own, once they got the rest of it squared away. That was the key, then. Tell them enough so they could work out the rest for themselves.

Do you know that house, back at the other end of the field?

Better. Give them a starting point. Set them on the right track. Start with the house, and the field. Start with what lies behind it, and beneath it. Good. He had a plan, then.

In another time and under different circumstances, he hadn't cared much for plans; but now was as good a time as any to give organized foresight a shot. With a little more thinking, he trimmed his plan down to just two words. Two words would get things going. Two words would show them where to begin.

A huge wheeled vehicle came roaring around a curve, and he froze. He knew the sound; he'd heard it for years, always in the faraway world above. Still, it startled him to meet it so close and see the source. The thing was rounder than any cart he'd ever seen, and it moved like a train without any tracks—fast and rough over the rocky, dusty strip of road.

Behind a pane of curved glass, a pair of distorted outlines indicated people within the fast-moving car. One of them pointed, the car swerved, and the two right wheels slid off into the grass.

They saw me.

He withdrew, back to the tree line. He didn't want to frighten everyone off before he could share his brief message. If they ran away before he could speak, all this trouble would have been for nothing.

The wayward wheels crawled back onto the dirt, flinging gravel out behind them.

He watched the thing retreat. Carefully then. He would make his way to the gathering the old way, the scout's way. He hadn't been much of a scout, truth be known; but if he could watch them for a bit it might be easier to approach them. It might be easier to speak to the group if he knew what sort of people were in it.

He stumbled and caught himself, wincing with the effort; but the wince was more a habit than a physical reaction. Nothing hurt, exactly, but tremendous concentration was required to pull himself together. Holding everything in one piece, it was like flexing a muscle—not quite so hard or short-lived as holding in a breath of air, but not so easy that he could keep it up for long.

His fingers crushed themselves into a fist, driving his dirty-looking nails into his palm. He barely felt it. He had to watch himself squeeze the knuckles tight or else he wouldn't have believed it. Nothing felt like anything. Something told him that if he ran his head into the nearest oak, it wouldn't matter to either the tree or his skull.

A loud, sudden laugh from the nearby party reminded him why he was doing this.

Find someone to tell.

Forget the rest. Hold it together long enough to talk.

Between the branches he spied a flapping white tablecloth trimmed with red and blue. A stray napkin swayed to the grass, and a high-heeled shoe stabbed it into the earth. An older woman in a powder-blue suit bent her knee and plucked the napkin away. She turned to a man beside her and accepted a very thin plate loaded with brightly colored food. Behind them, there were twenty or so rows of chairs lined up neatly, and most of these chairs were occupied by other people with similar plates of food.

If he could read, then the banner hanging over the gathering might have told him something helpful, or then again, it might have only confused him. He wondered what it said. One word looked familiar; it was a long word beginning with a "C." He felt he ought to recognize it, but he didn't; so he decided not to dwell on it. Letters had never been his strong suit.

It didn't matter, anyway. He'd found the party he was looking for, and they were a promising bunch of folks. They were older, so some of them were bound to be respectable; but they were not so old that others wouldn't take them seriously.

The longer he watched, the more certain he became. Yes.

These people would listen. He skirted the edge of the clearing, darting from tree to tree, drawing closer, trying to see their faces.

One man in particular looked like a promising contact. He had a certain leanness in his cheeks, and a slouch that struck the ghost as being familiar in some unspecific, mostly forgotten way. This man was standing beside a woman with bright blond hair that sat immobile on her head like a round yellow crown. She scratched at her wedding ring and tugged at her cuff while the thin-faced man talked to two other men.

The lurking shade closed his eyes and thought hard, willing his form as close to solid as he could come. He forced himself to recall as much detail as he could, conjuring up the dull gray jacket and with it the tarnished buttons, the shapeless pants, and his badly battered cap.

When he was dressed, and when he was as ready as he could make himself, he stepped forward into the sunny patch of grass.

At first, no one noticed.

He was still a few yards from the group, so he drew himself closer to them, nearer to the one who had caught his attention. The ghost moved with care, so as not to startle them. He fixed his eyes on the thin, casually slumping man with the bored-looking wife and pulled himself towards the neat forest of metal chairs.

The wife spotted him first.

He knew she saw him—she froze her idle scratching and polite, agreeable nodding to stare directly at him. The ghost paused, not wanting to frighten her into a scream.

To her credit, she did not cry out. Her eyes widened and her head cocked to the right, but she lifted her hand to her lips and covered them up as if she wasn't sure what might pass through.

"Evan," she breathed between her fingers.

"Dear?" her husband answered fast from the middle of his conversation. He dropped the syllable without looking at her.

"Oh, Evan, "she repeated, this time reaching out to touch his arm. "My God, but look at him. "

"What?"

"Look at him. Look at him, Evan. Doesn't he look like—"

Evan sighed and turned from his group. "Look at *who*, darling?"

"*Him.* "

The figure in question stretched himself up to his full height, and held up his chin. He assumed a stance of formal attention and waited.

Throughout the gathering, all the small conversations dried up and all the happily chatting faces went limp. Evan dropped his plastic glass. It toppled to the grass with a splash and a thud, spilling purple punch across his new shoes—though he wouldn't notice the stain for days.

Satisfied that he had everyone's full, undivided attention, the ghost opened his mouth. But no sound followed. Frustrated, he closed his mouth and opened it again.

Still, nothing.

Just two words, he swore to himself. *Why can't I say it?*

He shook his head and tried a third time, but he couldn't utter a single, raspy gasp. It made him angry: all that preparation, all that effort, and all that trouble, and here he was, right where he'd meant to go, but he couldn't tell them a damn thing. And to make things worse, he could feel his hold slipping. It would not be long before he lost control over the people's shocked silence and his own physical form.

No words, then. Quickly. Before the moment had time to pass.

He raised his right arm and pointed, as hard as he could. He aimed his hand across the pretty clearing, and beyond the trees beside it, and over the creek and through the fields of waving green grass to a point that no one could see.

And then he disappeared.

TWO

TWO STEPS BACK

I bet myself a dollar that he'd pull a picture out of his wallet within fifteen seconds of introducing himself. I only won fifty cents from that wager: he pulled it from his jacket pocket instead.

"Eden? I'm Gary. This is my little girl. Her name's Casey."

"She was beautiful," I replied, contradicting his verb choice.

If he noticed, he didn't bother to correct me. "Yes."

The man thumbed at the photograph in a sad sham of removing a smudge. He dug the pads of his thumbs into the glossy the way they all do—as if, should he rub hard enough, he might thrust his way through and find flesh beneath the paper.

"It's been over a year."

"I'm sorry, Gary." I'd learned it was best if I began apologizing early on in these conversations. Things sometimes went more smoothly if they'd grown accustomed to hearing it by the time I had to break their hearts.

Gary put the picture down on the round, marble-top table between us and smoothed it with his palm. "No, I'm sorry. You

15

were just trying to have a cup of coffee and I'm bothering you."

I put my mug down and closed my book. "It's okay."

"I guess you get this a lot, don't you?"

"Yeah," I admitted. *And it never gets any easier.*

He dragged his attention away from the photo. At least he looked me in the eyes when he said the next part. "I was hoping you could help. Is there any way you could talk to her for me? I just want to know she's all right."

Sometimes they don't ask so directly. Sometimes they're so torn between being desperate and being ashamed that they stare at their hands, or at the floor. It's all they can do to mumble their plea, and they often try to phrase it as though they can't imagine I might say yes in a million years… because God knows they don't believe in that sort of thing, anyway.

But just in case, they have to ask.

"I would be…" I stalled, and started again. "I would love to help you, but I don't think I can. And it's not because I don't want to, because I do. But—"

He cut me off there, and he lifted a brown satchel into his lap. "Oh, I know you need information, and I've brought it. I've got all the newspaper clippings from her kidnapping, and I've got the follow-up articles about the guy who did it; and I don't know how this works exactly, so I brought some of her things for you to touch if that helps."

"Gary—"

"I've got her first tooth, too." Out from the bag he lifted a blue plastic container on a cord. "She got a dollar for it. It's clean, don't worry. It's a couple of years old now. Here."

I didn't object fast enough. He clasped my hand in his and the tiny pebble tooth toppled down. I closed my fingers to keep from dropping it.

"Let me try to explain, please. I need for you to understand."

He nodded hard, nearly shaking his glasses loose.

I took a deep breath.

"One time, when I was in high school, we had a new guy join our class. The teacher made him stand up and tell everyone who he was and where he was from. His name was Jake, as it turns out, and he'd transferred to our school from Texas.

"This one girl sitting behind him got all excited when she heard the 'Texas' part. When he sat down, she poked him on the shoulder and told him, 'I've got a cousin who lives in Texas. Her name is Amy Abernathy. Do you know her?' And everyone laughed at her." I stopped there, seeing if he'd pick up the prompt.

"I bet they did. That was a pretty stupid question." Gary fidgeted and picked up his daughter's picture, fussing with it again.

"Well, under different circumstances it might not have been so dumb. Say, maybe her cousin mentioned someone with the same name as the new guy. It would be a coincidence if it turned out they knew each other, but it wouldn't be a miracle or anything. Right?"

"Right," he said, but his heart wasn't in the agreement. I think he knew where I was headed.

"Or maybe if she was from another country, and she didn't understand that Texas is a huge place with millions of people in it—then it wouldn't be such a crazy question for her to ask either. Maybe, for all she knew, Texas was no bigger than a city block."

"But it is. Much bigger."

"Yes, it is." I put the little tooth back into its case and pushed the case back to Gary's side of the table. "Do you get what I mean?"

He tapped a fingernail at the tooth case for a few seconds,

trying to decide how best to argue. "But being dead isn't like being in Texas," he finally said, and I could hear stubbornness working its way into his voice.

"You're right, it's not."

"Then why won't you try to talk to Casey for me?" He said the words slowly; he needed time to fortify each consonant against whatever I might say next.

"Gary, if Casey were in Texas, I would know where to begin looking for her. I could drive out there—I could look her up in the phone book. But imagine, for a second, that she could be anywhere at all in the entire world. But wherever she is, there aren't any phones, and no matter how loud I shout, she won't hear me."

"Eden—"

"And for that matter, there's a better-than-average chance that she's not even here anymore. Listen—when most people die, they don't hang around. I don't know where they go, and I don't know how far away it is, but it's someplace that's... well, it's not *here*."

"But *some* of them stay. You know they do. You've seen them."

"Yes, some of them do. And the ones who do are free to make contact with me if they like, but I don't have the foggiest idea how to bring them around. Do you understand?"

Clearly, he did not. "But you could *try*. You could ask around, or something. If you really wanted to."

"Ask around? Gary, now we're right back to the Texas analogy. Let me ask you something, and I am asking in all seriousness—without any intention of making fun of you."

"Go ahead."

"Have you prayed to Casey at all? And I'm using the word 'pray' in the very broadest sense—I mean, have you tried to talk to her yourself?" I already knew he had. Of course he had. They always do. I think it's part of the "bargaining" stage of grief.

"I wouldn't say I've been praying to her, but I've asked… if she might come have a word with me."

"And you've never heard, or felt, or seen anything to indicate she heard you?"

"No. But that's why I came to you."

I took another deep breath, and then a third. I was getting frustrated with this poor man, and I knew that we were coming to a point in our conversation where he was only going to try my patience more. "Why would it be different if I tried to call her? You're her father, and I'm a total stranger. I don't believe that she could hear me any better than she can hear you."

"But you could see her if she *did* come. Couldn't you? And I can't."

"I think that probably, yes, I could see her if she answered you. But I also think that you'd get some sense of her presence too. Or maybe not, I don't know. What I'm trying to tell you is this, Gary: unless she's standing beside you right this second, there's no way at all for me to communicate with her."

He dropped the tooth container into his satchel and clutched the picture with both hands. "She isn't, then? She's not here with me?"

I could have fed him a line about how she was always with him in his heart, but such a trite sentiment would have only made us both angry. He wanted to know if his daughter was with him still—in a literal, if intangible, sense. We both knew the answer already, but someone had to say it out loud. That was the real reason he'd tracked me down.

I tried to say it gently. "If Casey were still here and she knew you were trying to reach her, she'd stay close to you. She was a daddy's girl, right?" It was an easy guess.

"Oh yes." He was crying now, fat and quiet tears.

I pushed my napkin against his knuckles, and he took it. "And if she needed something, or if she was in some kind of trouble, you'd be the go-to guy, wouldn't you?"

He pressed the napkin to his face and bobbed his head.

"You said you came here because you wanted to know if she was all right. Well, I think it's safe to assume that she is. If she wasn't, she'd be trying to tell you. But she's not trying to communicate, at least not that I can see."

The mug-sized square of ephemeral coffeehouse napkin proved no match for Gary's grief, so I fumbled for my purse and managed to scare up a couple of proper tissues.

"You're not even going to try then, are you?" he sniffled, stuffing the picture back into his jacket pocket. "Is it because I didn't offer you any money? I don't have much but—"

"Money? I didn't ask you for any money."

I felt like I was sitting in the front car of a roller coaster, and cresting that first big hump. *Here we go.* Once money's come up, there's nothing I can say or do to keep the talk from plummeting downhill. This is always the hardest part, and it always makes me angry, because it hurts my feelings.

"Of course you didn't. Because then it would be extortion, wouldn't it? That's why all the TV commercials for the psychic lines say in the small print, 'for entertainment purposes only.' That way, if they're wrong you can't sue them. But you pretend to be the real thing—you're like one of those escort service girls who acts like no money needs to change hands in order to get results. I get it. I see."

Ah, now we were rolling. Which to get defensive about first—

the implication that I was a fraud, or the comparison to a hooker?

And I know, I know. The man was in pain, and he came to me seeking some comfort. I should have forgiven him for his misdirected anger; I should have been tolerant of his agony, and forgiven his terrible manners for his loss. I should have tried to help him. For what it's worth, I *did* forgive him. And I *was* tolerant. And I *did* try to help him. Yet for all that, I was still just a lying whore because I wouldn't tell the man what he wanted to hear.

I folded my hands around my coffee cup and sat back in the ironwork chair. "First of all I have *never,* not even once, claimed to be a medium. On the contrary, I've spent the last year of my life hiding—rather unsuccessfully, it would seem—from people like you who want to assign me that title. And second, I wouldn't take your money if you threw it at me. If I could help you, I would—and I'd do it for nothing. But I can't. I'm sorry for your loss, but there's nothing I can do for you. If you're not okay with that, you need to leave."

He stood to leave, still crying. Still grasping my tissues.

I exhaled my entire collection of deeply drawn breaths as the door closed behind him.

Similar scenarios had played themselves out so frequently that I'd given up hope for a different ending. Sometimes it took longer for the bereaved to go from grief-stricken and vulnerable to wishing that I, personally, were dead, but the end result was always the same.

And I don't know how they find me—it's not like I put an ad in the paper. Maybe they track me down through online rumors, or my name is written on a bathroom wall somewhere. I wonder sometimes what the gossip says. Does it mention me by name? There has to be more to it than "Biracial Southern girl chats up dead people. Come visit the Scenic City and see if you can sucker her into a reading."

If I could find it myself, I'd delete or wash away every word.

My coffee had gone tepid. I wandered over to the counter and talked someone into trashing it in the sink for me, then reclaimed the cup for a fresh hit of caffeine.

Behind me, the glass door swooshed open again, and I heard the electric hum of a familiar wheelchair. As usual, the sound of the chair was shadowed closely by four paws clapping on the tile floor.

"Hey, Karl," I said over my shoulder as I pumped myself a refill from the air pot on the counter. "And hey, Cowboy," I added towards the shaggy brute beside him. I finished my top-off and reached for the creamer.

Karl joysticked himself up to me so that his floppy, feathered cowboy hat hovered beside my shoulder. His diligent sheltie sidekick assumed a politely seated position on the floor.

"You've sure got a way with people." He grinned. "You make 'em cry faster than that Barbara Walters woman."

"Thanks. I think." I grabbed a brown plastic stirring stick and swirled my beverage until it turned a uniform beige. I faced him then, leaning my rear against the counter. "And what brings you two old coots downtown today? Anything special?"

"Just you, beautiful. I've got a weakness for brunettes, you know." He winked and wiggled his graying mustache at me.

"And blondes. And redheads." I reached down and tugged at the brim of his hat, winking back without any real mirth. "And I bet you say that to all the girls who chase people out of the shop in tears."

His laugh was a rough, low sound that managed to carry a

Southern accent even without any vowels. That man could clear his throat in a thunderstorm and you'd be able to hear he was a local.

"You've got me there. But I mean it—I was hoping you'd be out and about. Join you at your table?" He and Cowboy were already halfway to Gary's freshly vacated spot, and I wouldn't have told him no anyway. Instead, I pulled the seat out to make room for his chair and kicked my purse under the table so Cowboy wouldn't have to lie on it.

"You want some coffee?"

"Got some." He waved a foam to-go cup with one hand and a newspaper with the other. "Have you looked at today's paper?"

"Not likely. Haven't needed to line any litter boxes since this morning."

He snorted, and Cowboy's ears perked, then settled again. "Then I guess no one else has showed you yet."

"Showed me what?" I asked as a matter of formality, but just as I'd known that Gary would have a photograph on him, I might have known that Karl would have a ghost story. If he hadn't been holding the newspaper, I'd have guessed he'd come to me bearing a new bad joke. Not a dirty or off-color joke, just a *bad* joke—one that would take at least ten minutes to wend its slow, painful way to a punch line.

"This article about what happened at the battlefield over Decoration Day."

I like Karl's jokes better than his ghost stories, but it was nothing personal, and it had nothing to do with his easygoing narrative style. It's like I said once before about there being no such thing as old news in the South. Likewise, there is no such thing as a private matter.

On the Internet someplace there's a list of things you'll never hear a Southerner say. I've seen it, and I think it's funny—though I'd love to add in the phrase "But it was none of my business, so I didn't ask." News or a damn good story will always find its way out, so ever since the whole mess with Malachi I've been a lightning rod for spooky anecdotes.

All of that having been said, by the time Karl showed me the article I had heard no fewer than a dozen versions of the Decoration Day incident at the Chickamauga Battlefield.

The story made the rounds in the valley with a speed that would shame a wildfire. Of course it expanded with each retelling until the saga came to include a regiment of skeletal Union ghosts, a couple of soldierless spook horses, a bloody-headed drummer boy, and at least two bugling wraiths who foretold the imminent rebirth and rise of the Confederacy.

So you had to understand my skepticism.

"You just look right here—they hid it on the third page, but it made it in all the same." Karl unfolded the *Times Free Press* and sorted it out, seeking a certain picture and finding it. He bent the third page double, nudged my coffee cup out of the way, and pushed the paper forward.

"'No Leads Yet in the Disappearance of Ryan Boynton.'"

"No, not that one." He tapped the paper, down below the headline I'd just read.

"'Mystery at Battlefield Park,'" I tried again, and he approved. "Sounds like a Nancy Drew title."

He patted at the columns with two long, bony fingers. "Go on and read it. Look what it says about Decoration Day."

"'The first unusual incident took place at a Sons of Confederate Veterans gathering, attended by nearly sixty people who claimed

24

their picnic was visited by a ghost. According to eyewitnesses, the specter of a young soldier approached the group and tried to speak, but he seemed unable to communicate. Before he vanished, the ghost pointed at the woods.

"'One witness, Edna-Anne Macomber, insists that the soldier bore a strong resemblance to her husband at the age of twenty—prompting speculation that the unexpected visitor may have been her husband's great-uncle. "He had the same-shaped face, and the same way of standing. You could've knocked me over with a feather when I saw him there. He looked right at us," Mrs. Macomber claims. "And he knew it too. That's why he chose us, I think. He knew Evan when he saw him."

"'Jeremiah Macomber fought with the Deas Brigade for the 19th Alabama regiment. He died in the Battle of Chickamauga on the first day of fighting, September 19, 1863.'"

I put the paper down and shrugged. "That wouldn't be too surprising, I guess. Maybe that *is* what drew old Jeremiah out in the first place—he spotted the family resemblance."

Karl got all excited. "You think it's true? You think some old soldier crashed the picnic?" He shifted around in his chair and gripped the brim of his hat with glee.

"I can't say it'd shock me." I tried and failed to remember a few details from a long-ago school trip to the battlefield visitors' center. "How many people died out there, anyway?"

"A *lot*." He beamed.

"I should've paid better attention in history class. But we know that a *lot* of people died under violent and painful circumstances. I'd be astounded if there *weren't* any ghosts out there."

"But you don't hear a lot of ghost stories about the battlefield. You get stories about Old Green Eyes instead."

"Yeah," I said, though that fact was something I'd always found strange. Thousands and thousands of dead soldiers are buried in the park, and most of the scary stories passed around campfires were about a made-up monster instead of the logical legions of war dead.

Karl must have been thinking the same thing. "There's a couple of stories about the tower in that field, and there's one or two about weeping widows roaming the grounds looking for their husbands; but for the most part Green Eyes gets all the good lines."

"The villain always does."

"Now *that's* true. I wonder why?"

I tossed my head to the left in half a shrug. "I couldn't tell you."

"Do you believe in him?" he asked, leaning forward. I'd given him an inch, and here he came chasing after me for a mile.

A year or two before I might have said no, but I'd had my horizons broadened a bit since then. "I don't know. I've talked to people who'd swear on their mothers' graves they'd seen him, but that doesn't mean anything. One of them was Mike, for God's sake."

"Mike's the one who got drunk and fell off the roof of the library?"

"That's him," I confirmed. "He was trying to prove he could rock-climb at three in the morning. He used to live out by the battlefield, in the subdivision on the other side of the train tracks. You know—there on the edge of the park. Mike and his brother have a million and one Green Eyes stories, but since most of them start off with a case of beer I'm not inclined to take them very seriously."

Karl tapped the paper again. "But *this*—this looks like something you could sink your teeth into, doesn't it? This is the sort of thing that you could maybe confirm, at least some of the little details."

"Maybe." I crooked my neck and examined the picture posted beside the story. The square black-and-white frame held a shot of a starry-eyed older woman with her arms crossed beneath her breasts. Edna-Anne, I gathered, even before I checked the caption. "I wonder if there are any pictures of this Jeremiah guy? Something you could show people for comparison's sake. If Edna-Anne could pull him out of a line-up, that'd be something."

"There might be pictures, there might be. And if there are, you can bet Tripp and Dana will dig them up."

I started to ask who he meant, but the answer dawned on me before I could broach the question. "The Gruesome Twosome? Are they coming here to look into this? Oh, good *grief.*"

"What?" He brushed his hand to his chest in pretended affront. Then he said exactly what I should have expected from someone who'd never left the valley. "But they're *famous.* And I hear that the people at the battlefield actually asked them to come out and look into this. Rumor has it, they're going to bring all that fancy equipment and set up for a few nights. Taking pictures, and getting readings and things."

"They must be working on another book."

Dana and Tripp Marshall were such well-known ghost hunters that even I had heard of them. Their shtick had a one-two punch: she had left an engineering career with NASA, and he was a psychic who claimed to have worked for the FBI. Their first taste of notoriety came courtesy of an old episode of *Unsolved Mysteries,* and since then they'd made the rounds of every niche cable show and prime-time paranormal investigative special on the tube.

"Did you ever read *They Speak from Beyond*? That thing scared the pants off of me."

"I missed that one," I halfway lied. I had picked it up from a display in a bookstore and made it through a couple of chapters before putting it down. I didn't like the feel of it; the authors were trying so hard to sell the audience on the phenomenon that I wondered if they believed anything they were saying.

People who already believe simply *know,* and they don't feel compelled to proselytize. People who *know* tell their stories like Edna-Anne Macomber, with a simple certainty that doesn't much mind if it's mocked.

"But why would they come *here*?" I asked. "Famous ghost hunters with a Civil War fetish usually go to higher-publicity fields like Gettysburg or Manassas. We don't have ghost stories at Chickamauga, remember? And Old Green Eyes, whatever he may be, isn't usually good enough fodder for big shots like the Marshalls."

"Finish the article." He grinned like a maniac. "Something new is going on down there."

"Karl, nothing *new* has happened down there in a hundred years." But even as I argued, I scanned for the place where I'd left off. "Well, all right. I stand corrected. 'Since the Memorial Day incident last week, a dozen new sightings of pointing ghosts have been reported. Though descriptions vary, the encounters are all similar. Witnesses say that the ghosts either appear in front of them or approach them, and then point at a distant location before disappearing.'"

He barely let me finish. "You know what I heard? I heard that a couple of the park rangers were so freaked out they quit their jobs."

"Did you hear this from the same source that told you the Marshalls were coming?" I asked, reading the dull concluding paragraph to myself and handing the paper back to him.

"No, I heard it elsewhere. My doctor's son had an internship out there, and he dropped it yesterday because he was too scared to keep going to work. And one of the guys who works here"—he jerked his head towards the barista counter—"his sister is married to one of the guys who keeps the grounds. I'm telling you, strange things are going on out there. You'll see—they won't be able to keep it page-three quiet for long, not at this rate. Before long, everyone's going to know about it and they're going to have to do something."

I tried not to laugh, in case he would have taken it the wrong way. "And what precisely would you recommend that 'they' do, anyway? These guys are dead. There's not a whole lot to threaten them with if they don't want to leave."

"I'm not saying they should be threatened, my dear. But it sure would be nice if there was someone hanging around who could just walk up and ask them what they wanted. That's all I mean."

"That's what Tripp and Dana are for. Let the celebrities handle this one. I only talk to my own dearly departed kin, if I can help it." I felt a damp tickle down near my ankle, and I nearly kicked with surprise. Cowboy was sniffing at my pants leg. I reached down and scratched at his head.

"Woman, haven't you got a curious bone in your body?"

"I've got a couple hundred of them," I assured him. "With change to spare."

"Then why not go on out there? Just take a look around and see what there is to see? You never know—you might be able to help those poor folks who can't seem to rest."

I could have handed him one reason for each guilty, curious bone, but I only offered him the most pressing one. "That guy who was leaving when you came in a few minutes ago. Did you see him?"

"Yeah, I did." He said it with the exact same inflections as the speaker in the old Ray Stevens song about the streaker.

"Didn't look happy, did he?"

"No ma'am, he didn't."

"Do you know how he found me?"

Karl shook his head.

"Neither do I. But he's the second one this month, and I've got to tell you, Karl, I really, really hate it when they find me. There's nothing I can do for them, and feeling sorry for them only makes them mad."

I found myself flailing for something to fidget with, and spotting my coffee stirrer, I picked it up. I twisted it around my index finger. "I don't want any more weird presents of baby teeth, or friendship bracelets, or tiny lockets with a first snipping of hair. It's awful—and it's not getting any less awful as they keep on coming."

"That's probably a good thing."

"From a moral perspective, sure. But from a personal standpoint, it sucks—and I want it to stop. Or, at the very least, I'd like to keep it at a slow trickle. You don't…" I paused to reconsider my phrasing. "You should see their faces. There's this split second when they figure out all at once that I'm not going to tell them what they want to hear."

I swallowed, and stuffed the coffee stirrer into my mouth, pinching it between my teeth. "And you realize, don't you, that if I were to get mixed up with these high-profile spook hunters, it would only get worse."

"I get it. A whole lot worse, maybe."

"Maybe." We both sat quietly for a minute, him fussing with the paper's corner and me nibbling the small brown straw down to a frayed, flattened bit of trash. "Sometimes I think maybe I ought to leave, and go someplace where people don't know about me at all. It might be easier. Or better. I don't know."

He reached around the table and patted at my knee. "Aw, don't say that. The brain-drain around here is bad enough; we don't need all the beauty leaving the valley, too. But you know, you wouldn't have to get involved with those two old crazies if you didn't want to. You could still poke around a little, see what's up for yourself."

"Or for you?"

"Or for me, sure. You're always welcome to go exploring for *me*. I'd love to sneak on out there myself, but these days…" He stopped and caught himself before the words went slow or sad. He laughed instead, slapping at the arm of his chair. "These days I'd need one hell of an extension cord, wouldn't I?"

"A cord, or a jet pack strapped to the back of that thing. You could run down Old Green Eyes and ask him yourself what's going on out there."

He laughed harder then, and Cowboy's tail thumped an optimistic beat against my shin. "A jet pack! And maybe a couple of pairs of roller skates for Cowboy so I could pull him along behind me—but then again, he'd probably just ride in my lap like a big baby. You should've seen him at the Riverbend fireworks this year. He spent the whole thing with his nose buried under my arm. Oh, hang on—I've run dry. Let me grab a refill." He took his foam cup in one hand and gripped the wheelchair's joystick with the other and swiveled himself away from me.

Despite the fact that Karl's destination was less than six feet away, Cowboy took it upon himself to rise and dash after him.

While Karl busied himself at the counter, pumping on the

air pots, I fiddled with the newspaper. He was right, and it was a damn good story.

I checked the last paragraph again and failed to see any mention of Tripp and Dana Marshall, so there was still hope that Karl's sources had been incorrect on that final point. I didn't have a solid reason to dislike the Marshalls so hard sight unseen, but that didn't stop me. I hated the thought of them coming to Chattanooga, bringing their cameras and spotlights and publicity crews.

Interacting with ghosts was something to be done quietly, and in private if possible—or so I liked to think. As awkwardly as I sometimes handled my strange abilities, I tried to take them seriously; and it made me uncomfortable to watch others treat my poorly guarded secret like a well-paying parlor trick.

Then again, my reservations may have been as simple as an old-fashioned distrust of outsiders. But if rumor proved true and they were on their way, I would get my chance to see if my suspicion was warranted.

THREE

HOME SWEET

"Professional jealousy, that's what it is," Dave joked.

"I beg your pardon?"

My uncle turned up the volume on the television, that we might better hear the news. It was all over the local affiliates, which was funny for an investigation that was ostensibly hush-hush. A skinny blond anchorwoman repeated the Marshalls' vow to "get to the bottom of things."

"Disdain, perhaps—but never jealousy," I corrected. "It's revolting, the way they capitalize on things like this."

"Revolting?" Lulu tapped me with her hip as she squeezed by, carrying a tray of nachos. She set the heaping snacks on the coffee table and went back towards the kitchen. "That's a strong word for it. They're some kind of scientists, aren't they?"

"Yeah, and I'm Big Bird."

Lu took a bite of a chip loaded with beans and jalapeños, chewed it, and swallowed without flinching. "I don't know. You might be. I'm surprised at you, really. I'd think you might be warm to the idea of having someone else in town for the crazies to talk at. For that matter, it might do *you* good to have someone to talk at."

"Speaking of being talked at, it happened again today." I reached past her to pick up a handful of chips that seemed mostly devoid of hot peppers, and I took a nibble. I winced, even though only the barest trace of pepper juice hit my tongue.

I might have said more about it—I might have told them about Gary and the tooth—but Dave flashed me a look that made me think better of it. He rose and headed towards the kitchen, and I followed him.

He opened the refrigerator door and stood inside the patch of dim light and cold air. "Something else happened again today too," he said quietly, and not happily.

"Dare I ask?"

"Do you have to?"

I wasn't sure how to respond. It was one of those moments where I didn't know what I'd done to perturb him, and I didn't want to start confessing to things until he gave me a hint. I cycled through a mental checklist of things he might scold me for, but I couldn't come up with anything he may have caught me doing.

He looked over the fridge door, checking to make sure Lu was still in the living room. We could both see her feet, propped up on the coffee table beside the plate of chips. I watched Dave decide that the coast was as clear as it was going to get.

"Someone called for you," he said. "It was some guy who claimed he was a friend of Harry's."

"Oh. What did he want?"

"To talk to you, I imagine. It's the third time this month the same guy has called. Is there anything you feel like you ought to tell me, kid?" He leaned on the door, eyes still holding the partial scene in the living room.

"No," I said in perfect truthfulness. I most certainly did *not* want to tell him that I'd warned Malachi to quit calling my cell phone, and that it now appeared the bastard was obeying the letter of the command, if not the spirit.

"Eden, are you in some kind of trouble? Because if you are, you can tell me, and if you want, I'll keep it quiet."

"Dave, I appreciate the offer, but I am not in any trouble whatsoever—not to the best of my knowledge." Again, I answered with pure honesty. "I'll call down to St Augustine tomorrow and ask Harry what's up. I'm sure it's no big deal. If something was wrong I'm sure my mystery caller would have left a message."

This too was true, though I also planned to give Harry full permission to beat Malachi senseless the next time he thought about phoning.

"What are you two doing in there?" Lu hollered.

"Where's the sour cream?" I shouted back.

"We're out. But there's some salsa behind the milk. Grab that and some napkins—and come back in here. Let's start this movie, already."

I reached around Dave to seize the salsa and the opportunity to flee, before he could interrogate me further.

So far as anyone officially knew, my half-brother and cousin Malachi was dead—murdered by the crazy old man who had lived at the clapboard house in the swamp. Not much in the way of remains had survived the fire, but I'd insisted with great fervor and earnestness that he'd been there in the hopes that it would keep the cops from trying to locate him elsewhere. In retrospect, I'm not entirely sure why I went to such lengths to protect him, but that's how family works sometimes. Even when they don't deserve it, you cover their asses.

Maybe I should have told Lu and Dave what really happened down in Florida, but I hadn't, and I couldn't imagine a situation where I could bring it up. I didn't want to have to defend myself to them—and I would certainly have to, if I came clean—until I had a better excuse than "It sounded like a good idea at the time."

Malachi wasn't exactly making it easy for me.

He'd called my cell phone every week until I finally switched it out for another model with a new number. The new number hadn't stopped him though. I don't know how he got it, but he did, and he called it like clockwork. About one time out of every four I'd answer, and we'd verbally hopscotch through an awkward, meaningless conversation that served no purpose other than to make us both uncomfortable.

He'd sometimes hinted that he wanted to come up here, but I kept telling him not to.

"Let things die down," I'd tried to tell him. "Give it a year or two. Then we'll meet up someplace in Georgia and do lunch, if that's what you want." But he always wanted more than lunch. He wanted a family.

I bet he was driving Harry nuts. But that's what the old guy gets for taking Malachi down there to St Augustine. If Harry'd had any sense, he would have left my brother for the cops; instead, he let me talk him into taking Malachi to Florida and hiding him in the monastery there.

But that night I tried to put them both out of my head, because I had nachos in the living room, Lu and Dave on the sofa, and *Young Frankenstein* in the DVD player. Everything else could wait.

✳ ✳ ✳

The next day, Lu and Dave drove down to Athens, Georgia, to catch a concert. I ordered them to make a romantic weekend of it, but they were way ahead of me: hotel reservations and a room service menu had already been secured. I was a little surprised by my relief at learning that they'd be gone for so long; or perhaps I was only glad to know that they were far enough away that I could make a phone call in peace.

The call itself began easily enough. I dialed Harry's cell and wondered idly if his ringtone was set to any particular music.

"Harold here," he answered, and I was glad. I'd half expected Malachi to pick up, just because I didn't want to talk to him and the universe occasionally allies against me that way.

"And Eden here," I responded. "How goes it down there, old man?"

He laughed a little and cleared his throat. "Oh, more of the same. But what brings you to the phone? Malachi says he can't get you on the line to save his life these days."

"I'm glad to hear he's noticed."

"Not taking the hint, huh? I thought you might be avoiding him. I told him to give you some breathing room, but he's so damn eager to make friends, he won't listen."

"He's started calling me at home, Harry. You've got to make him stop. When it's just the phone I've got in my purse, I can ignore him till the cows come home; but if he keeps looking for me here, I'm going to have a whole lot of elaborate lying to do. As it is, Dave already suspects something."

"What have you told him?"

"Nothing, except what we agreed on. I've got my fingers crossed that he thinks I'm hiding a boyfriend, but I'm probably wrong and he's half an idea closer to the truth. I don't think he ever bought the story as we laid it out, not one hundred percent. Even if he doesn't think I'm *lying*, he might suspect that I don't know the whole story. When I logged on to the Internet here the other day, there were some links in the history folder that suggested one of them had been looking to dig up news stories about last year. It might've been Lu, but my money's on Dave."

"Any particular reason?"

"No, just a hunch. I think Lu already knows more than she lets on, but she's happy with whatever fiction makes the most sense. Everything's back to abnormal, and she doesn't care. Dave's curious, though. I think he feels left out of the loop." Funny. I hadn't realized that part until I said it out loud.

"Makes sense," Harry agreed. "Why don't you fill him in a little? Throw him a bone?"

"Which bone exactly would you have me throw him? The one about how my homicidal half-brother isn't really dead—or the one about me hacking up my undead grandfather in self-defense? Hell, maybe we should clue him in on *all* that hocus-pocus at the shack. That'd make a great dinner conversation, don't you think?"

"Eden…"

"I could explain how since that night I can see dead people so well I sometimes can't tell them apart from the living, and, oh yes, by the way, did you notice I haven't been sick since then? Haven't had so much as a bruise or a paper cut? How am I supposed to explain all this to him when I'm not sure what happened myself?"

"Oh settle *down*. You don't have to tell him much, maybe just talk to him about it some—even if you've got to be vague. He almost lost his two favorite women, and he doesn't know why or how. I can hardly blame the man for being curious."

"I guess." I shifted the phone to my other shoulder and sat

down on the arm of the couch.

"It's sweet, though. The way you want to protect him, when he thinks he's protecting you."

"I'm a real sweet girl, or so they tell me."

"Who?"

"Okay, nobody really. You might actually be the first."

He grunted with amusement. "*That,* I believe. Hey, since I've got you on the phone, I don't suppose you've heard about that nonsense at the battlefield, have you?"

I groaned. "I live on *top* of a rock, Harry—not under one. How did *you* hear about it? Surely it hasn't made anything past the local news?"

"I couldn't say. I didn't hear about it on the news; I heard about it via the Marshalls. They're up there right now, aren't they?"

"If they aren't, they will be soon. And that's just what the battlefield needs—more ghost hunters. Damn Yankees ought to stay home and chase their own ghosts."

"Those damn Yankees are from one of the Carolinas, I believe."

I shook my head, as if he could hear it rattle. "And what, pray tell, is your interest in the Marshalls?"

"Purely professional, I assure you. They did some fascinating research into a case in England a few years back. Friends of a friend. You know how it is. They're not so bad, once you get to know them. Dana's a tad abrasive, but you'd really like Tripp if you gave him a chance."

"I'll take your word for it. They were on the news here last night, throwing slogans around. If I hear how they're going to 'get to the bottom of things' one more time, I'm going to start screaming. They're not going to get to the bottom of squat."

"So why don't *you,* then?"

I'd walked right into that one, but I was prepared to walk right out of it, too. "Because I'm not interested in getting to the bottom of it. There's probably nothing to get to the bottom *of.* It's a battlefield, Harry. People died there. It's haunted. End of dull and uncomplicated story."

"You're a terrible liar," he accused.

"No, I'm an *excellent* liar. You're hearing what you want to hear. I'm done with ghosts. I'm tired of them. I see them plenty enough as it is; I'm not about to go looking for more. They're like those crazy homeless people who hang out downtown—if you give them five seconds of attention once, they never leave you alone."

"I doubt that's a fair comparison."

"It might be. What do you know, anyway?"

"Quite a lot that might surprise you," he said. A very vacant pause followed, and I couldn't tell if he was being dramatic or if he'd stopped to think.

The silence bothered me, so I filled it in. "I'm going to let the Marshalls take care of the battlefield. It's not my problem. Hell, it's probably not anybody's problem. Some people saw some ghosts. Who cares?"

"The ghosts care, apparently. They seem to be going out of their way to try and communicate, but their success has been limited so far. It might be something important. In fact, I have to think that it *must* be—if the reports are right, and the sightings are so consistent.

"Really, dear," he went on, "you're in such a unique position to assist them. It's a shame you don't want to help."

"I bet the Marshalls don't want any help."

"They might. I could make some phone calls."

"Don't you *dare.* They're probably fakes, anyway."

"No," he insisted with a suddenness that surprised me.

"They're not fakes. They're not as gifted as they want to believe they are, and they're publicity whores of the highest caliber, but they do get real results. That's one reason I think you should see about contacting them, or offering to help their investigation. It might do you good to meet other people like yourself."

"And you want to hook me up with a play-date? Honestly."

He let slide another one of those pauses, and I almost interrupted him when he continued. "You know," he said, "you're not alone. There are other people who can see things and tell things that most people wouldn't believe. You ought to find a few of them and make some friends; it isn't that hard. The social circles are small, but they exist. I could give you a phone number or two."

"I watch late-night TV every now and again. I've got access to all the 1-900 numbers I can stand, thanks." I tried to sound flippant, but it came off too dry to be careless.

"There's no need to be catty. I'm not trying to hook you up with a psychic shrink; I'm trying to explain that there are people out there outside your immediate gene pool who might understand what it's like."

"To what end? I don't need any pen pals, Harry."

"For your own well-being, or peace of mind. You're entirely too isolated up there in Chattanooga. It'll make you crazy, being your kind of different and having no one to share it with."

"Crazy like Malachi?"

I almost heard Harry's eyes roll. "He *is* an easy example, yes."

In the end, the phone call was pleasant, but less than productive. By the time we hung up, I was unconvinced that he'd put a stop to Malachi's pestering—and he was unconvinced that I was uninterested in the battlefield.

We were both right to be suspicious.

FOUR

ABC

The city of Chattanooga shifts and swells around the university, which is tucked away downtown. It used to be located in the middle of a nice suburb; but time and economic stagnation have taken their toll, and now the school perches on the edge of a ghetto. This less-savory part of town is shrinking away from the school in slow, baby steps; but the change will take more time yet, partly because investors around here don't have a lick of sense. Real estate progress in the valley tends to swing one of two stupid ways: companies build in the wrong place, or they tear down the wrong things to start building.

But the university, downtown in the middle of the ghetto, is a marvel of hodgepodge architecture if ever there was one. As the school expanded, it ate up a couple of blocks unintended for academia, including an old hospital, a strip of historic suburbia, and a couple of cemeteries.

I parked out in front of one of them. A battered stone-and-ironwork fence hypothetically keeps the college kids at bay,

42

and though I'd challenged the fence's authority before with easy success, that night I was not there to visit with the dead.

Jamie's nighttime poetry workshop was held on the second floor of the building across the street.

I'd gotten the world's most pitiful phone call from him earlier that afternoon. His car was in the shop; he promised to buy me a drink and the burger of my choice if I'd pick him up and give him a ride to the Pickle Barrel. An acquaintance of ours was having a birthday party there, and the thing about Pickle Barrel birthday parties is that *everybody* stops by. Being on a first-name basis with the birthday person is not so much required; and, in fact, it might come as a genuine surprise.

Around here, a party's a party—and I'd had my fill of coffee for the week. A night's worth of alcohol would break up the monotony.

Jamie was late, as usual.

I leaned against the stairwell wall and tapped the back of my head against the plaster. I could hear him arguing with another student, and I could imagine him waving his hands and tossing his head—wielding his expansive mane as a weapon to invade the personal bubble of his opponent. Jamie's not a huge guy, but he's in excellent shape; and the way he throws himself around with all that manic, mobile black hair, people tend not to notice that he's only five foot ten. He takes up a *lot* of psychic space.

I thought about leaving him and letting him hoof it. The party wasn't but a mile or two away as the crow flies, and if he was feeling argumentative, I wasn't sure I wanted his company. He's usually fine so long as he knows you don't plan to sleep with him, but when he's on his high horse he can be more trouble than he's worth. I was still weighing the pros and cons of going ahead alone

43

when he burst from the workshop room in full princess mode.

"Eden, darling. Take me away from these *philistines*." He tossed his satchel across his back and flashed one last ferocious glance at the stragglers still within the classroom. Then he squeezed my forearm and nearly dragged me down the stairs to escape.

"Philistines? Is that the new word of the week?"

"It is *now*."

"Tore up your latest performance piece, huh?"

"Like piranhas on a quarter-pounder." Someone less egomaniacal might have sighed at this point, but Jamie was indignant, and he snorted instead. "There's just no explaining to this batch of six-toed inbreds that some poems are meant to be heard. It's not the same if you simply read them. Mere words on mere paper have no *soul*. They have no *fire*."

"They have no *you*," I clarified. "But you can't force a roomful of academics to become your own personal audience, you know."

"Says who?" he grumbled, stalking to the passenger side of my car and waiting for me to pop the locks.

I opened my door and hit the button to let him in. "Says them, apparently. You're going to fail the class if you can't play nice. Maybe you should try a little harder to... I don't know. Be less antagonistic. Fit in or something."

"Because I don't care—and I am too *brilliant* to fit in. This whole thing is ridiculous. I have more artistic genius in my right nut then they've got in that whole circle of posing wannabes. I shouldn't have to have a degree to validate my creativity. I don't need a piece of paper to prove that I'm great."

"Sounds like you don't need any humility, either."

"Who needs humility when you've got talent?"

"People who need jobs."

"Bitch," he spit.

"Bitch? That's all you've got? You must be losing your edge."

He nattered fussily at me all the way downtown, which wasn't very far, thank heaven. We took the sidewalk around to the front of the flatiron-shaped restaurant and bar. It's built on the end of an old city block that once housed—what else?—a hotel. The hotel is long gone, and the space has been parceled out to several other businesses, including the Pickle Barrel.

The Barrel is an eclectic little joint. It's not big enough to serve as host to a party of any size, but that never stops anyone from holding them there. The place is a local landmark, and half the city would be inconsolable if it were to close.

The first floor is all dim yellow lights, beat-to-hell hardwoods, and badly scratched windows. None of the tables are the same size, and they've all been lovingly carved with the same slogans you find spray-painted on overpasses. Most of these tables wobble, and all of them are warped to some state other than flat. By the time evening comes around, there are rarely enough chairs to go around, so some patrons always wind up sitting on benches that were once padded but now leak foam stuffing onto the ground.

Up by the bar a colorful jukebox lists a number of diverse titles, but every time I've ever been inside, Dire Straits has been playing. If it's not the Romeo and Juliet song, it's "Money for Nothing."

Behind the jukebox, a circular, ironwork staircase of narrow width and dubious stability leads to the roof. Parties usually begin upstairs, because there's more room to spread out. Also, the rickety metal stairs serve as a good litmus test to determine who's sober enough to leave. If you can make it down that treacherous spiral without breaking your neck, you're probably okay to drive.

We skipped the popular (yet uncomfortable) corner seat and made for the stairs. Already we could hear familiar voices up on the roof. Our heads crested the second floor in time to see a waitress arrive with a fresh round of drinks, sparking a happy holler from the birthday boy.

I didn't know Chris well, but his brother Mike used to date the daughter of a friend of Lu's. Jamie didn't know Chris or any of his near relations, and he wasn't particularly well liked among some members of the group; but he had a long-standing interest in Mike's best friend's sister—who might be in attendance.

In this city, that's plenty enough connection to crash a shindig.

About thirty people had camped upstairs, sprawling amoeba-style around most of the round metal tables. I knew most of the attendees in that vaguely acquainted sort of way in which most people here know everyone else in their age group—which is to say, I'd seen them around either the coffee shop or the university.

Jamie and I pulled up chairs and snagged the waitress while we had the chance. I put in an order for a fully loaded cheeseburger and a Coke, and Jamie ordered a half-carafe of wine.

It wasn't until the waitress had made her tired way down the stairs that I realized the topic of the conversation we'd wandered into.

"I heard it from Dave. He quit his job out there on Thursday," my friend Benny, a thin guy with glasses, announced without his eyes ever leaving his sketchbook. I wondered how he could see well enough to draw, but he seemed to be doing fine with a ray or two cast by the nearby streetlamp.

"Which Dave?" Jamie asked.

Ben tapped his pencil against the sketchbook's spiral. "Dave

Young. Katie's ex-boyfriend—you'd know him if you saw him. He's Josh's cousin, the one who used to be in the army."

Nods of recognition went round the tables. Chris, the spectacularly drunk birthday boy, sloshed beer over his wrists and added his own two cents. "You mean the one who works out at the battlefield?"

"Yes, baby." His girlfriend, Angie, dabbed at the patch of beer now freshly decorating her knee. "That's the one. What did he say about it, Benny? Is it true about the ghosts?"

Our resident artist squinted down at his paper. "Dave said they were talking about closing down the park for a while."

"They can't close the park!" Chris's equally inebriated sibling Mike gasped what we all were thinking. "That park's been open for two hundred years!"

"Well, a hundred and fifteen. Since almost thirty years after the war," Ben corrected him. "But they're saying that they need to keep people out of it until they find out what's going on. They don't want to get sued because someone has a wreck in the park or a heart attack from seeing a ghost."

"Surely you can't sue a national park?" I asked, but no one seemed to hear me, or maybe no one knew the answer.

"They can't keep us out of that park," Chris swore.

"They sure as hell can't," his brother Mike agreed. "We should go down there right now and—"

"No, no, no. I don't think so." Angie took his beer away and set it down on the table before she could get any wetter. She'd be driving both of them home later, so she was sticking with soda. "Not tonight, anyway. Maybe this weekend, say Saturday night, we'll pull a party together and go out there. That might be fun."

"The park closes at sundown, doesn't it?"

Everyone got quiet and turned to stare at me. Several of them said in chorus, "So?"

Benny folded his sketchbook closed and tucked the mechanical pencil into his shirt pocket. "There's a back way onto the grounds. Everybody knows about it."

"*I* don't," I assured him, but that only opened me up to the invitation I didn't want to get.

"We could show you. Hey, that would be neat—you're into ghosts, right?" Angie handed Mike his beer back and scooted her chair closer to mine. She looked excited and frightened at once. Her straight blond hair dipped past her ears and fell into her face. She tucked it back into place. "Do you want to come with us?"

"Um, I don't know. I might be busy Saturday."

"But you're the local ghost expert," Mike chimed in, punctuating the sentence with a mighty belch. "You've got to come along to protect us."

"Protect you? From ghosts?"

Angie tapped my side with her elbow. "From themselves, more likely. You really oughta come. Have you ever been there?"

"Yeah, a couple of times. A long time ago."

Besides one or two elementary school field trips, Dave and Lu had driven me out there when I was in high school. I'd been doing a paper for history class. The place had looked dull to me then—all empty and neatly mowed, with statues and obelisks peppering the landscape.

"Have you ever gone there *at night*?" Jamie leaned in close to ask.

"No. And I don't have any burning desire to, either."

They dog-piled on me then, teasing and goading. They insisted that it was easy as pie to sneak in at night, through the suburbs on the edge of the property. They told me all about how *spooky* it was—and how *haunted* it was, and how much *fun* it would be to go. "Spoken like people who have never actually seen a ghost," I observed, and they just laughed.

"Look, if you're serious about this," I said, because I didn't believe for a moment that they were, "you need to put more thought into it than this. You can't just drag a couple dozen people onto federally protected land in the middle of the night. You're not exactly a bunch of ninjas when you're stone sober—God knows you'd have the cops all over you before you could say 'Old Green Eyes.'"

"Ooh, Old Green Eyes!" Mike gurgled. "I saw him once. Long time ago."

"Bullshit," someone said from the fringe of the circle.

We all turned to regard our waitress, who had returned with my food and Jamie's wine. She sat it down in front of us without making eye contact with anyone, then stood up straight and tucked her tray under her arm.

"If you'd actually seen him," she practically whispered, "you'd never cross the Georgia state line again."

Everyone got quiet then. A couple of people misunderstood her enough to think she was being pissy. But I knew true fear when I saw it.

FIVE

DOWN BY THE RIVER

I'd abandoned Jamie to my tab and a ride home from someone else and was walking back to my car when my cell vibrated. Usually I leave it turned off and let all incoming calls go straight to voicemail, but since Lu and Dave were out of town, I'd left it active. Accidents and emergencies happen, and I'd have hated for them to be unable to reach me if they needed to.

I held up the phone and pressed a button to illuminate the caller's number. It began with a 423 area code, so it was local, but I didn't recognize the remaining seven digits. I don't give out the number to many people, so I don't usually ignore it. Curiosity got the better of me.

"Hello?"

"Eden, you've got to help me!" The words tumbled fast, buzzing into my ear over an imperfect connection. My stomach lurched. I held the phone back and checked the number again—yes, it was definitely local.

"Malachi?"

I was downtown on a city sidewalk, and even though it was late I was well within view of the still-crowded Pickle Barrel, so I was probably within hearing distance of anyone seated up on the roof. I lowered my voice and turned my head away from the restaurant.

"Malachi, where are you?"

He answered me too quickly to be understood. He was keeping his words soft, as if he too was afraid of being overheard.

"Stop it stop it *stop* it," I ordered. "Wait just a second."

I withdrew my keys from my pocket and let myself inside the car. When I closed the door behind me I hit the locks, halfheartedly paranoid. Clutching the phone between my ear and my shoulder, I strapped myself in and started the engine.

"Okay. One more time. What's going on—and where are you?"

"You've got to help me!" he repeated, hissing in his fright or worry.

"I think I got that part. Keep talking, I'm listening."

"I'm at Moccasin Bend."

I nearly dropped the phone. "You're *where*?"

"I'm at the Bend. You've got to come get me." He sounded like he was about to cry; and if he wasn't, I planned to give him something to cry about when I caught up to him.

"Are you insane? Hell, what am I saying—of *course* you're insane! That's why they sent you there in the first place! You came up here, didn't you? I told you to stay in Florida, but you wouldn't listen; you came up here, and you got caught. Christ, I swear to God—"

"Don't talk that way, Eden."

"How in the hell do you expect me to get you out of there? If I show up saying nice things about you, they're likely to chuck me inside with you. Call Harry or something. Call a lawyer. Call Eliza, if she's still alive—but the craziest thing you could possibly do is call—"

"Would you listen to me, please? I'm not *inside* the hospital. I'm just on the grounds. I'm outside. I tried to get in but I couldn't. And now my car won't start and I'm stuck. Can you please come and get me?"

I had no choice but to go quiet. I was too confused and surprised to say anything else, until he prompted me again.

"Please? You can run me out to the airport if you want, and I'll be on the next plane back to Florida. You can call Harry and let him yell at me. You can do whatever you want—just please don't leave me here tonight. I'm wet, I'm cold, and I think I've been bitten by a snake."

"A snake?"

"It might have been a copperhead. I couldn't see it."

Pulling to a stop in front of a red light, I rubbed at my eyes and then, very slowly, I beat my head up and down on the steering wheel. "When were you bitten by a snake, Malachi?"

"Huh? I don't know. Maybe it was, I don't know… What time is it now?"

I glanced down at the blue LED on my dashboard. "It's after midnight."

"About thirty minutes ago. It happened before I tried to see Kitty. But I couldn't talk to her. Something's happened to her. She's scared, Eden. And I'm scared. I think something's out here, on the grounds. Something is…" His voice fuzzed in and out, and I missed the last half of the sentence.

"Malachi? Malachi?"

"Come and get me, *please*?"

The light had turned green; but there was no one behind me, so I took another moment to hit my forehead on the wheel some more. If there had been anyone else Malachi could have called, he would have. If he'd had anyone in the world other than me, I wouldn't have been beating a groove above my eyebrows.

But he didn't have anyone else, and no one knew it better than I did.

Headlights spilled towards me, reflecting off my rearview mirror. I lifted my head and took my foot off the brake. I put my right blinker on and turned onto Market Street.

The fact that he continued to speak lucidly—well, lucidly for Malachi—inclined me to think he hadn't been bitten by a copperhead, but he was scared and alone, and I couldn't bring myself to hang up on him. I sighed hard.

"Where are you?"

"Oh thank you, thank you Eden—I owe you one. I owe you big. When will you be out here?"

"First…" I pronounced every letter in the small word, for I was determined to keep my cool. "First you have to tell me where you are."

"I told you, I'm at the Bend. I'm outside. There's a payphone, but I've got to get off of it before somebody sees me."

The Bend.

Like the Barrel, a place recognizable even without its first name. I knew roughly where it was, but I wasn't one hundred percent positive how to reach it. That's the beauty of city planning here—there wasn't any.

Moccasin Bend—the state mental-health facility—is located upon Moccasin Bend, a thumb-shaped peninsula created by a sharp crook in the Tennessee River. From the brow of Lookout

Mountain the river rather decidedly resembles a snake, and thus the name, or so I guessed. Since it's surrounded on three of its four sides by running water, I had to assume that there would be but one way out there short of swimming—and I wasn't sure what that one way would be.

"Malachi, I know you're at the Bend. But I need for you to be more specific. I've never been there before, and I'm not sure I can find it. How did you get there?"

"Okay, okay." He was excited now, knowing I was coming for him. "Okay, go downtown."

"I *am* downtown."

"North or south of the river?"

"South. I'm a block or two over from Miller Park."

"Okay. Go towards the river. Go over the river, I mean. Go over the drawbridge to the north side, and go left at that first stoplight there. Do you know where I mean?"

"Frasier Avenue, yeah. I know what you're talking about."

"There's that road that runs underneath the interstate, and it dumps onto the road right there to the left of the stoplight. There are signs talking about it being a bike route to Moccasin Bend. Follow the signs. That's how I got here. It's kind of confusing, though."

"That rings a bell, now that you mention it." I'd thought about trying to scribble down some notes, but I didn't have anything handy in the car and I had a pretty good idea of what he was talking about anyway. There are a lot of scenic bike routes around the valley, and if one ran out to the Bend, so much the better.

"It's dark out here, Eden. Please hurry."

"I'm doing my best. Now where do you want me to pick you up?"

"I'm on the road—" And here it sounded like he dropped the phone, or he was shifting to hide himself. "I'm not out to the sign yet. I'll try to get all the way to the sign before you get here."

"*What* sign?"

"There's a sign that marks the entrance. It's two signs, actually. Big concrete ones that look like they were put up in the sixties. You have to pass them to get onto the grounds."

"And you'll meet me at the signs?"

"I'll try to."

I shifted the phone to my other ear. "Malachi, so help me God if I get to those signs and you're not there, I'm turning around and driving home. Do you hear me?"

"I hear you," he whined. "I'll try to be there, but it's farther out than you'd think. I'll come out to the signs as fast as I can."

"All right then, so will I." I hung up then, tossing my cell phone onto the passenger's seat and clutching the steering wheel so tight I thought I might bend it.

I tried to picture the Bend in my mind, and compare its location to my mental map of the area. Once I got to Manufacturers Road, if I kept bearing west and south towards the river, I'd have to hit upon the entrance eventually—or so I hoped.

As I neared the edge of the peninsula, I found myself in a darkness that mocked my headlights for their woeful inadequacy. I passed a big liquor store on my left, but it was closed; and on my right I saw a few enormous factory buildings in various states of repair.

In front of me there was nothing at all, except for a strip of pavement that slithered off between the trees. I turned on my brights, kept my eyes open for signs, and hoped for the best. The road was growing less linear and flat by the foot, so I drove more carefully than I usually do. Every curve was blind, and every hill promised obstacles just beyond my vision.

There were also about a thousand signs—but none of them seemed to tell me exactly what I wanted to know. I thought I'd hit pay dirt when I spied a brown sign with a cyclist on it, but while the path might have eventually brought me to the Bend, it was unpaved; my car isn't exactly made for off-road excursions, so I thought the better of roughing it. Besides, Malachi had said he'd driven to the compound, and I didn't see any evidence of tire tracks, so the right way must lie elsewhere.

Up and down Riverside Drive I wandered. I wasn't lost—I could see the river through the trees—but I didn't know how to get where I needed to be, so I may as well have been. For a mad moment or two I thought about stopping for directions, but I didn't see so much as a gas station or a bar, and even if I had, how would I have broached the question? "Pardon me, ma'am or sir. I realize that it's well after visiting hours, but I'm trying to find my way to the crazy bin. I don't suppose you could help me out?"

I'd end up talking to the cops faster than you could say "One flew over the cuckoo's nest."

On a whim, I yanked my car to a sharp left turn. "Well, Malachi, at least I'm giving you plenty of time to get to the entrance. And by God, you'd better be there." A gold glow up ahead suggested lights, and I got my hopes up in time to be disappointed by a water treatment plant. But past the plant the road evened out into a promising-looking straightaway, so I stuck with it. If I was going the wrong direction, at least I was somewhere near civilized electricity.

I didn't see the river anymore, so I chose to assume that I was on the peninsula and bearing the right way. As I drove, I began setting limits for myself and counting them out loud: "When this next song on the radio is over, I'm going to turn around. If I don't see any hint of the place within another five minutes, I'm giving up."

But I didn't stick to any of them. By instinct or by suspicion, I kept driving until I spied the two big signs that told me I'd found the right place.

I slowed the car and cut the lights, drawing to an idling stop on the pseudo-shoulder beside the main drag.

No spindly-limbed half-sibling of mine stepped out from behind the signs or from the woods beside them.

I pressed the ball of my foot on the gas pedal, revving the engine to get his attention with a rush of subtle volume. I stared hard at the two signs, back and forth between them, and then again to the trees on either side. Nothing.

I lifted my palm, intending to shove it against the horn. But I changed my mind. I put the car in park and rolled all four windows down.

"Malachi? Malachi, are you out there?"

Up a nearby hill I saw a large building of indeterminate size and purpose. There weren't any lights on, and I wanted to keep it that way, so I kept my voice down to a hard whisper. "Malachi, you bastard."

He wasn't there.

I knew it. I'd given him nothing but time as I wandered around trying to follow the river, but the dumb son of a bitch hadn't been able to make it anyway. He was truly and completely useless, and I decided on the spot that if I did find him, I was going to punch him in the head.

Mad—and, against my will, a bit worried—I threw the car back into gear and pulled back onto the road. So far I'd been lucky and I'd hardly seen another vehicle; but I couldn't trust that luck to hold.

I couldn't reasonably hope that no one would be coming or going between the river and the hospital, so I had to choose a strategy.

I could poke along with the windows open, hissing Malachi's name to the forest; or I could pretend that I was minding my own business and zipping along at the speed limit like a perfectly innocent person on a perfectly ordinary errand. I didn't know which approach would work better, and I didn't know what I'd do if I actually reached the hospital. Would I be able to turn around? Would I have to pass some kind of checkpoint?

I tried to think up a story to hand to any potential guards, but I was having trouble coming up with anything plausible, and I kept forgetting to hiss out the window.

"Come out, come out wherever you are, you jackass," I mumbled, just in time to catch a speed bump entirely too fast.

I nearly drew to a complete halt out of pure surprise.

Who puts a speed bump in the middle of a straight shot? The Bend people, apparently. And they didn't quit with one, oh no. They spaced them out every fifty yards, so every time I got up to third gear I'd have to slow right back down again.

With every yellow-painted hump I became that much angrier at Malachi, and that much closer to the hospital—the point of no return.

Before long I could see it at the end of the road. The place was lit up like an old gas station, bright but not warm. From a distance everything looked square and sharp. It was all straight lines and right angles. Efficient and unfriendly.

Even as I dreaded getting closer I strained to see it better, but that only meant that I wasn't watching the road when Malachi lunged in front of me.

Someone had given him a haircut to tame that blond haystack

of a head, but he wasn't dressing any better and he hadn't gained an ounce. His lanky, clumsy frame stepped into my headlights with arms waving. He thrust himself in front of me far too late for me to avoid hitting him.

I swerved left across the opposing lane, but not before I winged him hard enough to make him yelp.

The car began to slide. Around I spun in a badly drawn circle, my headlights casting a swiveling carnival glare at the trees, the signs, and the knee-high grass. I came to a stop with a neck-whipping jerk when my front right fender knocked itself still against a trunk. Some precious part of the Death Nugget crumpled, and something plastic shattered.

And for a few seconds, everything was quiet.

I unbuckled my seat belt and opened the door. A pinging chime sounded to remind me that my lights were on. I turned them off, then stepped out of the car one shaky leg at a time.

Malachi came limping up, clutching his thigh and panting.

"Are you okay?" he asked—using his "outdoor voice," as a grade-school teacher would have put it.

I slapped his arm hard enough to smart. "What the hell is wrong with you? Shut up!"

"Sorry! I'm sorry."

"Not half as sorry as you're going to be," I grumbled, closing the car door so the dome light would extinguish itself. "What do you think you're doing? Christ, my car. Holy shit, Malachi, look at what you've done to my car."

"Technically, I think it's the tree that did the damage—unless you've got a dent in your bumper from where you struck *me*." He sulked a feeble defense, but if he thought he could make me feel guilty he was barking up a *very* wrong tree.

"My front bumper is fine and I barely nicked you. But this?" I ran my hands along the damaged panel. "This is *not* fine. This is not fine at *all*."

"You can't even see it. Come on, let's get out of here. You can check it out when it's light. Look, your headlight isn't even broken—just the blinker on the side."

Off in the distance I thought I heard a car's engine. I waved him quiet and listened. The last thing we needed was a good Samaritan.

"Eden," he whined my name, making the "E" too long.

"Shut *up*. I think someone's coming." But even as I said it, the rumble faded and I knew I was mistaken.

"We have to get out of here."

"I know. But first I need to make sure my car is in one piece enough to drive. What were you thinking? I mean *seriously*? I thought you were supposed to be over at the signs." I opened my car door again, kneeling on the front seat to reach into the glove compartment for my flashlight.

"I couldn't make it. I tried, I swear. But I couldn't do it. I got scared. Kitty was talking about a man wandering around outside near the river, and I thought I saw him. Except…"

"Except what?" I kicked my door closed again and snapped the light on.

This time he actually whispered. "Except I think maybe it wasn't a man. I think it was something else."

"Really?" I asked, more out of conversational habit than real curiosity. I was preoccupied with examining the damage. "Oh, my poor little Nugget," I breathed, running my hands along the battered metal.

"Really. I don't think he saw me, though. Or maybe he did,

I don't know. If he *did* see me, he didn't care that I was there. He freaked me out, Eden. I started running, but I got turned around in the dark, and I slid down the bank into the river. That's when I got bitten by the snake."

I glanced up at him and pointed the light at his torso. Only then did I notice that his pants were wet, and one of his arms was black with mud. "The world's most harmless copperhead?"

"It *might've* been a copperhead. You don't know."

"Where did it bite you?"

He held out his muddy elbow and pointed at a spot just below it. I saw some scraping and a bit of dirty blood, but nothing that cried out to me, "festering snakebite."

"I think you'll live," I told him. "But that's only in the event that I decide not to kill you. Look at this!"

I aimed the light at my front tire. Though the car's frame appeared, in my limited inspection, to be all right, the rim of the wheel-well was bent sharply inward. "If we try to leave with it like this, we're going to have a blowout."

Malachi rubbed his wounded arm, then rubbed at his thigh too. "What do we do?"

Again I thought I heard an engine, or voices, or some indication that we weren't alone. I flipped the light off and grabbed his unhurt arm, pulling him back behind the car. As the moments passed, I began to feel stupid. No cars came along, and no inquisitive neighbors came out to investigate our crash.

Surely *someone* had heard us; but then again we seemed to be in the middle of nowhere. The closest sign of human habitation was the hospital, and we were half a mile away from it yet.

"Do you hear that?" I asked him, bringing my voice as low and soft as I could and still be heard.

"No?"

"Me neither."

I didn't hear anything. Not a sound. No traffic, but no insects or birds, either. I fancied I could maybe hear the river if I listened hard enough, or maybe it was a different rushing hum and I was only mistaking it for water.

Whatever it was or was not, I didn't like it.

"Malachi, you said your car broke down. What car are you talking about, and where is it?"

"I bought it. For five hundred bucks, cash. I knew it wouldn't last forever, but I hoped it would get me as far as here. And it did, so I guess I can't complain."

"Fine. I'll complain for the both of us. Where is it?"

"Around on the other side of the hospital. I pushed it off the road and into the trees so no one would hear me coming. When I tried to leave, it wouldn't start. I don't know what's wrong with it. But I'm not going back to it," he added quickly. "I'm not walking back up there. No way. That's where *he* was. *He* was wandering around, talking to himself. No way. They can have the thing and sell it for scrap. I'll eat the loss. But I'm not going back there."

"Yeah, yeah. I heard you. Not going back. But I don't suppose you had a crowbar or anything in that car, did you?"

"No, I don't think so."

"You're not just saying that because you're afraid to go back there?"

"*No!* Eden—"

"Okay, fine. Of course not. That would be too easy. Okay. Then this is what we're going to do: you and I are going to find a branch, or a sturdy stick, or something like that. It can't be too big, but it has to be solid enough to lever that rim away from the tire. Got it?"

"Uh-huh."

"Good. Now stay close," I ordered, implying that I didn't want him going all girly on me, but the truth was less noble. I was getting nervous too. That rushing, rumbling sound that was neither engine nor water was getting louder in my ears, and I didn't like it. It made my head feel stuffy, and almost sleepy despite the adrenaline that I knew must be coursing through my heart.

"You don't hear anything?" I asked him again.

He shook his head. "Just the river. It's right on the other side of these trees."

"The river," I repeated. I didn't believe him, but there was no sense in both of us acting panicky, so I kept my concerns to myself, swallowing them back with a sigh. "This sucks."

"I'm sorry."

"I know. Be quiet."

"Okay."

"Stay close," I told him again. I pointed the light at the ground and let him grip the back hem of my shirt. "All we need is one good stick, and then we're out of here."

"I think we just missed the shift change."

"What?"

"The shift change. At the hospital. Everyone who's coming or going has probably done so by now," he said, twisting his fist in my shirt. "Unless they're late."

"Good to know," I murmured. "But still. Let's hurry up."

I swept the beam back and forth on the ground at my feet, kicking leaves and rocks out of my path as I went. The rushing noise came and went, close and far depending on how I turned my head. It was as if I were trying to tune into a radio station whose signal was too weak to come through clearly.

"This is ridiculous." I pushed my feet through another foot or two of undergrowth and stopped. "Everything is too small and twiggy or too damn big. Maybe we can pull something down off a tree or something."

"I don't think we should do that."

"Why?"

"I really don't think we should disturb anything out here. Eden, are you sure we have to do this? Your car didn't look too bad. Can't we just—"

"No, we *can't*. We'll blow out a tire before we even get back on the road. And what did I say about keeping quiet?"

He sucked his breath in, and I thought he was jokingly complying with my request until I took another step and he caught me by the shirttail. "What are you doing? Let go or keep up."

He only tightened his hold on my poor T-shirt and tugged me back towards him.

I turned around and smacked his hand. "What the hell is wrong with you?" I growled, pretending not to know a loaded question when I asked one.

"I saw him," he said, more quietly than I'd ever heard him speak before. If I'd been another six inches away, I couldn't have heard him.

I brought the light up until it aimed its halogen beam at his chest. "Who? Where?"

He lifted one long, skinny hand and waggled it as if he were trying to shake something off it. "Over there. I saw his eyes. He's going that way. Wow, he moves so fast."

Malachi dropped the end of my shirt and took a half-step back.

"Malachi," I said with a warning.

I didn't disbelieve him, exactly, but I didn't want him to

hightail it from fright. "Malachi, calm down."

I wanted to say more, but I stopped and shook my head like I was dislodging water from my ears. The low, insistent static sound hummed stronger now. By now I was all but certain that the white noise was no river rush. It was too hard to think when I heard it. It was too hard to concentrate on anything else.

"I have to go. We have to go."

"Malachi. Malachi, don't run."

"We have to go."

"*Malachi,* calm down. Stay here for just a minute—"

"No," he gasped, and he turned to run.

I caught his arm and whipped him back; and because I couldn't think of anything else that would slow him down, I hit him as hard as I could. My knuckles caught him in the temple, or maybe on his brow-bone; I couldn't tell. Either way, down he went. He sort of caught himself on his knees and elbows, and crumpled down to lie on his shoulder.

"Shit." I rubbed the back of my hand against my stomach and knelt down beside Malachi.

"What'd you do that for?" he slurred, holding his palms against his eye.

"I didn't mean to," I answered, and it was almost true.

A small spark flashed over to my left and was gone. I swung my light around to catch its source. Between the trees something moved away from us, or past us, and was gone.

"Did you see that?" I asked my prone companion.

"I see stars, like in a cartoon, only they're smaller. Brighter," he answered dreamily. At least he didn't sound afraid anymore.

"Good. Good then. You stay here and look at the stars. I'll be right back."

I underwent a moment of crisis trying to decide whether to bring the light or leave it with him, then took it and put it into his hand by prying his fingers apart and wrapping them around the barrel. "Hold this," I told him.

"What?"

"Hold it, until I get back. Wave it around so I can find you again. Okay?"

"'Kay."

"And don't turn it off."

"Turn it off."

"*Don't* turn it—oh hell. Never mind. Give it here. Give it back." I wrested it out of his hand and set it down a few feet away, aimed at the sky. "Lie here and stay out of trouble. I'll be back in a minute. I'm leaving this here so I can find my way back to you. Don't touch it."

"'Kay."

I turned my back on my prostrate brother and gazed between the trees, looking to catch that flash of motion again. It was more like a fast burst of light, so I thought I might have better luck seeing it without the flashlight—and besides, if I took the thing with me I'd never find Malachi again.

I didn't plan to wander far, anyway. If I didn't find anything soon, I'd give up and go.

But I wanted to know what the watery white noise meant, and I wanted to see what moved in the trees. No person walked so fast, or so quiet; and it'd had ample opportunity to jump us if that was its intent. Instead it ignored us—brushed past us towards the river. If it saw us at all, it did not care that we were there.

I swiveled my head left and right, focusing, trying to pinpoint the inconsistent sound. Over to the left, maybe. It was stronger in that direction. I took a step or two that way, and I grew more certain.

Enough glow remained behind me to cast deep shadows in pillars around the trees, but even with the haphazard optical effect I spotted the gleam again.

I stumbled towards it, tripping over anything bigger than a quarter and scuffing my palms on every trunk that caught me. But the rush had reached a roar and compelled me forwards, even as the last of the light I'd left with Malachi faded dim enough to be useless behind me.

Before me a form came together on the riverbank, or it might have been only that I saw it better as my eyes adjusted to the gloom. I thought it must be tall—a good head and a half taller than me, so at least seven feet or better—and I thought it was wearing a cloak or something else that flowed long around its back. Its shoulders were hunched, and its arms were wrapped around them.

It was rocking back and forth and mumbling, but I couldn't understand what it was saying. The words didn't make any sense from my distant position, and something about the cadence suggested I might not sort them out even if I drew closer.

I did move closer, forward from the trees and nearer to the river's edge.

I couldn't hear what the tall thing was saying, but I could understand it all the same. There were words in the swirling ambient noise, or if not words then something else very close to words—the chunks of ideas that inspire that which is spoken or written.

It's not a cloak he's wearing, I thought as I circled away from the trees and down to the water. *It's hair.* It fell long and thick down to waist-level, and it swayed like a curtain.

"I can hear you," I said.

It ignored me. *He* ignored me, I decided—assigning a more personal pronoun. He seated himself and wrapped his arms around his knees; he was still nodding back and forth as he sighed his monologue.

A deal is a deal. The last was dead, and I gave my word.

I couldn't tell if he said it aloud or if I only heard it that way, but I understood him well enough regardless. "What deal?" I asked, but he didn't turn around.

But was it the right thing to do?

"Was—was what right?"

Still he did not respond. I didn't expect him to; he was not talking to me, and if he heard me address him, he didn't deign to acknowledge it. But I wished he would turn around. I wanted to know what he was, and what he looked like.

He did turn, a three-quarters shift that showed me an indistinct profile and one warm-bright eye. It made me think of a cat's eye, the way his socket pulled all the dim light together and concentrated it into a dull, certain gleam the color of a cut lime.

He almost seemed to address me then, or it might have been only that he spoke to himself while facing my direction.

No. The dead are my children. I owe them more than this.

Louder and louder the buzzing, roaring, humming sound that accompanied him. My eyes watered, and I pulled my hands up to rub them hard. The vibration became something that knocked my teeth together and made my cheeks numb, and when it stopped I let my hands fall to my sides from pure surprise.

Whoever he was, whatever he was, he was gone.

And I was in the dark—alone, except for the odd slapping

of a fish against the water's surface a few yards away. I yawned to stretch my jaws, and my ears popped.

"Eden?"

Malachi's voice sounded closer than I expected. I felt like I'd moved a mile or more away from him, but a wobbly column of light wiggled through the trees and pointed at the sky.

"Eden, where did you go? Did he get you? Eden?"

"No one *got* me."

"What?"

"Hang on, I'm coming back. Keep holding that up."

I caught my foot on something heavy, and I crouched on one knee. I'd found a half-buried branch that might or might not suit my car-fixing purposes, so I kicked at it until I dislodged it.

"You hit me," Malachi accused when I returned to him. He aimed the flashlight directly into my face.

"Yes. Get that thing out of my eyes."

He lowered the light and ducked his head. "Sorry. Hey, you found a stick."

"Yes, I found a stick. Come on. Let's get back to the car. We need to get out of here." I took the light away from him and used my stick to push him in front of me. "Move it. If we're lucky, no one's seen it yet. If we're even luckier, this thing won't fall apart when I shove it up under the tire rim."

"Did you see him? Did you?"

I nodded, aiming with the stick. "This way. Yeah. I saw him."

He went back to that low-pitched whisper he'd used on me before. "He's awful, isn't he? Is that what all the ghosts are like?"

"Awful?" I thought about it for a minute, but chose to disagree. "No. He's very different, though. He's no ghost; he's something else. I don't know *what*."

"I thought he was awful."

I remembered that one reflecting eye and wondered if Malachi wasn't right, but I couldn't make myself believe he was correct this time. "He's different, and strange. But not awful. At least I don't think so."

"You must not have seen his eyes."

"Not both of them exactly, no."

We scrambled back to the car in time to duck away from incoming headlights. Thankfully, they did not stop for us—though they slowed long enough to make me worry. I had a feeling the driver was pausing for a cell phone call, or making a mental note to send out security later on.

I handed the flashlight to Malachi and made him train it on the badly battered wheel-well while I wielded the stick. I slid it between the tire and the dented metal; slowly, carefully so as not to destroy the stick or further damage the metal, I levered the rim away from the tire. When I was confident that the tire would not explode upon my first ninety-degree turn, I tossed the stick into the trees and unlocked the doors.

"Get in. Now."

I didn't have to tell him twice. He yanked the door open and threw himself inside before I had time to offer him a rag or a towel to clean himself up with. I crawled into the driver's seat and turned the key with a wish and a prayer.

The Death Nugget started up immediately and without incident.

I flicked the headlights on and noted that the right one aimed in an altogether incorrect direction, but that was better than if it were smashed. I accelerated slowly out of the grass and mud, sliding a tad but catching solid ground soon enough.

In a moment we were back on the road and trying to look innocuous.

We didn't speak for five or ten minutes, and when we did it was all I could do not to start swearing at him.

"Why did you hit me?" he asked, tempting me to do it again.

"Because you didn't follow directions."

"It hurt."

"It was supposed to hurt," I grumbled back, even though it wasn't true. I'd meant to stop him, not hurt him—and if one was a side effect of the other, then that was tough luck. "And don't whine at me like I've done you some great wrong. I *did* drive all the way out here in the middle of the night to pick your ass up, and I *have* wrecked my car on your sorry behalf."

"Your car's not wrecked."

"I beg your pardon?"

"You're driving it, aren't you? The car's not wrecked."

"All the same"—I spied a sign that pointed to 27 and was greatly relieved to follow its winding ramp—"I'm going to have a lot of explaining to do when Lu and Dave get home. And *you* are really lucky they're out of town right now."

"Thanks for getting me, though. I know you didn't have to. And I'm sorry about the car." He leaned his head against the window and closed his eyes. This was a man prepared to be yelled at. He was too pitiful for words.

"What are you—? Hey, put your seat belt on."

He reached around himself and dragged the belt into place, fastening it by his left hip.

"What are you doing up here? Not just the Bend, but here— Tennessee. You're supposed to be dead; and I've got to tell you, this isn't the best of all possible places you could choose to lie low.

People remember folks like you, you know."

He didn't say anything until we were on the bridge, headed out of town. I'd promised him a ride to the airport, and that was where I was taking him.

"I did it because you wouldn't talk to me."

I wasn't sure how to respond to that, so I didn't. I waited, and he kept on talking.

"I needed to know some things, and I thought you could help me. But you wouldn't talk to me, and I could only think of one other person who might know something."

"Who?"

"Her name's Kitty. She's been in the Bend for twenty years, so I figured she'd still be there if I came up for a visit. She's kind of like you. She sees things."

The thought of that made me uncomfortable. "And that's why she's in the Bend?"

He shook his head. "Oh no—she's in the Bend because she killed her sister's two children. She thought they were possessed by the devil, so she drugged them and shut them in the garage with the car running and they died from the gas. *That's* why she's there. But also, she sees things."

"Huh."

"I met her when I was in the Bend after… well, a long time ago. I thought she could maybe tell me something if you wouldn't."

"What did you want to know about?"

"My mother."

"Oh." We both quit talking then. It took me a minute to work out all the sides of his quest, and when I did I felt like a heel.

Back in the swamp, Avery had implied very strongly that Malachi's mother, Rachel, was dead. He'd all but said that she was the entity who roamed Pine Breeze, looking for her husband's lover—my own mother. I couldn't remember if he'd said it outright or if he'd only hinted, but either way Malachi wouldn't have bought it without some investigation.

I couldn't blame him, there. I'd want to know, too. I'd want someone to check it out for me, especially if I happened to be related to somebody who had a knack for chatting with the dead. And if that relative was uncooperative, I could certainly understand why he might reach for a surrogate psychic—even if it was someone like Kitty.

"I thought maybe," he went on, rolling his forehead on the glass and leaving a crescent smudge of sweat and dirt, "maybe you could go up there to the old hospital and see if it's her. You could tell me if she's there. I need to know."

There was no delicate way to handle the truth, but I gave him my own opinion as gently as I could. "You know that I've been there, and I met the… the ghost." I didn't have a better word for the vicious presence there, so I assigned it one he'd recognize. "The ghost mistook me for my mother, and then it got mad at me. It chased me away like it hated me, personally. I don't think that it wants to hear from me again, whoever it once was; and I think that the odds are good that Avery was telling the truth. He had no reason to lie."

"My mother didn't believe in ghosts."

"Lots of people don't, and then they become one. I've found that the experience broadens their thinking somewhat."

We drove on in silence for another mile.

"I don't know if you're aware or not," I finally broached. "But Pine Breeze was torn down last year."

"It was?"

"Yes. It's gone—completely leveled. The paper said that nothing's left but a few foundations, some stone walls, and the dirt roads that ran between them. For what it's worth, I bet that whatever walked the Pine Breeze dormitories has probably gone too."

"Why?"

"There's nothing left to haunt. If it *was* Rachel, then she probably left when they demolished the place." I used her name because I couldn't bring myself to call the thing at Pine Breeze his mother.

Then Malachi actually brought up an interesting point. "If she was looking for your mother," he said slowly, "and she's a ghost, how come she didn't know your mother's dead?"

I considered my conversation with Gary a day or two before, and had nothing better to offer Malachi than a quick rehash. "I guess it's just because not everyone sticks around. Maybe my mom passed on, and Rachel stayed. I don't know. But with the old sanitarium gone now, I can't imagine that she'd remain there."

At least I hoped not. It seemed too weird and miserable a fate to walk the same grounds for eternity, hunting for someone long gone who won't return.

The thoughts rambling around in Malachi's head came wandering out his mouth. "But if my mother's dead, when did she die? Why didn't I hear about it? Aunt Eliza said she ran off with a cult when I was a kid, but Mother used to send me stuff sometimes, every now and again. For the first few years, anyway."

"Then what?" I asked. "Did it all stop at once, or did the contact taper off?"

He thought about it, then kind of shrugged. "Hard to say. It was always sporadic; sometimes she'd write or call more often than others. I remember once she sent me three letters and a package within a month… but then she'd go for a year or so and I wouldn't hear from her."

"So…" I started a sentence but lost the thought before I got too far. I was trying to think in too many different directions at once.

After a protracted delay on my part, he said, "So?"

"So we're going to the airport." I said it out loud in time to notice that I was about to miss the exit. Thank God it was late, and there wasn't much traffic. I cut across two lanes and dashed up the ramp onto the proper strip of highway.

"Are you sure?"

"Are you kidding?"

"I was thinking, I mean, I was hoping that I could stay up here for a few days or something. Not with you," he added quickly. "At a hotel room someplace. I only want to look around and see if I can't find Mother, if that was her out there."

"I told you, Pine Breeze is gone."

"I know. I believe you. But you don't know if it was her, or if she's still there. You're only guessing, and I really need to know. What if it *is* her? What if she's stuck there and she doesn't know she can leave? I could tell her, maybe. Maybe she'd recognize me. Maybe I could talk to her."

I don't know why it irked and surprised me that he'd be stubborn about it. It's all anyone wants—from me or from the universe, or from fate, or whatever they want to call it. Everybody wants a second chance to say their piece to someone who's beyond hearing it.

"Give me one day," he begged, turning in the seat to raise one leg up beneath himself as he shifted his torso to face me. "Twenty-four hours. All I want to do is run up there to the ruins—that's all I came here to do."

"There *aren't* any ruins. There's nothing. And if that was all you wanted, why did you go out to the Bend?"

"A couple of reasons." He crossed his arms.

"Well, now is the time to discuss them," I said. "Because you've got another five minutes or so before we get to the airport; and if you don't convince me by then, you're completely out of luck."

"I went back to the Bend because I couldn't find Pine Breeze when I went looking for it, and you wouldn't talk to me. Kitty grew up around here. I thought she'd help me find it."

"Ah, so you're back to blaming me for this."

"No, I'm not. Sheesh! Why do you always think everyone's blaming you for everything? I didn't want to go out there by myself, that's all, and I don't know anyone else up here. I thought Kitty would be a good choice, because she can see ghosts—or she says she can, anyway."

"This is the woman who killed her sister's kids?"

"Uh-huh. She's really nice once you get to know her."

"I'm sure."

"Well she *is*. And she's not under very heavy security there. I thought I could spring her for a night and then sneak her back in, or something. It wouldn't be too hard, probably. Or it wouldn't have been, anyway, if they hadn't moved her since I was there. It took me almost an hour to find her. They moved her over to solitary."

"How come?"

"How should I know? I've been in Florida for the last year, remember? That's just what I found out when I got there. She wasn't in her old room, so I had to go looking for her."

He shook his head and peered anxiously out the window as an airplane swooped down low, loud and blinking over the road, coming in for a landing. "She's never been a problem patient. But the file I found in records storage said she'd started making a big fuss, saying over and over again that *he* was there. She called him the Hairy Man, and I think that's who we saw today. She's not *that* kind of crazy. She saw him too, and he scared her."

"Yeah," I said, not really affirming anything at all, but feeling the need to agree.

"Yeah," he said it back.

I turned into the airport complex and made sure I was in the right lane. It's not a big airport by any means, but it's laid out in such a way that it's easy to wind up driving someplace you didn't intend.

"Wait a minute." I stopped myself before pulling into the airport's parking lot. "We can't put you on a plane, can we?"

"Why not? I don't have any scissors, or anything…" He patted at his pants pockets.

"And I bet you don't have an ID, either—at least not anything that won't have you arrested as soon as you fork it over."

"Oh. Um. No. I don't. You're probably right. I guess I'll just have to stay here for a few days, huh?"

"Fat chance, buster. The Greyhound station is right over there. And it'll be cheaper, anyway."

Neither one of us spoke while I wound my way into the parking lot across from the airport runway. I took the car out of gear and removed my keys, but did not open the door. I closed my eyes and put my head back, leaning it against the seat.

I think Malachi was sucking in his breath and holding it in his throat. I only noticed him doing it because it's something I do when I'm nervous. This small thing we had in common made me hold my words for a few seconds. It made me reluctant to be too mean.

"It goes like this," I finally told him. "First of all, I'm sorry I didn't answer the phone more often, and I'm sorry I didn't at least hear you out before ignoring you. But that doesn't change the fact that you shouldn't be here—for a million and one reasons that I trust I don't have to elaborate upon. Also, you shouldn't have come up here alone. You should have at least come with Harry."

"Harry said no when I asked if he'd come here with me. He said I should leave you alone and stay out of state a while longer."

"Yes, he's a sharp guy. I know you want to know about Pine Breeze and whether the presence there was your mom; so I understand your impatience, but it was still a terrible idea for you to venture this way by yourself."

"But Harry—"

"I heard you. Let *me* talk to him and see if I can change his mind. I bet I can. Give me maybe a week—can you do that?" I lifted my head and swiveled it to look him in the eye. "But not today. Not tomorrow. Lu and Dave will be back tomorrow night, and I just can't deal with that much lying in a forty-eight-hour period. I'm already working on a story about the car—"

"A deer," he interjected. "You can say you swerved to avoid hitting a deer."

"I'm more likely to tell them a skunk." I used enough droll overtone to imply a bad joke, but he missed the punch line altogether and I was sort of glad. I had felt dumb for it as soon as I said it. Going after his feelings with a rusty steak knife wasn't going to get anyone anywhere.

"A skunk would work, yeah. No one wants to hit a skunk. You'd never get the smell off the hood."

"Right. A skunk, then. But I'm not going to throw you into the mix too. Give me a week or two to work on Harry, and then

I can tell them that he's coming up and I'll be getting together with *him*. I can even, if I have to, arrange for him to meet them for coffee or something. It's far less conspicuously dishonest, and therefore more likely to work."

He dropped his jaw and arranged some objecting syllables to launch from it, but I stopped him before he got going good. "And between now and then, I will make a point of going out to the hill where Pine Breeze used to be. I'll poke around and see if anything turns up. And if anyone or anything makes itself known, you'll be the first one I inform."

Malachi sagged in the seat. "I was really hoping we could do it tonight."

"Well, we can't. And we're not. I believe you when you said you couldn't find it, because God knows that even when it was standing it was a pain to locate unless you knew exactly where it was. And at night? There's nothing anywhere around there, Malachi. No streetlamps. No stores. No people, except those who live farther on down the hill—and they would probably call the cops if they saw headlights going that way at this hour."

"So you're making me leave."

"Yes, I'm making you leave. But I'm also telling you that I'm open to the idea of you coming back. And I'm making you a series of promises that go contrary to all common sense. I promise you this: I'll answer the phone when you call, assuming you don't abuse the privilege. I promise I'll go up to the hill and look for your mother. I promise I'll talk to Harry and see if he won't bring you up here for a fact-finding mission sometime soon. But at the same time, I am most definitely making you leave before you get either one of us into any more trouble."

He sulked hard, but I stood firm.

"I don't have any more money."

"I will buy you a bus ticket."

"Now?"

"Yes. Right now. Get out. You didn't bring any stuff, did you?"

"No. Just an overnight bag, and I think I lost it in the river when I fell in and got bitten by the snake."

"Marvelous. Now come on. You can clean yourself up in the bathroom while I arrange a ticket for you. I don't know how soon I'll be able to arrange your departure, but there ought to be something going south before morning comes. I hope." *The sooner the better,* I added to myself. The longer he stayed in the Tennessee Valley, the more trouble he was likely to get himself into.

We went inside together and parted company while I hit the nearest service desk. Malachi slunk out of the restroom a few minutes later, and I handed him the packet. "The good news is, you've only got two hours to stew here."

"And the bad?"

"It's going to take you a while to get home—but it was the best I could do on short notice. I got you as far as Orlando by 6:45 tomorrow night. Here's fifty bucks. Get a magazine or something when they stop. Maybe a razor, or a fresh T-shirt. You'll be okay. And I'll call Harry in the morning"—I glanced at my watch and winced—"well, later on in the morning, and let him know you're coming. He'll have to drive down and pick you up, but it's not that far and it shouldn't be a problem."

"All right."

"All right." Everything had been said, at least everything pragmatic and utilitarian. He was set. The bus was waiting. But the dead air between us seemed to call for something more, so I stammered on a little. "So… are we good, here?"

"We...? Um, I guess. I'm good, yeah." He was disappointed; that much was obvious. But he wasn't at the bottom of the river or back in the Bend with a lifetime membership, so things could have been much worse. He knew it, but he didn't pretend to like it.

We stood there awkwardly, trapped in one of those moments where two ordinary people might hug and say proper goodbyes. But between the pair of us, all we managed was a half-hearted shoulder swat and wishes of good luck and safe travels. I also extracted, with some difficulty, a promise from Malachi that he would not leave the station until his bus saw fit to collect him.

And he dragged out of me the assurance that yes, I wanted him to call me when he'd arrived safely. But that was all the familial intimacy we were able to conjure up on such short notice. He'd spent half his life trying to kill me, after all. Understanding the misunderstanding doesn't make everything spontaneously uncomplicated.

I left him then, wandering back to my car and taking another moment to scope the damage. I could hardly stand to look at it. It would have to wait until daylight, which—it occurred to me—was only another couple of hours away. Lu and Dave would arrive later still, and I was glad I had time to work on my story. "A skunk," I'd told Malachi.

It was as good an alibi as any.

SIX

THE DISPLACED

Daylight didn't make my car look any better, but it gave me a better idea of the damage. Like so many aspects of the previous evening, it could have been worse. As Malachi had pointed out, and last night had demonstrated, the Nugget was still drivable. All the damage was cosmetic save the unbalanced headlight, and a few minutes rifling through the garage turned up a funny-shaped screwdriver that corrected that. My informal tweaking might not hold for long, but it would work for the time being.

Harry's response to my 8:00 a.m. phone call was predictably irate. At some point I actually set the phone down and poured myself some cereal while he raved, and when he finished I tried to smooth things over between bites of Wheaties.

It hadn't worked as well as I would have liked, but before we hung up I had badgered Harry into a definite maybe as far as coming up for a visit with my wayward brother was concerned. I don't know if I'd sold him on the idea or not, but I'd held up my end of the bargain and tried.

And now, I had other things to think about.

I had an idea or two I wanted to chase before my aunt and uncle returned from their concert in Georgia, so I headed towards town and made for the library. I was going crazy wondering about the thing I'd seen at the Bend; it reminded me of something I'd seen or read a long time ago. I already knew who and what the thing at the Bend had to be, but I wanted some reinforcement for my theory.

The dead are my children, the long-haired creature had said.

He was a caretaker. A guardian. I remembered the way he'd faced me briefly, and how that eye I'd seen had burned such a catlike shade.

I told the woman at the book desk that I wanted some books on local lore—preferably with ghost stories, or information on Appalachian cryptozoology. I probably should have stopped myself at "ghost stories," but my unshakable impression that I was dealing with something other than a ghost made me tack on the rest.

The librarian looked at me like I was insane; but I was accustomed to that, so it was easy to ignore.

"Cryptozoology," I repeated, prepared to explain.

"I know what the word means, sweetheart," she said. "And we've got a section with books like that up on the second floor. I don't know if you'll find anything as specific as 'Appalachian cryptozoology,' but there are plenty of books that talk about area hauntings. We've probably got a whole shelf of stuff dedicated to the Bell Witch alone."

"The Bell Witch? She's not exactly local."

"It happened outside of Nashville, and that's local enough for Chattanooga library classification."

The librarian took a scrap of paper and jotted down a few

Dewey numbers. "Check around here," she said as she handed it to me.

I thanked her, took the wide, carpeted stairs up a flight, and checked the rows of books against the scrawled note I held. I glanced down the aisles and saw practically no one; the place was deserted save for the odd homeless person napping in a chair, or the stray library worker shuffling along with a cartload of tomes to be shelved.

I found the row the librarian had indicated and slid between the tall bookcases, tilting my head to the left to read the spines.

The first shelf I spied was stuffed mostly with small-press products about mysterious happenings at Civil War battlefields in the greater Chattanooga area. I saw several titles about ghosts left by "The Battle Above the Clouds" on Lookout Mountain, and a couple more on the subject of Missionary Ridge or Cameron Hill. Half a dozen wanted to tell me about ghost regiments, lost troops, or spectral officers who had never relinquished command.

Almost everything else was about the Bell Witch. Some people claim that the Blair Witch movies were based on the haunting of the Bell family. I couldn't say if that's true, but you'd be hard-pressed to find anyone in Tennessee who doesn't know about how Andrew Jackson passed through Tennessee one time and swore until his dying day that he'd rather face the entire British Army than spend one more night at the Bell farm, so I guess she may as well qualify as local legend. But I wasn't interested in the unfortunate Bell family.

I ran my finger along the musty lines of books until I caught the word I was hoping for.

"Chickamauga."

I slid the book free, even as I spotted another one right next to it with the same subject. I flipped to the back and scrolled my eyes along the helpful columns of words and numbers—Battle, Boynton, Cherokee, Repeating Rifles, Van Derveer—until I found what I really wanted.

Green Eyes, (Old) Green Eyes. 33, 34, 35, 37–40.

What I found on the noted pages was mostly sensationalistic and unhelpful. It didn't tell me anything new, anyway. I was already aware that Green Eyes hung out at the battlefield and that he'd been known to chase trespassers out of the park. The book offered me nothing in the way of proper speculation, so I set it aside and reached for the next one.

Better. The next book suggested that the first sightings of Green Eyes took place in the days after the battle. Scouts sent from the government to assess the clean-up situation reported seeing a tall creature with glowing green eyes roaming among the unburied dead. More contemporary reports indicated that he'd caused at least two automobile accidents in the park during the 1970s, each time having emerged from the fog to startle unsuspecting drivers—both of whom wrecked into the same tree, if the stories were to be believed.

I noted that the reports did not declare that the drivers had been chased from the grounds; they said only that they'd seen the creature, who had turned and vanished back into the trees. I wondered if these sightings had taken place at night or during the day. Old police reports might tell me, if I could get my hands on them. It might be important.

But I was sure I was missing a detail I'd heard before in passing. As I turned countless pages I read a dozen different theories, some more plausible than others. According to one source he was the spirit animal of a lost regiment nicknamed "The Tigers"; and another put forth a rather fanciful tearjerker about a Confederate widow with a pair of emerald earrings. "Even now she climbs the Wilder Tower and watches from the windows for her husband's return," I read aloud. I couldn't keep from adding my own follow-up commentary: "Somehow I doubt it." I didn't know much about the battlefield, but I was fairly certain that the Wilder Tower and the rest of the monuments had not been erected until years and years after the war took place.

I was beginning to wonder if I'd made up the elusive detail in order to fit my encounter when I found a third, older book that featured a chapter on Chickamauga. *Civil War Ghosts of the American South* was published in 1968, and it encouraged me by referring to the post-war Green Eyes sightings as "The first European sightings." It went on to assert that the Cherokees seemed to already know of the creature's existence.

> *Old Green Eyes has been described in various ways by many different witnesses. Some say that he had a face like an ape and enormous canine teeth, while others have said that he looked like an ordinary man except for his significant height and his glowing gaze. Many have suggested that he was wearing a cloak, or that he had a head of very long hair... but everyone seems to agree upon his luminescent green eyes.*

I stopped. That was it. That was *him*.

Well really, who else could it have been?

The dead are my children.

A more rational, disinterested observer might have said that I was merely succumbing to the insistent suggestion of the last few weeks and their strange events. Everyone who was interested in ghosts had Chickamauga on the brain, and in local thinking "Chickamauga" went hand in hand with "Old Green Eyes."

My hypothetical disinterested observer would have made a good point, but I would have dismissed it anyway.

I sat down on the hard Berber-carpeted floor and crossed my legs, pulling down a couple more books and scanning for more information. The more I read, the more convinced of my guess I became.

Many people believed that Green Eyes was not a ghost. The more reliable accounts almost never told of meeting him as a spiritual sighting, but a decidedly physical one. He was something solid, but something different. He was something tall, they all agreed, and either had very long hair or was covered in it.

Yes, yes, yes. All of these things. And I'd seen him. I'd seen Green Eyes.

So what was he doing away from the battlefield? Why Moccasin Bend, of all places?

I dragged *Civil War Ghosts of the American South* into my lap again and reread the pertinent passages. "The Cherokee Indians seemed unsurprised to hear of the creature roaming the battlefield."

I sat still, thinking. Moccasin Bend. I wanted to think it had more significance than being merely a mental-health facility and a snaky twist in the river, but nothing came to mind. Downstairs, there were computers with Internet access. I shelved the books I didn't want, then brought the three or four I did want with me to the first floor.

I opened a search window and tried a few word combinations, just to see what would turn up. Mostly I got a bunch of boring

.org sites about the state facility there; but on a whim I entered "Moccasin Bend" and "Cherokee."

I clicked a couple of links and was skeptical of what I found. I reminded myself that not everything on the Web is true, and kept clicking. A third and a fourth link all revealed similar information. I looked at the site addresses and poked around for signs of a hoax, but I couldn't find any.

That didn't mean I believed a word of it.

Even if it explained rather neatly what Green Eyes might be doing there, it was still the sort of thing that even Ed Wood would think twice about.

Behind me I heard the buzz of a wheelchair and I turned, hoping to see Karl, but instead an older woman went zipping by with a bagful of books hanging off her chair. But my desire to consult Karl had been sparked. If I remembered correctly, he was part Native American himself. Even if he wasn't Cherokee, he might know whether the online articles were true or not.

I didn't have any better ideas, anyway, so I left my books on the counter by the computer monitor and went back to my car. The coffee shop where Karl usually lurked was closed on Sundays, but I knew what his backup would be.

I tracked him down a few blocks away in the Bluff View Art District, up a hill and around a corner from his usual spot. He was parked with Cowboy in a pretty flagstone courtyard with an artsy stone fountain. The pair of them were presiding over a game of chess taking place outside the auxiliary coffee shop.

He waved when he saw me, inviting me over to the table. The chess players and the dog ignored me, but Karl was as chipper as ever.

"How you doing there, girl?"

"Fat and happy, darling. Have you got a minute?"

"For you? I've got all day. Pull up a chair."

I did as instructed, and I wasted no time.

"Karl, this may sound like a weird question, but I thought you might know the answer."

"Ask away," he invited, shifting his chair to make me a little more room.

"It's about Moccasin Bend. I heard someplace that it used to be—" I hesitated, because I felt stupid saying it out loud where the whole world could hear me. "Did it *really* used to be an Indian burial ground?"

One of the chess players cocked an eyebrow and nodded. Karl did the same. "Back in the day, it was a sacred site for the Cherokee people. There was a lot of controversy over the government putting the hospital there. It's protected ground, or so they say. Like a park, I think. But once upon a time, yes, it was holy territory."

"You're joking."

"'Fraid not."

"So what you're telling me is that the government built... *a mental hospital... on top of a sacred Indian burial ground* ?"

"Yes ma'am."

I blinked slowly and shook my head. "Had these people never seen a horror movie? Never read any Stephen King?"

"Apparently not. Why're you so interested in Moccasin Bend all of a sudden anyway, kid?"

I balked, unsure of how much to share. "I heard something strange was going on over there, that's all. Someone I know who worked out there heard some stories." That was more true than not; Malachi had lived there for years, and I knew they'd put him to work in some menial capacity.

Both of the chess players laughed, even as one of them lost a bishop. The guy playing white looked up at me and said, "No one ever works out there long without gaining a story or two. It's like working at the battlefield."

"Funny you should make that connection," I mumbled, but Karl heard me.

"You picked up something about Old Green Eyes?" he asked, lowering his voice just enough to make everyone around our table lean back and strain to hear us.

"Oh, I wouldn't say *that*."

"Then what *would* you say?"

"I'd say that the world's a funny place, Karl. And for now, I'd leave it at that."

SEVEN

RISING AGAIN

SAND MOUNTAIN, ALABAMA, SEVEN WEEKS EARLIER

Pete Buford was thirty-two years old when he was released from the Silverdale Correctional Facility. They turned him loose with a regular set of clothes, and his Uncle Rudy picked him up to take him back up Sand Mountain to Henegar, Alabama, from whence he'd originally come.

Two women were conspicuously absent from his homecoming.

One of them, the girl he was once going to marry, had mailed him a Dear John letter two years previously; and the other had died of a heart attack a month after he'd gone in. Pete still thought the whole thing had been terrifically unfair. It should've gone the other way around, he thought. Allie should have been the one to bite it, and his mother should've been there to make him chicken dumplings to welcome him back to freedom.

As it was, no one was waiting at home and there would be no dumplings, though Rudy was kind enough to run by the KFC drive-through and pick up a bucket of the Colonel's finest.

They talked a little. Mostly it was idle chit-chat about what had become of the house and who had made off with what after Pete's mother had died. Rudy admitted that while he'd kept the place up as best he could, it wasn't in the greatest shape.

"Needs a new roof, for one thing," he said. "I'm running out of pots for when it rains. And you can't just let it fall wherever it wants. That floor's old enough, and the wood's getting weak in places."

"I was going to fix it for her," Pete mumbled.

"I remember that."

Pete had been *going* to do a lot of things in the new millennium, but he'd only managed to follow through on the one that got him sent down the river. It was his dumb sister's boyfriend's idea. The whole scheme was that loser's fault.

Brady, the chump his sister had been hanging on at the time, he'd heard about a way to make shit-tons of money driving stolen cars up to Canada and back. It had something to do with crossing the border and getting them reregistered, so they could be resold legally in the States. The plan had sounded a little complicated, but Pete hadn't asked too many questions because he was afraid of looking stupid.

Everyone said the plan was brilliant and foolproof, so Pete didn't argue when Everyone stood up to shake hands.

Ten years, the judge declared when they caught him in the hot Cadillac Escalade, but Everyone said he'd never serve it all, and on that particular occasion Everyone had been right. They'd turned him loose in four and a half—partly because he'd been good and partly because the county was running out of room. Moving stolen property around wasn't a violent act; and with that in mind, the State of Tennessee had paroled him in favor of incarcerating some guy who killed little boys and dressed up in their clothes while finger-painting with the contents of their stomachs.

Despite his issues with the State of Tennessee, Pete had to admit they'd made a good judgment call on that one.

Pete might have driven a stolen Escalade through Murfreesboro with intent to take it across state lines, and he might have had a joint on him at the time, and he might even have tried to run from the cops for a few miles before wrecking the Caddy against a hotel manager's office... but he hadn't killed any little boys to make art with their innards, and he wasn't likely to, either.

All Pete wanted to do was go home.

Despite Rudy's warnings about the house's condition, Pete didn't think it looked much different than the last time he'd seen it. Leaky roof, battered porch, and all, it was a sight for sore eyes.

A big brown dog sleeping on the porch lifted its head when Rudy's battered old Nova rumbled up into the driveway. The dog thumped its tail up and down a few times and yawned, then climbed to its feet and stretched.

"That's not Digger," Pete observed. "Where's my dog?"

Rudy shook his head. "No, that's Princess. I'm real sorry—I didn't realize you didn't know, but I guess nobody told you. Digger got hit by a car not long after your mother died. He was a good dog, though. I liked him. I liked having him here when I first moved in; he was the only one who wasn't calling up yelling at me because Aunt Somebody-or-another took your mother's something-or-other, and didn't I know Sue would've wanted someone else to have it? I swear and be damned."

"Man." He said it as a vague, general curse.

"Yeah," his uncle agreed. "But for what it's worth, I did like that dog. I took care of him, but he was restless once you were gone and Sue died. I felt real bad about it."

They simultaneously closed their car doors and approached the smallish yellow house with the wide gray porch.

"I picked up Princess at the county fair. Some kid was giving away free puppies, and I thought how it'd be nice to have a dog around again, so I took one. She's mostly bloodhound, I think, and the rest is just a little of 'dis, and a little of 'dat."

Princess snuffled her large head against Pete's hand and deemed him worthy of a lick. She barked at Rudy, and he gave her a rough ear rubbing that delighted her. "I know she's a little ugly," Rudy said, gently slapping his hand against the dog's side. "But she's all right."

"She's not that ugly. Not as ugly as Digger was."

"I wasn't going to say that out of respect for the dead, but you may be right at that. The ugly ones make the best dogs—I don't care what anyone says—and I don't understand the people who breed them to look at them. But come on in. I'll get you a Coke if you want one."

"I'll take one, if you don't mind."

"I don't mind. And I need for you to know, that whatever the lawyer papers say this house is as much yours as mine. It was your home long before I took it on, and it's your home as long as you need for it to be."

"Thanks, Uncle Rudy."

"You know, I didn't move any of your stuff, either. It's all back there in your room. I know you were packing up to move out with Allie when all the bad things happened, but I didn't move any of it and I didn't let your sister take it, either."

"She tried?"

"Yeah, she tried. But I told her that stuff wasn't hers, and she couldn't have it. It was halfway her fault anyhow, what happened to you. Her fault and Brady's."

Pete appreciated the sentiment, but he knew better and it only made him sad. "No, Uncle Rudy. No one made me do a damn thing. Laura's a bitch and more, but it wasn't her fault—just her dumb idea. She'll get hers someday."

Rudy stood before the fireplace and watched his nephew closely for a moment. "That's a good attitude to have about it. I think maybe you'll come out okay yet. Have you got any thoughts about where you might want to work once you get settled in?"

He stared at the door to his mother's bedroom, and then over to the door that marked his own.

"No, not yet."

Rudy saw him looking and hastily said, "If you want to swap out and take your mother's room, I understand. I only took it because it was the big one with the bathroom, and there wasn't anyone else here anyway."

"No, that's okay. I don't care. My own bed'll be fine."

"I imagine it gets hot in there. I've got an extra fan I kept in the kitchen; you take it into your room and turn it on yourself at night so you can sleep."

"Air conditioning still broke?" Pete asked, though the answer was obvious enough and it had been broken long before he'd been in prison.

"Haven't had the money to see about fixing it."

"I figured."

"You know how it is."

"Yeah, I do. I think I'll go ahead and take that fan now, if you don't mind. The chicken's weighing heavy on me, and a nap out here in the quiet would feel good."

Pete took the fan and plugged it in at the foot of his bed, turning it on full blast and letting it swing back and forth to blow away the worst of the heat. When he sat down on the mattress it squeaked and sagged. The bedding hadn't been washed in God-knew-how-long, but Pete didn't really care.

All things considered, he felt pretty lucky.

His sister had long since wandered off into the sunset to make trouble for someone else; Allie was busy cheating on some other guy; and the only roommate he had to worry about at the moment was his mother's older brother, who was possibly the nicest man in the world.

Or maybe he was being nice because he was afraid that Pete would claim the house for himself and throw his aging uncle out—but Pete didn't think so. Rudy never thought that way. Calculated self-preservation had never come naturally to him, any more than it came naturally to Pete.

"We're a bunch of half-assed suckers," he said to himself. "We don't get good ideas of our own, so we don't know how to sort out the bad ones when we see them."

Later that night the two men sat in front of the television with its foil-wrapped bunny-ear antenna. The local news came in fairly clear on one station, so they watched that instead of fiddling with the antenna to see if they could find something better.

"Damn shame," Rudy said.

"About the battlefield?"

"Yeah. That ain't right."

Once again—for the second time that year—vandals had raided the battlefield, spray-painting monuments and defacing the old buildings that still stood. Park rangers were complaining about how they'd only recently finished cleaning off the last of the previous graffiti, and now it was going to cost thousands of dollars to clean up the new mess.

"They never seem to make it to Snodgrass Hill though, do they?"

"What?" Pete asked.

"Snodgrass Hill. The kids with the paint, they never make it that far. They always get chased off. You know why, don't you?"

"Sure. It's Old Green Eyes."

Everyone knew Old Green Eyes kept an eye on the battlefield. Pete always wondered why people ever went there at all when they weren't supposed to. Besides risking the wrath of the local boogeyman, why bother pissing all over a bunch of statues? What was the point?

Rudy rose and flipped the television off with the back of his hand. "It's offensive, is what it is. It's not right."

"Nope. Hey, someone in our family died there, didn't he? At Chickamauga, I mean. Didn't we have a grandfather or somebody who died in the war?"

His uncle turned around and almost glared. "The Bufords sent half a dozen boys to war, and only got two of them back. And one of them, yes, was killed at Chickamauga. That's another reason it's so wrong. You don't dishonor the dead that way. Not our dead—and not theirs either," he said, meaning the Union soldiers too.

The way he said it, Pete imagined that his uncle thought there was no way on Earth any good Southern kids could be up to this sort of badness, and the culprits must be the spawn of Yankee transplants.

"It shouldn't be this way," Rudy breathed, popping the top on another Coke.

"What way?"

"*This* way." He waved his hand in a circle big enough to encompass the living room, the house, the town, the whole state. The whole South.

"It's not so bad," Pete almost whined. "The house needs some work, I guess, but we'll fix it up now that I'm back."

Rudy snorted.

"There shouldn't be any need for it. We ought to still be living off money from our great-great-grandparents. We should've been richer than those bastards who waited out the war on top of the mountains in Chattanooga."

"They got hit up on the mountains too, though." Pete thought he remembered something from school, a trip to a house on Lookout. A guide had told him a story about the way both sides had fought, back and forth, using the house as a point of reference to gauge their progress.

"I guess."

Pete crooked his head. "Well, what do you mean, then? When was anyone in our family rich?"

"Never." Rudy reached like he meant to turn the TV back on, then changed his mind. "But we were close. And we almost had… it was something like an inheritance. It should've been ours."

"An inheritance? From who?"

"From Jefferson Davis himself." Rudy said it with finality, but he stood by the kitchen door and clutched at the frame like he might say more if Pete waited long enough.

"You never said we were related to him," he offered weakly. He knew there wasn't any relation, but he wanted to say something anyway. In general, if Rudy wanted you to know something, he told it to you without leaving you to wonder; so Pete didn't want to ask any questions. But Jefferson Davis? That wasn't the sort of name you dropped if you didn't want someone else to pick it up.

"You heard me. It was a trust—between the people of the South and the men who tried to set her free. And we were in on it. We should've reaped those rewards, even after."

"After? Oh."

"Yeah, you know what I mean. *After*."

Pete shifted himself and stood. "I guess I'll get another Coke."

"I'll get it for you; I'm going back in there anyway. What kind you want?"

"Do we have any Mountain Dew left?"

Rudy bobbed his head. "A couple. Hang on."

A minute later Pete heard the click and fizz of a tab being pulled. He probably didn't need the caffeine so late at night, but he didn't let that stop him. He took the can when his uncle brought it out.

"There's a story to it," Rudy said simply, taking a swig off his own can of soda. He glanced down at his nephew's Mountain Dew and added, "You won't be sleeping for a while. You want to hear it?"

"I think I do, yeah."

"I can't believe your mother never told you. Well, then again, I don't know how much she ever knew about it. But they were her kin too. My own mother used to tell me about them before bedtime at night, on Fridays when we didn't have to get up and go to school the next day."

"Them *who*, Uncle Rudy?"

He took another swig and came back into the living room, sitting himself down into the chair opposite the couch. The elderly springs groaned beneath his weight, and a small puff of polyfoam filler escaped the armrest.

"The brothers."

EIGHT

THE MIDNIGHT RUN

"I thought you didn't want to go," Jamie reminded me. He pursed his lips prettily and blew on the froth of his half-fat soy latte, not because it was hot, but because he was flirting with a girl who was standing in line at the coffee bar. He was in full on, loose-bloused Casanova mode, and it would have been amusing if I didn't need his attention.

I flicked my middle finger at his elbow. "I didn't. But now I think I do."

Benny was sitting at the table with us, peering down through his glasses at his sketchbook, as usual. "Why? What changed your mind?" He scratched a finishing flourish with his pencil and set the book aside.

I retrieved the notes I'd made in the library and leaned in closer to both of them. "I've got a theory."

"A theory? You going to share this theory with us?"

I opened my mouth to spill, but then I wasn't sure. "Well, it's not so much a theory as a good starting point for a theory."

Jamie licked foam off his upper lip and sat his mug down. He actually gave the photocopies a cursory inspection, which implied that the girl in line must have been ignoring him. "What do you mean by that?"

"Exactly what I said. Do you want to hear it or not?"

Both of the guys nodded, so I filled them in.

"These ghosts, the ones that are popping up like dandelions all over the battlefield—we've never seen anything like them before because of Green Eyes."

"I thought you didn't believe in Green Eyes," Jamie accused. He sneaked a glance back at the counter and was apparently disappointed by whatever he saw there.

"I never said that. I professed a healthy skepticism regarding the subject, that's all."

Benny opened up his backpack and dropped his sketchbook and pencils inside. "What changed your mind?"

What the hell. I figured I may as well join the ranks of the initiated and fess up. "I saw him. That's what changed my mind."

"Isn't that something?" Jamie half-sighed a laugh. "Everyone else is seeing ghosts, but *you* of all people see monsters."

"When did you go out to the battlefield?" Benny asked.

I shook my head. "I didn't."

"Then where did you see him?"

"You guys aren't going to believe this, but I saw him out at Moccasin Bend."

They widened their eyes and glanced at each other, then back to me. Benny asked the question they both had waiting on deck. "So how did you know it was Green Eyes? I thought Green Eyes never left the battlefield. That's pretty much his chief identifying feature, except for, uh, the eyes."

"That's what I thought too—or that's what I heard, anyway."

Jamie scrunched his forehead. "What were you doing out at the Bend?"

"It's a long story. But I know it was Green Eyes. I got a real good look at him, and I don't think I could have mistaken him for anyone else." I flipped through the photocopies and called their attention to the parts I'd underlined.

"All of this—what these books are describing—this is him. This is the… thing that I saw. He wasn't exactly a person, but he sure as hell wasn't a ghost. And he had all this hair. And of course there were his eyes."

The guys looked at me across the table, not exactly disbelieving, but not exactly believing me either. Maybe I really did need other spook-seeing crazies to talk with. I didn't like to think so, but the blank faces at the table had me frustrated.

"Oh come *on*. How many giant, hair-covered creatures with glowing green eyes can there possibly *be* in this part of the country? The Bend is only about fifteen miles away from the battlefield, so unless we've got some kind of wacky colony going on, I'm going to go ahead and make the crazy leap that it must be the same guy."

"But why?" Jamie swigged at the latte and looked over at Benny for support. "Why would he leave the battlefield, for one thing; and for another, why would he go to the Bend? It doesn't make any sense."

"I know it doesn't make any sense." Hearing it out loud only reaffirmed that point for me. "That's why it's not a full-fledged theory yet, boys. I can't imagine why he would have left the battlefield. According to everything I've read on the subject, he's been out there since well before there were any European settlers in the area. I couldn't tell you what it would take to chase him off.

But if he did leave, where *else* would he go? Did you guys know that the Bend used to be a sacred Indian site?"

"Um, *yeah*. I thought everyone knew that." Jamie ran his tongue over the side of his cup and stole another glance at the counter.

"I didn't know it, but that's not the point. The point is, the Bend is probably the closest religious site to the battlefield—and if Green Eyes was some sort of Cherokee, um…" How to finish up that thought? He wasn't a spirit, and I didn't imagine he was a god. "Associate. If he was originally an Indian associate of some kind, then he might have gone looking for them when he left the battlefield."

"Associate?" Benny zipped up his backpack and pulled it into his lap. "As if they conjured him up to do their taxes?"

"Shut up," I told him. "You know what I mean. I don't know what he is, and I don't know what he wants, but the Native Americans seem to have known a whole lot more about him than we do. I think he's confused. I think he might even be afraid. The point is, he took off. He left his post, and *that* is why the ghosts are coming out."

"Because he's gone? Like, you think that he was somehow suppressing them?"

"Suppressing them? What? No, I don't think so. I don't think it's like that. Everyone talks about him like he's a guardian. A protector. I think they're upset that he's gone. Something has bothered them enough to wake them up and send them on the move, and I don't think it would have happened if Green Eyes had been there."

"Maybe he helps them rest," Benny suggested.

Jamie furrowed his eyebrows. "Paranormal Valium?"

"Seriously, think about it—everyone talks about the battlefield being haunted, but until these last few weeks no one ever talked about ghosts. Not as much as you'd expect, anyway. It's a pretty quiet spot, all things considered."

"Except for Green Eyes." Jamie pointed at Benny with his coffee stirrer.

"Except for Green Eyes," I agreed. "But now he's gone. And I want to know why."

The guys stared thoughtfully at me, Benny probably thinking about a midnight run to the battlefield and Jamie likely wondering if it would be too obvious for him to check out the girl at the counter again.

"So... are we on? Are Chris and Mike still game to go out there?"

"Oh, yeah," Benny nodded. "They'll get out to Chickamauga, anyway. But there's no telling if they'll ever make it onto the field. The Great Battlefield Excursion is set to begin—and probably end—at a bonfire party over at Ted's. But I'm sure you could nab a few of the more sober bodies and walk across the train tracks to spook central."

Ted was an older, peripheral member of the downtown group. Most of his popularity revolved around his gift for hosting big parties that involved lots of alcohol. He lived out in the sticks of north Georgia, far enough from civilization that a bonfire wasn't out of the question; and he was close enough to the battlefield that the more adventurous partiers could wander off to scare themselves in the fog and overgrown greenery of the fields.

"Ted's place, huh? That's cool," I said, but I was privately wondering if I might be better off beginning from a less raucous starting point. But I didn't want to drive out there alone since my knowledge of the area could best be described as "slim to none," and I wasn't certain I wanted to wander the place by myself.

"Tomorrow night," Jamie added. "Starts around dark-thirty. I don't have a ride yet or anything, so if you're driving out there, could I hitch along with you?"

"Me too? I know how to get to Ted's if you don't."

Benny guessed right; I didn't have the faintest idea how to get there. I'd heard about the bonfire parties, but I'd never attended one.

I shrugged. "Sure, that's fine—but only if you can promise me you'll stay sober."

"What?" They said it in chorus, almost in harmony.

"If I'm going to drive all the way down there and let you two tag along, you've got to at least keep me company on the battlefield."

"What, are you scared to go out there by yourself?"

I recoiled. "Scared? I'm practical. I've never been out there at night before, and I understand it's a tad illegal to march around there after closing."

Benny sniffed. "If they were that serious about keeping people out, they'd fence the place off or something."

"Are you kidding? It's huge. Entirely too big to fence off." Jamie argued. He sat back in his chair and made a show of flexing his arms as he folded them across his chest. "Besides, there are miles of space where it runs into private property."

The girl from the counter walked past us then, carrying a to-go cup. The glass door swung shut behind her, and Jamie partially relaxed. "I've been there, you know. I used to date a girl who lived out that way. We used to go out to the Wilder Tower and get stoned after slams."

I almost asked him if he'd ever seen Green Eyes, but if he had, I would have heard about it already.

"So you know your way around?"

"Yes. Like the back of my hand—if it were green, grassy, and covered with fog."

"And you want me to give you a ride."

"My car sucks, and I don't have any money for gas. That's a yes."

"Benny, do you know your way around?"

"Not at all." He beamed. "If that means I get to drink."

"Fine." If I could choose between them, I would've picked Benny as a guide, but if he wasn't showing off for anyone, Jamie was all right. "You're both in. But when I'm ready to leave, we leave—or else you find another way back to town. Deal?"

"Deal."

"Okay, it's a deal."

"Then meet me here tomorrow night, around dark-thirty. We'll be fashionably late, like everyone else."

The guys were as good as their word, and the next night we all met up at our usual spot. They both beat me there by half an hour or more, but that wasn't surprising. They practically lived there. Benny had left the sketchpad at home but still toted his backpack. This time it was loaded up with flashlights, plus cigarettes, a tape recorder, a camera, and a host of other things I hadn't thought about.

"Holy crap, doll-baby. You're turning this into a proper research expedition, aren't you?"

He grinned and pulled out a plastic bag filled with batteries. "Those Marshalls have got nothing on me."

Ah, yes. The Marshalls.

I sincerely hoped we wouldn't run into them out in the field.

Maybe they confined their work to the daylight. I thought I'd read someplace that they insisted that phenomena could take place at any hour, so they often worked between nine and five. It was the only sensible idea I'd ever heard connected with the duo.

But Jamie brought up the possibility before I had a chance to change the subject. "Maybe we'll run into them out there. That might be fun. We could scare the shit out of them."

"Really? You think?" I rolled my eyes and used my own backpack to nudge him towards the door. "Yeah, I'm sure we could freak out a couple of people who investigate ghosts for a living."

He lifted one nostril and dipped his chin to the left. "I thought you said they were phonies."

"They are. Probably. I guess. I don't really know," I finally admitted. "Whether they are or not, they make a living checking out places that scare the bejesus out of other people."

"I bet people have tried to con them before, anyway." Benny skipped over to my car and claimed the passenger's seat. "Odds are, they've seen it all."

Jamie was gracious enough not to sulk as he opened the back door. "They haven't seen Green Eyes."

"Neither have you," I said.

I climbed into the driver's seat and started the engine. "If we see them, we're going to very quietly run off in the other direction. The last thing we need is to get caught by people who actually have *permission* to be out there."

"Oh, nobody would do anything to us. The cops would just tell us to leave, and what could the Marshalls do except call the cops?" Benny stretched out, crossing his knees and adjusting his glasses.

"Got any bail money on you? Because I don't think I've got enough to go around." I said it with what I hoped sounded like grim confidence, but in truth I was worried.

It was one thing to wander around abandoned structures on private property; but the battlefield is a national park, and I couldn't help but think that the penalties for trespassing might be stiffer than a night in the clink. I'd heard that you could be thrown out of the park or arrested if they caught you with a shovel. And God help you if they caught you with a metal detector.

"You don't have any spray paint or weaponry in that bag, do you Benny?" I asked, making a mental note to remove my climber's knife from my own bag. In case we did get caught, I wanted to keep the number of potential charges down to a minimum.

"No. Just what you saw, unless you count the flashlight. It's pretty heavy."

"Unless you wield it like a nightstick, I think you'll be okay. Jamie? What about you?"

"I'm absolutely unarmed, save for my trusty flask, which is filled to the top with a highly flammable liquid," he announced from the backseat.

"Oh, whatever. Keep your cigarette lighter in your pocket and we'll be fine."

The battlefield proper is only ten or twelve miles away from downtown Chattanooga, but the most direct route is through downtown Rossville, so it took twenty or thirty minutes to get there. Ted's mobile home was behind the park in a suburb that backed up against the protected grounds, and Jamie knew the way as well as he'd said he did. I parked in a makeshift lot that looked like it might have been a construction site by day.

Ted's party was a hit.

Behind the trailer a great orange glow rose up into the darkness, and voices laughed back and forth over some music.

We didn't bother to go inside.

Out back, someone had found an extension cord long enough to run a boom box out to the yard. A local "slightly too heavy to be top-forty" station was coming on strong, and the fire was blazing even stronger. I had to wonder what the hell they'd been feeding it. As I looked for someone to ask, a burly, dark-haired fellow came stomping out of the night.

If I remembered correctly, his name was Brian. If I observed correctly, he was carrying the corner of a small wooden shed on his shoulder. It looked like he'd simply chosen a section, kicked it free, and walked away with it.

With a heave and a grunt, he tossed the angular segment of wood into the bonfire. The pit exploded into bright sparks and set to work peeling the paint free from the boards.

"Wow."

"Yeah," Benny agreed.

"Good," Jamie said. "We're right on time."

About fifteen people were gathered around the fire—some sitting on blankets, some standing and toasting marshmallows and hot dogs. I recognized most of them; all but a few had been at the Pickle Barrel a few nights before. Those who were sober enough to realize that the party had newcomers yelped, cheered, and waved. Those who were not happily ignored us.

Ted came out within a few moments of our arrival. He emerged from the mobile home looking exactly like the last person you'd ever expect to see step out of a trailer. In a gray suit with a red striped tie, he smiled down upon the proceedings as though it were a cocktail party at the Four Seasons instead of a weekend barn-burning with s'mores.

"Eden!" He opened his arms and swept me in for a highly

stylized hug, then nodded to my companions. "And gentlemen. Welcome to the soirée. Could I interest you in a hot dog, or a coat hanger upon which to cook it?"

Benny said no, but Jamie was game. "Sure. Could I trouble you for mustard—if you have anything that isn't primary yellow?"

"Dijon okay?"

"Perfect. Thank you."

He took a wire hanger and began to untwist it while Ted went back inside for a tray of cookables.

"Don't fill up on wieners," I warned him. "I want to get moving before it gets too late."

"Don't worry. But let me have one or two. I skipped supper."

"Hurry up."

While I watched the fire and waited on Jamie to finish eating, Benny grabbed a beer and sat down on one of the square-beam railroad ties that had been laid out around the fire. The light glinted off his glasses, so I couldn't see his eyes.

"How do you want to do this?" he asked me.

I wasn't sure, so I wandered over to the other side of the fire and sat down next to him. "I don't have any great plan. I thought I'd go over to the battlefield and look for ghosts. They obviously want to communicate. Maybe they'll have an easier time talking to me than the people they've addressed so far."

"Maybe." He nodded. "What all do you want to bring?"

"My own bad self—but beyond that I don't know. You came way better prepared than I did. Should I assume that you've done this before?"

"Oh, yeah. But not in a while. And not with anyone like you. No psychics or anything, I mean."

"You ever catch any ghosts?"

He adjusted the edge of his glasses and gazed into the fire. "We got some good orb photographs, and we captured some good ghost activity on audiotape."

"But did you, personally, ever get anything out of it?"

"Once," he said. Benny pulled the glasses off and wiped them with the end of his shirt, polishing the lenses though they didn't seem to need it. "Something talked to me. Addressed me by name. It scared the crap out of me, if you want to know the truth."

"Is that why you quit hunting?"

"No. The people I used to go with moved away, and I didn't want to go by myself. But you understand that. Otherwise you wouldn't be out here now. You'd be out *there*." Benny flipped his wrist in the direction of the battlefield.

"You're right," I admitted. "And thanks for coming with me, by the way. I appreciate the company."

"Anytime. I'm happy to give this another go."

"Let's bring, well—what have we got?" He pulled his backpack up onto his knees, and I pulled my own battered leather bag off my shoulder and sat it in front of me. We opened our bags.

"There's plenty of light out here tonight. Let's just bring one flashlight, and only use it if we really need to. We're more likely to be spotted than we are to spot anything if we go bouncing around the battlefield with half a dozen—what's that?"

Benny held up a camouflage-green light with a right-angle crook at the top. "I got it from an army surplus store. Check it." He unscrewed a cap on the light's bottom, and three circular plastic discs fell out. One was clear but textured, one was blue, and one was red.

"What are those for?"

He unscrewed a ring around the bulb and slipped the red disc over the light source. "The clear one is for floodlight instead of spotlight, the blue one is for… something else, maybe signaling or something, and the red one is for covert operations, such as the one we'll be undertaking this evening."

I took the light when he handed it to me, and I pushed the switch with my thumb.

"From a distance, red light is harder to see than ordinary white light," he explained. "We won't be such an obvious target, but we'll still be able to see the ground in front of us."

"Right on." I smiled, fiddling with a nubby button beneath the main switch. "What does this do?"

"It's a pulse button. You use it when you're signaling. It's faster than flipping the switch over and over again."

"Ah. And you said you had a tape recorder?"

"Yes ma'am. I'm afraid it's digital, though."

"Why do you say that like it's a bad thing?"

Benny popped open the back of the recorder and checked the batteries. "It's not necessarily *bad,* but it isn't ideal. It's better if you've got a regular tape device, because that way if you get anything good, you have something for the authorities to examine."

"But we're not looking to prove anything to the authorities. I'm not, anyway. I just want to find out what's going on. I want to know why Green Eyes left, and I don't care if that message comes across on a microchip or a minicassette."

"Fair enough." He set the recorder down beside his bag, next to the modified flashlight.

I rifled through my own bag and turned up nothing more practical than a tube of lip gloss and a keychain-sized vial of pepper spray. I added the spray to our pile, put my car keys in my pocket, and closed the bag up again.

"Let's leave it at this, shall we? And we can put the rest of this stuff in my car—unless you want to leave it at the mercy of the bonfire party."

"Okay, but I want to bring my knife, too."

"No weapons. No way. Seriously. Bad idea. How did you sneak that past me, anyway?"

"We are *not* going to get caught," he argued.

"You don't know that. Look at this party, Benny. There's a bonfire. In a pseudo-suburban neighborhood. Someone could call the cops at any moment, and if we're as close to the battlefield as you guys say—"

"It's right around the corner, over the railroad tracks."

"Okay, then if it's that close, there's no reason to push our luck. No weaponry. It's not going to be any good against ghosts, anyway. By definition, they are already dead. They are unimpressed by the stabby."

"I'm not worried about the ghosts," he sulked.

"I already told you Green Eyes isn't there anymore, so you don't have to worry about him, either."

Jamie came up behind us then, one cheek still bulging from his most recent bite of hot dog. "Oh, but Green Eyes and the ghosts are the least of your worries out there." He swallowed the last of it, and the rest of his half-joked warning came out less garbled. "And I'm not talking about catching an accidental ride in a paddy wagon."

"He's right," Benny agreed. "The real trouble comes from other mortal, human idiots."

Jamie bobbed his head and sucked the end of his coat hanger, then dabbed at his lips with a striped paper napkin. "Weekend Satanists."

"Half a dozen ley lines cross these fields. Paranormal

enthusiasts come out here from all over the country and—"
Benny was interrupted by a smash and a hiss, and a hearty cheer
from whoever had thrown the beer bottle into the fire. "And other
morons get drunk and come out here too."

I'd heard of ley lines before, and I knew they had something to
do with energy currents; but I didn't want an in-depth education
on the subject, so I didn't ask for clarification. "This is crazy," I
said. "The park is *closed* because people are too scared to go
anywhere near it lately, and you're worried that we're going to run
into supernatural sightseers?"

"In abundance," he assured me. "Especially now, with all
the publicity it's been getting. We won't be able to swing a stick
without hitting someone with an infrared camera and a Time Life
book on the Civil War."

"Such an optimist *you* are," I muttered, shouldering my bag
with one arm and using the other to gather up our paraphernalia.
"You guys do what you like, but I'm not setting foot on that
battlefield with any object that could *possibly* be misconstrued as
a weapon, a metal detector, or a shovel. Got it? Now are you in, or
are you out?"

"I'm in," Jamie said right away. "It'll be an adventure, and
I'm not the sort of paranoid nutter with the need to wear blades
everywhere anyway. My wit is sharp enough to… Ooh, you've got
mace! Do I get to carry mace too?"

"It's pepper spray. And this is the only one I have, so the
answer is no. Benny? You still game?"

He sighed heavily, and mostly for show. "Fine. But if we end
up disemboweled by drunken rednecks, don't say I didn't warn
you. Let's go drop this junk off in your car, if that's the way you
want it."

"Since I don't want that bulky, sinister Brian fellow throwing any of my personal property into the blaze, then yes, that's the way I want it."

"Can I keep my trusty flask, since you won't let me have the mace?"

"It isn't mace. And you're allowed to bring the flask if I'm allowed to have a swig."

He offered the pretty stainless-steel container without hesitation. I took a deep swallow, then wished I'd sniffed it first. "Thanks, but that's disgusting. What is it?"

"Fine Irish whiskey."

"Ew."

He shrugged and threw back another gulp. "More for me. This way, gang. To the railroad tracks or bust."

We swung by the car on the way, locking our extras inside. I brought a small but mighty flashlight to use as backup in case we ran into trouble, but other than that we took only the army light, the pepper spray, and the handheld digital recorder.

We made our exit quietly, lest we acquire a larger party than we wanted. By the time we reached the end of the street, the glow of Ted's shindig seemed very far away.

We walked in a row, with Benny in the middle. He aimed the red beam at the ground, and we followed it as quietly as we could, stepping with care and keeping our mouths closed. We were all listening—for other people, for other things. We didn't know what we expected to find, but we sure as hell weren't going to let it sneak up on us, whatever it turned out to be.

Jamie reached out for Benny's flashlight-holding hand and guided it off to the right, where a graveled area sloped upward off the road. "The tracks," he whispered.

Once he'd pointed them out, they were hard to miss. A pair of big, reflective railroad signs glinted in the red light and warned of potential trains. And behind the signs something else loomed black and huge against the sky.

The Tower.

The Wilder Tower, it was properly called, but like the Pickle Barrel and Moccasin Bend, people tended to drop the descriptor. The monument had become an archetype unto itself, and it would not be mistaken for any other.

Our footsteps ground over the gravel and skipped past the tracks into the parking lot at the Tower's base. An expository plaque discussed some of the monument's finer historical points. Over to our left I could just barely make out the shadows of oversized statues. If I squinted hard enough, one of them looked like a horse.

Benny, Jamie, and I stood still in a small, close triangle. Benny turned off the flashlight.

As our eyes adjusted to the night, we could see one another fairly well; but beyond a few yards we were all but blind.

Jamie leaned his head until his mouth was an inch from my ear. "There's a field that way," he breathed, pointing past the Tower. "And a road."

Benny crowded closer to us and brought his voice down low. "What should we do now? Do y'all see anything?"

"No," Jamie and I answered together, but both of the guys looked at me.

"You don't see anything we don't?" Jamie asked, and I shook my head.

"Not a thing."

I might have been leading the charge, but I wasn't sure how to proceed. I gestured for the light. Benny gave it to me and I turned it on, casting its limited beam in a circle around us.

Over in the Tower's shadow there were large stone blocks that served as benches. I cocked my head towards them and nudged Benny's arm. "Let's sit down over there. We can break out the recorder and see if we get any response. Maybe we'll invite somebody out that way."

Together we shuffled up the asphalt and onto the grass, settling on a chilly bench. We turned off the light, and Benny pressed a button.

"How does this work?" I asked. "I've never done this before."

"What *is* this?" Jamie wanted to know. "What's that for?"

"EVP," Benny replied. "Electronic Voice Phenomenon. We're trying to get ghosts to come talk to us."

"Does that actually *work*?"

"Sometimes."

I couldn't vouch for it one way or another. If I understood correctly, investigators usually used EVP to record ghost voices because they couldn't hear them otherwise. Only upon playing back the tapes did the words become clear. As you might imagine, I've never had much use for that method of inquiry.

"What do we do?"

In the dim glow of the incomplete moon, I watched Benny's face harden. He might not have been positive how this should happen, but he wasn't about to let *us* know that.

"We invite them—anyone who wants to speak."

"How?" Jamie asked, saving me the trouble of doing so.

"We just, well… Eden, keep your eyes open. Speak up if you see anything. You'll probably know first if we're making any headway."

He brought his voice up from a hoarse whisper then, with

barely enough volume and clarity to lift itself into the realm of a normal speaking voice. Although I knew he was still being carefully quiet, there on the stone-silent battlefield he might as well have been shouting. "Residents of this place, hear us and know that we listen."

"You made that up just now," Jamie murmured, but I hit his arm and he shut up. I didn't care if Benny made it up on the spot or if he read it off the back of a cereal box, so long as it worked.

"We invite you to join us," he continued, his eyes swooping back and forth between the field beyond the Tower and the bulky, shadowy monuments in the clearing up the hill. "We know that you wish to communicate with the living, and we offer you our audience. Eden, do you see anything?"

"Not yet."

"Okay." He brought the recorder up with one hand, holding it loosely between his fingers, thumb ready to press the record button at a moment's notice. "If anyone out there has a message he'd like to give, we invite you to come forward. We invite you to speak. Is there anyone present who will offer us counsel?"

Off to the left, by the monuments up the hill, I thought I saw something move. It was hard to say; the black almost-shapes appeared to wiggle and shift if you stared at them too long. But I wrote it off to a trick of the eyes and brain until a more deliberate motion assured me that I was seeing no illusion.

From a few feet off the ground, something swept itself up in an arc and dropped down, landing firm on the grass.

"Benny?" I whispered, pressing my shoulder against his. "What are those statues over there, the ones that go up the hill? I can see them, barely, but I can't tell what they are."

"I don't remember."

Jamie joined the huddle. "They're statues of people, I think. And a big one of a horse."

The horse.

By sheer optical stubbornness I discerned a prancing equine shape, and beside it the figure who had moved—the figure who had dismounted a moment before.

"Keep talking, Benny."

"Is it working?"

"Maybe. Just keep talking."

"Come and sit with us. Come and speak with us. Tell us what you want. Maybe we can help you." He slid his thumb against the record button and it snapped into place.

The figure by the horse had begun walking towards us, and as it moved our way another dash of motion suggested we might have more company coming. In the field beyond the Tower the grass rustled and parted, but I could not see what disturbed it. I returned my attention to the first faint, chalky-pale figure and saw that he'd come much closer, much faster than I expected.

"A man," I gasped.

Benny nearly dropped the recorder. "What?"

"A man," I said again, though when he drew nearer I thought I must be wrong. He couldn't have been any older than fourteen when he'd died, if his present form was any indication. Around his cheeks there was a softness, and his skin showed no signs of shaving.

"He's in a uniform."

"Blue or gray?" Jamie asked, seeking the object of my attention but apparently seeing nothing. "Where is he?"

"It's a little dark to tell," I scolded. But he shifted as he approached, and I saw the glint of a Confederate States logo on a low-riding buckle. He squatted down a few feet in front of the bench where I sat, meeting my eye level. "He's a Confederate."

Following my lead, Benny aimed the recorder in the direction of my gaze. "Hello and welcome." His words cracked around the edges, and his fingers shook around the recorder's buttons, but he held it together all the same.

The ghost nodded as if he understood.

"What's going on?" Jamie demanded, and the soldier tried to answer.

His mouth moved but I could detect no sound, and it was too dark to lip-read with any real success.

"This isn't going to work, is it?" I asked.

He straightened to his full height, then shook his head.

Jamie poked at my ribs. "Ask yes-or-no questions."

"Good point," I conceded.

The ghost looked up and over my shoulder, stretching out his neck to see around the Tower.

I chased that gaze into the field behind us and saw that another two or three trails were whisking and parting their way through the knee-high grass. Our guest did not appear concerned, so I decided not to worry about it… but I couldn't help but feel a sense of urgency as the others closed in. We were getting the attention we wanted, but before long we might also glean some attention that we didn't.

I asked the first thing that popped to mind. "Green Eyes is gone, isn't he?"

Benny thrust the recorder forward even farther, nearly under the nose of our visitor.

The ghost seemed surprised that I knew this. He mouthed a few words and heartily bobbed his head in the affirmative.

"He says yes," I translated for my companions.

"Why would Green Eyes leave?" Jamie wondered aloud, echoing our earlier conversation on the subject.

The ghost heard the question and tried to answer it, but again I could hear nothing. I hoped Benny's voice recorder was picking up something I wasn't.

"Yes or no, Jamie. Yes or no," I reminded him. "Are you upset that Green Eyes is gone?"

Yes. A definite yes.

"And you want him to come back?"

Another yes.

"Do you know where he's gone?"

No.

"If you did know, could you go and get him?"

Uncertain. Then no.

I felt a small gust, like someone had blown across my ear, and when I turned around there were two more ghosts behind us. One of them was nearly in Jamie's lap, but I decided not to mention this to him. He was playing it cool—cooler than Benny, anyway—but I didn't know how far he could be trusted not to lose it.

"Two more," I said quietly.

Both boys swiveled their heads back and forth.

"You still don't see them?"

"No." Benny was shaking, but he wasn't running yet. "But the grass over in the field. It's moving around like someone's walking this way. And I think..." He put out his hand, and it passed through the shoulder of one of the newcomers, "I think I can feel them. I feel *something*."

"Remember the recorder," I said, hoping it would get him to focus on something else, and figuring there was no need to tell him that the "something" he felt was the inside of a dead man.

"Oh, yeah." He held it up again, having allowed it to droop forgotten down to his knee. He didn't know where to aim it anymore, so he waved it back and forth, then settled on his original subject.

One of the other soldiers seemed to want my attention. I kept feeling his chilly breath on the back of my neck. I turned on the bench and faced him. "Do you agree with this guy?" I waved a thumb back at the first soldier.

He nodded. So did his companion.

Both of them were wearing more elaborate uniforms than the first. I thought they must be officers; and when I looked more closely I was almost certain that one had fought for the Union and the other for the South. I was somehow reassured to see that the war colors had come to mean so little.

"So Green Eyes is gone, and now you're all awake."

Yes, yes, yes.

And suddenly, all three heads snapped to attention and stared hard at something beyond the edge of our vision. The three of them looked back and forth between each other and then to me.

You.

It was a small-enough word that I understood the shape of the ghost's lips. He pointed at me, his hand coming so close to my face that he might have touched me—and I wondered if I would feel it the way Benny had.

I knew then that they understood the others could not see them.

He said another word, and I think it was "go."

I acted on that assumption. "Where?"

All three lifted one arm and pointed in the same direction. It didn't help. It could have been east, west, or simply "behind you." I couldn't tell. I didn't know well enough where I was to say more than that they were all in agreement.

I would have asked them for clarification, but that's when the gunshot sounded.

We three living jumped as if we were the ones who'd been hit. We reached for each other in that primal way, reacting to that instinctive electricity that seizes your nervous system when you're still too afraid to speak, but past the point where you can only hold still.

Our spectral companions vanished, and we wished we could do likewise.

We stood and fell over ourselves; I banged my leg against the bench with a fervor that promised a bruise, and Benny tripped and joined me. "Calm down!" I hissed. "Everybody calm down. We don't know what—" And I was cut off by another shockingly loud round.

I wasn't sure what the battlefield did to acoustics, but I sure couldn't tell where the commotion was coming from, and I doubted either of the guys could, either.

"Out. Everybody. Out of here."

"What are the ghosts doing?" Jamie asked as he started to run.

"I don't know; they're gone. Benny?"

"Right behind you."

"Where's the light? I can't see for shit."

The red circle clicked on and waggled wildly on the ground at our feet as we ran, back over the railroad tracks and back down the street towards the warmly glowing bonfire behind the mobile home. Behind us I could have sworn I heard another shot, and an indistinct commotion came fast on its heels.

"Are we being chased?" Jamie panted.

I checked over my shoulder and saw nothing at all. "I don't think so."

"Maybe we shouldn't run, then." He stumbled to a slower jog, and Benny and I both outpaced him within seconds.

"You're on *crack*," Benny swore.

We tore around the dirt driveway and skidded back to Ted's place. If anyone noticed we'd been missing for twenty minutes, no one said anything, but the gunshots had been heard over the festivities, and there was much discussion.

"Hunters?" Very Drunk Mike suggested, but no one bothered to agree. Not on federal property, and not in suburbia.

"Maybe we should call it a night," someone else suggested, and many heads nodded.

"Somebody help me put out this fire, then." Ted walked over to an outdoor faucet and turned it on. He grabbed the end of a hose as it began to sputter, and pointed out a pair of shovels leaning against the building. "Anyone want to take those and start throwing dirt?"

Burly Brian and Chris from the Pickle Barrel volunteered, and together the three of them began an assault on the enormous fire.

In the distance we heard sirens. The prospect of police prompted a few of the drinkers to slink out while the slinking was good. I knew at least two of them weren't of age, so I couldn't say I blamed them, but I hoped they weren't driving.

Things seemed to be breaking up, despite the early hour for a weekend. I thought we ought to do the same. The guys agreed, so after thanking Ted for hosting us, we split.

NINE

BROTHER AGAINST...

SAND MOUNTAIN, ALABAMA, SEVEN WEEKS EARLIER

"It was supposed to be a legacy, and an insurance policy. It was supposed to help and protect those of us who had been most loyal and most trustworthy. Jefferson Davis gave us more than a mission—it was a *trust*."

Rudy began to pace back and forth. He never paced unless he was talking about something important, and since he rarely bothered discussing anything more important than sports scores or the rising price of cigarettes, Pete had never seen it before.

Back and forth he went, from the kitchen door to the table past the television and back again. He rubbed the back of his head, thumbing the thinning hair against his collar. He punctuated his sentences with pauses and twists of his bony hips that brought him to face his nephew.

Pete was transfixed.

"People make fun of our name now, because of what they've

seen on TV and how they think we talk and what they think we're like. But Buford is a damn fine name, and it's one to be proud of. You've heard that before. But maybe you didn't know it. Not really. Not if no one ever told you, and if your mother didn't and I haven't up till now, then I guess nobody ever did."

"Go on, then," Pete said, more for conversational contribution than out of impatience.

"Well, I will. Back in the war, two of the Bufords—brothers, not cousins—were promoted high for good service. And one of them, Andrew, was a bank man. He worked with money somehow. He was good with numbers that way. Went to school somewhere out east and north, but I don't know where.

"Anyway, Andrew and his brother William were recruited by the Confederacy, and they both worked as spies. It was easiest for Andrew, since he'd gone to school up north; so William went west."

"Why?" Pete asked. "What was going on out west?"

Rudy flapped his hand dismissively. "All kinds of things, but that's not what the story's about. Where our part of the story really picks up is, unfortunately, when the South began to go down." He stopped by the television and leaned on it with one hand, causing the bench it sat on to creak.

"Everyone knew. Some of them pretended they didn't, or acted like they couldn't see it coming, but after a while, it was clear as day. We couldn't win. There were just too damn many of them. They were siphoning them out of the slums in the big cities— throwing them into the army and sending them to shoot us even as they got off the boats, trying to immigrate. Lots of Italians and Irish. Lots of others too, who didn't have much choice, or didn't know they did. They threw them at us. Those bastards like Sherman, they didn't care how many men died because they knew there were always more poor back where they had come from. And there were more coming in every day.

"It wasn't the same for us. We couldn't compete with that. But we knew it before Appomattox. And we started making *plans*."

"Plans?" Pete asked without as much enthusiasm as his uncle might have expected. But Pete didn't like plans. Plans had gotten him into all the trouble he'd ever known.

"Plans—with men like Andrew and William. They took men they knew they could trust, men who understood the way the world worked… and they starting doing the only thing they could."

He paused, for drama's sake, and Pete leaned forward.

"They started moving the gold."

"Gold?"

"The treasury of the Confederacy. If the Union got it, every ounce would have been lost for good. The war was clearly going to end against us; but it didn't have to break us too. We couldn't let them take everything. We were going to need that money to rebuild—we would need it to start over. And we weren't going to let them have it."

Pete frowned. "So… so what did we do? Where did we put it?"

Rudy let go of the television and turned away towards the kitchen. "Here and there."

"What, that's all? Here and there?" Now Pete was getting pissed. What a stupid story, one without even an ending that was worth tacking on. "Nobody knows, do they?"

"Not exactly, but don't be like that about it. That's what I'm trying to tell you. They sent it off, but they didn't just drop it into a hole and shoot all the diggers. They made *plans*. They took *precautions*." He pointed a stern finger at Pete's chest. "And *your* ancestors were part of it."

"Andrew and William knew where the money went?"

"Some of it, anyway. Davis didn't just write out a check for the whole amount and hand it off to some flunky. They split it up. They broke it into big chunks, and sent it in different directions. Andrew was a bank man, and he kept the ledgers. He kept all the records of where the money was going to go and how it was going to get there. And I think that they put the Buford brothers in charge of the chunk of change that went out west. William had already spent time out there, and he could've made arrangements someplace. And Andrew was coming along behind him. I think, with the paperwork."

"So what happened? Where did the gold go?"

"You'd have to ask Andrew. But you can't, because he's dead."

Pete threw himself back against the couch and tossed his hands into the air. "Then what's it all about? Why are you all wound up about it, if nobody knows and it don't matter now?"

"Well it *would* matter."

"How do you figure that? Those brothers have been dead for a hundred years now, and—"

"One hundred and forty, more like it. But if anyone knew where either of them finally fell down, it could mean a whole world and a ton of gold—that's why it matters. William, we might never know. Rumor has it he ran off to Mexico after the war, but I don't know if that's true or if he died with the secret in his mouth."

"And Andrew?"

"Andrew went down at Chickamauga."

"You *lie*."

"You know I don't." Rudy snapped his fingers. "And I can

prove it. There's a letter. I mean, there *was* a letter. Your mother had a photocopy of it. She found it in some archives and ended up donating it to the museum out there at the battlefield. But she copied it before she got rid of it."

He shuffled off into his sister's bedroom and opened drawers, closing them hard when he didn't find what he wanted. A minute later he whooped a cheer and came triumphantly back to the living room, waving a folded sheet of paper that had once been white.

"Here it is, right here." He held it under Pete's nose and whipped it back up to his own face, peering hard at the narrow, crooked handwriting. "It's hard to read."

"Let me see it," Pete asked, holding out his hand.

"No, I've got it. I've got the gist of it, anyway. It's from some young private Andrew knew. He's the one who wrote the family after Andrew died. It was the kind thing to do; soldiers who lived tried to do that much for the loved ones of those who died, and this fellow Bentley did that for us."

"Bentley?"

"It's a family name; don't you mock it."

"Sorry, sir."

"Now Bentley was there at the battlefield, and he was one of the lucky ones who made it home. This is what he said. He said, 'Dear Mr. or Mrs. Buford, I am sorry to write you with news like this. I was out at the fields with your son on the nineteenth of September, and I am sorry to tell you that he was killed in the woods out behind the cabin at Dyer's farm, and there he is buried with too many others.' This next part is hard to make out, but it says something about him fighting bravely. Or maybe boldly—it's tough to read. Anyway, he then goes on about how hard the war has been on everyone, and how many friends he's lost, and how he counted Andrew among them."

But Pete was confused. "He died fighting at a farm?"

"Well yes, boy. All those fields out there, those were farms back then. There was Dyer, and Snodgrass, and Poe, and a few other families too, I think. Some of those old homes still stand. The park preserved them."

"Really?"

"Really."

And then the wheels began turning. "And we know, pretty much, where Andrew's buried?"

Rudy laughed. "Well, Son, there's 'pretty much' and then there's the battlefield—which is miles and miles square. Dyer's farm is sitting between a big open field and some woods. I went out there a few times and looked around; I wasn't looking to dig or anything, 'cause you can't do that out there, and I don't figure I'd know Andrew's body if I found it. But maybe I'd know his father's pocket watch, and maybe I'd know the ledger."

"There was a ledger?"

"Yes, I told you—there was a ledger. And as far as I know, no one ever did find it. It's not in the museum there, either. Some of the artifacts taken off the battlefield were put into that visitors' center, but I went through that thing a dozen times and I never saw it. They might have some stuff downstairs in storage, but if they do, I don't know how to get to it."

"But you thought about it."

Rudy nodded. "Yeah. I've thought about it. It's hard not to." He quit pacing altogether, then, and dropped himself onto the couch beside Pete. They both stared straight ahead without speaking for a few moments.

Pete broke the quiet first. "You said there was a pocket watch, too?"

"A family heirloom-type piece. Real silver, or that's how I hear it—and it was engraved with Andrew's father's initials: C. L. B. It might be nice to see that watch, and it might even be worth some money. But that wouldn't be a drop in the bucket compared with that ledger and the gold it ought to lead to."

"How much do you think that gold would be worth now?"

Rudy shook his head, then leaned it back against the wall. "I couldn't tell you. Millions, at least. If anyone knew where it was, or if anyone knew where Andrew's ledger was."

"And the ledger is probably with his body."

"So far as anybody knows. As I said, it might be in the museum. A tour guide there told me they keep some things in storage, so they can switch out the exhibits every once in a while."

"Huh." Pete leaned his head back too, settling his skull against the thin wood paneling with a thump. "Isn't that *something*?"

Rudy sat forward then, and slapped Pete on the leg. "Yeah, it's something all right. But it's nothing, too. And it's tragic, on top of that. Because it doesn't mean shit to us now. It doesn't mean a thing."

But that night Pete lay awake and stared at the ceiling.

He was *not* forming a plan. He hated plans. Besides, he didn't have enough information to make a plan.

Not yet.

TEN

WHAT WHISPERS

According to the news, police were canvassing the battlefield looking for the shooter, who had nearly killed a cameraman working with the Marshalls. We hadn't been alone out there, but I was glad we hadn't run into them.

Dave and Lu were home when I returned from the party. I thought about hiding yet another story from them, but then thought the better of it. I felt like the secrets were getting out of control, so I told them the truth. Luckily, they kept the freaking out to a minimum—though they both expressed some concern about my "habits" of late, bringing up my battered fender in a way that made me feel all the more guilty.

"But nothing happened," I assured them. "There was no danger where we were. And to be on the safe side, after it happened we put out the fire and called it an early night."

"Did you see anything?" Lu wanted to know.

I told her no, of course not. "It was dark. And we were a couple of blocks away at the party. None of us saw a thing."

"You only heard the shots."

"That's right. Three of them, I think. But it was a long ways off from where we were. We weren't even sure what the first one was, when we heard it. Where did they say the fun went down, over near the park entrance?"

Dave checked the paper again. "Near the cabin at Dyer's field, this says."

"Where's that?" Lu asked.

"I don't have the foggiest idea."

"Middle of the park, it sounds like from the article. So not too far from you, but not so close. Where does Ted live?"

"In the neighborhood behind the Wilder Tower."

Lu frowned. "Which one is Ted again?"

"The gay Republican," I said. "Wears suits all the time. Calls you Louise and always has a get-rich-quick scheme. You'd know him if you saw him."

"Oh yes, *him*. With the briefcase. Always talks like he's selling something."

I smiled and let them chat over breakfast, thinking that the less they asked me, the better. Fewer questions, fewer awkward evasions, less worrying on the part of my guardians. A good formula all around.

While they finished eating, I went to my room and loaded up my bag. I planned to be gone for the afternoon, and I didn't want to have to run home for anything. Going up and down the mountain can be a real pain, depending on the traffic and the time of day. It's better to leave prepared.

"Where are you going?" Lu asked as I made for the door.

"Benny's place. Down in Red Bank. I'm helping him with a project he's working on. We may catch a movie later on tonight with some people, so don't wait up or anything."

"All right." She tossed me my cell phone from the end table by the couch. "Call if you're going to come home past dawn."

I was just glad she hadn't asked me "What project?" "Will do," I said, adding the phone to my already-stuffed bag and forcing the zipper closed. "Does anyone need anything while I'm off the mountain?"

"No ma'am," Dave answered, propping his feet up on the coffee table and opening the newspaper. "We're all good."

I was almost to the door when Lu had to throw in another question. "Are you going to get your car looked at today?"

I cringed. The Nugget ran fine, so the body work could wait. "Not today. Maybe tomorrow. More likely next Monday."

"Is the headlight okay?"

"It's fine. I promise I'll get an estimate soon."

"You let us know, so one of us can come down the mountain with you. You'll probably have to leave it for a couple of days."

That was another reason I was putting off the inevitable. I hated the thought of being without my own transportation. The mountain was a boring-enough place when I had a car; the thought of being stuck there with no recourse but the kindness or whims of my aunt and uncle was too much to bear.

I made my exit a hasty one, before they could delay me with more queries. I'd told Benny I'd be over at his apartment by eleven. When I got to his front door, I heard a series of sharp digital explosions that implied he was shooting zombies on his gaming console, and not sleeping late.

I rapped on the brown-painted door with the back of my hand.

He pulled the door open and used his leg to hold aside a shaggy gray kitten with big gold eyes. "You're early," Benny observed. "Come on in, but watch out for Tiggy. She'll make a run for it if you're not careful."

Assuming that Tiggy was the four-legged thing trying to climb up my shin, I picked her up and carried her into the living room. She wiggled with glee.

"New kitten?" I asked.

"Travis's kitten. I'm kitten-sitting for the rest of the week."

"Fun." I scratched the cat's chin and she purred.

Benny nodded. "Yeah, it is, kind of. I might get one of those once Travis reclaims this one. She's pretty good company. Slept on my head last night."

"*On* your head?"

"On my head. Fell asleep facedown in my ear, purring. It was cool. I think I want one now."

I held the fluffy little feline up and bounced her gently, trying to gauge her weight. "It's cool when she's this small—she weighs about as much as a can of Coke. But once she grows up, you might prefer other sleeping arrangements."

"Maybe," he conceded. He reached down with one bare toe and turned the video game system off, then walked across the room to a dining nook that was occupied by a beat-up desk and a bookcase. With a sweep of his hand he indicated a sprawling set-up of computer and electronics equipment. "You want to hear what we got at the battlefield?"

"Hell yes, I do." But the haphazard amalgam of boxes, wires, and plugs made me wonder. "Are you going to play it on this? What is all this?"

He tweaked the corner of his glasses and sat down on what looked like an orphaned piano stool. "What did you think I was going to play it on?"

"I don't know… the tape recorder?"

"Sure, I did that first. But it's hard to make out what's going on. This," he said, cocking his head at the monitor, "is FrankenHal."

"FrankenHal?"

"FrankenHal. 'Hal' for the computer in the movie—you know, 'Open the pod bay doors, Hal.' And 'Franken' for 'Frankenstein,' because this system is basically a highlights version of four other computers that I gutted and raided. It's a lot more powerful than it looks. Don't let the case from 1995 fool you. Early Bill Gates Beige is just a color. Many wonders lurk within."

"Many wonders?"

"A fast-as-hell processor. Shit-tons of memory. A hard drive that could crack nuts. And best of all, for our purposes, some very expensive audio editing software that I did not pay for."

"Ah. And the rest of this stuff—over here on the bookcase?"

"External drives. A CD burner. Extra parts. And that thing on the end that looks like a little hot plate is a mug-warmer my grandmother gave me for Christmas. So that's not part of FrankenHal."

I peeked into the mug that sat on the unplugged plate. "So this isn't FrankenHal's penicillin experiment?"

"Probably not."

Benny jammed his thumb hard into a button. With a few awakening beeps, a promising bright line of jittering life, and the hum of cooling fans spinning into action, FrankenHal was in service. Benny picked a plain silver disc up off the edge of the bookcase and inserted it into an outstretched tray.

"I saved these as .wav files. We got several really good sound bites, and a bunch of lesser-quality ones, too. Maybe you can make some sense out of them. I cleaned them up as much as I could, but it still sounds like shouted Greek to me."

"Shouted?"

He nodded, and the disc began to whir. "They're shouting, trying to make us hear them. It's wild. Next time we'll know, though. We can tell them to speak more quietly so we can understand them. A lot of the more unclear bits sound like somebody screaming into a bucket."

"Are they really that bad?"

"Sometimes, it sounds like the bucket is underwater."

"Ah."

Tiggy writhed out of the light hug in which I held her and squirmed her way to the floor so she could sit next to Benny. He patted the top of her head with one hand while he worked his mouse with the other.

Before long, he had all the right programs running and a black rectangular box in the center of the screen. "Pull up a chair," he suggested.

I grabbed the nearest stray from the dining set and pulled it close. "Dazzle me," I dared him.

"All right, I *will*. This first one is one of the best. At the beginning of the clip, you'll hear Jamie asking, 'Why would Green Eyes leave?' And then someone tries to answer him. I'm not going to tell you what I think it said—I don't want to lead you into drawing the same conclusions I did."

"Fair enough. I'm ready. Hit 'play.'"

He reached out and turned up the volume on a pair of speakers that loosely flanked the monitor. Then he clicked the mouse, and a bar at the bottom of the rectangle began to move in step with the clip.

"Why would Green Eyes leave?" That was Jamie's voice, clear as day and very loud through the cranked-up speakers.

Bargainwasup.

"Whoa." I leaned forward. The words were faint and fast, but firm, like they were being shouted from a great distance away. "Play that again."

Bargainwasup.

A human voice, very far off. I remembered, though—the ghost had stood immediately in front of me.

Benny clicked the button again. *Bargainwasup.*

"What does that sound like to you?"

I picked up the kitten and moved her aside so I could scoot my chair closer. "It sounds like, 'Bargain was up.' The bargain was up. There was some kind of bargain? Is that what you hear, too?"

"Yeah, it is." He was getting excited now. "So we agree on that one. Okay. This is another of the good ones. This is right after you told me to remember the recorder, because I'd let it fall down at my side. You said we had two more visitors. I held it up again. This is what it caught."

Behindinthefield.

"Behind in the field," I said quickly. I understood this one more clearly than the first. More of a frantic whisper, these four words might have been hissed directly into the microphone.

"Not the world's most helpful message, though."

"Or the most grammatical," Benny agreed. "Behind in the field. I don't get it. Behind what?"

"And in which field?" I added. "The whole place is made up of fields."

"There are a lot of woods, too."

"Well, yeah. That's true. Still, that leaves about half the park."

"We should get a list."

"Where would we do that?"

Benny made a few clicks and drags, and another file readied itself. "At the visitors' center, I bet. They've got a million pamphlets and brochures. We should go out there during the day—"

"We can't. Remember? The place is shut down."

"Oh, yeah. I forgot. Anyway, here's another one. This one isn't as clear as the other two. I've got a theory about what they're trying to say, but I'll wait until you've gotten an earful before I say anything."

"All right." I jumped as Tiggy grabbed my ankle and began to scale me like a scratching post. I pulled her into my lap and stroked the back of her head until she purred. "Hit it."

"This one we recorded after you said, 'So Green Eyes is gone, and now you're all awake.' There seemed to be some confusion. You said there was more than one of them."

"That's right. They were talking among themselves, but I couldn't tell what they were saying."

"Give this one a listen."

He leaned over to the left so I had a better view of the screen. The wavering line in the black rectangle swung frantically when my own voice said, '...you're all awake,' went still for a second or two, and then jolted again.

It sounded short and sharp—two jagged syllables that began with a "b" and closed with an "n."

B—n.

A few moments later, a second, quieter voice chimed in with something equally dim.

Fen—vrrr.

The line quit bouncing and trailed to a slim horizontal slice.

"What the hell was that?" I asked.

140

Benny didn't answer, but he tapped the play button again.

B—n... fen—vrrr.

I stopped petting the kitten, who was on the cusp of a nap anyway and didn't mind. "I can't understand that at all. You said you had a theory, though?"

"Listen again. Come on—listen hard." He turned the speaker up another notch, just about as far as it went. "One more time."

On a third listen, I thought I heard a vowel in the first word, but I couldn't swear to it; and the second part sounded a little like the word "fender," but that didn't make any sense either.

I shook my head. "Sorry, Ben. I can't make heads or tails out of it."

He swiveled on the piano stool and faced me. He bit his lower lip and looked back at the screen. "Okay, so I lied. I can't make it out either. I was hoping you'd be able to pin it down."

"Nope. Try another one. What else have you got on there?"

"A couple more. Hang on." A few more tabs and adjustments later, and the box was ready to play. "This one came before you said, 'Do you agree with this guy?' You'll hear yourself towards the end, but right before that there's a couple of whispers that overlap. I think it's two voices, or that's how it sounds to me. I spent a lot of time cleaning this one up, but part of it is still pretty fuzzy."

"That's all right. Let 'er rip."

"Here it goes. Okay."

Ey... ereagain... ows...

I heard the rest of it the way Benny suggested, like a second voice was speaking at the same time.

Iah... ows.

At which point my own overly loud words kicked in. Benny played the segment back a couple of times, and on the third hearing I was pretty sure about the first part. "I think the first few words are, 'They're here again.'"

"Good. That's how I heard it too. What about the rest of it? That second part that comes in midway—what about that?"

"*That* part I'm not so positive about. The second word sounds like 'outs,' sort of. And the first word is maybe 'I,' but I don't know."

As Benny ran the clip again, both of us strained our ears towards the speakers.

They're here again... outs... I... outs

"I don't think it's 'outs,'" I confessed. "It must be something else. What do you make of that 'I' sound?"

"It sounds to me like 'dire,' the way a bad situation is 'dire,' you know? Or maybe it's 'tire,' like they're 'tired.' You said something about them being awake—maybe they were telling you that yeah, they're awake—but they're tired."

"Do dead people get tired?"

"You tell me."

"I can't. Put it through one more time."

He obliged with a flick of his finger.

"Dire," I said aloud, and the word fit as well as anything else. "Tire." Said quickly, even by the living, the two words would be hard to distinguish. The consonants were close phonetic cousins to be so far apart in the alphabet. "Something is dire. No. No, wait a minute. Have you got a newspaper?"

"Um," he looked around the minimalist clutter of the living room and then told me to wait. He slipped a pair of sandals on his feet and darted out the front door. Tiggy raised her head when he turned the knob, but she didn't bolt. My lap was warm enough to hold her until he returned, paper in hand.

"My neighbor's," he explained. "They're out of town and

they won't be back until tomorrow anyway. They'll never know the difference."

On the front page, beneath the red rubber band that held the wad together, the paper announced, "Shooting at Chickamauga Battlefield."

"It made the front page," he observed.

"I know. Dave was reading about it this morning, I think. He mentioned it." I snapped the rubber band free and unrolled the fat bulk of paper. "He mentioned a place. A name. *There*."

I dropped my finger down onto the print, just below a follow-up story on a missing person case.

Benny adjusted his glasses and peered closely at the paragraph indicated. "Near the cabin at Dyer's field," he read.

"And what's another word for cabin? 'House.' I think that the missing word is 'house.' "

He abandoned the paper to me, and Tiggy abandoned my lap because it wasn't big enough to hold both her and the *Times Free Press*. I kept reading until I heard the recording buzz over the speakers.

They're here again... house... Dyer house.

"I think you're right. So, roughly—'They're here again at the Dyer house.' Who's here again?"

I waved the front page at him.

"The Marshalls. Last night was their third night of investigation; and the shots were fired while they were on the road—the one that runs alongside Dyer's field."

"Ah." Benny grinned. "Which, one might assume, is where the Dyer's house is located. You think the ghosts were trying to warn us?"

I grunted a negative. "Warn us? I doubt it. The Dyer house is a ways off from where we were. I remember those two ghosts now, and how they were talking to each other. I think they were just exchanging information between themselves. The one dead guy was telling the other dead guy, 'Hey, those nuts are back, over by the house.' And the other one says, as if to clarify, 'The Dyer house.' That's more logical than anything we've gotten so far, isn't it?"

"Absolutely. Much more logical than, 'The bargain was up.' What does that mean, anyway? If it wasn't so clear I'd think we must've misheard it. But that's what it says, plain as can be."

"God only knows. Was that all of it, or is there more?"

"That's all of it."

Benny toyed with the computer while I quickly scanned the rest of the article, reading key parts out loud.

"It says that one bullet landed in a cameraman. Or an assistant. One of their people, anyway. The other two or three shots—they don't seem to know how many were fired—either went wild or hit trees."

"Did the guy die?"

"No, he lived. He'll be okay. He took it in the shoulder, through his back," I continued. "'The identity of the shooter is not known, nor is any motive suspected.'"

"Huh." Benny pressed a button, and the computer's CD tray extended. With two fingers he lifted the disc out and slipped it into a sleeve; then he put the sleeve into a case on the bookshelf. "That's interesting, but not real helpful. We're going to need to go back."

"I agree. When? And under what conditions? Have you got any suggestions?"

He swiveled in the stool and leaned his back up against the desk. "Since it's still closed, we'll have to go at night, obviously."

"We should pick a different trespassing point. Something closer to Dyer's field. Can we do that?"

"I don't know. But I can find out. Let me blow some time on the Internet this afternoon before I go to work. I'm betting I can score us some maps or directions or something, unless you'd rather do the honors."

"You can do it—or get Jamie to look it up with you. You guys know the area a lot better than I do. You get us directions, and I'll get us supplies. Equipment. Whatever we need."

"Be careful what you offer. You could end up spending thousands of dollars," he warned, but I spied the gleam in his eyes. I didn't have thousands of dollars to throw at the project, but I could throw a few hundred at it without starving; and the prospect of a proper investigation would keep Benny on board indefinitely, which pleased me.

"For starters, I was thinking we could pick up some infrared film. I don't know if Dave has any good filters for working with IR, but it'll probably give us some extra image information in the dark all the same. The pictures might not be as clear as they'd be in the daytime, but they'll be a heck of a lot better than snapping shots in the dark without a flash."

"What will they look like? Like crazy negatives? Like, black and white?"

I shrugged. "It'll depend on whether or not Dave's got color filters and if I remember how to use them properly. Anyway, we may not want to get too close to the Dyer house if there's shooting around there, but I'll borrow one of his good cameras with a telephoto lens—and we'll be able to spy like the pros."

"I like the sound of *that*. But where would we buy infrared film around here?"

"I don't know—but Dave would."

It occurred to me that Dave would also demand to know what I wanted it for, but if I could corner him when Lu wasn't there, I might be able to get away with telling him the truth. Then I glanced down at the paper, and that big shooting emblazoned on the front, and I changed my mind.

"On second thought, I'll call around. Do you have a phone book?"

"Sure."

Twenty minutes of curious dialing turned up a photography supply store downtown, only a few minutes away. They had the film we wanted in stock, and the price was right.

"I'll drive," I announced, and Benny agreed. Once his shift started, he'd be driving a cab all night. He was happy to let me take the wheel.

I wasn't positive I knew where the camera shop was, but the man on the phone said it was across the street from Jimmy's Diner, on the same block as the United Way building.

I didn't remember having ever seen a camera shop there before, but then again, downtown Chattanooga is full of nooks and crannies. The block in question was one of the oldest in town, and had been on the verge of falling in on itself until it was bought and restored a few years back. Nothing delighted me more than to see a set of men with sandblasters methodically stripping the paint off and letting the original red brick show through because if they were bothering to clear it off, then they probably weren't going to tear it down.

I would have hated to see the old place go.

Parking downtown is something of a pain, especially in the old parts where the streets run one way and the lots are few and far between. After a few minutes of searching, I finally found a space a block up from Jimmy's Diner. Benny closed his eyes while I parallel parked nose-down on the very steep incline.

"Oh ye of little faith," I grumbled, sliding the Death Nugget in roughly—but accurately—between the white lines. I yanked the parking brake up and climbed out onto a highly sloped street.

"There's Jimmy's." Benny declared the obvious. "And that must be the camera place."

"Wow. Little hole-in-the-wall, isn't it?"

"Who cares? As long as they've got the film."

"Right."

A bell that hung from the door frame jingled when we pushed the door. Despite the antique appearance of the narrow storefront, the inside of the shop was reassuringly bright and populated with an assortment of shiny, high-tech devices.

At the counter, two men and a woman were excitedly sifting through a set of pictures that I presumed they'd recently had developed. They huddled together and slapped through the photos, sorting them into piles. "That's a good one; put that one over here," a man in a dark red windbreaker said.

Behind the counter, a thin guy in a collared shirt with a corporate logo looked up and greeted us. "Can I help you?"

"Yes," I said, approaching the counter. "I called a few minutes ago asking about infrared film?"

The other three customers abruptly stopped talking.

"That's right. And it's funny, too," the clerk said. He ducked his head at our fellow camera shop patrons. "They were here after the same thing. Two requests for it in one day; and we almost never sell any of the stuff."

The woman lifted her head from the glossy rectangles on the

counter and gazed upon Benny and me with suspicion.

Once I got a good look at her, I realized why: we were sharing a camera shop with Tripp and Dana Marshall.

I didn't know who the third man was—possibly a replacement for the assistant who had been shot—but the other two were unmistakable. They'd been all over the news for weeks, and they were exactly the sort of people who would have a pretty good idea what we needed the infrared film for.

Benny lifted his right hand and mustered a four-fingered wave. "Hi there." He couldn't have looked guiltier if he'd been wearing a T-shirt that said, "I want to believe."

But as far as I was concerned, our desire for infrared film was none of the Marshalls' business. I pretended that I hadn't seen them, I didn't know who they were, and, for that matter, couldn't care less what they thought we were up to.

"How many rolls did you need?"

"Three ought to do it," I told him, and I dug out my credit card while Benny fawned shyly over the Marshalls. I stretched over with my toe to nudge my friend into silence, but it was already too late. He was out of reach, and his mouth had started to run.

"You're Tripp and Dana, aren't you? I've read all your books," he began. "And I loved your special on the Sci-Fi Channel, the one about the ship that was sunk in that bay by the lighthouse."

I cringed. If they hadn't guessed our plans before, they could surely do so now.

"Thank you," Dana murmured. The look on her face said she was shaking his hand only because she could not politely refuse to do so. She was a small, blond woman, at least six or seven inches shorter than me and as thin and tight as a strand of licorice. Her hair was cropped close in a frosted do that should have given her a pixie-like air, but instead only made her look a little mean. Twenty more pounds and a few curls would have made her appearance infinitely more personable.

"I'm Ben Scott," he introduced himself. "And I don't mean to sound stupid, and I don't want to bother you, but I'm a huge fan."

"Oh, it's never a bother to meet a fan. Guys like you keep us in this crazy business." Tripp stepped out from behind his wife and likewise extended a handshake.

He was only marginally taller than Dana—about Benny's height—and if I surmised correctly, he was a handful of years older. The first streaks of gray were working their way through the hair at his temples; and although he wasn't heavy, he was soft.

"It's a real pleasure," Benny gushed on.

I kept my mouth shut and signed the receipt that would give us the film and let us leave, but Tripp seemed as happy to keep on talking as my friend was.

"This must be the only place in town that carries this film, huh? We called around all over before we hit pay dirt. It's a good price too. Much cheaper than it was up north. A few rolls of this stuff in Chicago cost nearly twice as much. Of course, it's a tax write-off for us, but still. You've gotta buy it before you can cash it out through Uncle Sam."

"What were you doing in Chicago? Are you guys doing another special, or another book?"

"Something like that," Dana said vaguely, as if she wanted to hurry up and leave as much as I did. She was definitely not the PR end of the operation, but for the moment I appreciated it.

"Oh, yes. We wrapped up a show that's going to be a two-hour jobbie on TLC in a few months. We had a wonderful time making it. Are you familiar with the wreck of the *Eastland*?"

Benny seemed thrilled for the opportunity to show his fan colors. "That day cruise boat that sank in the river, and killed all those people back in the nineteen-teens? I read something about it a long time ago. I've heard that to this day the police get frequent phone calls from people who hear voices crying for help from the water by the dock."

"It's true!" Tripp beamed. "We even got two of them to go on tape. I couldn't believe it; usually guys like that don't want their names associated with projects like ours, but every once in a while you find a few who aren't afraid to stand up and call it like they saw it."

"That's incredible. Really incredible."

By that time I was holding a brown paper bag filled with film, shaking it, and making obvious "come on, let's go" head motions. Dana caught on before Benny did, though, and she reached for her husband's elbow.

"Well, it was nice to meet you, but we really need to get going now."

"It was great to meet you." Benny smiled from ear to ear. "And I can't wait to see what you come up with out at the battlefield. We're all really excited to have you here. I hope you can get to the bottom of things."

Dana paused to frown at him. "Mmm. Yes. Well. We're doing our best. Things would probably go more smoothly for us if we had the battlefield all to ourselves, though."

I stepped forward a little too fast with the righteous indignation. "I beg your pardon?"

"The shooting," Benny said quickly. "Yeah, we heard about that. You've got to keep an eye out over there. Out here, everybody and their brother knows about the battlefield, and people are getting curious and paranoid. I hope your cameraman is okay."

Trip nodded gravely. "The doctors say he'll be fine, and they're going to release him from the hospital tomorrow morning if things go well. But I have to tell you, the whole thing has been quite a shock. The rangers did warn us that there was a big problem with trespassing out there, and that we had more to fear from curiosity seekers than from any ghosts—but that's always the case. There's never anything to fear from the dead."

I was tempted to argue with him, but I bit it back. I wasn't sure how to contradict him anyway. For all I knew, he was right. He and his wife *were* the professionals here, after all. What did I know?

"But there's plenty to learn from them," his wife concluded, and I had every reason to believe that our conversation had drawn to a close. She guided his arm towards the door, and I laid a hand on Benny's shoulder to encourage him to head the same way. After some mutual "bye"s and another round of "nice to meet you"s, the Marshalls and their associate went their way and we went ours.

Benny glowed all the way back to the car. "That was *awesome.* They were really nice, weren't they? Really? I mean really. That was amazing. Aw, *man*—I should've asked them to sign something."

"Like what?"

"Like—oh shit. We should've had them sign some of the film! We could've had ghost-hunting paraphernalia signed by Tripp and Dana Marshall! Okay, now I'm just kicking myself. I really should've thought of that. At least the receipt. We should've had them sign the receipt."

I rolled my eyes and shook my head. "Yeah, because right now it's only *highly probable* that they're going to have the cops keeping a lookout for us at the battlefield—but if we'd played our cards right, we could've had them calling the Feds to arrest us on the spot. Well, now I'm just sick with disappointment. Maybe, if we run, we can catch up to them and briefly explain our plans."

"There's no need to be like that. They seemed cool. And who's to say that we were going ghost-hunting with this film? For all they know we could be bird-watching."

"Bird-watching? At night? For what—owls?"

"Yes. That'll be our story. Owls. Owls, and bats. We're bat-watchers."

"You need *help*."

Benny shrugged happily. "And food, too. Are you hungry?"

I sighed. Let him be giddy. There was no sense in bringing him down. "Sure. Fine. I could eat. What are you in the mood for?"

"Jimmy's is right there. Let's do that. Have you ever eaten there?"

"No, but I've gone there for coffee. Do they have regular diner-type food?"

"Yes, and some Greek food too. Good gyros. Let's go."

Together we waited for traffic to slow, then skipped across the street. Jimmy's Diner is something of a local landmark, or at least its location is. Supposedly the chrome and 1950s nook was built to be the very first Krystal hamburger shop in the country. And since Krystal still has its corporate headquarters just a few blocks away, local legend might actually be local history. If it wasn't *the* first, it was definitely one of the first.

Inside everything was early space-aged chic—with red vinyl seats, chrome-trimmed tables, and gleaming tile floors. We took a table by a window overlooking the sidewalk. Our waitress was wearing a uniform that could have been seamlessly accessorized with roller skates. She handed us menus and went back behind the bar to get us Cokes.

Right about then my cell phone began to vibrate against a tube of lipstick in my purse, making a buzzing, clanking noise. "Hang on a second," I advised Benny. I fished the thing free and pressed the lit button.

"Hello?"

"So you went back there? And you didn't find anything?"

"Oh, there you are... um..." I glanced up at my companion, who was eagerly scanning the plastic-coated menu. No one in my social circle knew about my continued correspondence with my half-brother, of course, so I searched for a greeting that wouldn't require me to name the caller. "Hey there. Nice to talk to you too, so *soon* after last we chatted. And it *is* soon. Too soon for me to have addressed any of your concerns or ideas."

"Oh." The word was a two-letter study in dejection. "So you haven't been out there yet?"

"Don't be that way—you've just got to give me a little time. I promised, didn't I?"

"Yeah."

"And I'll follow through; don't worry. But some stuff is going on out here right now, and I simply haven't had a chance to look into it for you... but I will. Probably this coming weekend."

He was silent for long enough for his pause to be called "awkward." "You're not just telling me what I want to hear, are you?"

"No, I am not leading you on. I'd only tell you what you wanted to hear if it happened to be the truth. It's better than reinforcing a lie."

"A lot of people would disagree with you."

"And those people are welcome to mislead others to their hearts' content. But I'm afraid that I don't offer any sort of reality discount, even for family. You're going to have to be satisfied with the facts."

"But I don't have any facts to be satisfied with. I don't even know for sure if she's alive or dead. At least if she was still there, and if you could talk to her… that would be something. I'd know that much. But I don't."

It was my turn to be quiet too long.

"I'm sorry," I said, because I didn't know what else to throw out to plug the conversation gap. "I wish I could help you with that one, but I can't. Maybe it should be a project that you and Harry work on—playing detective, seeing if you can't find out where she went and what happened to her. In fact, I officially make that your mission between now and next weekend. Go and do some research. I bet between you and Harry, you can find something."

Our waitress returned, whipping out her tickets and clicking the end of a pen.

"Look, I've got to go. We're in a restaurant. We can talk about this later, if you want."

"You promise?"

"Yeah, I promise. Call me early next week if you don't hear from me."

"Okay. Talk to you later."

"Later," I echoed, and hung up.

Benny ordered a gyro and fries, and since I hadn't had time to look up anything fancier, I went with a cheeseburger.

"Who was that?" Benny asked, sipping at his soda.

I answered honestly, and vaguely. "A cousin of mine. I've been doing some research for him. Long story."

"Oh. Cool."

"So you're working tonight," I changed the subject. "What time do you get off?"

"Midnight-ish. And don't you dare go out to the battlefield without me."

"I won't, I won't. Don't worry." I stuffed my cell phone back into my purse, then wadded up the top of the brown bag of film and mashed that in there too. "I'll have to sweet-talk Dave into loaning me one of his cameras first anyway. If I ask for it and then run off at midnight, I think he might twig onto the fact that I don't want it for bird-watching."

"Bat-watching."

"Oh, let it go. You're going to have to be a bit less crazy if I'm going to use you as an excuse. Maybe I should just use Jamie as an excuse instead anyway. He's been bugging me to take headshots of him."

"Why?"

"He wants to release an album of spoken word pieces. He plans to burn a few CDs and carry them around with him to slams—sell them to the crowd and try to cover a few expenses that way. He wanted a headshot for the back of the sleeve."

"Are you sure? He seems more the kind of guy who'd put his picture on the front."

"Point taken. I don't know. But he knows Dave's got lots of equipment, and he was asking me about it a few weeks ago. This may be the perfect excuse to nab a camera."

Benny took another fizzy swig. "Do you even know how to use a camera?"

"Yes." I scowled, then pulled my own drink close. "Of course I do. Back in high school I went through a phase where I thought photography might be the thing for me."

"Was it?"

"Not exactly. I'm not bad, but I'm no Dave."

Our waitress walked by, and we both looked up hoping that she bore a tray. She did, but it wasn't for us.

"What did you take pictures of?" Benny asked, still eyeing the grill behind the counter.

"Cats, mostly."

"Cats?"

"Cats. I like cats. I think they're pretty. I also did a lot of the typical crap—you know, close-ups of roses and things. I lost interest in it after a few months, but I can still work a shutter when the chips are down."

"I could go for some chips right now."

"Be patient," I told him, but the longer we sat there, the hungrier I got too. The place smelled great, and a cheeseburger was sounding better by the minute.

Before long we were rescued by two steaming plates loaded with our orders. Between greedy bites, we worked out a plan.

It would be best to wait a few nights before going back out to the battlefield, considering that the Marshalls were going to be on high guard. Having a crew member take a bullet would set a group on edge, I imagined; and Benny's none-too-subtle fanboy display was only going to reinforce the sense that they weren't alone out there.

With this in mind, we agreed to meet up again Friday afternoon, sometime before sunset. We'd grab Jamie and take him too, since he still knew the area better than either of us did, and he still seemed interested in accompanying us. Together we would select a vantage point near Dyer's field. I'd bring the camera, a small tripod, and a remote.

"I'll bring some camo gear," Benny offered.

"What for?"

"You want to just leave all that expensive equipment lying around in the woods, for anyone to find and steal? We can build an improvised blind, somewhere in the woods along the edge of the field. We'll need a relatively clear view through the trees, though, so we won't be able to hide *too* deep."

I thought hard for a minute. "Are there any woods along the edge of the field?"

"What else would surround a field out there? They're all surrounded by trees."

"I don't know. A road, maybe?"

"Okay, right. A road, maybe." He waved a fork in a dismissive gesture and used it to stab a fat, crinkled fry. "But unless the road goes all the way around the thing like the Talladega track, there are going to be *some* trees for us to hide in."

I chewed another bite of burger and wondered how this was going to work out. Following a hard swallow, I said, "Let's see— army surplus gear, surveillance equipment, federally protected property…"

"It's a recipe for wackiness," Benny agreed. "We're going to have to be careful."

"We'll need to be more than careful. We'll need to be *ninjas*, for God's sake. We are going to be in some serious shit if anyone catches us, you know that, right?"

"This is the part where you remind me again about the 'no weapons' part, isn't it?"

Now that he mentioned it, this was as good a time as any to reinforce that point. "Precisely. Remember that we are doing this unarmed. Completely. Totally. Utterly. I want *nothing* on your person that could even be wildly misconstrued as something you brought in order to stab somebody with."

"Got it."

"Or shoot somebody with."

"Not a problem."

"Or bludgeon somebody with."

"No blunt objects. I get it."

"I'm not kidding, Benny. If we get caught it'll be bad enough without any illegal accoutrements."

"But"—he raised his fork on high again, jabbing it in the air for punctuation purposes—"consider this, my friend: now we *know* that somebody else is out there on that battlefield, and he— or, for all I know, *they*—are not following your rules."

"You're right. I know you're right."

"And something tells me that he or they will shoot at us as easily as they shot at the Marshalls."

"This is true. However, if there's a gun-toting maniac roaming the battlefield, a couple of knives aren't going to help us much anyway, are they? If someone is shooting at us in the dark and we get hit, a knife is going to serve no purpose at all except to leave us as a pair of very sharp corpses."

"I can live with that."

"No, you can't—which is the point."

"No pun intended?"

"Oh shut *up*, Benny."

ELEVEN

DIGGING FOR MORE

SAND MOUNTAIN, ALABAMA, SIX WEEKS EARLIER

Rudy went into town for some reason or another, and while he was gone Pete snuck into his mother's old room. He didn't know why he was sneaking, but he felt like sneaking was called for. The room was not his—it had never *been* his. Now it wasn't even his mother's.

Pete didn't know where Rudy kept the letters, but a few minutes of digging through cedar-scented drawers turned up a likely-looking manila envelope. Inside he found the aging photocopies of dirty paper covered with chicken-scratch handwriting.

He sat down on the ugly, patchwork comforter that covered his mother's old bed, and he began to read.

The reading was slow going at first. Reading had never been Pete's best subject, and the dead Confederate's tiny, slanted script was difficult to make out in some parts, nearly impossible in others.

He needed more information.

Down the road within walking distance there was a library, but it wasn't much of one—a little branch that consisted of one big room, two smaller ones, and a couple of reference desks. But the librarian was a helpful woman—a pretty, younger woman with long brown hair clipped back in a barrette. Her round face was all smiles when he showed her the old letters. She walked him over to the computers and helped him with a search engine.

"Genealogy is such a popular thing these days," she said, pointing and clicking with dexterity that Pete could only dream about. He couldn't even type beyond the two-finger hunt-and-peck method. "And that's real interesting, about your family. Lots of people around here had family in the war, of course, but that you've still got record of this stuff, that's neat. Do you know where the original documents came from?"

"No," Pete admitted, watching her long white hand palm the mouse around the worn red pad. "Well, then again, I think my uncle said something about a museum. One for the battlefield."

"The one at the visitors' center there? Out at Chickamauga?"

"I think so, but I don't really know. That's where my uncle thinks it went, anyhow."

"That could be. It's a nice set-up out there." She brushed her hair off her shoulders and squinted at the monitor, and Pete thought about how the library's set-up wasn't half bad either.

"You've been out there?"

"Once or twice. Hasn't everybody within a hundred miles?"

"Probably. But the museum there, it's a good one?"

She shrugged. "It's not bad. It's not like something you'd find in Atlanta or anything, but there's more there than you'd expect. And some old nut donated his antique gun collection, so the museum has a big wing dedicated to that, too."

Pete turned the photocopy over in his hands. "Do you think they'd have something like this out on display? So I could look at the original?"

"Maybe. I don't know. I don't see why not. And if it's not out on display, there are rangers who work there that could tell you about it if you asked. A bunch of the collection objects are kept down in the basement, I hear."

"In the basement?"

"I guess they don't have room for it all out in the open. I bet they switch it around from time to time, changing out the exhibits for people who come by regularly. So that way, it's not the same thing every time they visit. You should take this out there. I bet the folks who work there would love to see it, and they'd know a whole lot more about it than I would."

"Thank you, ma'am," Pete said, rising from the uncomfortable plastic chair. "I may just do that. I appreciate your time."

"That's what I'm here for." She smiled up at him, and he almost blushed as he hurried his way out.

When Rudy got home from wherever he'd been, Pete asked if he could borrow the car. Rudy rubbed the keys between his thumb and forefinger, worrying them thoughtfully.

"What do you want it for?" he asked.

Pete already had his answer planned out. "Job hunting."

"Dressed like that?"

"Well, I didn't mean right *now*. I was gonna clean up first." He wiped his hand self-consciously across his forehead and back through his hair. He was still wearing the same dirty clothes he had on when he'd walked to the library. "And besides," he added, "I'm not trying out for a big insurance company or anything. I thought I'd drive down to St Elmo and try my luck at the foundry."

"That's not a bad idea."

"No sir, I didn't think so either."

"Well, you take it, then. Just be real careful. It's pulling to the right. I need to get it realigned, when I get the money."

And Pete went down the mountain and into the city; or rather, he went *through* the city and down into Rossville, just on the other side of the state line. According to the signs on the interstate, you could get to the battlefield by such a route.

Pete took the signs at their word, and about twelve miles south of Chattanooga, he found himself driving onto park property.

He hadn't been sure what to expect, but the rolling hills, tended grass, and paved bike trails felt anticlimactic somehow. *My ancestors died here,* he thought. *And a whole lot of other people's ancestors, too.* It felt funny to putter through the lawns and see people with picnic gear seeking out patches of sun.

Off to the right of the main road there was a big, antebellum-house-shaped building with cannons in front of it. Pete took a guess that this was the visitors' center and museum. He parked the loud old car in the lot, lining up the hood with a pyramid made of stacked cannonballs.

He got out of the car then, retrieving his yellow envelope from the passenger's seat and tucking it under his arm.

Up the stairs and inside, past the glass front doors, there were walls lined with paintings and photographs. Most of it was standard portraiture of long-gone generals and colonels and morbid Mathew Brady samplings; but in the panels between the displays the walls were adorned with large plaques offering episodic history lessons in a big bold font.

Flags hung down from the ceiling like so much bunting, and

a donation box asked where you were visiting from. A clear plastic sheet over the top had slots for all the states in the Union, with a change-sized hole in case you wanted to represent your home locale with a bit of cash.

The Georgia bin was stuffed pretty full of dollars and quarters, and the Tennessee one was too. Kentucky also had a smattering of spare change, and a few Alabamans had come by as well.

Otherwise, the pickings were slim.

Pete shoved his hand down into his pocket and pulled out a few nickels. He pushed them through the Alabama hole and moved on to read the informative wall coverings.

He walked the wall slowly, reading closely, pulling the words into his chest and feeling his ribs expand with pride. This was the first national military park in the country. Thirty-five thousand soldiers had died on these grounds, and surviving veterans of the conflict had petitioned Congress to see the land protected. Two men in particular had spearheaded the drive: General H. V. Boynton and Ferdinand Van Derveer. Together they lobbied until the funds were raised and the territory was set aside in 1890.

He followed the script around to the left, momentarily skipping the park guide's island at the juncture of the three main hallways.

In the next room he found more historical graffiti, and artifacts too. A black munitions cart had been carefully restored and placed in the mini-museum, as well as a full gray uniform, some cannonballs, a journal or two, and a wealth of buttons and insignia—accompanied by historical photographs that had been blown up and posted beside them.

"Chattanooga, as seen from Missionary Ridge," one caption read. The city looked like a mud pit crisscrossed by railroad tracks, and Pete thought to himself that it didn't look like something anyone in his right mind would fight over.

But there were other notes too, about the city's importance as a transportation hub and center for the distribution of goods. The trains that chugged through the dirty little mud pit were feeding ammunition and food to the entire South, thus the North's interest in getting a good grip on the place.

Once he felt like he'd absorbed everything worthwhile from the left corridor displays, Pete returned to the park ranger cube and asked if he could have a map.

A blond lady in a beige-and-black uniform handed him a pamphlet that unfolded into a multicolored diagram of the grounds. It noted bike trails, street names, and numbered all the significant monuments, cross-referencing them on the back.

"What does that mean, the 'significant monuments'?" Pete asked.

"There are too many monuments to list them all on a handout bill," the lady told him, pointing at the map with a plastic pen. "Most of the big monuments you see along the trails were paid for by veterans of assorted regiments, or by their families. Many of the other ones are off the beaten path; some of them are even out in the middle of the woods."

"Why?"

"Because representatives of Van Derveer and Boynton were trying to mark the spots where Chickamauga's major players fell. Sometimes people died out in the open, and sometimes they dropped in out-of-the-way places."

"So some of those spots are out in the woods."

"That's right. The places where brigade commanders fell are marked by the big pyramids of cannonballs fifteen high; and headquarters are marked by smaller stacks of cannonballs seven high. Of course we're not one hundred percent sure about a lot of them, but what can you do?"

"What do you mean?" Pete asked, displeased with the implications. If no one was sure where the bigwigs had died, the odds were better than good that nobody knew a thing about the mortal remains of Andrew Buford.

"When the park was being laid out and populated with monuments, the veterans came through and pointed out the places where they thought these men had died. But this was twenty or thirty years after the battles happened. That's why we tend to view the monuments as approximations instead of historical fact."

"All right. But there aren't any monuments to the regular Joes, are there?"

She grinned patiently from underneath a fluffy set of bangs. "Almost all of the monuments in the park are dedicated to the regular Joes. Look out the window there, across the field—that's the Florida monument, to all the regular Joes who came from that state to fight. And down the way there's the Ohio monument, to all *those* regular Joes. Many of the monuments list names and—"

"But none of them talk about where specific soldiers died, do they? Not unless they were officers."

"No, I'm sorry." She shook her head. "Is there some special reason you're asking?"

"I'm doing some"—he thought of the librarian back on Sand Mountain—"genealogical research. On my family. I had some family members who died here."

Her eyes went wide, then blinked slowly with fresh understanding. "Oh. I see. You want to know exactly where a relative died. A grandfather?"

"An uncle. I'd like to know where he's buried, anyway." A new thought wormed its way up and out into the conversation. "Hey, what about graves? Are there big patches out here where there are mass graves? They didn't take the bodies away to bury them, did they?"

"Pretty much everyone who died here is buried here, with a few exceptions. Wealthier families would sometimes try to have bodies shipped home for burial, but given the lack of refrigerated cargo transport back then, you can just guess how well *that* went. Poorly or improperly sealed wood caskets, long train trips across a couple of states… things got ugly. By the time your poor unfortunate family member made it home, you wouldn't be able to recognize him."

Pete grunted. "Ew."

"Yeah," the ranger agreed, happy to be off on a fond and obscure subject. "In fact, a lot of people don't know this, but the practice of embalming as a science really took off in this country for exactly that reason. They didn't use formaldehyde back then, though. They pumped the bodies full of arsenic. But the point is, most of them who died here, stayed here."

"Oh."

"And out here, it was especially bad. After the fighting it took over a month for anyone to come this way for clean-up."

Pete winced. "Clean-up?"

"Burying everybody. It took 'em that long to get out here and get working. That's why we really prefer that visitors stay on the trails or on the paved roads. There are places in this park where you'll bust an ankle wandering around off the beaten path. The old graves collapse in on themselves after a while, and it leaves the terrain all messed up. It's especially bad out between the trees, because fallen leaves hide how uneven the ground is. People think it's all right, so they maybe wander back to see one of those smaller monuments hidden in the woods... and then, oh, no. Twisted ankles. Scraped-up palms. Trouble for everybody."

"Wow."

"Yeah. Wow. So you've got family who died out here?"

"Yes ma'am. And I've got these letters here. I've got copies of them, I mean. They belonged to my mother before she died, and I heard that the originals went to your museum here some years ago."

"Let me see those," she offered, fluttering her hands at him in a gentle grasping way.

Pete pulled the letters out and handed them forward. "Do these read familiar to you?"

She examined them, holding them up so close that they touched the tips of her voluminous hair. "I couldn't say for sure," she eventually said. "We get a lot of stuff like this in the collection. I don't suppose you'd be interested in leaving them here for a couple of days and letting me poke around some?"

He shuffled his feet and scratched at the back of his neck. "I'd rather not, if it's all the same to you. They were my mother's, and she died not long ago. I could make you copies, though. Could I leave you some copies of these?"

"Sure you can. That would be great. And you know where else you may want to check? Go out to the university in Chattanooga. Their library has a collection of letters and things like these, and they bought out a few of our items a couple years ago. Check with them, and see if your papers ended up in the school library."

"I'll do that, ma'am. Thank you for your help." Before he left, he stopped himself and turned around for one more question.

"While I'm here, though, could you point me at Dyer's field?"

"Yes I can, sweetheart. You just follow this road out here—right out front, you see it? Follow that up about a mile or three, and you'll see the Dyer's cabin on the left. It's not much, but it's still there."

"What does it look like?"

"It looks like a little brown cabin. You can't miss it."

"Got it. Thank you, ma'am."

Pete folded up the pamphlets and stuffed the lot of them into his back pocket, where they bulged like a wallet. He went back out to his car and pumped on the gas and twisted the key until the engine gargled to life, then pulled out onto the smoothly paved road that ran alongside the visitors' center.

Every so often, a smaller road would split off into a half circle, offering a place to park or picnic. Pete found one such turn-off across from Dyer's field and hauled his vehicle away from the main thoroughfare.

With a slam and a kick, he closed the car door behind him and squinted across the field.

It wasn't remarkable. The field was just a big rectangular stretch of bright green grass flanked on three sides by trees. All in all, the field was maybe half a mile square by Pete's best estimate.

At the far end of the field was a small brown cabin, exactly as it had been described. The backside of the house was only a few yards away from the tree line. Pete began walking towards it, figuring it would get bigger as he neared it. He was mistaken.

Up close and personal, the cabin was about the size of his living room.

The door was barred off, but left open so visitors could climb up on a stair and peek inside. A few period-appropriate pieces of furniture adorned the thing, but it was basically empty.

Pete was underwhelmed.

He climbed down off the stair and checked out the field surrounding it. Contrary to the park ranger's suggestion, he didn't see any dips for old graves, or uneven turf. Maybe the grass needed to be mowed closer.

He wished he'd thought to bring the letters with him from the car, but he didn't want to walk all the way back across the road, so he decided to trust his memory. The message from the soldier had said Andrew died in the woods behind the cabin—Pete was pretty sure of that. But there were a *lot* of woods behind the cabin.

Back behind the little old shack he poked his head between the trees and saw a shiny hunk of granite next to a pyramid of cannonballs. He didn't see any signs telling him not to trespass or to stay on the trails, so he decided to take his chances and get a closer look.

His footsteps crunched through the dropped leaves and over fallen branches. Birds called from tree to tree, and squirrels scattered from his path. *What a perfectly normal place,* he thought, *for so many people to be buried here.*

Between two gigantic trunks, a podium-shaped slab of polished gray stone announced a shift in line formation and a forced retreat by the Alabama regiment that Andrew had been in.

The black pyramid beside it stood for the loss of the troop's commander, Thomas Winder, who had fallen on this spot—or approximately on this spot, Pete remembered—on the nineteenth of September.

"Same day as Andrew," Pete said aloud. "That fits with the letter, anyway. Maybe he's somewhere around here, too."

He slowly turned himself in a full circle, looking for any sign of shallow graves or a divine hint. Pete didn't really believe in divine hints, but he was open to the possibility. Nothing short of a divine hint was going to get him anywhere today.

"I'll never find him. Not without..." He stopped himself. Not without what? What sort of equipment might be required to find a specific body underground, buried with many other bodies? Even a metal detector wouldn't turn up anything more interesting than buttons or bullets.

Or, maybe...

Pete quit his calculating pivot and held stock-still.

Or maybe a silver watch. But talk about your *long* shots.

If Andrew had been wearing or carrying the watch on the battlefield, and *if* he had been somewhere near this commander when he died, and *if* no one came along and decided to liberate that silver watch from Andrew's corpse while it lay exposed for over a month... then maybe.

Maybe.

Maybe an ordinary metal detector might do the trick.

Pete didn't know where he might come by this piece of equipment, but he figured it couldn't be that hard to find. Pete knew that a detector was likely to sound off at all kinds of trinkets, medals, buckles, and lead shot, but his dim idea of how the machines worked made him think that a detector might make a louder bleep for a bigger item.

He could experiment. It wouldn't be that difficult, he didn't think.

Pete was elated by his own genius. He smiled so high the corners of his lips almost greeted his eyebrows.

* * *

Back at home, he began making phone calls. The army surplus store didn't have anything he could use; and the people at Sears could hook him up, but the price was well beyond his reach. There was an industrial supply rental place out in Henegar, though. The kid on the phone didn't know if they had anything or not, but they were open and Rudy wasn't yet home or in need of the car.

Pete sped into town and pulled up at Marty's Industrial Supply. Inside, the store was a dirty tangle of specialty saws, drilling equipment, plumbing peripherals, and more.

An older man with a tall shock of gray hair offered his assistance.

"I spoke to someone on the phone about finding a metal detector," Pete explained.

The old man wheezed and nodded. "A metal detector? We may have one in the back. You looking to rent, or buy?"

"Just rent."

"Okay, then. Come on back. Let's see what we have."

Together they climbed through the metalwork jungle and fought their way into a room even more dense than the storefront. Tile and concrete dust filled the air, and the old man gave another little wheeze.

"Sorry 'bout the mess. We don't get a lot of call for these things, not too often. You going looking for bullets?"

"Bullets?" Pete thought fast. He hadn't realized he might need a story.

"Bullets, you know. From the war. That's what people usually want these for, though you know you can't take 'em into the state parks. They'll arrest you, and throw you to the Feds."

Yes, Pete had known—but in his excitement he'd forgotten that one niggling fact. "Sure, that's what I need it for, but this is a

171

private property thing. A friend of mine down in the valley, he's thinking about putting in a pool."

"Started digging and turned up some goodies?"

Pete nodded vigorously, even though the storekeeper was facing away from him, picking through a pile of miscellaneous hardware. "Sure enough. Some lead ball shot, and the like. Probably nothing too wild, but he thought he'd take a look to be sure."

"You never know. Where's your friend live?"

"Um, on the ridge. Up on the ridge there, over the East Ridge Tunnel." He fervently hoped the location sounded reasonable, or that the shop guy didn't know enough to realize that it wasn't.

"Near the Georgia line. I see. You're right, I bet, and it's nothing too wild. Sure might be interesting to look, though. Your friend, he may want to keep an eye out for other things, too—Indian things. Artifacts and the like. Stuff this baby won't register."

He lifted a long-handled machine with a dinner-plate-sized head out from behind a lawn mower cart. Using the end of his shirt, he wiped off some of the dust and gave the thing a good shake.

"You'll need to charge the batteries on it, or put in some new ones; but she'll still run for you, I bet. Watch out like I said for those Indian things." Then he lowered his voice, despite the fact that they were alone. "And if you find some, don't say anything to anybody. Boy, if the state gets wind that you've got Indian doodads on your land, you'll be in some real trouble. They'll dig up your house if they feel like it, just to get at the useless history that *might* be hidden underneath it. You mark my words. If you find them, you keep it to yourself. Don't even dig 'em up. Leave 'em in the dirt where they are. If they turn up on one of those Internet sites, people will want to know how you got them. And you can't sell those things for shit, anyway."

"I'll keep that in mind. Thanks."

The price on the detector wasn't as bad as Pete had feared. He had enough left over from the fifty Rudy had given him for gas and lunch to cover the rental, so he stashed the thing in the trunk and took it home.

Something told him that Rudy wouldn't approve too heartily of Pete's exciting new plan—and that was fair enough, because Pete had to admit that his batting average hadn't always been so close to a thousand.

But there wasn't much to lose, and there was so much to gain.

Having visited the battlefield, Pete was more confident than ever that a secret excursion wouldn't be tough. The place was huge—bigger than he'd imagined by far—and the few rangers on duty seemed to congregate in the museum. He hadn't seen anyone driving around scoping the grounds, or any guided tours going on anyplace.

Pete thought back to the news story from a couple of nights before. Hell, if a band of jackass kids with paint could storm the place, one lone man shouldn't have any trouble at all.

That night while Rudy watched TV, Pete scared up an oversized knapsack that a cousin of his had gotten from the army. The thing was a monster, about four feet long and designed like a duffel bag in hideous pond-scum green. It easily held the metal detector when the handle was collapsed, and it also had plenty of room for a small shovel and a flashlight.

"I'll need the car again tomorrow if I can take it," Pete broached, with as much nonchalance as he could muster.

Rudy looked up from his fast-food takeout. "What for? And how'd things go at the foundry? Did you have any luck?"

"Yes and no. The guy I needed to talk at wasn't there today.

They told me to come back." Pete made a mental note to visit the foundry as well. He'd have to do it eventually, and if he didn't do it before long, Rudy was going to get suspicious.

"All right, then. I can ride with Albert." He pointed at the keys, sitting on top of the television.

"Thanks, Uncle Rudy. I appreciate it."

The next day Pete went to the city and stopped by the foundry like he'd told Rudy he intended. He filled out an application and talked to the guy in charge, who struck him as being neither committal nor hostile. By the end of the week, Pete would hear something, one way or another.

He stopped for a snack-food lunch at a gas station. There he used the remainder of his money to put more gas in the car, and killed some time checking the air in the tires, making sure the oil wasn't low, cleaning the windshield, and throwing away some of the trash that had accumulated on the floorboards.

The battlefield park closed at sunset.

If he timed things right, Pete would arrive within an hour of that deadline, and by his calculations, the place ought to be fairly empty by then. The day-trippers and bicyclers would have packed things up; and if he was extra lucky, the rangers would all be busy closing down the visitors' center.

Pete knew about the suburbs on the other side of the train tracks. On the map he'd gotten from the blond ranger, it looked like the distance between homestead and federal preserve was thinnest by the Wilder Monument.

He checked the round number by the train tracks and read the blurb on the back. The Wilder Monument—that was the tall white tower. He remembered seeing it in pictures or in the past.

Assuming the map was right, there was a set of train tracks directly in front of the Wilder Tower, and on the other side of those tracks lay private property. It might be a good place to park.

Of course, it might also be a long way to run back to the vehicle in case of trouble, but if he gauged the distance directly, it wasn't more than three-quarters of a mile. Pete could run that far carrying a whole lot more than a metal detector and a shovel, and he could run it *fast* if someone was chasing him.

He chuckled to himself, thinking he could make the dash even faster if some*thing* were chasing him; but it was funny how little he believed in Old Green Eyes anymore.

Maybe he'd never believed in the ghoul to begin with. It was just an old bedtime story, anyway.

Even so, once the thought had sprung up, it was hard to kick it back down. He wished he'd thought to bring one of Rudy's guns with him. Oh well. It was too far to drive back up Sand Mountain this close to dusk.

Instead, he heaved the oversized satchel carefully out of the trunk and put it on the passenger's seat. Within twenty minutes he'd backtracked his way through the bordering neighborhood, and within five more he found a run-down little house with an abandoned look and a Crye-Leike Realtors for sale sign in the front yard.

He parked on the street in front of that house, retrieved his satchel, and slung it onto his back.

Wax paper, potato chip bags, and the occasional coiled mound of dog shit suggested that the Wilder Tower had hosted visitors earlier in the day; but by the time he crossed the train tracks and walked up the gray sidewalks, it was deserted. He wandered past it, sticking to the main paths, since—at least for the moment—

he wasn't doing anything wrong. The park wasn't yet closed, and Pete wasn't yet digging on federally protected land. No sense in sneaking until it was absolutely necessary.

Through the thick fields of thigh-high grass he walked, sticking to the concrete and seeing absolutely no one. When he reached the main road, two cars crawled by, one in each direction.

When both cars had passed out of sight, he crossed the street and approached the Dyer cabin. He tossed a furtive glance in all four directions and, seeing not a soul, ducked back into the trees.

The monuments were far enough back that they'd be nearly invisible from the road and very difficult to see from the cabin. The sky was dimming into dark, but he had another half hour of light left at least, and the flashlight to hold him over after that.

He felt safe there beneath the canopy—but not quite safe enough to use the metal detector's headphones.

With a swift twist of the dial, the detector came to life.

Another swift twist brought the volume down to an acceptable level, and a series of bleeps, pings, and pops whined forth from the black box on the handle.

Although Pete had thought about experimenting with the detector, learning how to use it and how to judge the noises, he hadn't gotten around to it. For one thing, Rudy had been home; and for another, he didn't know how much battery life was left in the old nine-volt and he didn't want to waste it. For thing number three, he'd completely forgotten.

A crash course would have to suffice.

Weeeoooooo, weeeeoooo. Pop.

He swung the flat, round head slowly back and forth, waving it a few inches over the turf. The head hovered like a UFO, grazing the grass tips. It breezed to and fro, left to right. The machine talked as it swayed.

Pop pop pop. Vvzzzzz. Weeeoooo.

Weeeoooo.

Pete began having fun with it. He pretended it was music. Made some steps, keeping time.

After a few minutes, he homed in on something solid. That's how it felt, anyway, and since his first trip with the detector was an experiment and a crash course all in one, he decided that further investigation was in order.

Lacking anything else to mark his target, he dropped the metal detector with the round end flat on the promising spot and returned to his bag. From inside he withdrew a small garden shovel, and then went back to the possible lucky spot. With one foot on the shovel's metal edge, he pushed the blade into the ground—just an inch or two. He didn't want to disturb anything important, and he didn't know how far down the important stuff might lie. Small shovelfuls, then. An inch or two deep. A gentle toe-push forward.

But it was getting hard to see.

Pete left his little hole and went back to the bag, where he pulled out the flashlight and turned it on. Night hadn't fallen hard yet, but the trees hanging over him cast a shadow, and the first fuzzings of a gray-white fog were beginning to pool near the ground.

With the help of the light, by the time it was perfectly dark Pete had unearthed two bottle caps, a dozen earthworms, and one shapeless, nubby lump that *might* have been an old piece of lead shot. Then again, it might have been anything.

Pete thought he should quit while he was ahead. He could always come back. He had plenty of time. The outing had not been altogether useless; he knew what to expect, now. He knew what to listen for. Next time, he could really get started.

Both of the bottle caps and the odd lump of lead went into his front pocket, but the worms he left where he found them—turning the earth back over them and patting it with the back of the shovel.

He straightened up and stuffed the shovel and detector back into his duffel bag, fiddling with the light as he heaved the pack onto his shoulders.

"Hmm," he grunted.

More than darkness filled up the spaces between the trees. Suddenly and slowly, the dense stew of fog had arrived full force, swallowing the forest, the fields, and everything else. The light wasn't going to be a whole lot of help.

But Pete knew what they said about how you don't drive with headlights bright when it's foggy. He aimed the beam towards the ground. That was enough to see his feet, and a patch all around them. It wasn't particularly scary, being engulfed in the pale, humid air. If anything, he found it reassuring.

Given how little he could see, the odds of being spotted and stopped were next to nothing.

Not by any park ranger or cops, anyway.

His brain choked on that thought for a moment, and he almost ran headlong into a tree. At the last second he sidestepped it, and shook his head back and forth hard. Against his better judgment, he lifted the light and pointed it around him at chest level. Nothing but blank whiteness reflected back.

Through the thick screen Pete spied a couple more tree trunks all around him in every direction. He was only a few yards from the Dyer's cabin. He ought to walk free of the trees any second.

But the next dash of stumbling steps only brought Pete into more trunks, and more fog, and more twiggy grass.

"Well," he said aloud, mostly to hear his own voice. "Well. It's okay anyhow."

Any given direction gone far enough would bring him into either a clearing or suburbia, so being lost wasn't such a concern. That's what he told himself. That's what kept his hands steady as they clenched the flashlight. The important thing was to not accidentally walk in circles.

He shifted his shoulders, and the pack creaked. Its contents clanked together.

Otherwise, there was no sound.

Even his breath came without a huff or a wheeze. Even his feet did not rustle. Only then did Pete realize he'd stopped walking. He was holding perfectly still, perfectly quiet. Flashlight pointed at his shoes. Listening for all he was worth.

He squeezed his eyes into a frown, squinting to make out anything at all beyond three feet away.

"This must be…" He'd prepared to make an observation to himself about the way blind people feel, but the internal warning system that had immobilized him forced his jaw to close.

He must have heard something and not realized it. He must have seen something and not noticed. Something must have yelled "danger" to his most primitive wiring, but Pete didn't know what it was.

Other trespassers, possibly. Other vandals.

Or something else.

Pete tossed his head again, trying to shake a thought loose. Other people didn't bother him much. If he met any other people, then that was okay, since anyone else out there at that time of night was likely to be as dishonest as Pete was, and would understand that nobody wanted a ruckus. But he didn't like the idea of any *something* else.

Between the fog, the leafy canopy, and the late hour, Pete Buford now found himself in proper all-the-way dark.

"This sucks," he wanted to say, but didn't.

To his left, and up through the trees, he heard a leaf crunch.

All the baby-fine hairs on the back of Pete's neck began to rise, and his arm hairs followed.

From near the same place, but maybe closer, a stick broke.

He was being watched. He knew it, as surely as he knew he wasn't supposed to be on the battlefield after dark, and as surely as he knew that he would be going back to jail if anyone with a badge found him.

Through the wispy places where the white blanket thinned, he thought he saw a light—just for an instant. But it was gone as soon as he'd registered it.

Another cluster of leaves crumpled beneath something heavy. Definitely closer. Not Pete's imagination.

There it was again, the telltale wink.

Not a ghost, Pete told himself. Not a ghost. Ghosts don't have feet to break twigs. Ghosts don't step hard enough to mash leaves. Definitely not a ghost. Definitely just some other person.

A louder crack popped through the silence. An acorn, or a bigger stick. Something small and crunchy giving way beneath something bigger and denser.

Another person who had a right to be there—somebody like a cop or a ranger—would have identified himself by now. He would have told him to come out with his hands up. Keeping this in mind, Pete did the bravest thing he'd ever done. With great deliberation, he swiveled his flashlight and pressed the lens into his chest, cutting off its illumination. A dull red ring marked where the circular head crushed against his shirt.

When he looked out again, he knew he was not alone.

A yellow-green gleam the color of a margarita peeked out through the low-lying cloud, or maybe there were two gleams. Maybe they were eyes. The matching lights disappeared in a slow contraction, then returned—reinforcing Pete's initial impression.

Surely not, he thought.

When the blink was finished and the lights burned again, Pete was all the more certain that these were no eyes. They hovered too high off the ground. Any head that would host them must belong to a giant seven or eight feet tall. But somehow this assessment didn't soothe Pete any.

A name was floating around in his skull, itching to surface. A label for this giant thing, invisible through the fog, rattled about in Pete's chattering mouth.

There's no such thing. There's no such thing as Old Green Eyes.

The lights went out, or the eyes closed. The red circle on Pete's chest was the only glow. He clutched the flashlight hard, jamming it against his rib cage—not quite brave enough to lift the light again and scan the trees.

An owl. Maybe.

A stick broke with a crackling snap. Farther to the left. Nearly behind him.

Owls don't walk around on the ground, do they?

Leaves rustled, as if a low branch were being nudged aside.

He was being circled. Stalked.

"Who—who's there?" He gulped. He cleared his throat and said it again, clearer. Louder. "Who's there?"

The question echoed back to him, reflecting off the fog like his flashlight beam. *Who's there?*

"This isn't funny." His voice made him bolder, hearing the normal sound disturbing the perfect quiet. "Hey. This isn't funny."

In his ears, his heart beat hard. The throb sounded deep, and slow, and heavy with bass. But that didn't seem right—the steady pump and rhythmic, weighty pulse. Pete could feel his heart knocking against his sternum not far from the flashlight he still hugged close. His heart did not sound slow. His heart did not sound steady. It sounded like a wounded animal thrashing in a cage.

Still the thick pounding filled his ears.

Not mine. Not mine.

A scuffing noise, like a foot dragging through dirt, scratched itself out over to Pete's right.

"You stay away from me!" Pete ordered, clutching the light against his chest. "You'd better do it! I'm armed!"

The dual glow burned again, closer still and very, very high for a pair of things that resembled eyes. One word came back in a hiss of an echo: *armed.* A rushing fuzz like TV static rose up hard and filled Pete's ears.

A gust of wind crashed against Pete's side, shocking him into motion. He nearly dropped the flashlight, but caught it and pointed it at the ground. One foot in front of the other, he began a terrified dash, but a tree older than his grandparents reared out of the cloud. He plowed into the trunk face- and shoulder-first.

Armed.

Dazed but afraid, Pete straightened himself up, ignored the wild blue pain in his shoulder, and spun the light around.

Armed.

The eyes soared forward, dipping down as if their owner was diving towards Pete's head. He screeched and staggered over a tree root and around a trunk, struggling to put that trunk between himself and the incoming horror.

"I'm not armed, not armed!" he repeated, gasping as he ran. The way the word kept floating back to him—it made him wonder. "I'm not armed. I was lying! Leave me alone. God, let me go. Leave me alone!"

He started another crazed dash and collided with another tree, falling this time. He scooped himself up, forced his legs to rise beneath him, and hauled the light around to lead him.

The unnatural wind and humming breath buffeted Pete still, blowing him onward and forward. The light was almost less than useless to him, but he wielded it like a weapon, since he had no other.

The green eyes followed—from behind, from the left, and from the right.

"Get away from me!"

Pete thrust his hands in front of him, not wanting to make hasty friends with another tree. His wrists and fingers battered against wood, and his feet tripped over every obstacle before him. But every glance over his swelling shoulder reminded him why he ran.

Waving his hands and the light, he ran on; and after a few minutes it occurred to him that he really was running—straight and unhindered. He'd left the forest. He'd run clear.

He'd been *herded* clear.

His shoes were slapping against a paved surface before he realized that fact. His toes were catching on the asphalt before he knew he'd been manipulated.

Pete fell, catching himself on his hands and one knee. The duffel bag, which latched at the top, flew open, and the metal detector slid forward, knocking him in the head. He slung an arm around to stuff it back in, but an enormous hand wrapped itself around his forearm.

Whoever the hand belonged to was inhumanly strong.

With a flick of a mighty wrist, Pete found himself back down on the ground. His light rolled away, tipping off the side of the road and into a shallow ditch. He cringed then, and cowered, embracing the oversized bag and trying to stuff the detector and shovel back into place.

"Leave me alone," he whimpered. "Leave me alone!"

Leave us alone.

Not exactly an echo that time, the three words were tossed back at him. The speaker, or whisperer, stood tremendously tall over Pete's crouching form. Between the hour and the fog, Pete couldn't make out any details save the glimmering eyes that shone like an animal's.

The brute was huge and wide, and his form seemed unstable or uncertain. As Pete stared, he thought that the reason might be a long jacket or cape hanging down around the thing's shoulders. It was hard to tell.

Leave us alone, it repeated. *Go, and do not return.*

"What… what are you?"

Green Eyes—for what else could Pete call it?—leaned down closer, stepping within an arm's reach.

I am the Sentry. And I know what you are.

The voice was so strange and so darkly soft that Pete wasn't certain how he was hearing it. It might have been breathed, it was so quiet; but it may have been growled, it was so thick.

184

You will not dig here. You will let them rest. Come to this place again, and I will kill you.

Though he was relieved to infer that no killing would take place on this particular occasion, Pete was still on the asphalt, hiding behind his bag.

"Why?" he asked, but Green Eyes had turned, and the smoldering eyes were no longer to be seen—just the mighty creature's retreating shoulders, heaving in time to his footsteps as he slipped through the shadows.

You know why. It's the old pact.

TWELVE

VISITING UNANNOUNCED

I had plenty of time to kill before Benny'd be off work, so on a whim I wandered back to Greyfriar's to get coffee and a newspaper. I'd need to go back up the mountain to nab one of Dave's cameras, but I had eight hours to run that errand; so I picked a quiet corner, back down the brick-lined hall towards the roasting room, and there I called Malachi.

I wanted to ask him for a few details on his friend in the Bend, Kitty. He'd said she had been rambling about "the Hairy Man" and had been moved over to solitary. If I could get in and talk to her, she might be able to tell me more about the Bend's elusive visitor.

I didn't know how it worked there. I wondered if you could just walk up and ask to see a patient or if it was more like jail, where you need to be on an approved list and can only show up at certain times.

Malachi could have told me, but the one time I wanted to talk to him, he wasn't home.

I hung up and fiddled with my phone. Like Lu always said, it never hurt to ask—but I didn't even know this woman's last name. And the more I thought about it, the less certain I was that I knew her proper first name either. Who names a kid "Kitty," anyway? I hoped for her sake that it was a nickname.

I pulled my mini-notebook out of my bag and flipped it open on the marble-top bistro table beside my coffee cup.

What did I know about the woman, anyway? She'd killed her sister's kids. Two kids? I went ahead and wrote that down, though I wasn't positive I'd remembered correctly. Her name or nickname was Kitty. She'd been remanded to Moccasin Bend, presumably for life. This probably meant that the crime had taken place in Tennessee somewhere.

Was this enough to turn up a news story if I ran an Internet search?

Possibly. But possibly not.

My coffee needed refreshing, so I went over to the air pots and selected the shade-grown Nicaraguan. Beside the swiveling plastic condiments tray, someone had abandoned a local free magazine.

I picked it up and took it back to my table, idly flipping through it while I sipped at the South American brew.

Page three hosted an article I couldn't skip, a page of accumulated anecdotes about the battlefield. Sensationalistic or not, I decided I could write up my trash reading to research. Most of the stories were a paragraph or less, and many of them involved silly showdowns or outrageous chases.

Four of them I paid attention to. I recognized the themes, and they had an understated ring of truth. Quiet ghosts, pointing arms. All in all, not terribly informative. The quick tales told me nothing I didn't already know. The ghosts wanted to communicate, but they weren't sure how to go about doing so. Well, we'd see if we could help them with that problem tonight.

I checked my watch. It wasn't even suppertime.

I closed the magazine and downed the last of my coffee. The library was only a few blocks away, and I couldn't think of anything better to do; so I tossed my bag over my shoulder and began to walk. It was an unseasonably nice day, after all—not too hot, not too humid. Plenty of sun, and just enough shade to break up the glare.

The farther you walk away from the river, the emptier downtown looks. Most of the storefronts are a hundred years old or more, and on some blocks fewer than one in four is occupied. But if you keep going past the emptiness, the longer you walk, the brighter the buildings get—at least in patches. Between the stretches of nothing, the odd bank building gleams, and once you get down to the TVA headquarters, the place looks positively civilized again.

Across the street from the library something new was going up where once there had been a parking lot. Construction had eaten a lane on all four sides of the block, and street parking wasn't what it used to be.

I passed a pair of older men relaxing on the concrete stairs and entered the ugly old building via the squeaky glass door. I parked myself in front of an available monitor, which I luckily didn't have to clear any porn off of before starting, and began my surfing in earnest.

A few quick searches turned up a handful of old news stories, but nothing that sounded like a promising match for Malachi's friend.

I tried again, adding the words "Moccasin Bend" to the mix, but again I struck out. A few more combinations led me to someone's blog, and after scanning a few paragraphs I learned that the author was a volunteer at the Bend.

A candy striper in a psych ward? I kept reading but didn't learn much more. She filed paperwork and managed activities, occasionally handing out mail or meds. It didn't sound too complicated, but I wasn't sure how she'd gone about getting this volunteer position.

Maybe I could go on out there and ask. Benny wouldn't be off work until midnight, and Jamie wouldn't be meeting me until after his date ended—around eleven if he was lucky, around nine-thirty if she was smart.

I checked my watch again. I had time.

I logged off the computer and left the library, happily forming a new plan.

Once I'd tracked down Moccasin Bend in the middle of the night, it was much easier to find the place in broad daylight.

My second impression of the Bend was no better than my first, the sun didn't do anything at all to improve the premises. Everything was still white and cold in the shadow of the mountain.

The buildings made a perfect ugly box at the end of the thumb-shaped peninsula, each one more or less the same. The compound looked like a neurotic collage of toy blocks, with all of the sharp edges but none of the color or charm. I drove between them slowly, looking up at every building front for clues as to how I might go about getting inside.

The visitors' parking lot seemed like a good starting point.

I pulled in and settled the Death Nugget into a space, then left it for the nearest and most promising-looking administrative building.

Inside, the floors were intermittently shiny, due to a half-assed wax job on wide, dirty tiles; and the russet orange Naugahyde waiting area chairs were older than I was. A variety of uniformed personnel darted through the main room and through a pair of double doors. Behind a window in the wall an old attendant with a gray bouffant hairdo looked up at me, clearly wondering who I might be and what I might want.

I nodded a greeting. She nodded back, and returned her attention to the computer monitor in front of her.

There was a clipboard on the window shelf, and it clearly held a stack of sign-in sheets for comers and goers. I perused it for information and inspiration. "Can I help you, darlin'?" the attendant asked.

"I'm here to volunteer," I said.

She brightened, then, looking up from the computer monitor as if all might have suddenly become clear. "Oh, you're here with the church? The outreach program, I mean?"

"Yes," I lied, because it was easy. My original plan had been to show up and see what becoming a volunteer involved, but if I could skip that step and fib my way in, so much the better. "I'm here with Kitty's old church," I continued, riding the tall tale along its logical track.

It was a safe bet that once upon a time, Kitty'd had a church. Almost everyone around here does, and besides, the woman had committed her crimes in the name of God. It would also be a fair guess that representatives of that church might visit every so often, if only to make sure God hadn't relayed any further instructions.

The woman in the window scrunched a fold down between her eyes, but it wasn't an unfriendly one. After all, I came from a *church*. I must be okay.

"I didn't realize they were sending anyone today. Usually the church folks come out on Wednesdays or Thursdays."

"Well, we heard that Kitty wasn't doing so well lately, and since I was out this way I thought I'd swing on by and see if I couldn't cheer her up, if that's all right with the hospital here."

The attendant, whose name tag read PAM, folded her arms and leaned forward, mashing together a ponderous pair of breasts until they nearly climbed out the top of her shirt. "You know, that's true," she agreed with a slight air of gossipy concern. "The poor thing's been all kinds of wound up for the last week or two. We're not sure what's gotten into her. They had her in solitary for a while, but they moved her back to a regular room yesterday. This one's upstairs, though. She insisted, and we got tired of listening to her holler."

"Maybe she could use a bit of company… or some prayer," I added as an afterthought—since I was from a church and all.

"Sure, sure. Bless her heart."

"But if now's not a good time, I could come back." Time to add a touch of honesty, since I wasn't interested enough in talking to Kitty to get in trouble over it. "I'm new to this, so I've never been here before. I guess I'd need to fill out some paperwork or something?"

"Well, if you're with the church it shouldn't be too big of a thing." She turned and rifled around in a drawer. "I can give you one of their passes and just let you sign in. Kitty's not a high-risk patient. I'll send you back with an orderly if you'll give me a minute here."

She invited me to leave my purse with her at the front desk. This struck me as a reasonable precaution, so I handed it over without a fuss. She put a tag on it and set it on a counter.

Not a high-risk patient, Pam had said. I wondered exactly

what one had to do in order to achieve the *high-risk* designation, if not kill a couple of kids. Of course, upon reflection I realized that the mere attempted murder of a kid must warrant even less stringent measures—which would account for how Malachi had gotten loose a few years previously.

After a moment, Pam beckoned me over and handed me a laminated visitor's pass with a metal clip that I attached to the bottom hem of my shirt. She flagged down a skinny, sloppily dressed orderly and gave him the fifty-cent version of my story. "Okay," he said. "Back this way."

It turned out that Kitty was being housed in the next building over. First I was led through the rabbit warren of the main building while the orderly ran an errand, then back out a side door. My guide swiped a card at the next entrance and ushered me through a big metal door with a little square window. And then I was officially inside.

The place wasn't as bad as I expected. I didn't see any moaning mentally disabled people having pills forced down their throats; there weren't any Nurse Ratcheds immediately visible in the corridors. Everything felt old and unkempt, though. Leftover 1960s architecture and decorative aesthetics made me feel at times like I was at the bottom of a retirement home's swimming pool: surrounded by aqua blue, dirty almond, and the odd trimming of institutional mint green. The hospital was clean and more or less tidy, but definitely showing its age around the edges.

In the back of my head hummed an irritating reminder about how Malachi had lived here for years. It must have been a strange way to pass the days, I thought, surrounded by technicians and nurses in pajama-like uniforms, taking calming medicines out of tiny Dixie cups.

I imagined that things could have been worse, but if it were me, I think I would have died of boredom.

My tour guide, the oblivious white rabbit, asked another caregiver if she knew where Kitty might be. "Is she out in the TV room, or did she stay inside her space today?"

A tall black woman with a lean, muscular body like a runner glanced down at my visitor's pass. She cocked her head off to the right. "Kitty stayed in."

"Okay," the orderly said. "Come on, then."

I followed him pretty close, ducking behind him to clear the way for the occasional briskly stepping doctor or empty gurney. A wide set of double doors opened before we reached them, having been triggered from the other side by the handicapped button. A patient scooted forward in his wheelchair, moving past without giving us a second look.

Down another maze-like run of halls, doors, and up a flight of stairs we went without speaking. I got the strong impression that I was interrupting this guy's routine, and while he wasn't going to slap me for it, he could have done without my accompaniment.

Finally, at the end of a linoleum-tiled strip, we stopped at a door and the orderly knocked. "Miss Kitty," he called, addressing her like the brothel madam in a spaghetti Western. "You've got a visitor."

He slipped a card-key into the slot below the knob. A green light popped and the door came open. "How do you feel about that, Miss Kitty? Are you up for a visitor today?"

The woman underneath the windowsill didn't answer him either way.

"She, uh, she usually lets you know if she doesn't want to be sociable. You might not get much talking out of her, though—and what you do get may or may not make a lot of sense. I'm not sure what's been wrong with her lately. She's been doing better since we moved her up here, though. Haven't you, Kitty?"

If she heard and understood him, she couldn't be bothered to show it.

"She didn't like being on the first floor," the orderly explained. "She's been calmer up here."

"Huh," I said.

"Yeah. Anyway, I'll be back in about twenty minutes. If you have any problems or need any help, hit the red button over there by the door and someone'll come around faster. Will that work for you? Are you comfortable with that?"

"Sure," I answered, though I wasn't certain if he was asking me or Kitty. I figured one of us might as well throw him a bone. He wasn't looking at either of us, but was flipping papers on his clipboard, and when I told him all would be well, he left us, closing the door and flashing me a hasty thumbs-up sign at the small rectangular window.

The room where Kitty lived was about half again as big as a dormitory room, with a full window lined from the inside by something like extra-sturdy chicken wire; on the outside it was laced with a series of thin metal bars. Thick white paint coated the cement-block walls, and in places those walls were covered with pieces of paper affixed with tape. The sheets looked like articles to me, or handwritten letters. I didn't see any pictures, not of Kitty or her family, or even anything snipped from a magazine.

"Hello," I said to her.

I stood in one spot, sliding my weight from one leg to the other because I didn't want to approach her without permission.

So this was what happened to you if you saw things. This was what happened if you couldn't make it work for you like Dana and Tripp, turn it into a business or a show. Was there no middle ground for people like me? Surely it couldn't be one thing or the other—you either ended up on television, or... well...

You ended up someplace like this.

Kitty was coiled with her arms around her shins, knees pulled up to her right temple. A straight plait of blond hair went down past her waist, the ends trailing on the floor where she was sitting, dangling in the crooks of her arms and spilling over her face. If I looked hard, I could see faint highlights of early gray winding their way through the locks.

She didn't lift her head up from her knees, and I couldn't see her face.

"I was wondering if I could talk to you for a few minutes," I went on, not sure what the protocol for this sort of thing was. I looked up at the speaker beside the door and noted that none of the little lights were lit, but this did not prevent me from wondering if anyone was listening in.

If the room was being monitored, there was nothing to be done about it except to hurry up and talk before anyone came to remove me.

"Here's the thing," I told Kitty, who hadn't budged and did not seem remotely interested in carrying on a conversation. "I'm here because I wanted to talk to you about Green Eyes."

I thought her smooth, gold-draped head might have twitched, so I paused. But she offered me no further acknowledgment. I stepped forward a couple of feet until I'd reached the foot of her bed.

"Could I just sit here, for a minute? If you don't want me to touch your stuff or anything I understand, but I'd really love it if we could chat. And… if you're not going to answer, I'm going to take that as 'Sure, make yourself comfortable.' Speak now or forever hold your peace. Okay then. I'm going to park right here and keep on talking. Feel free to jump in anytime."

She made a small sigh, or grunt, or it might have been the first syllable of a cynical laugh. I couldn't tell.

"Okay. Okay. Right." I folded and unfolded my hands, laying my elbows on the top of my thighs and leaning in her direction while I spoke. "I don't know if you're aware or not, but you had another visitor a few nights ago. He didn't make it all the way inside, but he really wanted to see you and say hello. So I'll start by passing along his greetings."

Technically, I didn't think Malachi had told me to tell her anything; but I didn't think it would hurt, and it might even get her attention.

"He used to live here too, in the Bend." I shuffled my buns along the bed and lowered my voice, for all the good it would do me if anyone was tuning in through the monitoring system. "His name is Malachi. I'm his…" I started to tell her the truth, but on the chance that someone *was* eavesdropping I changed my mind. "He's an old friend of mine."

Two muffled words rose up from the half-fetal figure balanced on the floor like an egg. "Malachi's dead."

I waited to see if she had anything else to add, but she didn't. "Is that so?" I asked, and I asked it carefully because something about her voice told me that she didn't believe it when she said it.

"S'what I heard. It was on the news, about a year ago."

Again I looked over to the speaker on the wall. Nothing indicated that we were being overheard, but I wanted to play it cautious all the same. "Maybe he is, and maybe he isn't—but he was coming to talk to you the other night. Were you two good friends?"

I thought maybe I'd lost her again; it took a full ten or fifteen seconds for her to respond. "Don't know about *good* friends. He was all right. Thought I was crazy, though."

"But you knew what he was in here for, right?"

She nodded, rubbing her forehead against her leg in the process.

"Then maybe you should take a look at me, and hear me out. I started this on the wrong foot, maybe, with a fib. Let me begin again—Malachi's not exactly a friend of mine, but he and I have come to an understanding. He's the one who told me about you."

Since everything with this woman happened in slow motion, I let the conversation lull drag on while she slowly swiveled her eyes up from her lap and over to the bed where I was sitting.

She was a pretty woman in a corn-fed sort of way—big blue eyes and good bone structure, like thirty years ago she might have gone on an album cover for the Mamas & the Papas.

Kitty fixed me in a stare that wasn't precisely blank, but apathetic. "You're his sister, then," she said. "That must be some *interesting* understanding."

"Yeah," I confirmed. "It is. But it works all right."

Unwrapping her arms one at a time, and unfolding her legs in a similar fashion, Kitty stretched herself out. She pivoted on her tailbone and reassembled herself into the same crunched position, this time facing out at me.

"What'd Malachi want?" she asked.

I gave the talk-box one last look and gave up. If they could hear me, they could hear me and there wouldn't be much stopping them. Maybe, so far as they were concerned, it would just be chatter—one lunatic to another. Let 'em listen, then. Let them hear us.

I leaned in forward, closer to her but only by inches. "He wanted to talk to you—see if you could answer some questions for him. He ran into some trouble looking for you, though, because they'd moved you since he was here last. I ended up picking him up and sending him home."

"Then what do *you* want?"

"I want to talk to you about why they moved you upstairs here. Are you more comfortable up above ground level?"

She shrugged. "I guess. Yeah." She clutched absently at her knee, halfway between scratching at it and rubbing it.

"It puts you farther off the street, and away from the Hairy Man, doesn't it?"

Her eyes narrowed sharply, leaving a slit of blue and white. "If you're here to make fun of me, you can just—"

"No," I cut her off quick. "No, nothing like that, I swear. Sort of the opposite, in fact. I need to ask some questions, and I don't want *you* to make fun of *me*. Can we agree to that, and can you hear me out?"

Kitty thought about it, and twisted her chin in a motion that might have been a nod, except it dipped sideways. "I guess," she mumbled. "But don't you make fun of me. If you make fun of me, I'll go to sleep and I won't talk to you. I don't have any more patience for that sort of thing. I've been here too long, and I'm too old."

"I promise," I repeated. "I swear."

"Okay then. But I'm not stupid. Don't treat me like I'm stupid."

"I won't, if you don't treat me like one of these doctors here. You can tell me exactly what you mean, and whatever you know, and I'm more likely to believe you than anyone you've ever met in your life. When I came out here to get Malachi, we had some problems with the car. We got stuck over by the woods for a little bit, and before we could get out, I saw the Hairy Man you were talking about."

Her eyes didn't open any wider, but she didn't curl up and implode into silence, either. "You saw him, huh?"

"Yeah, I saw him. And I've got some thoughts about who and what he might be. But I bet you've seen him more than I have, and I wanted to know if you could tell me anything about him before I go jumping to conclusions."

"Malachi said that you saw stuff. He thought it made you wicked."

"He's had a change of heart on that matter. It nearly killed him, I think, but we've come to terms. I *do* see stuff. And I want to talk to you, because you see stuff too."

She digested this, and then did her funny tic of a nod. "What did you see?" she asked. "Tell me. People don't ever tell me what *they* see—they only ask what *I* see. So you talk first."

The faint hint of hunger in her face made me uncomfortable; it reminded me how short the distance was between us, and I understood a little too well her desire to listen. After all, who ever reads the cards for the fortune teller?

I gave her the rundown from the beginning, when I got the frantic phone call from Malachi, and filled her in regarding the small wreck. She let out a laugh when I told her how he had run out in front of me and I'd gone off the road.

"That sounds like something he'd do," she interjected.

"No kidding. It shouldn't have surprised me as much as it did. But once I stopped and we checked out the car, I began to hear this noise—it's hard to describe, like TV static, kind of. Or like a radio stuck between stations."

Kitty bobbed her head, but didn't offer any additional commentary.

"It got louder and louder as he got closer. Even Malachi heard it, which sort of surprised me. But Malachi, he—well, he got his head hit, and I had to leave him for a minute. I went following the noise, and I saw the Hairy Man sitting down by the river. He was talking to himself. Have you ever heard him talking?"

"Not exactly," she admitted. "You don't 'hear' it really. You feel it in your ears."

"That's a good way of putting it. I felt it in my ears, then. He wasn't talking to me, I don't think, but he didn't seem to care if I could hear him, either."

"What did he say?"

"He said, 'The dead are my children,' and that he shouldn't have left them. I think I know what he meant, but I'm not sure. That's why I came here. I wanted to know if you knew anything that might flesh out what I've gathered. So please—if there's anything you can contribute to this, I'd really appreciate it."

She wrinkled her toes up until they cracked, and then lay one long leg down so her foot was pointing at me. She didn't bother to meet my eyes. She didn't need to. "Why did you really come here, anyway? You already know who he is. You guessed it before you got home that night, like I'd guessed it too, a few weeks ago. Is it just that you want to say it out loud, and not be laughed at? 'Cause I understand, if that's all it is."

It was my turn to stay silent for too long.

"It's not that, exactly," I said.

"What is it, then? Don't you know anyone else like you? Have you got a mother, or a sister—or brother? Anyone else who sees?"

If we were really playing turns, this would have been her

round to keep quiet, but she had me twice in a row. "No," I finally confessed. "I guess I really don't."

Kitty hunched her shoulders in a shifting shrug. "Makes it hard to get a second opinion, don't it?"

"It does."

She closed her eyes and opened them, too slowly to call it a blink. "I don't blame you for coming. It's hard, when it's only you—and you don't have anyone else to ask. It's hard, when you think you're the only one who can hear it. And if you listen long enough, and no one else butts in to say, 'Hey, I heard it too,' I think after a while you start to misunderstand."

I would have been tempted to call killing children something more dire than a misunderstanding, but I wasn't in a position to be too judgmental, so I let it lie. The elephant in the room remained unmentioned.

"These days, I try to tune it all out," she continued. "I thought it'd get better once I came here. I thought maybe if they closed me away, I wouldn't hear anything at all, and then it wouldn't matter who was talking because the walls are very thick. They don't want to let me out, so I thought it'd be okay if they kept me *in*. But I didn't know they'd put me *here*."

"What's so bad about—oh. Never mind. Not the ideal location for someone who's sensitive, I don't guess. Indian burial ground, and all that."

She nodded. "There's a lot of negative energy here, that's for sure. It's very… draining, sometimes. But in time, I got used to it. I can ignore almost anything, these days. But I couldn't ignore *him*… "

She didn't put a period after the pronoun. We each waited for the other to go ahead and say his name. I caved first. "Green Eyes, you mean."

Kitty went ahead and laughed. "There you go. That wasn't so hard, was it?"

"I don't suppose it was." I shook my head. "Not hard, but weird."

"Have you told anyone else?"

"Yeah, actually I've got a couple of friends who are pretty open-minded. We're doing some investigation on our own—"

"Not with those people on TV?"

"The Marshalls?" I rolled my eyes. "Oh *hell* no. We ran into them today, downtown. It was awkward. I think they know what we're up to, and that's unfortunate. Discretion being the better part of valor, and all."

Kitty rolled her head back and forth, like she was trying to crack her neck the way she'd popped her toes. "But your friends, do they believe you?"

"I think they do, yes."

"It's like faith, though. They believe without knowing."

"Something like that, but I don't think there's anything but good intention behind it. They want to believe, at least, and knowing me gives them a little bit of an excuse. We got some evidence the other night, at the battlefield."

"Evidence? You going to go to the newspapers?"

I shook my head and waved my hand at her. "Oh no. Not *that* kind of evidence—not empirical evidence or anything. Nothing that would stand up to scrutiny."

She offered me a thin-lipped smirk. "Not much in the way of evidence, then, is it?"

"Not to anyone who wasn't there, no. We took a tape recorder out to the battlefield and asked the ghosts there if they'd talk to us and tell us what's going on out there. We picked up some voices. But I couldn't prove to someone who wasn't there that the voices we got were really spirits. You'll have to take my word for it, is all."

"What's going on out there—you mean, with all the pointing? I saw that on the news the other day, how they point and disappear into nothing."

I knew they'd been pointing, yes, but I hadn't thought of it as a theme until Kitty put it that way. "What do you think they're pointing at?"

"Some place. Some thing. I don't know."

"Dyer's field, maybe," I said, mostly to myself. "We think there might be something fishy going on at Dyer's field."

"You never know. Could be. You're right for sure about the Green Eyes thing, though. I saw him. I didn't know at first it was him, because, well, you know. You don't think 'Green Eyes' except for when you think of the battlefield. Someplace else it takes you a while to figure him out. Jesus, but he's scary."

I rocked my rear back and forth, sliding away from an uncomfortable spring. "I don't think I'd call him scary, except that he's different. Really, really different. He's not like the ghosts I'm used to seeing here and there. He's something more solid. More real."

She agreed, but in a way that disagreed with my assessment. "And more able to hurt you if he wants to."

"What makes you think he wants to hurt you?"

"I don't know if he does or not, but if a ghost wanted to hurt me, there wouldn't be much it could do about it, except scare me. But the thing out there"—she wagged her shoulder towards the window—"if he wanted to do something bad, he *could*."

"You're right, I guess. But so long as he's uninterested in

molesting the rest of us, I'd prefer to think of him as 'mysterious' and not 'sinister,' if I can help it."

"Think of him however you want. He's dangerous, and horrible, and I want as much thick sanitarium wall and floor and tight metal bars between me and him as I can get."

Out in the hall I heard a muffled pair of soft-shoed footsteps, and I knew our time was all but up. Kitty heard them too. I was almost disappointed; I felt like we were only just starting to communicate, and I think she would have rather kept talking as well.

"Let me know how it works out," she said, beginning her slow curl back into the cramped position I'd found her in. "You can come back, if you want. I don't mind. We could talk, if you want. I'm tired of talking to all these crazies."

I didn't make her any promises, but I thanked her for her time and let the orderly lead me away. I fled the premises with a sense of relief, and a touch of sadness.

I was terribly glad to go.

THIRTEEN

BACK TO THE BATTLEFIELD

I met Benny at his home about twenty minutes after midnight, after calling Lu and Dave and telling them I'd be out for another few hours. God bless them for not asking any questions; I think when I told them Jamie was involved they assumed I'd gone out dancing, which I do almost exclusively when Jamie drags me. We usually go to the gay bar out in the bad part of town, because the drinks are strong, the music is good, and the worst thing that happens to Jamie there is that he gets hit on because he acts gay—which he finds more palatable than just plain getting *hit* because he acts gay. This is a tough town for a guy to be so femme in, and if there's anything I respect about Jamie it's that he doesn't let that stop him from doing as he pleases. Dave and Lu think he's funny, and they don't mind if I stay out late with him—which aided my small deception.

My uncle hadn't noticed that I'd made off with one of his older cameras. I figured the missing equipment would fly under his radar, since I'd selected an older manual number that he'd set aside for a newer model a year or two before.

I was pretty sure I remembered how to use it.

Jamie was waiting at Benny's too, as previously arranged. Between us, we ran through a final rundown and made sure we had everything we needed. We even played back some of the EVP for Jamie, who hadn't heard it yet.

"You think we'll catch more of the same?" he asked, clicking the mouse on the play key again.

"I don't know. Maybe. Maybe not." I reached around him and picked up the tape recorder, and I stuffed it into my bag. "If we're lucky, maybe some generous dead guy will recognize us from last time as friends, not foes, and lead us to where the action is."

"What about the Marshalls?" Benny let fly a half-smile that said he didn't object too deeply to the thought of running into them.

"Let's hope we miss them altogether," I said, hoping to nip his apparent enthusiasm in the bud. I didn't want any subconscious sabotage, and I sure as hell didn't want to meet the Marshalls any more up close and personal than we had earlier.

"But what if we *do* run into them?" he pressed.

"Then we will run the other way and hope they don't see us. Back me up here, Jamie."

"Sure. What she said."

"Thanks, I guess. I've got the camera. You got the film?"

Benny shook the baggie until the canisters fell out. "I got the film."

I tossed my head over at Jamie. "What've you got?"

"Passion. Charm. Talent. And an irrepressible desire to charge around a battlefield while I'm being pursued by the dead."

"Okay," I agreed. "If that's all you've got, it'll have to do. We ready?"

"We ready," they said, and I believed them. Benny was carrying his same khaki bag with the military flashlight and assorted peripherals; I had the tape recorder and a camera bag with Dave's manual camera and the infrared film clattering around next to it. We were as ready as we were going to get.

I drove, for the same reasons I always drive: Benny drives for a living and refuses to do so during his extracurricular activities, and Jamie's car is a piece of shit that none of us trust to go fifty feet without exploding.

At least he offered to chip in for gas money, a gesture which was appreciated, if refused. I had a full tank, and he needed the five bucks worse than I did.

We made it out to the battlefield just before 1:00 a.m. and parked back near Ted's place. In the event that we were stopped by authorities, Ted wouldn't care if we used him as an excuse for being there. And even if no one believed us, it was good to have a backup plan. Saying that we had wandered over to the battlefield while visiting a friend was less incriminating than admitting, "We drove all the way out from north Chattanooga for the sole purpose of trespassing on federally protected property."

So that was our story, and we were sticking to it.

The excursion began cleanly. There was no sign of anyone else in the fringe neighborhood—a crowded maze of half-paved streets interspersed with trailers, and without regular streetlights.

We kept it low-key, just the crunch of our shoes where there was no asphalt. Benny's flashlight led us with its telltale red halo, drawing us back to our starting point at the Tower. Dyer's field was off to the right and across a road, but we liked being able to approach the position by skimming through the edge of the tree line.

"Do you see anything?" Benny asked, hunching down in

front of us as if making himself shorter would make us all more difficult to see.

"No," I whispered back. "Not yet. You?"

"*We* don't see ghosts, remember?"

I nudged his back with my knuckles. "Maybe not, but you might see the Marshalls' field party. I can't be on the lookout for everything at once. Work with me, here."

"Oh yeah," Jamie breathed. "*Them.*"

I'd loaded the camera with the infrared film before we'd left the car. It hung around my neck on a festively embroidered, hippie-looking strap Dave must have picked up in 1970. As I walked, I tugged on the strap to shorten it so the heavy apparatus wouldn't bang up and down against my breasts. I liked it better up high, perched above my sternum.

"Need a hand?" Jamie offered.

"Got it, you perv. Thanks."

"Where are we going?" Jamie asked, tapping my shoulder.

"Dyer's field. Right?"

"Right," Benny backed me up.

"Why?" Jamie asked.

"Because," I said, too loud. I cleared my throat and lowered it again, continuing the conversation in our best "inside" voices. "Because something's going on over there, and we're going to find out what."

"Are we sure?"

"No," Benny and I answered at once.

We walked on without talking for another few minutes before a sudden stop caused us to collide into one another. We had to halt—we'd reached the edge of the Tower area, and the woods had made way for the two-lane road. We retreated en masse back into the trees.

The three of us huddled, bringing our heads together to plot our course of action. One way or another, we were going to have to brave a big open space.

The field itself was no more than fifty yards away, but that field had been mowed to a knee-high state of grassy uniformity. It was a giant rectangle several acres across, one side marked by the road, and the other sealed off by a dark strip of trees. Another crop of dense woods topped off the short side closest to us. The side farthest away was difficult to discern, and it was only when we tried to see it and failed that we realized the fog was rolling in.

"What is it about that damn fog?" Jamie swore, following the misting boil with a suspicious squint.

Benny and I did too, shaking our heads in time. The fog was a creepy and inscrutable sign; it was often said to mean that strange things and ghostly happenings were afoot. I knew it *really* only meant that we were stuck in a low-lying cloud, but hey, whatever makes you quiver around a campfire.

From a more practical standpoint, it meant we needed to stay close together or risk getting lost.

"Well," I said, lifting the camera and popping the lens cap into my back pocket. "If we wait a few minutes, it might make for good cover."

Jamie did a terrible job of trying to hide the fact that he thought I was crazy. "You want to hang around until the fog gets *thicker*?"

"Yes. Yes I do."

Benny made a noise that was just short of a sigh and a whimper. "It makes sense. I guess. But it's not thick enough yet. Let's hang out over here for a while. Hey, does that camera have a good zoom?"

"Good enough, I bet." I crouched down and balanced my elbow on my upper thigh, sighting the camera through the trunks. "Let's get a little closer to the edge and see if we can't catch anything before it gets too cloudy down here. Turn off the light, darling, would you please?"

Together we crept as quiet as we could closer to the road and the end of the trees. All of us went down into a crouch or a kneel. I pulled the camera up again and watched the field across the road, scanning the cabin, the tree line, the grass. I wanted to bring the view closer, but I'd have to settle for the magnification I had on hand.

I reached my finger around to the shutter, but a faint hum made me change my mind. The flash was warming up. I flicked it off and aimed the camera back across the road again, feeling stupid—but not so stupid as I would have if it'd actually gone off.

Over by the cabin I thought I saw a smudge of motion. I snapped a picture. The click seemed unnaturally loud, though I knew it wasn't.

"Did you get something?" Jamie's lips were almost touching my ears, but he was speaking so quietly I barely heard him.

"Not sure," I said back. "Move. Give me room."

Benny had been crowding in too. Both of the boys backed up.

The second time I was certain I'd seen honest-to-God movement. I snapped another couple of pictures, then moved my focus. I swayed the lens to the left by short degrees, pausing to take more pictures of any hint of activity. I couldn't tell if I was seeing tendrils of fog or tatters of old uniforms; it might have been wind waving the grass, or it could have been something else. I was too far away to judge, and even as I peered through the lens the battlefield cloud was gathering itself into a cottony mass.

I clicked another three or four pictures before deciding the cause was lost, then reached into my pocket to nab the lens cap.

"Hey, look." Jamie knocked his arm against mine.

I followed his gaze to the far side of the field, across the street and down at the bottom end of the rectangle.

Several distinct shapes moved through the soupy air, without a lot of caution but plenty of purpose. At a distance it looked like they were carrying things between them, but it was hard to be sure. They were definitely not hiding, though. They stomped along the shoulder of the paved strip, loud and careless, talking among themselves in ordinary voices. It reminded me of a Girl Scout excursion I'd taken as a kid, when our leader had told us to go ahead and make all the noise we could, in order to scare away snakes.

They're more afraid of you than you are of them, after all.

But I didn't think the party on the other end of the field was trying to scare off snakes. They had bigger worries to nurse.

"Do they *want* to draw the attention of every armed lunatic on the battlefield?" Benny asked. "Didn't they learn their lesson losing a cameraman?"

"Yeah, I think they did," I said. "Look at them. They're announcing their presence—making a point of not sneaking up on anybody."

"Oh, I get it. They're giving the crazies time to get out of their way."

"Exactly."

Jamie raised an eyebrow. "I guess they're not worried about chasing off the ghosts."

I shook my head. "I doubt it. If anything, they probably think the noise might draw them out. They're killing two birds with one stone."

"Why aren't *we* doing that?" Benny demanded, louder than before.

I pulled him towards me by his neck and put a hand over his mouth. "Because *we* aren't supposed to be here. *They* won't get arrested if anyone finds *them* here."

"Oh, yeah," he mumbled between my fingers.

"Keep it down," I reminded them both. "Something funny's going on over there," I said, pointing towards the cabin. I was certain, the harder I stared, that someone or something was moving, and when I closed my eyes to open my ears and let the night come in, I caught a faint, intermittent electric *bleep*.

Jamie shifted and rustled into a more favorable position. I put a hand on his arm and one on Benny's too, holding them both down and still by pure force of will. I needed to listen. I needed to get a better fix on that sound. It was familiar but not common, coming closer, going farther away in four- or five-second intervals.

I pulled them both in, so that our three heads could have nearly fit together in a shoebox. "Do you hear that?" I breathed, hoping they were close enough to read my lips in the dark, even if they couldn't hear me.

"Hear what?" they mouthed back, so it must have only been me.

It came and went, rose and fell, but not in an up-and-down motion—it made me think of swaying, of swinging back and forth. Or maybe it was something else. My mind wandered back to a sixth-grade science fair and a classmate's display of Morse code. Dash, dash. Dot. Beep. Bleep. Hum. Whir.

Similar. But not exactly that. This was slower, and less rhythmic.

I wagged my head. "I can't place it," I swore.

"Can't place *what*?" Benny pleaded.

I shook my head and lowered it. "Don't know. Hush."

"Holy shit," Jamie muttered. He lifted his arm and flapped his index finger towards the Marshalls and their crew, then over at the field. "You can hardly see them anymore."

He was right. In a matter of minutes, the fog had nearly hit its critical mass. It was heavy enough to touch, to brush aside in a cottony swirl if you reached out for it. The cloud was chilly and wet against our skin. I could practically *feel* my hair frizzing itself into an atomic black puff of humid rage.

Jamie grumbled something else—"Cold sauna of the damned," I think it was—and he was closer to the truth than he knew.

The chattering of the Marshall party overwhelmed the barely there electronica I had been hearing before. They were close enough now that if we leaped out and shouted "Boo!" they probably could have spotted us—fog or none. The fuzzy glow of their electric lamps gave them a wide yellow halo, a dome of fuzzy light that both revealed and distorted their location.

I had the distinct and unpleasant sensation of being trapped between a rock and a hard place. There was nothing to be done except hold still and watch.

The mobile bubble stopped. "I don't think we should go any farther," a man said in an ordinary speaking voice.

"Tripp," Benny blew the word into my ear.

"We're almost at the field. Or are we *at* the field? Dammit all, I can't tell. What crazy weather they get down here. I don't know how anybody stands it."

"It isn't all the weather," a woman answered, and I assumed it must be Dana. "This place is positively loaded with activity. I've never seen so much energy. I've never felt anything like it."

A third voice answered her. "I've never felt anything like a bullet in my ass, and I'd be happy to keep it that way if it's all the same to you. I say we stop at the field."

"Did you just now realize you're wearing a red shirt?"

"Yeah. Thanks for reminding me."

"Fine, we're stopping. This is close enough; we can set up our equipment here. I suppose it won't hurt the dead much to come across the street. Where's the cabin?"

"I'm not going near the cabin. That's where Matthew got shot. What if there's some wacko holing up in there?"

Dana again. "Look, the cabin is barred up—you can't get into it, okay? They keep it locked all the time these days, and no one but the rangers has keys to it. No one's hiding inside. Last time was just some fluke. You heard those kids at the camera place; every nut and his best friend comes out here wanting trouble."

"Let's get off the road and set up over by the picnic tables."

"Where?"

"We passed them a minute ago. It's across the street from the field, and it ought to be close enough."

"Honey, the EVP we got said to go to the field—not 'the picnic tables across the street from the field.' I think we should get closer. We could set up in the road alongside it, at least. It's not like there will be any cars coming."

So they'd gotten a message about Dyer's field too. It couldn't be coincidence, or at least I didn't think so. We must be in the right spot. A quick look at my companions told me they had both come to a similar conclusion. But this was the right spot... for what?

Swish. Swish.

The boys heard it too, though it was awfully soft. I raised the camera again and pointed it at the white wall between us and the cabin. I couldn't see anything, but the film might tell us something later.

Swish. Swish.

Legs, I thought. Parting tall grass with shins. One-two. One-two.

Swish. Swish.

"All right. Whatever. The picnic tables. Which direction is that? Christ, I can't see a thing."

"Turn around, dear. Look. We're still on the road. The picnic tables are behind us."

"I have never seen fog like this before in my life. No wonder this place scares the locals so bad. It's not enough that it's haunted silly—it's also got homicidal maniacs and pea-soup fog."

"Cannon smoke," said the third member of the party. "It looks like cannon smoke."

The other two were quiet, and might have been staring at him.

"Well, that *is* what it looks like. Isn't it?"

After another pointed pause, Dana said, "Charlie, you're entirely too sentimental for this job. Stop letting your imagination get the better of you."

"I still think it looks like cannon smoke."

"Think it all you like; just don't write it down and publish it."

Swish. Swish.

My friends and I exchanged nervous glances. Someone was coming, from over behind the cabin. Maybe nobody was holed up inside it, but someone was hanging around it; that much was certain. And whoever he was, he was on his way over.

He wasn't carrying a light so far as we could tell, but he didn't need much of one. The beacon dome of the Marshall party glowed beside the road. So long as no trees or small monuments got in the way, it would be easy enough to make a beeline for the group.

Jamie dropped one hand to the ground and propped himself on it to move closer to me. "What do you want to do?" he asked, so quietly that even Benny didn't hear it two feet away.

"It might be nothing," I replied, knowing as I said it that it wasn't likely true. If the swisher was an ordinary trespasser like ourselves, he'd probably avoid the Marshalls for fear of getting caught. We couldn't see them well at all, but for all we knew they'd brought a police escort of the strong-and-silent type. God knows *I* would have looked into a cop companion if I'd been them, after getting shot at once before. And just because we hadn't heard a fourth member of the group didn't mean they hadn't hired a uniformed representative.

But there's something about the supernatural that skews peoples' priorities. Ghosts have a way of making the real world and all its dangers seem small and unimportant.

Unthreatening.

Swish. Swish.

But the real world wasn't safe to ignore for too long, either.

Whoever he was, he was getting closer, and he was no ghost. He was no Green Eyes, either—of that much I was confident. And it was only a matter of moments until he reached the road.

The Marshalls were retreating to the picnic area, but the swisher was following them, pushing his feet through the grass. He moved slowly, as if to make as little noise as possible.

He was definitely creeping up on them.

Benny echoed Jamie's question, just as quietly, into my other ear. "What do we do?"

I shook my head, almost hitting Jamie with my cheek. "Don't know."

Let me think, I wanted to add, but the swishing stopped and a soft pat announced a foot setting down upon the road. The time for thinking was almost up. We needed to decide whether we were going to watch or interfere, and we needed to do so *quickly.*

"We've gotta warn them!" Benny whispered fiercely, almost too loud.

I agreed, though. I let go of his arm and dragged my fingers along the ground, searching for something to throw. A piece of asphalt the size of a peach pit caught itself under my thumb.

"Move," I told Jamie, who shifted his chest to give me room.

As hard as I could, I chucked the rock towards the Marshall party. My aim was bad in the low light and heavy fog, but the dome of electric light made them an easy goal.

I'm not sure who I hit or how hard I hit him, but one of the males cried out, "Hey!" A scuttling scratching noise followed when the rock clattered to the ground, and the Marshalls stopped. I think they were holding their breaths.

"What was that?" Dana demanded, not bothering to whisper.

"Who's there?"

"Show yourself!"

If the swisher was still moving towards them, I couldn't hear him. He must have stopped, but he *had* to be within a few yards of them. He'd made it to the road, and they'd not yet made it to the cement picnic tables.

A long moment of loaded silence followed, while all those within listening distance weighed their options.

Behind my neck I felt a soft rushing noise, like someone was blowing cold air there. When I looked back, I was startled by a familiar face, even as I was happy to see it.

The pitifully young Confederate soldier circled around

the boys to stand in front of us, looking for all the world like a projection of dusty light upon the fog. He moved his lips, but I couldn't read them; he pointed at the orb near the picnic tables, and then at another spot between the field and the nervous people within that orb.

I know, I mouthed, drawing the attention of Jamie and Benny. *What do we do?*

The soldier crouched down. He crooked his neck and looked intently at the army-green flashlight Benny was holding, although it was switched off. He seemed to give the object some consideration, then took one translucent hand and placed it over the unlit bulb, covering it completely. With the other hand, he indicated the Marshalls.

Two dull scrapes, one after the other, suggested the swisher was moving again—and this time, the Marshalls heard him.

"Oh, God. Who's there?" Dana asked, and for the first time I heard a real touch of fear in her words. The undead she could handle without any trouble, but the living were another story.

Click.

"Oh, God." Someone else said it this time, one of the men.

Benny gasped.

I clutched his arm, and the ghost clutched at his light—covering the lens with both hands and regarding me frantically. The time for thinking was past. Someone had cocked a weapon, and all bets were off.

"Stay down!" I commanded my comrades as I leaped to my feet. I suddenly understood the dead man's message, and whispering wasn't going to do anyone any good anymore.

"Marshalls!" I yelled as loud as I could. "Turn your lights off! *Now!*"

The cocked weapon fired, as loud as any musket and a dozen times as deadly. The blast came from in front of me and to my right. A few trees away, bark splintered and cracked.

I ducked back down to the ground just as the screaming started.

One lamp went out immediately, the light blob that marked the investigators shrinking by half, but the other stayed lit, and held aloft. The carrier started to run with the lamp, and what had previously been difficult to make out became a wild shadow-puppet theater of confusion.

Another shot rang out, then two more in quick succession.

The remaining light fell to the ground and shattered, eliminating the only clear target on the field. I hoped it had only been intentionally dropped, but I feared otherwise. I wished to God the fog would clear so that we would only be fighting the night for navigation. The fog and the darkness together were impenetrable and terrifying.

"Oh shit, oh shit, oh shit." Benny was scrambling on the ground, trying to gain his footing.

"Quiet!" I ordered, turning around to see what was happening. A fifth shot aimed itself in our direction. Behind me I heard the ping of a ricochet and felt something savage and hot streak across my collarbone. I grasped at the line of fire just south and right of my throat, and it was wet there. In contrast to the cold mist, the blood felt like lava on my shirt. I was bleeding on Dave's camera.

Shot number six went back towards the place where the Marshalls had been sitting ducks half a minute before.

There was running, and scuffling, and frightened wheezing— and these sounds were beginning to scatter. The group was breaking up, which, though unplanned, was surely wise.

"Tripp?"

"Tripp?"

"Dana?"

"Charlie, where's Tripp?"

Clatter, clatter, *spin*, plunk. Plunk. Plunk.

He was reloading. It was only a six-shooter.

"We have to move. We have to run," I said, pushing the boys apart, accidentally shoving Jamie into a tree trunk. "Split up. Now. Meet back at Ted's place. Whoever gets there first calls the cops."

I didn't have to tell them twice, which made me think that neither of them had seen that I was bleeding. I didn't believe for a moment that they would've left so easily if they'd known I was hurt.

I held still and leaned against the backside of the handiest tree, placing it between me and the shooter. The boys ran in opposite directions, crashing into every low-hanging limb, stump, rock, and root that was in their way. It's not easy running through the woods in the dark, and it's even tougher running through the woods, in the dark, in the fog, across uneven ground.

Harder still was running in the woods, in the dark, in the fog, across uneven ground, while wounded and holding my breath. Counting. Trying to calm myself down, even as I heard "plunk" number six and the steel wheel snapping back into place.

I closed my eyes and slid down, pressing my hands against the soaked spot on my chest. The ghost came up again and knelt beside me, looking at the injury and giving me a concerned expression that was kind, if not helpful. He stood again and parted his jacket so I could see the great red wound it concealed. I stared at the ancient injury with a special kind of horror, knowing that a

220

gut shot would not have killed him quickly.

But mine's only a grazing, I told myself, and prayed I wasn't lying. Just a skim. Not too bad.

I pushed my fingers around and felt a short channel of torn skin, but there was no entry hole that I could find. That much was reassuring, even if the sounds of screaming coming from behind me and two more revolver rounds were not.

"Tripp!" Dana was still shouting, and it sounded like she hadn't run far.

I didn't know where Charlie had gone, but the mad charging through trees somewhere off to my left suggested that he'd headed in roughly the same direction that Jamie had. That left the married couple and all their equipment behind—alone so far as I knew, and unprotected.

On the battlefield, acoustics are funny; things echo where it seems they shouldn't, and noises feel like they're hitting your head from all angles at once. Therefore, it was hard to pinpoint Dana's exact location. But depending on how much ammunition the shooter carried, his aim might not need to be precise.

"Oh my God! Oh my God!"

She wasn't getting any quieter, and it sounded like she'd stopped fleeing—she'd maybe even doubled back. Bad plan. Sticking around the field was a good way to get killed.

"Hey asshole! Come and get me!" It was Benny, but I couldn't tell where he was hollering from.

"Shut up," I whispered back, knowing he couldn't hear me. I held my position, but only because I didn't think the shooter's odds of catching me were very good so long as I stayed in the woods and kept low. Heaven knew he couldn't *see* me, and if I kept my mouth shut he wouldn't hear me, either. But Dana, frozen to

her place and panicking for all she was worth, was a very loud fish in a murky barrel.

The searing heat on my chest was either wearing its way down to a warm, dull line of pain, or I was getting used to the sensation and it didn't feel so bad.

I braced my back against the tree trunk and used it to slide myself upright, catching flaky bits of dirty bark all over my back. I felt shaky and scared stupid, but otherwise not too bad. I was not hurt bad. Not too bad. Not bad at all. I mumbled it like a mantra.

Up and around I flexed my right arm, testing the ligatures and making sure that my assessment had been correct: *just a graze*. The arm pulled my skin tight across the deep, nasty scratch, and it stung like hell, but it was nothing I couldn't live with.

There was always the possibility that I was in shock, and simply unable to process the extent of the damage, but, given the circumstances, I'd take what I could get.

I pushed myself away from the tree with my hip, stepping around it to face the direction of the distraught Dana Marshall. All the running, stumbling, crazily thrashing retreats had fled beyond earshot; and another round was fired—farther away this time, and back towards the field.

I cringed, remembering that Benny had taken off that way. I thought he'd hit the road and run along it. That way would be quieter and easier to navigate. There would be less chance of trees and rocks stopping him.

Surely he hadn't cut through the field?

Benny wasn't a big guy, but he was wiry and fast when he needed to be. I consoled myself with the thought that he must've gotten a good head start, and was surely halfway to the car by now. Also, he had the flashlight with the dim red beam. If he was far enough ahead, he could flip it on and make even better progress.

Bless his heart, the loony little bastard was leading trouble away from the rest of us.

I held my arms out in front of me and felt my way out of the woods, homing in on Dana. She was closer than I thought, maybe twenty yards from where the guys and I had been spying. I almost tripped over her, but grabbed her instead and fell down beside her. I whipped my stronger arm around her face to muffle the crying.

She tried to shriek, and gave me a mighty elbow jab that honestly winded me, but I was larger and stronger; I pinned one of my legs around her waist. "Shut up," I muttered into her ear, stronger than a whisper, so she could hear from my voice that I was a woman. "Shut up, or you'll get us both killed."

Dana nodded, and when I removed my arm she clapped her own hands over her mouth. Whatever was making her sob could not be stopped by willpower alone. When I unwrapped my leg from her lap I kicked something prone on the ground, and then I knew why.

I let her go, and felt my way along the body. His head was sticky, and in the dark it looked like tar had been poured over it. With a grimace, I ran my hands up Tripp's neck and felt around for a pulse. I only found gore, and a wound the size of a plum behind his right ear.

The shooter had made one remarkably lucky shot—two, if you counted hitting me. I prayed that those were the only two hits he'd made.

Once I'd forced Dana to muffle herself, things had gone quiet again in a very scary way.

Click.

Distant. Farther away than when he'd first begun shooting, but close enough still that he might get lucky again. I wiped my hands on my jeans and let my fingers crawl up Dana's face.

I took her chin and turned it towards the direction of the gunman's approach. Her chest shook and her face quivered, but she swallowed back everything she could and we held there, immobile.

Down, I gestured to her. *Down.*

With tedious, careful slowness we lowered ourselves until we were lying flat. I pushed the camera over to the side so it snuggled against my shoulder. Dana and I both put our chins on the ground and drew our limbs up close. The fog rolled over us in a damp, wooly blanket, obscuring everything beyond a small circle's diameter. He wouldn't be able to see us until he was literally on top of us.

I parted my lips and breathed through my mouth. Dana copied me, and I was glad. Her sinuses had filled as a result of the crying, and any trace of sniffles would give us both away.

Pat. Pat.

His feet hit the pavement again. He wasn't coming straight for us—probably because he couldn't remember or tell which way we were hiding—but he was advancing all the same. Dana closed her eyes, but I lifted my face up off the ground and saw, through the soup-thick mist, a humanoid shadow.

I was certain then that it was a living, breathing man: he moved in a top-heavy way, and the vague proportions I could make out implied hips that didn't sway.

I couldn't discern anything else. Not a hairstyle, not a distinguishing feature of his face, not a color of clothing. He was a nebulous blob, nothing more; and I hoped that we were less than that to him.

I was wearing dark jeans and a black shirt with my customary black boots. I didn't know what Dana was wearing, but a cautious glance told me it was fairly dark. I hoped we blended into the ground, a gravelly mix of cast-off asphalt and deep green grass.

Two more shapes formed in the fog. At first I held my breath; then I realized that these two were not like the shooter. They were dead.

Before us stood two soldiers in bulky, poorly cut uniforms—I couldn't see what color—but they saluted in sync, and dashed in front of the man with the gun. I don't know whether he could see them. God knew I barely could.

They left a trail, though—a wake of swirling air that pulled the fog into patterns of action. Maybe the man felt them, even if he couldn't hear them. They got his attention, at least. His heels swiveled in a full circle, and he fired a shot at no one who would care.

Dana whimpered under my arm, very softly, but he didn't hear her. He stepped forward, lurching away from us. His legs went swishing back into the grass, charging away in fits and starts, well out of my view.

I squeezed Dana's shoulder and slowly rose. I pulled her with me, but she hesitated, still clutching the form on the ground. We'd dropped down closer to Tripp than I thought. She must have been holding onto him while we were lying there.

I tugged a second time and she stood up, carefully.

She reached up to put her hands on my face, and I was struck by how small she was. "He's dead, isn't he?" she asked, in words so quiet I couldn't hear them—but I felt them all the same.

While she had her hands on either side of my jaw I nodded. I wanted to say something more, but we both knew there weren't any words that would help.

We listened. The murderer was somewhere across the road, in the grass.

We looked around, trying to get our bearings. It was impossible. We couldn't see more than three or four feet in any direction. If it were only dark, we might find a way out of the park; or if it were only foggy.

Between the two, we were pretty much screwed.

Huddled together, we took a few steps in each direction until we spied the edge of a cement picnic table. We crouched to take hold of it, and felt our way around it until I guessed we were facing the road, if the set-up was the way I remembered it.

Still hanging on to Dana's forearm, I tried to orient myself.

If I was correct and we were facing the road, then off to my right would be the way we came in, and to the left, along the road, would be the way back to the front of the park. Behind us, more woods. Around us, a fog so thick I could reach out and grab a handful of it… blended thoroughly with the lovely pitch dark that happens out in the middle of nowhere at nearly two in the morning.

The moon was out, but it may as well not have been.

I didn't know where Jamie and Benny were, and I was still bleeding. A warm trail of wet worked its way down my shirt, and the burning sting was spreading into a humid, nasty pain across my chest. But when I rubbed at the source it was numb, and what had at first seemed a ferocious scrape felt less disastrous.

Dana must have sensed my movement, because she reached out and touched me—landing a hand squarely on my chest and working her way up.

"You're hurt too," she said, though I didn't know who else she could mean besides her husband, who was well beyond hurt.

I nodded, and gripped her hand. "It's not bad. Come on."

"Where?"

"This way." We were both whispering and holding close. I had to lean down to reach her ear.

We would move most quietly if we could walk on the road, and if we followed the road far enough we would eventually hit the front of the park. Though the visitors' center would almost certainly be deserted, there was a main road right outside the entrance. One way or another, we'd flag somebody down for help, if Jamie and Benny hadn't done so already.

Together we crept off the grass onto gritty gravel, and then on to the asphalt.

A sliding wrong step brought us both to a halt, ears perked with fear.

Off to our right and across the road—in the middle of the field by the sound of it—someone came to attention. After a hesitation he came forward a few feet in our direction. Dana released my hand, and I thought she might do something stupid out of impulse; so I reached into my front pocket and pulled out the first thing I found—a tube of lip balm—and I cast it into the woods behind us. It knocked loud against a tree and fell to the ground, rolling to a stop in the underbrush.

Our stalker froze again; then he surged forward, tearing his legs through the grass. He chased the bait at a full-on charge, and that was our cue.

I could barely make out the edge of the road down to my left, trailing it in the dark by the slight texture change between grass and pavement. I saw it best in my peripheral vision, if I stared down hard at the road beneath us.

Dana wanted to run, but I held her back. She was wearing

hard-heeled shoes, and if she wasn't careful, they would clatter. For a few seconds we could enjoy the cover of our pursuer's headlong rush, but he'd slow down when he hit the trees.

"Tiptoes," I told her.

She seemed to understand, shifting her weight to the balls of her feet as she stepped.

We couldn't go too fast. We could barely see a thing, and the road was not perfectly even. The first skip or stumble and we'd be discovered.

My chest hurt, and my head was starting to hurt too, from all the fruitless squinting and staring into the diaphanous white darkness. Dana was dragging, and crying quietly. Somewhere behind us, sooner or later, a man with a gun was going to figure out he'd been duped; and his confusion might not last long enough for us to get far enough away to call ourselves safe.

But hope propelled me forward. I hoped I wasn't bleeding anymore, and I hoped that Dana could hold herself together just a little longer. I hoped that Benny and Jamie were okay. I hoped that the road wasn't as long as I was afraid it was, and that we weren't as far back in the park as I believed we were.

But lacking anything more concrete than hope, we pushed on—one foot in front of the other, shoving ourselves through the fog towards safety, wherever that might lie.

Behind us, he hit the trees and kept hunting, firing off at least two shots, maybe three. I'd quit counting once I heard him reloading. It wouldn't do us any good to play the odds of his barrel.

"Faster now," I said, pulling her, where before I'd been pushing her. Not too hard, not too fast, or I'd make her fall—but faster, all the same.

The road began to curve, and we followed it, panting with

fright and exhaustion. Adrenaline pushed us far, but after a point our bodies objected to the abuse. My own sense of lightheadedness was surely due in part to the bleeding, and the more I thought about it, the more I wondered if Dana hadn't been hit too. Maybe I'd misunderstood her earlier observation, and it wasn't her husband she'd been talking about.

"Faster," I said again anyway, because straggling would get us killed. "Faster."

Clumsy thrashing and a spat of swearing announced that the gunman was having a hard time in the trees. *Good,* I thought. *Let him get lost.* We were sticking to the road.

Around us the ghastly pale air swirled and writhed, parting to let us through and closing behind us. Under different circumstances I might have found it soothing or interesting, but given the situation, I found it inconvenient and downright terrifying.

I lifted my eyes up off the road for a moment and saw that we were not alone. Beside us and behind us new shapes appeared, curious and confused. Soldiers, officers, horses. A woman in a plain dress with a cinched waist. A black man. A boy with a drum. Next, next, next—all in rapid succession. Maybe a crowd, maybe only a dozen of them. It was hard to tell when I was concentrating in so many directions at once.

They weren't reaching or grasping, threatening or screaming. They were only curious. They crowded in, swarming us as we ran.

I ignored them. They weren't our problem right then.

I didn't know if Dana could see them or not, but if she could, she didn't say anything. She let me haul her along without objection, and with only the occasional faltering step.

Then a more familiar face reared out of the haze—I was almost coming to think of him as a friend, or at least a friendly acquaintance. The slight-figured Confederate boy held out an arm in the universal signal to stop.

I complied, jerking Dana against my chest in an impromptu hug to halt her as quickly and quietly as possible.

The soldier folded all of his fingers except for one into a fist, and he held that one up to his lips. Another symbol, universal. Easy to understand across a thousand miles or a hundred years. So too was Dana's responsive nod. She *did* see them, then. I decided to be glad for it. I decided that it would be easier if she saw them too, so I didn't have to explain.

When we weren't moving we could hear better, and now that we'd been stopped in our proverbial tracks, we could tell that maybe the swisher had gotten the idea he'd been had by the lip balm.

He was coming again. Not as fast as we were, and when we quit moving he quit too, for a few seconds. But he was behind us, closer than before. No longer swinging his arms at the tree trunks in the fog.

This way.

The ghost moved his lips with enough exaggeration that I could read them. He pointed, and waved.

Follow.

He was directing us off the road, into the woods—the same course that I'd prayed would get our mad swisher lost. But the mad swisher didn't have anyone showing him the way, not so far as I knew.

Dana was already tugging at my wrist, wanting to obey. Wanting to follow.

Well, she was the professional here. I was just an amateur with a correctly tuned ghost receiver.

And since I was out of ideas, I let the others take the reins. I wasn't even sure that the road we were on did lead out of the park—I only figured it might. But the dead definitely knew their way around better than I did.

We took simultaneous deep breaths and took off after the ghost, more noisily than I would have preferred, but with enough speed to possibly make up for the lapse in silence.

We fled faster. He followed faster.

But we had a good lead on him by then, and we had someone leading us. We reached the tree line in moments, and we dove on through the trunks. It was one thing to run around in the dark on an open stretch of road, but another thing entirely to navigate a woody obstacle course. Our progress slowed considerably, but again, we had a guide, and we had a lead.

Of course, our pursuer had a gun.

He fired it again, enough times to empty the thing. He was forced to stop long enough to jam a hand into his pockets and grab more ammunition, and we made good use of that time.

There were enough tree trunks between us and him that he didn't have much hope of hitting us, and we liked that. We wanted to extend that buffer as deep as we possibly could, so we kept going, tagging after our indefatigable leader as he whipped around the trees. Dana and I clung to each other still, yanking one another to the left, to the right, around and past and over—pulling each other's skin until we left red marks, digging in until we left scratches, anything but letting go.

Eventually we could no longer hear the determined footsteps dashing haphazardly along in our wake, but we didn't feel too relieved about evading him yet. Our guide was still pulling us farther into the park, and we kept after him.

Finally, the ache at my collarbone and the waning of my adrenaline had worn me down enough that I needed to call for a time out. Apparently that perpendicular hand signal is not as universal as a finger to the mouth, but the ghost caught on quick.

"Time out," I gasped, not too loud. "Time out. Can't run anymore. For a minute. Give me a minute."

Dana agreed. "Wait. Just wait. Oh God, we left Tripp."

"Tripp's dead," I said, with less tact than I might have scrounged up otherwise.

"I know," she said, and I thought she might start crying again, but she didn't. "I can't believe I ran off and left him."

"We couldn't have carried him, you know. And," I added, not meaning to sound so harsh, "he wouldn't have wanted you to stay and get killed. You know that, right?"

She wiped at her face with her forearm. Maybe she *was* crying again. She was hiding it well, if that was the case. I didn't hear a squeak or a sniffle. "Yeah. He would want me to run."

"Definitely," I panted.

Our guide obliged us, stopping to wait. He didn't look impatient or hurried at all anymore. The sense of urgency was gone. Assuming his goal had been to see us away to relative safety, this mission could be regarded as a success.

He approached us with something like idle inquisitiveness putting out a hand to me like he wanted to shake hello.

I lifted mine, unsure of what he intended or desired.

His hand went through mine, more or less, giving me a tiny twinge of a chill where what used to be his flesh met mine. He moved his fingers around mine as if trying to touch them. If he was trying to achieve some literal, physical impact, he failed.

"I don't think it will work with her," Dana said, sounding almost normal.

"What?" I asked, but the ghost clearly understood.

He turned his attention to her and offered the same hand.

Dana took it, and drew it forward. The ghost fell into her, a drifting, soft collision wherein Dana absorbed the spirit completely and easily. She had done this before.

She blinked, hard.

A few of the others had caught up to us by then—a black woman with a white bundle of something like laundry on her head, two of the enlisted men, and one of the officers. It was too dark to distinguish their uniforms. It was too foggy to tell them apart too well; but even as I remembered and noticed again the fog, it retreated.

Not everywhere, but around us the wall of white backed away, clearing us a patch—a small circle—and giving us room to see one another better.

"She's cold," Dana said, in a voice that was perfectly ordinary. It didn't sound like it belonged to anyone else at all, not the way they portray it in books and movies. It sounded like Dana.

"It's getting cold out here, yeah," I replied. "She should've brought a jacket."

"You're hurt."

I shrugged. "Not bad."

"Not now, no. It's closing up quick." Ah. The way he said "quick" it sounded almost like "quake," so there was some change after all—an accent to the vowels that didn't belong to Dana.

"Well, it's stopped bleeding anyway. I think."

"More than that. It's closing. What are you, anyway?"

"What do you mean? I'm not… I'm not anything. But I can

see you, obviously. All of you, when you come out like this."

He snorted. "That doesn't make you half so unusual as you think." The closing word sounded like "thank." "She can see, too," the soldier said, meaning Dana.

"I know I'm not the only one who can see—"

He interrupted me. "Lots of people can *see*. And lots of animals, too. But you've got something else here, don't you? The bullet didn't strike you too hard. It hit a tree first and came back. I saw it. But the wound is all closed up now, where the bullet skimmed you."

I fondled the sore spot and frowned. "How do you know? It's too dark to see a damn thing out here."

"With this woman's eyes, yes, it's too dark. But before, with my own, I could see it fine. I see the blood especially well. It glows, to us. It shines in the dark, like your tears, and your sweat does. We can see it fine. It reflects to us like a cat's eyes. If you ever come back like us, you'll see it too."

The blood was drying on my shirt, making the fabric crackle when I squeezed it. "I wasn't hurt bad. I was in shock before, but now I'm not. That's all. It's no big deal." I only sort of understood it myself, and to know that the dead could spot me as strange made me deeply uncomfortable. It was as if I were more like them, and less like the living.

He laughed, harsh and hoarse. "No big deal. If we'd had an army of men like you, we would've never lost. You're touched with something, whether you'll admit to it or not."

Another soldier joined the circle, chattering and pointing.

Dana's head shook. "I can't hear you," he told the ghost. "I don't know why. Maybe it's just been too long since we tried to speak. I, I like these clothes she's wearing, though. I like the pants."

I threw my head to the right, trying to bring the soldier's attention to the other ghost. "Hey, buddy, I can't hear him either, but I think he wants us to get a move-on."

"I can't…" Dana's head went back and forth again. "I can't lead you out this way. I can't see a thing. But I like her pants. I'll let go now. We'll take you to… there's a, at the front of the place there's a… there's a building. We'll take you there."

"Wait—don't let her go yet." I held Dana's body by the shoulders. "What's going on? If you can talk to us this way, well then, *talk*. What's going on at Dyer's field? Who's that asshole who's been shooting at us? Why did Green Eyes leave?"

"Green Eyes," he repeated. "That's what you call him. He's left us. He tried to keep the digging man away, but the bargain was up. The digging man isn't afraid of us because he can only barely see us—only sometimes, at that."

The soldier's mind was wandering; he seemed to have a hard time keeping a train of thought together. It sounded like a struggle to string the right words one after the other.

"The digging man—the man with the gun?"

"Uh-huh. That's him."

"So you've seen him before. And there was some bargain made with Green Eyes, that he'd stay here?"

Dana's body sagged back against a tree, and her knees began to fold. "A pact. Until the last descendant of the good general was gone. He watched us until the last one died."

"I don't understand," I said, which was possibly the understatement of the year. "Come on, stay with me now. I don't understand. Please keep talking."

But the ghostly newcomer waved his hand and shook his head hard, motioning for quiet again. Maybe the "digging man"

235

was closing in on us again, though I didn't hear anything to indicate it.

Dana was slipping down, falling asleep by the look of her. I didn't know what to do; I wasn't in the habit of babysitting channelers. I didn't have the first idea how to handle things, so I pretended she was fainting and I caught her.

"Please," I said again. "I don't understand."

"It's because… it's because we have no wings to the kingdom."

Then Dana's eyes rolled back in her head, and she went limp.

The soldier spirit rose out of her and re-formed into a more recognizable shape, though he too appeared disoriented by the experience. He was fuzzy around the edges, and indistinct where he'd once seemed solid.

I cushioned Dana as she fell, holding her up and against me. It wasn't hard. She couldn't have weighed a hundred pounds, soaking wet with rocks in her pockets. Her eyelashes fluttered against my neck.

"Come on, honey. Up and at 'em," I said into her ear. "Rise and shine, Dana. Come on."

She twitched against me, coming around enough to push me away and stand with the help of her friendly neighboring tree trunk. "Shit," she fussed, rubbing her knuckles against her temples. "Shit."

"Shhh," I responded, indicating the ghosts around us.

They were all holding still, as if they too could step and break a twig, or otherwise give us away.

Dana cleared her throat and bobbed her head to say she got it. It was time to hush up and run again. The ghosts retreated, except for our new friend, and as they backed away the fog closed in again—but this time I thought of it as cover instead of nuisance.

Dana took my hand again and staggered forward, close on the heels of the small soldier.

It must've been a shortcut; or then again, I might have misjudged the size of the park and our position in it. Within a few minutes of unchanging scenery—trees set in the white gelatin mold of the fog—we were back to the road, and in the distance I heard cars.

"Where are we?" I hissed, and the soldier pointed at something I couldn't see.

Hurry. Go.

And he left us.

We were alone in the dark, but we were free of the trees, and if we stayed on the road we'd run into something shortly. The visitors' center, I assumed.

Dana and I shuffled on, elbow to elbow, listening for the sound of trouble behind us. We weren't disappointed. A crash and a muttered "fuck" told us we were only literally out of the woods.

My companion picked up the pace without any prompting, and I kept it with her. The puttering hum of a bad muffler went zipping by, not too far away, and the sound was music to my ears. We pulled ourselves towards the intermittent vehicles with all the energy we could muster. The road wasn't busy—it wasn't rush hour traffic—but it was a main thoroughfare, and even in the middle of the night there would be someone.

Anyone.

I realized with some dismay that I didn't hear any sirens, and I hadn't seen any blue lights flashing. Where were Jamie and Benny? Had either of them made it to safety? The digging man, the swisher, the shooter—whatever I called him in my head—he couldn't have gotten them both.

He couldn't have.

He'd spent too much time chasing me and Dana to have doubled back and taken them both.

To our left, a big square shape loomed. The building was much closer than the main road, but it was probably unoccupied. Probably. I didn't have the faintest idea if there were park rangers who kept watch all night, but I didn't believe the odds were good. If anyone had heard the shooting, surely they would have called the police.

Or maybe not. The memory of a dimly recalled story flashed through my head—some tale of how gunshots were so common on the battlefield that the cops didn't heed those calls.

Ted had said something, once—he'd mentioned as a party story that he often heard people crying for help in his backyard. He said he'd heard groaning, and crying, and artillery fire; but when he called the police and told them, they told him to go back to bed and forget about it.

"Everyone hears them," they said. "But there's nothing we can or should do for them now."

Until I was running in the dark through the fog in the middle of the night, I hadn't believed him. I'd assumed he was regaling us with bonfire stories, like any good campfire host would.

Hell, maybe he'd been telling the truth. What a horrible thought.

Summoning assistance might require a more tangible, deliberate action. "This way." I pulled on Dana's arm. "To the center."

"There's no one there," she replied, and I nodded even though she couldn't see me.

"I know. That's okay. Hurry."

A sidewalk, or an offshoot of the road, went zipping up a hill. We took it, hobbling together up the incline and tripping simultaneously on a set of stairs. Dana fell towards a cannon and took me with her, but we recovered and found ourselves before the big glass doors at the now-dark entrance. I pressed my face up against the glass but saw nothing inside except flags hanging from the ceiling, plaques mounted on the walls, and a big ranger's desk in the back. A stubby lamp was lit on the ranger's desk, barely illuminating the place from within, but not giving enough light to really make it visible from the road.

Dana lifted an arm like she was going to beat on the glass, but I stopped her.

"No good," I swore. "Something bigger. Heavier. We need to nail this in one stroke."

She caught on quick.

"By the cannon," she said, and left me. A moment later she whispered through the fog. "Help me, goddammit."

I had thought all the cannonballs in the pyramids were welded together, but I've been wrong before. Dana had found a stray shell and was trying to lift it. They're smaller than you might expect, only about the size of a toy bowling ball, but a whole lot heavier than they look.

I worked my fingers under one end while Dana worked her fingers under the other, and between us we shimmied it over to the window. Off in the not-too-distant distance, the digging man slid off the road into the grass, either missing the sidewalk or not knowing it was there. He might have been tracking us by acoustics, in which case he was in for a mighty damp surprise before reaching us.

A splash declared that he'd found the creek, and the ensuing clatter as he worked his way up the short banks told us we were running out of time.

"One," I said, and swung my arms out.

Dana worked with me. "Two," she declared, helping me pick up the pace.

"Three!" We said it together, not bothering to keep it down.

We released the cannonball, and it pitched forward by the weight of its own inertia, plunging through the glass. Immediately, a ferociously loud alarm sounded—a violent clanging that matched my concept of a firehouse bell.

"Now what?" Dana shouted over the din.

I grabbed her wrist, and my grip slid down to catch on her hand. For what felt like the one millionth time that evening, without any destination in mind, we ran.

FOURTEEN

AFTERMATH

By the time the police arrived, Dana and I were inside the visitors' center, hiding behind the big, circular desk area that the rangers sit at during the day. I'd initially climbed over the counter because I thought maybe I'd find a weapon, or something, but there was no such luck to be had. The most exciting thing we found behind the counter was a *Playboy* magazine stuffed inside a historical journal.

The cops arrived within three minutes of us busting out the window, swarming the joint. We stood up and threw our hands in the air as soon as we heard them. Dana started crying.

We were interviewed, collectively and separately, for several hours. Jamie had showed up back at Ted's, where he'd called the authorities as promised; but it took them hearing the formal alarm before they'd sent anybody out.

I was worried about Benny for a while. He seemed to have vanished, and I was hard-pressed to tell anyone where he'd run off to, apart from a general direction where he might have gone. Someone with a flashlight found him about an hour later. He'd face-planted into a tree back in the far side of the park and knocked himself out cold.

After the ambulance had finished with him, he held an ice pack against his forehead and sat down next to me and Jamie. We sat on the steps of the visitors' center beside the big cannons and, between us, got most of the story out of our heads and into the cops' notebooks.

Thirty-five minutes after I called home, Lu and Dave arrived at the battlefield. You just have to know the local geography to know how impressive *that* little feat was. To make it from the top of Signal Mountain to north Georgia in that sort of time, well, they're lucky all the cops were down where we were and not running speed traps along the way.

I would have felt warm and fuzzy about their concern if they hadn't been so quiet once they got here.

Screaming I could have dealt with. Yelling would have been a relief. Instead, they kept their collective cool and chatted with the cops, confirming my address and other assorted contact information.

Both of them were dressed, though rumpled. Lu's socks didn't match, and Dave wore a determinedly ugly plaid thing tossed over a red T-shirt that said JOE'S CRAB SHACK.

Dana wandered off with someone in a uniform, and I didn't see her again for the rest of the night.

Looking up at Lu and Dave, I wondered if *I* was going to be okay.

Dave shot Jamie and Benny the sort of glare that is usually reserved for incoming suitors, and the guys dived off in opposite directions as if on cue. My aunt and uncle sat down on either side of me, replacing them.

For the moment, all the cops were off doing other things—milling around in that sort of way that implied that I wasn't allowed to go yet, but they were finished talking to me for the time being.

"So," Lu opened the floor. "Dancing, eh?"

"I didn't tell you I was dancing," I pointed out. "I just said I was going to be out late."

"Perhaps you should've corrected our assumption."

"Yeah." I stared down at the step between my knees, feeling like a little kid.

"You really had us worried," Dave piped up, staring straight ahead, just like I was.

"No I didn't," I argued. "You didn't know there was any trouble until the cops called you in. From where I'm sitting, I was *sparing* you two worry. That was the point of not correcting your assumption, anyway."

"Thanks," they said together, neither one of them sounding sincere.

We sat in a row—monkeys Hear No Evil, See No Evil, and Speak No Evil, respectively.

Lu stared off at one of the two ambulances. "Your friends okay?"

"They're okay. Benny knocked his head on a tree, but he'll live."

Dave dropped his head into his hands, propping his forehead up with his elbows on his knees. "Eden, somebody died out here tonight."

"I didn't mean it that way. It was a poor choice of words."

One of the other ambulances was closing up, and through the square window in the back I saw Dana's blond head. I was miserable, but there was no fixing anything now, so I'd be better off if I could keep my mouth shut.

Lu leaned around me, noticing the hole in my shirt for the first time, and the dark stain around it. "What's this?" she asked, and my mood sank even further.

"Nothing," I muttered.

"Nothing?" She had Dave's attention then, and they leaned in to poke at my chest.

"Well, you know. I've been running around in the dark, in the woods, and I'm sure I've finished the evening with more than a couple of scrapes. Bruises, and the like. It's no big deal."

Dave's voice lifted an octave. "No big deal? Look at this crusty mess. You were *bleeding*."

If it had been any other time, he'd have been answered with a menstrual joke. But he was Dave, and not someone else, so I saved it. It occurred to me that I needed to find a different way to deal with stress than resorting to bad humor. But it had been a rough night, and I was too tired to change my coping mechanism now.

"Leave me alone, y'all. I need a shower, my bed, and half a box of Band-Aids. And I'll be fine."

"Let me see it," Lu demanded, and I let her.

I tugged the neckline of my shirt down to reveal a flat white bandage, because I'd already run through the paramedic gauntlet. I love Lu and Dave, but I know them too well to let them get the drop on me. I'd had the patch put on before they could arrive and see the weirdness for themselves.

It was just one more part of the secret I'd carried out of the swamp in Florida. Getting hurt was bad enough; but they'd be even more alarmed if they knew how quickly the wound had closed itself.

"What's underneath *that*?" Dave asked, pointing now instead of poking. There's something so formal and official about medical tape; I knew good and well that neither one of them was going to make me take it off to satisfy their curiosity.

"A scratch."

"A scratch?"

"A bad scratch. But it didn't need stitches or anything, so it wasn't *that* bad."

I didn't mention how the paramedic had grilled me—how he'd called the ambulance driver over to look at me too. I didn't tell them how they hadn't believed me, at first; and I didn't say how they'd put their fingers through the hole in the shirt to convince themselves that the half-healed wound they found there was only an hour old.

It was weirder than they knew, and stranger than I was prepared to tell them.

I meant to change the subject, but Dave beat me to it.

"Is that my old camera?"

"Um. Yes."

"Is it broken?"

"I… I don't think so, no. Can we just go home now? I'll explain everything after some sleep, and I think they're mostly done with us here."

Lu looked around at the visitors' center parking lot—as far as she could see it, anyway. The fog had let up some as dawn was approaching, but it was still asserting a healthy presence.

"Where are you parked?" she asked.

"Back by Ted's place."

As if on cue, Ted appeared beside us. He was not perfectly coifed, but he was surprisingly well put-together for a man who'd been roused before dawn for an emergency phone call. He always was, though. There was something aesthetically mercenary about him that you either loved or found repulsive.

"And of course"—he inserted himself into our conversation, extending a hand to Lulu—"your lovely niece is welcome to leave it on my property for the time being."

"Forget it," I said.

"We'll drive you home," Dave said, patting my leg.

But I wasn't about to leave the Death Nugget thirty-five miles away from its driveway of preference. "No way. I'm not hurt. I'm tired as hell, but so are you two—and I've still got leftover adrenaline to keep me awake. Besides, I've got to run these two nutters home." I tipped my head at the boys.

Benny was still holding an ice pack to his head, and Jamie had a rat's nest of leaf litter stuck in his curly mane.

Lu looked them up and down, noticing for the first time that they were alone. Both of them looked back at her with perfect dejection.

Neither one of them had summoned any family assistance. Jamie's mother was old enough to be his grandmother and in poor health, so it didn't surprise me that he hadn't given her a call. And Benny was on the outs with all of his relations, save a much older brother. I didn't know the details and I'd never asked. It was none of my business. If he wanted me to know, he'd tell me.

"We can give them a ride," she said. "We'll run them home. We'll all fit in the car."

"You *could* run them home, but you're not going to. I brought them here, and I'll take them back," I insisted. "I'm not leaving my car out here. One of you would only have to bring me back to it tomorrow."

I stood up, brushing concrete dust off of my hands and onto my thighs. Everyone else sitting on the stairs—Dave, Lu, Jamie, and Benny—rose as well. Ted stood aside in a charming, deferential fashion that marked him as a salesman.

"My offer stands," he reminded me, and I thanked him but declined again.

"Thanks, man. But I don't want to have to come back for it. I do appreciate it, though. If you hadn't been home, we might've been in trouble."

I said it with a rueful sort of smile that I hoped told them all I was kidding. No one smiled back except Ted, but that was okay.

Lu tossed her hands up, then snaked one arm around Dave's wrist. "Suit yourself, if that's the way you want it. We're going to follow behind you, though. We're parked over by the Tower monument. I won't have you falling asleep at the wheel."

Or give you extra time to run off and get your story straight, I thought, but did not add aloud. It wouldn't have been fair. She was worried, and Dave was worried, and I had been the one to worry them.

"That's fine. We've got to walk that way to get to Ted's anyhow. Let me make sure the cops are done with us, and we can walk back to the car."

I confirmed with the nearest police officer that nothing more was required of any of us, though they had all of our contact information and would almost certainly be in touch. No surprise, there. They offered us a ride back to our car, but I declined on everyone's behalf.

I rejoined my friends and family. Benny withdrew the trusty flashlight from his bag and struggled to flick the black switch to turn it on. He was exhausted, and had a headache to boot.

I put out my hand, and he gave me the light. With some trouble of my own, I pushed the switch into place and aimed the beam at the ground. Everyone was kind enough to refrain from pointing out how badly the circle of light shook and wavered.

I was worn out, but not so much that I didn't appreciate it.

We left Lu and Dave at their vehicle, and the rest of us walked the extra half a block to Ted's in silence. Even Ted kept quiet, which was a little out of character, but he was a smarter guy than I sometimes gave him credit for.

I thanked him again for his assistance; then Jamie and Benny and I all piled back into the Nugget. We closed ourselves inside the smallish car and exhaled simultaneously.

I stuffed my hand into my pocket and dragged out my keys. They felt bulky and sharp in my hand. I fumbled with them, dropping them twice before my thumb found the right one.

"You sure you're okay to drive?" Jamie asked.

I nodded. "We're all okay. We're all just tired. Right?" I looked over to Benny, then over my shoulder at Jamie. "We are all okay, aren't we?"

They mumbled assent, though Benny put his hand to his head with a wince.

I leaned forward until my brow was creased against the steering wheel. "Let's go." Without looking, I jabbed the key into the ignition.

I couldn't keep Lu and Dave waiting.

Benny showed up on the mountain shortly after the first hint of daylight, begging to be let inside. He figured that since our number was unlisted, except for Dave's studio office, the reporters might have a harder time tracking me down. He figured right, sort of. Though Channel 3 had located Benny's home within an hour, it took them all of three to catch up with *me*.

Benny cowered in the kitchen when Lu opened the door.

"Hello, ma'am. I'm Nick Alders from WRCB. Is Eden available?"

I shook my head fiercely—*no, no, no*—but Lu just opened the door farther and invited the man inside.

"Baby," she said, "you went out and made this mess. You clean it up. Can I get you fellows anything?"

The heavily laden cameraman and reporter duo declined, but thanked her.

Tall, brunet, and violently tanned, Nick Alders beamed his big-toothed way into my living room, hand outstretched to shake mine.

There was no statement to be made by being rude, so I took it and obliged him. He dipped his head and called me "ma'am," same as he'd done to my aunt, but that was no surprise. He wanted to butter me up good and see what slipped out.

"Miss Moore, we were very much hoping we could have a moment of your time, to talk about the incident at the battlefield last night."

"Why me?" I asked, glancing into the kitchen and seeing no sign of Benny.

"Your friends have both declined to provide us with a report in the matter, but with all those rumors flying around, we sure would like to give you the opportunity to set the record straight."

"What rumors?"

The cameraman turned to set a blocky canvas bag down on the ground. He adjusted the equipment—pulling out digital memory cards and investigating his battery supply.

Nick didn't answer as fast as I would have liked; and when he did respond, he was vague. "Oh, you know how it is around here. People like to talk."

"I do know that for a fact," I agreed, with matched vagueness.

He flicked his eyes to the sofa as though he wanted me to adjourn to the seat, but I stood my ground. We were eye to eye and I liked it that way. I was tired and beat up from the previous evening, and pissy about the intrusion. And I felt stronger if I was ready to run, even when I didn't intend to.

"Would you care to sit down?" he asked.

"No thanks. I'm fine."

He cleared his throat and motioned to his assistant. "Well. All right, then. Would you um, hang on—Calvin, if you could just bring that up here I'd appreciate it, yeah, thanks—okay, Miss Moore, would you care to give us your take on the events at the battlefield last night?"

Again I looked over into the kitchen. I hadn't heard the door to the garage open or close, so I could only assume that Benny was crouched on the floor behind the counter.

I shrugged as Lu excused herself to the porch and left me to my journalistic fate. "What exactly do you want to know?"

"What would you like to tell us?"

"Tell you about *what*?"

His hundred-watt smile twitched. "Ma'am, I sure would love to be the one asking the questions, here."

"Then why don't you ask me something specific?"

Nick sighed—not in a pretty way, but with an aggravated hiss. "Turn that off for a second, Calvin, would you?"

Calvin obliged him, and when the red light went off on the camera Nick started again. "Because we don't know shit, that's why. Nobody knows what happened, and nobody's talking. I'm just trying to do my job here, honey, so if you're going to blow me off or dick around with my time, just say so now and I'll be out of your hair."

Out of the corner of my eye, I saw the top of Benny's rumpled head rear slightly over the edge of the counter.

"I find your candor refreshing, Nick. But if you want me to stand here and tell you the long and sordid story of what we were doing out there and how it all went to hell in a handbasket—"

"Oh, I don't need all of that," he interrupted me. "Maybe I exaggerated when I said we didn't know shit, precisely. Dana Marshall released a statement from the hospital."

She had? That was news to me, but I didn't announce it to him right away. "All right. How about this, then—we'll sit down and have a nice chat and you can tell me all about what you know, and then I'll maybe fill in a few gaps for you. But I don't like the camera. Leave the camera off and we'll talk."

"Deal. Camera's staying off. Is a tape recorder okay?"

"Yeah, that's okay." Mostly I didn't want anyone seeing me on TV. Again I thought of Gary and the little dead girl; and I thought of all the hopeful lovers, parents, and friends who had come before him. They were finding me one way or another, but I wasn't going to make it any easier for them.

"What about your friend over there, beside the fridge? Does he want in on this, or not?"

So he wasn't completely blind. That made one more point in the reporter's favor. "I'm guessing not. Benny?"

"Naw." He waved from behind the counter. "Y'all go ahead. I'm just looking for the chips. Down here. In these cupboards."

"Check the pantry. Up on your left."

"Thanks," he said, and sheepishly rose to fish around behind the pantry door.

"Salsa's in the fridge. Second shelf. Sour cream's in the door."

"I *got* it, okay?"

"Okay. Now Mr. Alders—"

"Call me Nick."

"Fine. Nick." I leaned back in the crook of the couch's right arm, striking a pose that might have looked open and friendly—though I didn't really intend it that way. I was making a point to take up as much space as possible.

"And I can call you Eden?"

"Knock yourself out. And let's start this with you telling me about Ms. Marshall's statement. I'm afraid I must've missed it."

He exchanged an eyebrow lift with the cameraman. "Surely it's not anything you don't already know. But since you asked, it was mostly typical stuff—it's a very difficult time for her and her crew, she's thankful that none of her local volunteers were hurt, and she appreciates everyone's thoughts and prayers. Nothing you wouldn't expect. Given the media coverage lately, we were all just confused to learn that they'd enlisted local help. I talked to her and her husband last week, and I got the distinct impression that they always brought their own people along."

In the kitchen, Benny dropped his freshly located bag of chips.

I was surprised too, but delighted that Dana had opted to cover for us. She hadn't needed to lie to the cops on our behalf, but it had been kind of her to do so. We'd been trespassing on federally protected land, and we'd gotten ourselves involved in a murder. I made a mental note to hunt her down and thank her later.

I nodded, half to myself and half to acknowledge I'd heard Nick. "You said she issued this from the hospital? Is she okay?"

"Didn't you know?"

"No. She got into the ambulance when they took Tripp away, and we haven't seen her since. I didn't even know what hospital she was brought to."

Nick's eyebrow stayed aloft. "Not keeping the closest of tabs on her, are you?"

"We were volunteers, remember? It's not like we've got to chase her down and make her pay us. Look, her husband had died and we didn't know her terribly well. The cops told us to go home. We didn't want to be in the way. There wasn't anything we could do."

Guilt rays emanated from Nick's pointed eyebrow. At the time, going home had felt like the only reasonable thing to do. But now I wished I'd asked more questions, or made a phone call or two.

"Sure," Nick said, jotting a note down in his palm-sized pad. "I understand. And she'll be fine. Minor cuts and contusions, and all that jazz. She checked out of Erlanger this morning. I guess she went back to her hotel, or went home. You guys will probably have an easier time finding her than I would, right now. So anyway— things were pretty crazy. Let's talk about those crazy things. It was late at night, the fog rolled in, and then what happened?"

"Then, we uh, we heard someone coming towards us. We couldn't see him, but we could hear him. He opened fire on us and we put the lights out so he'd have a harder time hitting us, but by then it was too late for Tripp. Listen, man. We panicked and split up. Dana and I ran one way, my friends ran two other ways, and I don't know what the hell happened to their camera guy. Eventually, me and Dana wound up back by the visitors' center, and we threw the cannonball at the window to set off the alarm. That's it. That's the whole thing in a nutshell. That's all I can tell you, but it's better than the nothing you've got so far, so I'm not going to apologize for it."

"Yes ma'am, and I thank you for it." Despite the tape recorder, Nick was scribbling notes again. "But let me ask, did you see the shooter at all? Were you able to give the police anything?"

I shook my head, and then rubbed at it with my fingertips. "No, I couldn't. Nobody could. You know what the fog's like out there." I figured he probably did. Everyone does.

He bobbed his head, and I continued. "Like I said, we put out the lights. We were an easy target when they were on, so we shut them off. It was a blind run. Couldn't see our hands in front of our faces."

"You must be the luckiest bunch in the world."

"Tell me about it."

"Why don't you tell *me* about it." He sounded like a shrink. "Seriously—everyone got away with insignificant injuries—"

"Except for Tripp," I scolded.

"Except for Tripp, yes—but the rest of you made it out without anything too serious. And you did it in the dark, in the fog, without lights. Do you know how far it is from Dyer's field to the visitors' center?"

"No, but—"

"It's a couple of miles. You two made it nearly two miles under preposterously bad conditions. You look fine to me, though I hear you had a bad scratch; and Dana's had stitches on her hands and elbows. I guess she fell or something. But still, really. The rest of you came out really well."

Benny piped up from the kitchen, arguing around the corn chip he was chewing. "I hit my head." He pointed at the bruise and the butterfly bandage.

"Okay, so that sets the tally at a set of stitches, a scratch, and a bump on the head. How did you do it?"

"I ran into a tree," Benny answered, though Nick had been looking at me when he asked the question. "Head first. Broke my glasses. I passed out cold, and woke up with a cop's flashlight in my face. Scared the crap out of me."

We both stared at Benny for a beat; then Nick returned his attention to me. "Right. So now we know how *he* did it—how did *you* do it?"

He knew already; I could tell by the way he was asking. He wanted to hear me say it out loud, though; he was dying to hear me say it out loud. He was positively *parched* to hear it. I wondered if somewhere, sometime, he'd seen something himself... and no one had believed him.

Nick leaned forward, almost tapping the intangible edge of my personal space, but not quite. "Come on," he begged. "We all know there's weird shit going on out there. That's what you people were doing on the battlefield in the first place, right? You were checking out the weird shit. Well, this is what I want to know: *did you see any weird shit?*"

I couldn't make up my mind. Instinctively I suspected he was one more thwarted believer, but rationally I knew he was a television reporter with a ferocious desire to scare the hell out of everyone watching the five o'clock news.

The front door opened, startling us all. Nick drew back onto his own designated couch cushion, and Benny dropped the salsa. It broke on the kitchen tile with a crunching splat.

"Dave." I exhaled, happy and relieved to see him. His arrival gave me another moment to consider my response.

"Babe." He nodded at me, and spied Benny's backside in the

kitchen—bending with a fistful of paper towels. "Ben?"

"Hello, Mr. Copeland," he said, without standing up straight or turning around.

My uncle sized up the man sharing the couch with me, and tossed a quick, dismissive glance at the apathetic assistant with the camera. "Ah," he said, and with his left hand he flicked an envelope towards me. "Don't let me interrupt. But when you're through, I'd like a word with you, please."

He left us, ducking out into the garage. I measured his words and decided that I wasn't nervous. I didn't feel a sense of "You're in trouble, young lady," so much as I got the impression that he wanted to show me whatever was in the envelope.

"I'm sorry," I prompted Nick. "You were saying?"

"Nice try. It was *your* turn to talk. What I want to know is, did you or did you not see anything unusual out there?"

He was a sharp little bastard; there was no missing that much. I leaned forward, meeting him halfway. Benny put his elbows on the counter and swung his head out into the dining room so he could hear my response better.

"It's like this," I began. "It was dark. *Real* dark. And there was more fog than I have ever personally encountered in my life. It doesn't matter what I saw, or what I think I saw, or what any given one of us saw, Nick. No one would ever believe us, and there's nothing you can say on the air or in print—there's nothing you can scrawl down in that notebook—that anyone is ever going to take seriously."

"But—"

"Nick, you seem like a cool guy, but there's nothing I can do to help you. Go chase something you can prove, or something you can get on camera. A man is dead, and he was killed by another man—not by a ghost, and not by Old Green Eyes. There's no story here except an ordinary murder."

He snorted. "Ordinary? Are you serious?"

"Ordinary enough," I insisted.

"You know, you keep referring to the killer as a 'he.' Are you sure you didn't see anything that could be of use to the authorities?"

I hesitated, and gave him the benefit of a moment's thought. "I think it was a man. I saw his shape through the fog. It was something about the way he moved, the way he carried himself. He moved like a man."

"Mr. Reynolds didn't say anything about that, though he said he thought he saw the shooter too."

"Mr. Reynolds?"

Nick bobbed his head left to right, and gave me another flash of the eyebrow. "The A/V guy? From the Marshall crew? With which you were 'volunteering'?"

I could hear the quotation marks around the word "volunteer." It was easy to guess that we'd made up half our story, and I couldn't tell whether or not he meant to imply a small spot of blackmail. I didn't care. He'd already let it slide that Dana had our back, so he could hint around all he wanted. Or maybe I was only being paranoid and defensive. It was hard to judge.

"Oh, yeah. Him. We barely knew him—last night was our first night on the job."

"Hell of a way to break into the biz, eh?"

"Tell me about it," I said, catching a glance from Benny—who also sent me a quick 'thumbs-up' for the fib-on-the-fly. "So, is Charlie okay?"

"He's fine. He made it out the back way, same as your other buddy, past the Tower and into the subdivision."

"And Dana?" I asked. "You said she checked out of Erlanger? Do you know where she went?"

Nick fluttered his notebook, flipping the pages closed with a whip of his wrist. "Back to her hotel? I told you, I don't know. I couldn't track her down. I thought you might know how to reach her, but I guess not. How did you ever meet the Marshalls, if you didn't know where they were staying?"

"At the camera store," Benny butted in with the truth, which was fine by me. "We ran into them while we were getting some film developed, and we started talking. They invited us out there. We met them there."

While Nick was looking at Benny, I flashed my pal a thumbs-up in return.

"Anyway, it's like I said—there's nothing I can tell you that you'll want to use. I'm sorry you've gone to so much trouble to find me up here, but I've said everything I'm going to."

He looked like he was going to press the issue, but I put him off with a moment of inspiration. "Let us catch up to Dana and see if we caught anything interesting with our equipment. There were cameras and digital voice recorders, so you never know. We might even turn up something we could fork over to your station." Whatever it took to get him off our case.

He leaned back with suspicion. "Didn't the cops keep that stuff? I know they've got at least the tape from Charlie's camera. He ditched it at the scene."

"They didn't take *mine*. And they didn't take the camera I had, either."

"And if you find anything, you'll give me first dibs?"

"You've got the scoop if you'll leave us alone for now. Come back in another few days and I'll see what I can do. No promises,"

I added with a warning finger. "No promises. But I'll try."

"Fucking-*A*. Seriously?"

"Swear to God." I offered him my hand, and we shook on it. He pressed a business card into my palm, and I took it as a means of facilitating his departure.

I couldn't believe it was that easy to get rid of him, but then again, the news around here is slower than molasses more often than not. Nick didn't talk like he was from around here; maybe he was looking for a little pizzazz to boost him into a big-city broadcast. I didn't think for a moment that I could give it to him, but if he was willing to bargain for it, I was willing to fake it.

Benny and I waved him and his cameraman away, standing on the stoop like two of the lesser-known Beverly Hillbillies. When the Channel 3 SUV pulled out of the driveway and into the street, we both relaxed and stepped back inside.

Dave had emerged into the living room behind us.

"You may end up wishing you hadn't promised him that," he said, brandishing the envelope.

"What've you got there?"

"Your pictures. Or *my* pictures, from *my* camera—however you choose to look at it."

"Let's say they're 'our' pictures, and call it a draw."

He slid his thumb underneath the sticky seal. "For the sake of argument, then. But if they sell to the *Enquirer*, profits are going sixty-forty in my favor. At least."

"But I bought the film!" I argued, mostly joking. "What's on those prints, anyway?"

"Much weirdness. Some of it's going to have to go to the cops, I think. I don't know what they'll be able to get out of it, but I wouldn't want them to accuse you of withholding evidence. They don't need to know I had doubles made, though."

He slapped a short stack of pictures into my hand. Benny swooped in close to look over my shoulder. Together we withdrew to the couch and began shuffling through the prints.

The first three or four were exactly what you'd expect—dark blobs upon dark blobs. But then shapes began to appear, including the very distinct outline of a human being in a loose-fitting jacket. He was carrying something, maybe two somethings. From one hand hung a baggy teardrop bag, and over his other shoulder there was something long and thin.

"A rifle?" Benny asked, poking the edge of the outline with his finger.

"Maybe, I don't know."

Dave held the photo out at arm's length. "What did it sound like he was shooting with?" he asked.

I knocked him with my shoulder. "As if I have *any* frame of reference to answer that question. It sounded like he was shooting with a gun. That's the best I can tell you—except he had to keep reloading it. It held six shots—I'm almost sure of it. But I couldn't tell you what kind it was."

Lu joined us, leaning herself against the doorway and sipping on a beverage she'd retrieved while we were seeing the newsmen off. "That shouldn't be too hard to find out, should it?"

"How you figure?" I wondered aloud.

"That Marshall fellow got shot, right?"

"Oh, yeah." Benny snapped his fingers and aimed them at her with an excited waggle. "There's a bullet in him. Once they dig that out, they'll be able to tell what kind of gun he was using."

"But that's not to say the police will share that information with *us*," I felt compelled to point out.

Lu nodded to concede the possibility, and came over to sit beside me on the arm of the couch. She peered over my shoulder at the photos, her hair falling almost down into my face.

Dave moved on to the next picture. "Right. So let's guess for guessing's sake that he's carrying a revolver and the long thing is something else. And he's also got a tote, or a sack or something."

"Could be anything at all," I said, and everyone agreed.

"The question is, is he bringing stuff *to* the battlefield or is he there to take things away from it? There's no telling." The next picture wasn't too much more enlightening. The same warm shape in the dark, posed in a crouch as if he was picking something up— or, as Dave had suggested, perhaps he was putting something down.

Benny ducked his head in close and said, "Look at *that*."

Lu swept her hair over her shoulder and off the back of my head. "It's someone's profile, pretty clear. That'll be something to hand the police. It's too bad you didn't zoom in closer on him."

"I didn't know how close I needed to zoom. I couldn't see anything at all."

"It's not a bad job, for a shot in the dark."

"Thanks, Dave."

"The profile's not what I meant," Benny corrected us. "I meant beside his face. Look at that. You can barely make it out but it's *there*."

We all squinted at the print. "What is that, an arm? A shoulder? Is there someone else with him?" Lu asked.

"Not someone else—some*thing* else," Benny announced. "We've got proof. Evidence, even, of life beyond the grave. *That*, my friends, is a ghost."

Lu performed her notorious shrug of indifference. "Looks like an arm to me."

"It's a ghost's arm. Check it out—look how it's not registering hot like the man with the bag is. It's incomplete, but it's there. See, there's an outline of a leg down here, and a boot. He's wearing boots. It's a ghost."

The rest of us kept quiet, not wanting to argue with him. It would have been difficult to argue, since it appeared he might be right; but as I'd said going into this amateur investigation, I never set out to prove the existence of the supernatural. I already knew about it. Proof was superfluous.

"This is the clearest shot of the shooter," Dave said. "It really needs to go to the authorities."

"But you said you had doubles."

"In fact, I do. And you can have one. Here." He fished it out of the back of the pile and presented it to Benny, who beamed like a halogen bulb.

"What about the negatives?"

"We'll see what the police have to say. Take what you can get, Mulder."

"Fine." He said it with a breath of a sulk, but the sulk was distracted by his new evidence. "And thanks. This is—this could be awesome. Are there more?"

"A couple. I didn't look through these that closely; I just glanced through them when I picked them up. Oh look, a stunning shot of Eden's shoe. And a stick."

"There were a *lot* of sticks."

"I'm sure there were." Lu tagged Dave's wrist to make him keep shuffling.

He complied and moved onto the next somewhat-clear image. Here we saw the man again, more nebulous than before. He was looking at or away from the camera, and his head was just a fuzzy oval. His chin was angled down though, looking at the earth; and whatever he'd had slung over his shoulder now hung from his hand.

"I think he's there to steal things, not hide them. Look at that," I said, taking the picture and shifting it to remove a bit of glare. "He's hunting for something on the ground. He's out there to find something specific. I wonder what he wants."

"That's the real question, isn't it?" Lu murmured, lifting the photo from my hand and holding it up to the light. "Benny, I believe there may be more ghostly outlines in this one, darling. Tell me, does that look like a face to you?"

"It does!" he cried happily, and Dave retrieved the double before he could even ask for it. "Are there any more?"

"Just the one, and I have to assume that this was just before all hell broke loose. Check it out—he's closer in this one, walking forward. Not exactly towards you, but in your general direction."

I touched the glossy edge of the picture. "He was headed for Dana and Tripp. Christ, they were sitting ducks out there. We tried to warn them, but they didn't get it until it was too late."

"There wasn't much you could've done," Lu assured me, patting my back.

"I know," I said, and I *did* know it, too. But that didn't make me feel any less bad for Dana, who was now a widow. And we'd only done the least that could be expected of us. It felt very insufficient.

"Things could've been much worse. You were very lucky," Lu reminded me, in a maternal sort of way that only annoyed me because it fed my guilt.

I didn't respond, even though she was right, and she meant well.

* * *

Benny and I caught up to Jamie on the roof of the Pickle Barrel around three that afternoon. We took a table at the farthest tip of the triangle-shaped seating area that gave us a good view without permitting anyone to see us well. Word was getting around, fast and furious. No secrets in the South except our secrets.

Everyone's secrets.

For all my intention of keeping a low profile, I had gone and gotten myself mixed up in the biggest story in the Tennessee Valley for the last eighty years. I appear to have a gift for it, much as it pisses me off.

The funny thing about Southern gossip is the way it stacks and builds, story upon story. It's like accumulating experience points in a video game; every new event gains you status and ability. The more people hear your name connected with local lore, the more they believe you're capable of, and the more narrative credit you're given.

I started out as a creepy little kid who saw ghosts. By the afternoon after Tripp's death, Lu and Dave were fielding phone calls from reporters seeking the city's premier medium, spiritual advisor, and Wiccan priestess.

You couldn't *buy* advertising like that, even if you wanted to.

But I was just looking to be left alone, and to eat a super-greasy cheeseburger in peace.

In the middle of the day, this could be done at the Barrel. Since it was before seven o'clock we wouldn't know any of the waitstaff, and the place was effectively empty except for us. Come nightfall, though, we'd probably have to find somewhere else to haunt if we meant to stay incognito.

While Benny shared the pictures with Jamie, I attended to my lunch, despite not having enough appetite to do it justice. Mostly

I picked at the tater tots and nibbled at the pot pie-sized burger until my phone rang.

I didn't recognize the digits on the display, but on a whim I answered it anyway in hopes that it wasn't someone from a network wanting a statement.

It wasn't. It was Dana.

"A woman at your home—your mother, I guess—she gave me this number. I hope you don't mind."

"No," I said quickly, without correcting her. "No, I don't mind. How are you? Where are you?"

"I'm at the Chattanoogan," she said, naming a newer, high-end hotel downtown. "I didn't have anywhere else to go, and they won't release Tripp... his body, I mean. They won't release it until after an autopsy. It may take a few days."

"Oh."

"So I can't go home. Charlie left this morning. I didn't have any reason to make him stay, and his wife was worried about him."

"That makes sense," I said lamely. The guys had stopped talking and were looking at me. They'd realized it wasn't Lu or Dave on the line, and were curious. I ineffectively waved them back to their own business, then removed my napkin from my lap and wadded it up, setting it on the table.

"Give me a minute," I told them as I stepped away from my seat and walked to the edge of the landing.

"I hope I haven't caught you at a bad time," Dana said, and I heard real hope in her voice—the kind you don't often get when someone's only saying it for the sake of politeness.

I leaned lightly against the ironwork railing, and stared down over Market Street and Eleventh. "No, not at all. I'm just finishing up lunch. I'm done now. I can talk. I'd *like* to talk."

Dana dove on in. "I wanted you to know, I told the police you were working with me. I don't know what you were doing out there really; but you probably saved my life, and I thought I owed you that much, at least."

"We appreciate it," I said. "I found out about it this morning, from a reporter who came by my house."

"Nick somebody?"

"Nick somebody, that's him. Alders," I confirmed.

"Chipper bastard, isn't he?"

I laughed, then smothered it because it felt wrong to laugh on the phone to a woman whose husband had just died. "Until the microphone was off, yes."

"He struck me as the sort of guy who rolls into the newsroom with a hangover, then tells the news while sitting behind the desk without wearing any pants."

Her assessment was pitch-perfect. "That's about the truth, I bet. And I mean it—thank you. We were out there for about the same reason as you. Hell, you met Benny, our fan-boy in residence. We were just trying to get to the bottom of it too."

"I thought that must be the case. And I saw later on, after the alarm went off and the ambulance was there—I thought I saw you had a camera around your neck, is that right?"

"Uh-huh." I shot a glimpse over at my friends, who were fawning over the arguable bits and pieces of the dead that had showed up in the images.

"I wondered if you got any pictures of the guy who did this. I thought, maybe we could get together and talk. Compare notes. Get a drink, I don't know."

"Sure. Sure we could."

I had a strong feeling that whatever motivated our shooter

was going to be something well outside the experience of local law enforcement—a possibility that had probably occurred to Dana, too. And who else would we talk to, if not each other? Kitty, out in the Bend?

"I want to understand," she said.

"I know you do. So do I."

"Is there a place we could go? Maybe this afternoon? Maybe now?"

I thought about telling her to head east a couple of blocks, but decided against it. It would be easier to go and pick her up than give her instructions. "I'll come and get you," I said instead. "I know where you are. That's the hotel with the bar in it, the Foundry. Meet me in the lobby, in say, ten minutes? I'm only a few streets away from you right now. We can get coffee, or something."

"I'll be there."

She hung up without any closing salutation, and I did likewise.

I went back to the table and my half-eaten food, and pulled a ten-dollar bill out of my pocket. "This ought to more than cover everything of mine," I said, and my friends nodded.

"Yours and a tip, too. You heading out?" Jamie asked.

"So soon?"

"Yes, Benny. So soon. That was Dana on the phone. We're going to compare notes. And I think maybe we'll talk about regular stuff, too. Give me the pictures, would you, darling? She'll want to see those, too. And, for heaven's sake, don't sulk. I'll bring them back. She's alone here, you know. She could use a friendly ear, and we're the closest things to friends she has in town."

"Poor woman," Jamie said, but whether he meant to be funny or not, I couldn't tell.

"You want us to hang around? Do we count as friends, too?"

Benny asked. He wanted me to say yes, but I wasn't comfortable enough with the situation to give him that.

"Why don't you give us an hour or two, then meet us over at Greyfriar's? We're just going there for coffee, unless she wants something stronger—and I wouldn't blame her if she did."

The compromise satisfied him, and Jamie too. I left them there and tiptoed down the curly ironwork stairs, back down to my car. I could've walked; the Chattanoogan was only half a mile away as the crow flies—if that. But I drove it to be prompt, and when I got there, Dana was sitting on the street curb instead of in the lobby inside.

I almost didn't recognize her.

She hadn't slept, or if she had, it hadn't done her any good.

"That was fast," she observed, rising to her feet and dusting her rear end off with her hands.

I popped the locks on the Death Nugget and leaned over to open the door for her. "I told you I wasn't far away. Climb in. Coffee's on me."

Dana Marshall settled herself into the seat and dragged the seat belt across her chest. "Thanks. I could use some, I think." She pulled down the visor mirror, but flipped it quickly back into place after catching her reflection. "I look like hell."

I thought about arguing with her for form's sake, but didn't. "So what? You've been through hell."

"So what, indeed. I don't give a damn if you don't."

I didn't.

The downtown area proper isn't very big, and my caffeine-hole of choice was only another three or four blocks towards the river. We reached it in as many minutes, delayed by construction and stoplights.

I parked down the street, across from a barbecue restaurant and a bus stop. "You hungry?" I asked.

She shook her head. "I don't think I could keep anything down right now."

"All right. The 'Friar's is right here."

"What do you recommend?" she asked, stepping past a hippie with a guitar and reaching for the door.

"It's all good. Get whatever you like. I'll cover it."

Inside the door, a gently frumpy man with a French accent discussed a game of chess with one of Karl's friends. I didn't know either of their names, but I nodded at them because I knew them on sight, and it would have been rude to ignore them. Dana meandered to the end of the counter with the order here sign and kept her eyes on the menu board mounted on the wall behind the counter.

"Can I help you? Oh, hey, Eden."

"Hey," I returned. "Hook her up with whatever she wants. It's on me, okay? I'll be right back."

I poked my head around the corner, checking out the back hall. The bathrooms, office, and roaster's room were a series of closed doors on either side; and the narrow, two-person bistro tables were unoccupied except for a dark-haired guy working on a laptop. He didn't glance up when I stepped into his field of view, and the muffin-sized headphones he wore implied that he wouldn't bother us even if he noticed us.

I dropped my purse onto the table farthest to the back, and I shrugged out of my light button-up sweater, hanging it on the back of the chair.

When I rejoined Dana, she'd decided against anything fancy and requested the largest cup of black coffee available. The girl on duty had given her a latte mug and told her to help herself to the air pots on the counter.

"Just give me a to-go cup," I said, thinking that their paper cups were larger than the mugs. I extracted enough dollar bills from my jeans pocket to cover everything. After paying, I dropped my change into a carafe labeled tip jar and pointed the back table out to Dana.

She topped off her mug of Yemen with a drop of half-and-half and followed my summoning finger, sinking into the little chair and putting her head down over the brew, facial-sauna style. I sat down across from her and began tearing yellow packets of sweetener.

For a while, we didn't talk. I stirred my coffee with the skinny brown straw, and she sucked down an entire mug's worth of beverage before I had time to get started on mine. She went back for another, and when she returned with this second cup, she felt awake enough for conversation.

"I knew who you were," she began, holding her elfin nose above the cup's rim. "In the photo place. Your friend didn't introduce you, but I knew who you were. I'd heard about you before."

"How?"

"Grapevine of the Dead. That's what I call it, all the gossip that works its way around in the field. Bits and pieces of truth and rumor that no one but us might take seriously."

I frowned into my French Roast. "What did you hear about me? I've been wondering for quite some time. People keep finding me, and I don't know how, and they're always so vague about how they knew to look here. It's… inconvenient."

"There's not much to hear. A young psychic in Chattanooga, mixed up in a murder investigation a year or two ago. I heard you were tall, with darkish skin and lots of dark hair. Different details leak their way to different sources. And you are by no means the first victim of the paranormal to prefer anonymity. In fact, the people who want to remain anonymous are the ones who are most likely to be legit."

"And I guess it's your business to ferret out the anonymous."

"Sometimes," she agreed between sips. "Sometimes the job is just a job like any other. Lots of research, lots of time-wasting. More travel than I'd prefer, but less than Tripp likes. Liked."

I flinched when she amended herself, and she must have, too—though I was careful to avert my eyes. It took her a few seconds to recover from his name, and from the verbs. She was more careful when she continued.

"He's always liked to travel. I'm more of a homebody, but it's worked out okay, up until now. My God, this is awkward." She stopped herself and set the mug down. "I shouldn't have put you in this position. This is just such a bad time… for everything. For anything."

She put her forehead in her hand and braced her elbow on the table.

"Maybe you're not ready for this. Maybe I should take you back to the hotel. You seem awfully tired," I said, pointing out the obvious.

Dana lifted her eyes and snagged mine. "What do you think is going on here?" she asked, ignoring my suggestion, or possibly not hearing it. "Really—who on Earth would do something like this? It's so fucking stupid—lurking in the middle of the night, ambushing anyone who comes near, even though they're not bothering anyone. We weren't bothering anyone, were we?"

"No."

"See? You were there—you *know*. We didn't sneak up on anybody, we weren't armed, and we weren't out to make any trouble. We were doing our job, and that job shouldn't have interfered with another living soul." Her eyes filled up but did not spill. She ducked her head over the cup and stared into the swirls there. "It doesn't make any goddamned sense."

I agreed wholeheartedly, and I told her so. "But why did you go back after the first person got hurt? I thought you'd have a police escort, at least."

"Oh, they *offered*," she growled. "But it's damned hard to work on something like this when you've got a uniformed skeptic tagging along, so we turned them down. They swept the battlefield that afternoon, though—or they said they did. There wasn't any sign of trouble, or any people who weren't supposed to be there. That's what they told us. They gave us the all-clear and said to be careful. It was supposed to be safe. It was supposed to be empty."

We descended into cranky silence again, until I remembered the pictures.

"I've got something to show you," I said a little too brightly, trying to change the conversation's current. "You were right, what you said on the phone. I *was* wearing my uncle's camera, and I got a few shots with the infrared film. The cops took one set of prints and the negatives, but we had doubles made."

I pulled the envelope out of my purse and scooted my chair closer to hers. We sifted through them together much the same way I had with Dave and Benny. They weren't very helpful from a mystery-solving standpoint, but they were distracting, which was enough.

"You said these are the doubles? So you don't have any other prints I could swipe from you?" She held the last photo by a corner, between her thumbnail and index fingertip.

"I'm afraid not, but I've got a scanner at home. I can e-mail digital copies to you, which isn't ideal, but it's better than nothing."

"That's fine," she said, handing them back to me in the same order I'd passed them to her. "No negatives, no originals, no proof. But no one really wants proof. If we had proof, we couldn't use disclaimers like 'for entertainment purposes only.' The networks are always happiest if things are disputable—don't ask me why. Maybe if we made guarantees for people, they'd sue."

I tucked the prints back into their envelope and put them into my purse. "Controversy makes better ratings, I guess."

"I'll never understand it. The older I get, the less sense people make to me—the living ones or the dead ones, either."

Dana threw back the last swallow of coffee from the bottom of the mug. "Do you think that's what we're dealing with? People? And before you answer me"—she leaned forward, pushing the mug to the side so there was nothing between us—"remember who you're talking to. I don't care how wacky your own theories are about the battlefield, I want to hear them. I want to *understand*. I want to know what you've got already, how you knew to come to Dyer's field."

I hemmed and hawed, but only out of habit. A small part of me was positively giddy at the thought of an interested peer, but I tried to keep myself from going too crazy with the opportunity. "I don't suppose anyone's told you about Old Green Eyes?" I began, thinking that someone, somewhere, must have—but not wanting to assume as much.

"Oh, sure," she said. "Haven't seen hide nor hair of him, though. Frankly, I've thought the stories I heard were a little weird; and considering some of the shit I've seen, that's saying something. He's the number-one bad guy there, isn't he?"

I shrugged with my coffee cup, creating a tiny tidal splash of caffeine. "I wouldn't call him the bad guy, necessarily, but he's definitely the most famous supernatural resident. Or he *was*, anyway. He's gone. I think that's why all the ghosts are out—they're upset that he's gone AWOL."

"You think?"

"I do. Some of the EVP we snagged backs up the theory, and besides, I think I know where he went. I just don't know why he went there. And I don't know how to bring him back."

"Talk to me," Dana said. She put her elbows back on the table and propped her head on one hand. "Tell me where he is, and let's go and get him."

I copied her position without realizing at first that I'd done so. "I don't think it's that easy."

"Why not?"

"Because it never is."

She wrapped her fingers around and through the handle of the mug, as if she was trying to decide about another round. Finally she decided what I always do—that there's no such thing as too much coffee—and excused herself.

"I'll be right back."

I twirled a coffee stirrer while I waited.

She returned in under a minute, sliding herself onto the chair with something that looked like fresh resolve. Despite the red streaks in her eyes and the dark circles under them, she looked more awake; but that might've only been the half a gallon of caffeine coursing through her veins.

"You said you got EVP," she said, downing another hearty swallow of brew.

"The other night, the first time your group was attacked. We were out there then, too—but not close enough to be involved. We were over on the other side of the Wilder Tower, by the suburbs. There was a party over there that night."

"And you used it as cover to sneak down the road into the fog."

"You got it."

Dana nodded, like she was stalling or thinking. "Did you get anything good? Off the EVP, I mean? It got you out to Dyer's field, anyway, I'm guessing."

"Right. Sort of. Between what we were able to decipher from the recordings and what happened to you guys, we put two and two together. How did you learn about it?"

"Same way. That, and the channeling—though it's hard to get much out of them that way. They find themselves in a body and get distracted by the sensation of it all. Besides, none of them seem to know much about what's going on either. Being dead doesn't make them omniscient."

I was relieved to hear someone else say it for once. "No kidding. I wish more people understood that."

"You and me both. But either they don't know, or they're not very good at communicating it. The best I got out of anyone was that the source of the problem looked to be coming from the old Dyer's place. But what would that have to do with the local chief spook going missing?"

"Well, while you were indisposed," I said, "I did get one potentially useful thing out of the ghost. He said something about Green Eyes watching the place until the last of the general's line had died. That's strange, but God knows I don't have any other theories about what would make the guardian leave his post."

"That's a funny thing to call him," she observed.

"It might be. But I think it's right. I saw him. Or I'm pretty sure I did."

Now she looked impressed. "You don't say? How'd you manage to pull that off? What, did he leave a forwarding address?"

"It was an accident. Dumb coincidence, that's all. I was out there for something else. Though in retrospect it makes perfect sense that he would've been there. There was nowhere else for him to go, after he left the battlefield."

Dana picked up on extra stirrer I'd brought and used it to swirl her coffee. "Okay, so where did you see him?"

"At the Bend. Moccasin Bend," I specified, remembering she wasn't local. "It's this spot a few miles from here; it used to be a sacred Native American burial site, hundreds of years ago."

She frowned. "And why would he go there? Was he some cohort of the natives?"

"Probably. They knew about him, anyway, before the incoming settlers did. There are legends about him from before there were any white people here. They knew about him, and cohabited with him, long before Chickamauga was set apart as a park. At the very least, I think he would've been more familiar with them than he was with us. I think that after he abandoned the battlefield, he went looking for them. And the only spot nearby he could remember was the Bend."

She grunted, a slight cough of agreement or approval. "All right. What's there at the Bend these days?"

"It's a mental institution for the criminally insane."

Dana let fly a cackle that shocked me with its abruptness. "That's brilliant," she gushed. "That is fucking *divine*."

"No kidding. I didn't believe it when I heard it at first, but I have been assured that it's true; and I've been out there myself. The place has a funny feel to it, if you know what I mean. Like something's restless there. I can't think of a better way to put it."

"You don't have to put it better; I get it. But more importantly, you saw Green Eyes out there? And you're sure it was him?"

"Sure enough," I said, hoping that my semi-certainty made the grade. "I can't imagine who or what else it would have been. At the time I didn't know yet that the battlefield had been left to its own devices, but the more I learned about the ghosts the more likely it seemed. Then, once we caught the EVP, the dead confirmed it for us—at least the part about him being gone. And then, when I heard him talking—"

"Wait, he *talked* to you? What is this thing?"

I flipped my hands up in a non-committal shrug. "I don't know. Not human, but not a ghost, either—not in any traditional sense. He's something solid, but mutable, or that's how he seems. I wonder if…"

"What?"

It sounded too stupid to say out loud, but again I tried to give Dana the benefit of the doubt. If I was going to say it to anybody, she was probably least likely to laugh in my face. "I wonder if he isn't the ghost of something *else*. Though really," I added, "I have no idea *what*."

She digested this without cracking a smile, though I watched her close and braced myself for one. "Okay. Maybe. Just because I've never heard of it, that doesn't mean it isn't possible. He really seemed that different to you?"

I nodded with vigor. "Whatever he is, whatever he *was*—he's never been human. Regardless, he seems to hold some measure of affection for us humans."

"How's that?"

"When he was talking, he said something about how the dead were his children. That's why I called him a guardian—it's like he feels a sense of responsibility for what happens out there."

"You may be right, but that brings us right back around to the original question: why did he leave in the first place? The last descendant of a general died? That's crazy. Assuming for the sake of discussion that it's true, how would Green Eyes even know about it?" Dana threw back the remaining contents of her cup, and laid her hand down over the top of it to head off any offers of refills.

Neither of us had an answer for that one, but we were distracted by the trotting tap of paws. Cowboy sidled down the narrow hall, with Karl close behind.

"Good afternoon, beautiful." He tipped his hat at me, and I nodded in return. "*Two* beautifuls," he amended his greeting, ducking the rim of his hat at Dana too. He recognized her quickly, as I might have known he would. He grasped the situation, but his manners wouldn't let him leave the obvious unmentioned. "Oh, dear. I hope I'm not interrupting anything. Ma'am, I heard the news about your husband, and I want you to know I'm awfully sorry for your loss."

"Thanks," she squeaked, leaving a bumpy silence in the word's wake.

"This is Karl," I introduced him. "And Karl, it looks like you know who Dana is."

"Yes ma'am I do," he said. "And again, I'm sorry to meet you under such sad circumstances, but otherwise, it would be a pleasure."

"Likewise, I'm sure."

"I don't mean to intrude," he assured us, and I knew he didn't, but I felt awkward on Dana's behalf, "but did I hear the pair of you talking about Old Green Eyes? Because I think it's just wonderful if the two of you are working together on that."

"We're comparing notes," I admitted, and then I proceeded to ramble, because I was uncomfortable. "We were talking about how strange it is that Green Eyes seems to have left the battlefield. He's been there for so long, it's weird that he would up and leave—right around the time he seems to be needed most, when there's some raving lunatic hanging around with a gun."

He pondered this for a minute, and I had to give him credit for not laughing at us for discussing such things so seriously. Then he fiddled some more with his hat's brim and said slowly, "Well now, that does seem peculiar. But then again, maybe his time there was up, and that's all. It may not be any more complicated than that."

Dana frowned, creating two perfect vertical creases between her eyebrows. "As if he was on some kind of time limit? Like he'd signed a contract, and it expired?"

Cowboy dropped his rear onto the ground and grumbled a little sigh, expecting that Karl might be a moment.

"Something like that. I don't know. You hear funny things about it, I'm just saying."

"Funny things?" I prompted him to continue, though Dana cast me a look that spelled mild irritation.

Karl played with his hat, pulling it off and into his lap. "Well—and pardon me for eavesdropping, ladies, but on my way back to the restroom I couldn't help catching just the tail end of what you were saying—I think maybe you're asking the wrong question when you start with why he's gone. You should start instead with why he was there *in the first place*."

Dana's irritation melted some. "That's fair."

"Look." Karl seemed in a hurry to move the subject on. "There are a thousand stories about what Green Eyes has been doing out there at the battlefield all this time—but most of the stories I heard when I was growing up, they talked about him like he was there fulfilling an obligation. I mean, he used to be a friend of the native people—"

"The same native people who were run out of this area on the Trail of Tears, right?" Dana interjected. "If he was a friend of theirs, why would he look out for the place after they were gone?"

"But he stayed, tied to the land if not the people. I don't know why, and I'm not pretending that I do—but after the Trail of Tears, and after Boynton and Van Derveer pushed the park through Congress, he *stayed*. And I think he must've had a good reason to."

Something about his apologetics set off a red flag in my subconscious, but I couldn't figure out what it was until Dana sorted it out for me.

"Wait—who?"

"Who what?"

She fluttered her hand in his direction, trying to draw the sentences back out of him again. "What you said just now. One of those names, it's familiar. The 'B' one."

"Boynton? That's the name of one of the fellows who set up the park, that's all."

I rejoined the conversation with an abruptness that surprised even me. "I've heard it someplace else lately, too. But I can't remember."

Cowboy whined, and Karl scratched at his hatless head. "Oh, you mean that murder case, I bet."

"A murder case?" Two related ideas were struggling to come

together, but I couldn't force them. I could feel them, though—like two mice underneath a rug, blindly running in circles and bound to collide with one another eventually.

"That boy. That Ryan boy. Boynton was his last name, too. Not surprising. Everyone's related here."

"No," I said. "Not surprising." But significant, maybe. "What happened to him? Do you know?"

Karl waved his hat, indicating the newspaper rack, I guess. "Oh, I'm not sure. He went missing a few weeks ago. Big-time football player at the McCallie school over there at the other end of town. They found his truck out in Rossville with blood all in it. Everyone figured he was dead, but it's only lately that the papers have come out and said so, calling it 'murder' instead of 'missing.' It's too bad, but I think we've all known for a while that he's not coming back."

His choice of words gave a jolt to the mice under my mental rug, and they charged towards one another.

The last was dead, and I gave my word.

The sentence came back to haunt me; it popped up before I could even place its origin. Before I dared connect the dots, I reached out and stopped Karl's gesturing hat with one hand.

"You probably won't know this, but did Ryan have any family?"

He looked at me with a confused yet willing tangle of eyebrows lifting high. "Well, I do know that, but only because the paper mentioned it. His parents died years ago in a car crash; he was at McCallie on a worthy student scholarship."

I let go of Karl's hat, and he replaced it on his head. "Ladies, if you'll excuse me, I was headed to the restroom."

We both nodded our permission, and he aimed the

power wheelchair at the men's room. Despite his lack of verbal instruction, the dog parked himself outside the door and assumed his best "good dog" stance of loyal attentiveness.

"You think they were related?" Dana asked in a lowered voice that only barely suggested the question mark at the end.

"They might've been." I drummed the plastic brown coffee stirrer against the table. "You know how people always make jokes about Southerners being related?"

"Are you about to tell me they're not just jokes? Because in North Carolina, they're just jokes."

I drummed the stick harder, against my cup, against the table, against a napkin. "Kind of. But I think what it really is, is that we admit to more relations than people do in other parts of the world. People talk about their 'cousins,' and they might mean their aunt's kids, or they may mean some far-distant relation three or four times removed."

"So what are you getting at?"

The last was dead, and I gave my word.

The phrase haunted me again, and I remembered the source perfectly. I remembered his reflecting eyes and his long, flowing hair. "Is that what he meant?" I asked myself, but I said it loud enough that Dana heard me.

"Who? What?"

"Old Green Eyes. One of the things he said before he disappeared was that the 'last' was dead. I didn't know what he meant, and I still don't know for sure… but what if this is who he means? Ooh, it's a long shot."

"No kidding, sweetheart."

"Well I'm not pretending it's a high probability; I'm just saying that it's possible the two are connected. It's perfect, or it might be." I chewed at my battered stirring straw.

We sat quiet, staring at everything around us except each other.

She caved first. "How would we find out?"

"I don't know. There might not be any good way. But let's pretend we know, for a minute," I begged her. "Let's say, for the sake of argument, that this Ryan kid was the last living relative of the old general who helped found the park."

"Okay, so what if we do?"

"So if we *do,* then we may as well—for the sake of argument— agree that Green Eyes was talking about Ryan when he said that the last one was dead."

Dana looked skeptical.

"Hang on." I cut myself off and hopped free from my seat. Out in the main lobby area there were always abandoned newspapers to be found, and I spied one in a flash. No one protested when I snatched it, so I rolled it up and brought it back to the table I shared with Dana. Within a few page flips, I'd located an update on the missing Boynton boy. I rotated the paper and pushed it up under her view.

"'No leads in the case of missing McCallie football star Ryan Boynton,'" she read.

"But if you look, if you keep going… Listen—he disappeared about a week before Decoration Day. That's right around the time the ghost sightings began in earnest; and, if we care to extrapolate, it's roughly the same time that Green Eyes left. The two could easily be related. Don't you think it's an incredible coincidence?"

"It's a coincidence," she agreed with a tepid shrug. "But I wouldn't say it's an incredible one."

I struggled to read the upside-down text on the sheet in front of her and defend my bright idea at the same time. "Yeah, but this kid could be the great-great-grand-something-or-another of the park's founder. He's murdered, and weird shit goes down at the battlefield."

She pushed the paper away, nearly tipping my empty cup. "But you're creating this coincidence—you're making a whole series of assumptions that are absolutely unverifiable."

"Like what?"

"Like, first and most obviously, we have no earthly idea if this Ryan kid is any relation to the dead soldier who helped establish the park. You said yourself—matching last names mean squat."

"Yes, but—"

"And second, we don't even know that he's dead—much less that he was murdered."

I shoved the *Times Free Press* back beneath her nose. "His truck was found filled with blood, broken glass, and bullet casings. If it wasn't him, then *somebody* probably died in that pickup cab. You don't find skull fragments of people who are still out walking around, and if he'd shot *himself*, then he'd've still been there when they found the truck."

"Probably," she conceded. "But not necessarily. There's always the possibility that Ryan did the shooting, and he has both disposed of the body and headed for the hills. You see what I'm saying?"

"I'm not asking you to embrace my theory without reservation; I'm asking you to think about it with an open mind. Isn't that what you're supposed to do for a living?"

She corrected me quickly. "Actually, it's always been my job to raise the sorts of questions and probabilities that escaped my *husband*. Eden, I'd think you know better than anyone how people who want to believe do so without a lot of critical evaluation. Don't fall into that trap."

"Why not?" I demanded. "I can afford to, so why shouldn't I? I realize that you've spent your career trying to validate your work, but you need to understand: I'm not working here. I don't do this for a living, and I don't do it for press, and I don't do it for journalistic integrity."

I paused, and sucked in a deep breath. I let it out and gathered another one before I'd gained the steam to keep going. "Having said that, I'm not entirely sure why I'm doing it at all, except that I'm not very good at anything else, and when it came down to it, I simply wanted to *know*. I wanted to go and find out what was happening because I could, and because of that, it felt like I *should*. But remember this—I don't have anything to prove to anyone except myself."

"That must be nice," she said with a lifted nostril.

I ignored her sarcasm. "It *is* nice, thanks. I don't have to document my sources, I don't have to catalog my findings, and I sure as hell don't have to justify my hunches."

"Is that what this is? A hunch?"

"Sure, it's a hunch. It might even be the world's most far-fetched hunch, but I plan to follow it anyway. And why won't you play along?" Before she could answer, I continued. "Do you want to legitimize your next television special, or do you want to know why your husband's dead? Because I can't help you with the one, but you've got nothing to lose by running with me on the other."

That stopped her, and I thought she might take a swing at me, but she didn't. "It'll be a waste of time," she murmured, after giving it a few seconds of thought.

"Well, what are you doing this afternoon? Say, right now?" I asked.

She caved, though not all the way and not without some petulance. "Fine. But even if you're right, what do you propose to do about it? Should we play cop and try to find the Boynton kid?"

She had me, there. I didn't have a plan; I just had a goofy theory that no one in her right mind would chase. "We need to…"

"Yes?"

Right about then Karl left the bathroom, tailed by the sound of flushing and his trusty sidekick. They scooted out and into the hallway, the man in the chair making friendly excuses and bidding us good afternoon. We smiled him off and returned to our discussion.

"Well, Ms. Spade, what are we going to do now?" She goaded me on, knowing I hadn't thought of anything stunning in the intervening minute and a half.

"Several things. Or there are several things we need to do, anyway, if I'm right."

"Go on."

I froze, thawed, and stuttered. "We've got to find out what happened to Ryan Boynton. If I'm right and he's been murdered, then we keep going. If I'm wrong, and he's huddled up in an outhouse with a shotgun, then we're completely off track and there's no sense in listening to another word that comes out of my mouth. But I bet if we found out where he was, and why he's gone, then we'll have a much better idea of why Green Eyes left his charges."

"And I guess we'll just leap ahead of the cops on the Boynton case, solve it, and be on our merry way before sunset?"

"Yes," I declared with perfect confidence, which was perfectly counter to what I actually felt. And then I heard Benny placing an order up at the counter.

"I'll have a latte in a large to-go cup, please. And have you seen Eden hanging around here?"

Karl answered him, from the table by the storefront window. "She's in the back with Mrs. Marshall. In the hall."

"Thanks."

Benny gave me the idea I'd been so fruitlessly clamoring for. "Yes," I repeated to Dana. "Yes, because we have access to resources that the cops *don't*."

Back at Benny's place, Dana, Jamie, and I gathered around FrankenHal and watched the lurching lines of the audio track as our EVP collection played. Dana frowned and listened hard. Jamie looked bored as he stroked Tiggy, who sat on his chest and purred.

Benny did his best not to appear nervous in the woman's presence, but he misclicked a couple of times and blamed it on his head injury. "There—that again. That part, there. What does that sound like to you? Doesn't it sound like 'Boynton'?"

"It definitely sounds like you saying 'you're all awake,' " Dana said, reaching around Benny's hand and taking the mouse away from him enough to play the clip again. "The rest, it could be 'Boynton,' I suppose."

"And the next part, the one I thought sounded like 'fender,' but with an extra syllable. I think it's Van Derveer. I think they're trying to say 'Boynton' and 'Van Derveer.' "

"That's not so far out," Jamie said. He'd already heard it once and didn't feel the need to impress Dana or prove anything, so he stayed on the fringes of the circle with the kitten.

I was happy for the backup. "No, it isn't. It's beautifully logical, and if it's right, then we may have all the answers we need right here."

"Again, I think you're reaching."

"Maybe she's right," Benny chimed in, but his loyalties were divided, and his enthusiasm wasn't high.

"Sure she's right. I *am* reaching. But come on. The ghosts were talking about a bargain, and about Dyer's field, and about a Boynton. My math isn't always spectacular, but I can put two and two together without any trouble, and right now I'm seeing four splashed all over the local news."

No one spoke until Dana looked up from the screen, clicking the audio player closed. "You think that kid is buried there. At Dyer's field."

"Well. Yeah. Yeah, I do. Can anybody think of a better hypothesis? Come on. Anybody?"

I didn't get an answer until Jamie put the kitten down. "But even if it's true, it's not like there's anything we can do about it."

"What? What are you talking about?" Benny asked, but Dana put a calming hand on his arm.

"Your friend's right. What are we going to do, go to the police?"

"Fuck yeah, we're going to the police!" he swore, but Jamie shook his head.

"And tell them what? We think there's a chance there's a dead body out there? On the battlefield? Good luck with that, man. Even if they believe us—and there's no good reason that they should—they aren't going to do much about it."

"No way," I bickered at him. "How could they *not* check into a tip like this? What are you talking about?"

Dana stepped in. "It's federally protected land. Can you imagine what the jurisdiction issues would be like? God only knows what paperwork hoops they'd have to jump through in order to excavate a grave there—even a new one. It's a stroke of genius to put a murder victim there, if in fact this is what's happened."

I was paralyzed by the infuriating truth of it all. "Damn, you're right. It'd be pulling teeth to get cops to go and check it out, even to see if we're right and there's a fresh grave at the cabin."

"And if *we* go and dig there, they'll arrest *us*."

"Or worse," Jamie said, though he didn't clarify the sentiment. "At this point, I think the best thing we can do for the case is to stay away from the park. There's nothing we can tell anyone that they'll take seriously. It makes for hip media coverage, but it's shit for investigating."

"Hip media coverage," I parroted. "That gives me an idea. Hang on a minute, will you?"

I excused myself and stepped outside, digging my cell phone out of my bag with one hand, and fishing for Nick Alders's business card with my other. I got his voicemail. I left him a message. I was vague but direct, hinting for all I was worth. I hung up.

Maybe he'd follow up, and maybe he wouldn't; but if nothing else I'd pointed someone unscrupulous and yet credible at my hunch. I hoped it would work, even as I knew it might not. If I was lucky, he'd follow up on it and draw attention to it with local law enforcement. If I wasn't, he'd ignore me.

But I was betting he'd at least look into it.

When I went back inside, Benny had stolen my seat and Jamie was leaning against the wall with his arms folded.

Dana had picked up the thread I'd dropped when I left, and

was kneading something more out of it. "What about this, then?" she asked, putting her hands out like she was about to tell us a story. "There are the Boyntons, whoever they are, and there's a bargain. Let's connect the dots, shall we? Let's say the bargain was with the Boyntons. So how about this: we've heard there was some kind of bargain made between the old general and the old monster. You yourself called Green Eyes a guardian and not a ghost. He's not a spirit; he's something else. And if he's protecting the place as part of an arrangement, who else would he have made the arrangement with?"

The room went silent again, and I said what the rest of us were probably thinking. "Keep talking. I'm listening."

"Well, what could be more pragmatic and dramatic than something like this? By the time the park was established, the Trail of Tears had happened decades before, so it's not like the native population was keeping the ghoul tied to the land."

"He might have been on his way out," I added. "He was going to follow them. But something made him stay."

Benny leaned his toe up against FrankenHal's power switch, and the machine dragged itself into darkness. "He must not have been all that resolved to leave, then."

I was willing to grant him that one. "I don't think he was. I saw him, remember? And he was talking to himself, more like arguing with himself. I don't think he ever really wanted to leave in the first place, but he didn't know what else to do once the Indians left."

"But you think someone gave him an excuse to stick around?" Jamie uncrossed his arms. "You think that's what this is about? We've got the world's most ambivalent supernatural freak on our hands?"

"I don't think 'ambivalent' is the right call. It'd be more accurate to call him 'unmotivated.'" I thought again to his hand-wringing mumbling, and his worrying, back-and-forth grumbles. "For all we know, he was never tied to the Cherokees, and like Karl said, he was connected to the land and not whoever lived there. They were here for a long time, and he got used to them, but things were changing. Everything was changing—the battlefield grounds had become farmland, and there were all these European settlers there."

Dana waved a pencil she'd picked up from Benny's desk. "He was disoriented. Confused. Didn't know whether to stay or go."

"But he'd stayed in the first place," I mentioned. "He stayed when they left, so he must not be bound to them very tightly. Again we come back to him being tied to the place, and not the population."

It was Jamie's turn. "But as the place changed, he was less sure he needed to stick around."

No one dared voice the next piece. No one except Dana. "Until someone gave him an excuse. Someone gave him a reason to stay where he wanted to be anyway. That's the obvious answer, isn't it?" She pulled her toes away from the kitten, who had abandoned Jamie to wander the floor.

Benny collected the tiny cat in his arms. "It's a good working theory. It fits all the facts, doesn't it? A modern-day Boynton disappears, or maybe dies, Green Eyes leaves, and the ghosts are agitated because there's no one left to keep an eye on the place. But why would they care if he came or went? They're dead."

I felt a momentary blitz of memory, thinking of Dana and the words she had given to the dead Confederate. "They have no wings to the kingdom, he said—the soldier at the battlefield.

Maybe they've stayed behind because they have to. I don't know. I haven't a clue how the afterlife works."

Dana rose to her feet, infusing the motion with a glorious hint of decisive finality. "Well then," she declared. "I think our next move is pretty obvious. We've got to go and find the green-eyed ghoul and ask him ourselves."

Everyone looked at me, since I was the only one who'd seen him up close and personal. She was right, and I knew it; but she was only half right, really. "No. We've got to do more than that. We've got to con him into coming *back*."

FIFTEEN

FRESH RESOLVE

CHICKAMAUGA, GEORGIA, SIX WEEKS EARLIER

Pete Buford was enraged, and he was afraid, and he'd spent too much of the last few years feeling helpless. When he left the battlefield he'd had a wet trail in his pants and the hot sting of terrified humiliation to lash him onward. It couldn't be like that. It couldn't be over so easily; he hadn't had a good idea in his entire life, and the one time he had a project—a real honest-to-God goal—it had been thwarted before it even got under way good.

There had to be an answer to it. There had to be a way around this obstacle.

He fumed and growled all the way to the car, then all the way to the trunk, where he dug out some rags. He scowled at the urine stains as they began to dry on his jeans. Pete grumbled at the gasoline can in the backseat and swore as he ripped the cap off.

He grimaced when he dumped it down his crotch. He wrinkled his nose at the pungent odor wafting up to his nostrils.

It made his eyes water, or maybe he was so mad he was almost crying. He wouldn't have admitted to either possibility.

The drive home was spent shaking, cursing, and stabbing his fingers at the half-broken radio that only wanted to pick up one or two stations.

He'd tell Uncle Rudy he'd run out of gas. He'd tell him he'd stopped with the can and spilled it. That would account for the smell. The rest would come out in the wash. The rest he could lie about if he had to.

He hated himself for running.

He'd run like a little girl, screaming away from the boogeyman.

But once he'd calmed down some, about halfway home, he decided to be honest with himself: it *had* been pretty fucking scary. He vibrated with anxiety, rubbing his foot against the gas pedal and making the old beater drive funnier than it usually did.

What the hell was that? he wondered. *I mean really, what the hell* was *that?*

It wasn't just that he'd never seen anything like it; he'd never even *heard* of anything like it. He'd never read about anything like that in a story, even.

On second thought, that wasn't true. Like everybody else in the valley, he'd heard stories about Old Green Eyes. But they weren't the sort of stories you believed—not if you were smart. Not if you were stupid, even. Not if you were the most gullible son of a bitch in the world—you didn't believe the Old Green Eyes stories.

Not for real.

You believed there was a ghost, maybe. You believed that there was spookiness out there on the battlefield. Thirty-five thousand people died there, isn't that what the park people had said? Thirty-five thousand people don't die violently anyplace and not leave a stain of some kind.

Pete believed in stains. He believed in marks.

He believed in places that gave you uncomfortable feelings because bad things had happened; and he believed in ghosts, if it came down to it. Why not? Lots of people claimed they'd seen them, all over the world. Pete had never personally seen a lot of things, but he was pretty sure they existed somewhere.

He'd never seen a kiwi bird, for example.

He'd read about kiwi birds in sixth grade, in Mr. Viar's biology class. Class had been held in a trailer classroom—one of the "temporary" buildings that stood for thirty years without air conditioning—and never did much to educate students at all. There'd been a chapter on birds, though, and about what makes a bird a bird. The teacher had said it wasn't flying, like Pete had thought it might be. Turned out, it was feathers that made a bird a bird. Even birds that can't fly are still birds, not just rats with beaks. Inside the biology textbook there had been a drawing of a brown bird that looked like a guinea pig on stilts, with a long pointed nose. The caption underneath had said it was a kiwi bird, and it didn't live anyplace in America. And even though it'd only been a drawing, not even a photograph, Pete had believed that the kiwi bird existed.

But this was different.

He'd heard stories about Green Eyes, and even though he'd never seen him personally, he'd believed them. But seeing the thing in person had been like meeting his first kiwi and finding out it was as big as a moose. Green Eyes was the most horrible thing Pete had ever heard of. He felt cheated by folklore's understatement. "Green Eyes" sounded like something ephemeral and floating—

spooky glowing orbs that hover and flutter and float, not anything like a monster.

What he'd seen, Pete reflected as he drove back up Sand Mountain, was something capable of doing real harm. This was a being that could grab, and choke, and pummel. It was something stronger than a man, and bigger than any man Pete had ever seen.

And it had chased him away.

One of Pete's more personal failings had always been an inability to leave well enough alone. The thought that he'd been chased away did worse to his ego than the soiled pants he'd disguised with the gasoline stink. Pete was not the sort of man to be chased away from a prize, much less one that was owed him or his family.

And the fact that he'd been chased at all suggested there might be something really good to be found. No one gets chased away from nothing.

Maybe Green Eyes knew about the treasure, and was guarding it for himself. In all the old stories, all the best treasures were guarded by fearsome creatures. But then he remembered that the gold itself almost certainly wasn't buried on the field, and this theory pretty much tanked.

Whether or not the beast was guarding anything was beside the point, anyway. Green Eyes was there. He was intimidating and possibly violent. Homicidal, even. And while Green Eyes was present on the battlefield, it seemed unlikely that Pete was going to get anywhere near the relics of his dead ancestor.

The trick was how to get *rid* of him.

When he realized this was all he needed to do, Pete brightened up some.

If he'd met the thing under different circumstances, his first instinct might have been to call the cops; but that course of action was clearly out of the question. Even if the cops believed him that something strange was going on out at the battlefield, what would they do? Arrest Green Eyes—assuming he was even catchable?

No, if anyone was going to nab the big bastard, it surely would've happened by now. If Pete's recollection served him, Green Eyes had been hanging around at least since the original battle. Nothing lives that long by being easy to catch.

So the cops were absolutely out. They'd never follow up on a tip from a criminal, anyway. So he might as well assume that the normal mortal channels were going to be closed to him. But there had to be another way.

All the way home, he turned the possibilities over in his mind. The odds of him scaring Green Eyes off weren't good, and besides, who knew what that thing was afraid of? Not Pete. The odds of killing him weren't much better, or at least Pete didn't think so. The creature was terrifically strong, and solid, but it didn't feel like he was *permanently* solid. Pete wasn't sure it would do any good to bring a gun.

A gun might be worth having, though. He mentally filed it away as something to try, if all else failed. But there had to be a better way. A more *definite* way.

This was going to require some serious thought.

Back at the homestead, Rudy was still up but on the verge of hitting the sack. The two men exchanged pleasantries—Rudy's were polite and concerned, and Pete's were largely white lies about the impending job at the foundry. They passed each other and retired to their respective sleeping quarters.

Pete dropped himself onto the squeaky, thin mattress and

stared at the ceiling with his hands under the back of his head. He'd been blessed with one good idea, and if he was going to follow through, he was going to need a second.

It was too much to hope for, but that didn't stop him from trying.

The next day, he went back to the library, but finding nothing helpful in the tiny, underfunded branch, he borrowed the car again and headed back down into the valley. He made a point of striking during broad daylight this time. He wanted another shot at the lady at the ranger's desk. It didn't matter if she looked at him like he was crazy.

He figured he couldn't be the first person who'd ever asked her about it, and he was right. The same blond lady in the beige uniform was working when he stopped by, and she greeted him in a formal, salaried way, though she didn't act like she remembered him.

The mention of the familiar lore subject brought a smile to her face, but it wasn't an unkind one. "Oh yes, dear Old Green Eyes. We get lots of questions about him. There's always someone writing a book or preparing to sneak onto grounds after hours looking for him."

"Have you ever seen him yourself?" Pete asked, trying to sound casual and succeeding more than not.

"Me? No. Well, I thought I did once, maybe. But Mel over in the gift shop said that if I only *thought* I saw him, I must've seen something else. He says that once you've gotten a look at him, you never wonder about it again."

Pete was tempted to agree with her coworker, but he kept the temptation to himself. "What's he doing here anyway, do you think?" he asked instead.

She tipped her head in a shrug, her heavily hairsprayed bangs refraining from budging. "Who knows? Some people think he just guards the battlefield and protects it from trouble. A lot of people think it had something to do with the Cherokees out here, like he used to be some kind of spirit guide, or whatever. I don't know. But if you talk to Mel—the gift shop manager—he could tell you about some of their old legends."

"There are Cherokee legends about Green Eyes?"

"Sort of. It depends on who you ask."

"You told me to ask Mel," Pete said. "What would *he* tell me?"

"He'd tell you that there are half a dozen myths tied into everyone's favorite battlefield spook. One of his favorites is about a strange creature with a glowing jewel on its head—I think he thinks that's where we get the leftover 'glowing green eyes' bit from."

It took Pete a minute to picture the connection, but when he did he nodded. "That's not a real far jump. Glowing jewels to glowing eyes. But you say this like you think maybe your buddy Mel is full of malarkey. If that's what he'd tell me, what would you tell me?"

She sat forward in her chair and folded her arms on the counter between them. "I'd tell you that it's a bunch of nonsense, but it's useful nonsense if it keeps idiot kids off the fields at night when we can't watch them so good. If what it takes to keep the place safe is a story about a green-eyed haint, well, that's nothing but all right with me."

A quick inspection of the gift shop failed to turn up anyone named Mel. Pete didn't consider it too big of a loss, though. The Indian angle had given him an idea.

Back in the pen, he'd known a guy, another non-violent offender like himself, who claimed to be part Cherokee and considered himself an authority on all things Native American. His back was covered with an elaborate eagle tattoo, and his arms were decorated with bear totems and symbols like that. He'd made a dreamcatcher in one of Silverdale's craft classes, and hung it up above his bed.

He even prayed to the Great Spirit, or some such shit.

Pete didn't begrudge people their beliefs, but like everyone else, he thought Orin was a jackass. Of course, that didn't have anything to do with the guy's professed beliefs. It had to do with the fact that Orin was a red-headed Irish guy with green eyes and freckles.

Orin always said being Indian was the same as being black, and all it took was a drop to make you dark underneath. If that was true, then it was a mighty slim drop that was swimming through Orin's veins.

But right about now, Pete didn't care if Orin did or did not have a drop of Cherokee blood worth claiming. Orin knew lots about Indians, and Pete needed an expert.

Orin had gotten out of Silverdale a year ahead of Pete, and if Pete knew Chattanooga, Orin would be right where he'd said he was never going back to.

Up on the north side of town there was a bar backed up against the big rock ridge everyone calls Signal Mountain. The bar was called Kilroy's, and to call it a hole-in-the-wall would be rude to respectable holes everywhere.

Orin's father owned Kilroy's, and he worked Kilroy's, and he had every intention of passing it down to his son... but Orin had no intention of accepting it. Except, he always found his way back there eventually. One day, his father would probably die and Orin would probably inherit it, and then he'd probably sell it as fast as he could and blow the money on a preposterous get-rich-quick scheme.

That reminded Pete—he was going to have to be careful about how he broached the subject. Orin could smell money a mile away, and Pete didn't want an accomplice. He wanted someone with information.

So he went to Kilroy's. It took him nearly an hour to find the place, snuggled against the ridge and in the shadow of a big strip mall. Pete didn't remember the strip mall, but it'd been a while since he'd been out that way, and a lot of things had been built in his absence.

Inside it was dark as hell. It took his eyes a minute to adjust, and when they did, there wasn't much more detail to greet him. The bar was half-empty, but to be fair it was still mid afternoon and there was no reason to expect a crowd. Pete couldn't blame Orin for disliking the place. It was filthy and bleak, and the neon advertisement signs within didn't do much to brighten things. The bar was sticky, and so was the floor. Pete watched his step.

He didn't know if the fat man at the bar was Orin's dad, and he didn't ask. He just asked for Orin, pretending that he knew all along the guy would be there. He was right. In the back, asleep in the stockroom, he found the red-haired Cherokee wannabe.

Orin sat up and slapped Pete's hand in a friendly greeting. "How the hell are you, man?" he asked, drawling out the vowels with alcohol and leftover sleep.

"I'm good, real good."

Pleasantries were exchanged and offers of beer were made. Pete wasn't a man to decline a freebie; so together the pair stepped to the counter, and Orin made arrangements to score them a couple of bottles.

The bartender, or Orin's father (Pete never did figure out which), opened the tops under the bar with a crank of his elbow. He set them on the counter and let the pair talk.

Orin looked just like Pete remembered, with his curly red hair tied into a bandana with a beer slogan. He had a new tattoo—a buffalo rearing up like a mustang. It reached from under his left armpit to his belly button. He showed it off with glee, even though it hadn't quite healed yet. It looked to Pete like it needed to stay covered for another week or two, but Pete didn't have any tattoos, so he didn't feel qualified to offer advice.

Instead he admired it, as politeness seemed to call for. "It looks real good," he said. He made note of the steam snorting from the creature's nose and talked about how it must've hurt.

"Naw, naw, it didn't hurt. Not like you'd think. Took forever, though. Felt like someone drawing on me with a red-hot fishhook. But not really bad. I almost fell asleep, on account of it took 'em so long."

"That's real good work. Where'd you get it done?"

"Downtown. A little place by the river. So what you come here for, anyway? Not that I'm not always happy to see an old friend," he added.

Pete thought that calling them "friends" was a little much, but he didn't object, because he'd come there wanting something. "Well, I'll tell you." He had a story ready and everything. "It's like this: a couple of stupid cousins of mine went out onto the battlefield down at Chickamauga the other day."

"Went down there? Were they up to no good?"

Pete lowered his head with associated shame. "I'm afraid they were. They're kids, you know, that's all. Stupid as a pair of bowling cleats, without a clean thought between them. They took some spray paint out there and tore the place up in a bad way. I'm more embarrassed about it than I could tell you. But I'm not here to apologize for them; I'm here to ask you if you might know something about what they... well, they think they saw something. It scared them to pieces; I mean, it scared the shit right out of them."

Orin straightened up on the stool; his mouth set itself in a knowing line. "They saw something out on the battlefield? They wouldn't be the first."

"I know it," Pete said. "And we both know they shouldn't have been out there. Their mother told them, too. She told them that they need to think of that place like a cemetery. It's a place where people died in a war, and it's where they're buried. There's no call to be disrespectful like that."

"None at all," his friend agreed. "But since they did it, it's no wonder they got scared."

"That's what I told them." Pete bobbed his mouth down to the beer and sucked down a gulp. "I said they deserved whatever it was they got from the place. And they're real sorry—I can see it in them, even though they didn't get caught. They've learned their lesson, boy don't you know."

"They should've."

"They did. But you know, I got thinking when they were talking about how strange it was that, what those kids said they saw... hell. I don't mind telling you, it would've scared the piss out of me if I'd seen it, too. Assuming, that is"—he felt compelled to call the story into doubt, if only to distance himself from it—"that the little shits were telling the truth."

"They saw Old Green Eyes, didn't they? And you can go on and tell me they did, and I won't laugh at you."

"All right then, I will tell you that. That's what they say they saw. They said he was taller than a man and had them glowing green eyes everyone talks about, just like the stories say he does."

Orin was unsurprised. "I can't honestly tell you that it unnerves me to hear it, either."

"You think he's real then, eh?"

"I know he's real. I believe with the certainty of the people who lived there long before the thieving Europeans came and took the land out from under them. They didn't believe he was there—they *knew* he was there. It's not no matter of faith when you see the fellow daily, now is it?"

"It's not."

"That's right. He's there, watching the land now like he did for the others before there was a park. It's his mission. It's his *duty.*"

"A duty?"

"A duty. He's tied to that place as surely as if he signed a lease. Or that's what some people like to say, anyhow."

Pete wished he'd clarify, but he wasn't sure how to ask him to without giving up too much information. Fortunately, Orin didn't need much prompting. "There was the Trail of Tears, you know?"

Pete nodded, because everyone knew about how thousands of Indians had left the south along the Trail. "But Green Eyes didn't leave when my people did. He stayed, tied to the place. And do you know why?"

"I don't," Pete confessed. "I've heard he made some sort of bargain, but I don't know what kind."

Bringing up the bargain Green Eyes had mentioned took some of the narrative wind out of Orin's sails. "Oh. You know about that, then."

"Only sort of. I mean, I know there was one, but I don't know anything about it."

"You mean you *heard* there was one. No one knows anything for sure. There's no one left alive from back then, so it's all passed into the realm of myth."

Orin sounded like he was trying to do the voiceover for a film.

"So then…" Pete had stalled, trying to recover the threads of his questioning. "He's staying around because he made a deal. With who?"

"With, well, with the park founders, at least. All of that happened some years after the war, but they were already having troubles with grave robbing and whatnot. The old guys who preserved the place, they were the ones who asked Green Eyes if he'd stick around and help keep the riffraff out."

"Now how would they wrangle him into something like that?"

Orin hunched his shoulders and tipped the neck of his beer bottle to his mouth. "You tell me. But supposedly that's how it happened."

Pete was not perfectly credulous. "But that's… well… I mean, what if he wants to leave? When does he get to go—or is he stuck here forever?"

"Naw, not forever. The way I heard it from my great-grandmother White Crow, it was more like Green Eyes would stay and watch the land until the last descendant of the generals had died or moved away from the valley. And then he was free to leave."

Pete did a miraculous job of not rolling his eyes at the likelihood of Orin having a grandmother named White Crow. Instead, he took the new snippet at face value and thought on it while he sipped at the beer. Behind him, a television monitor detailed a football game that neither man had any interest in, and behind the bar the tender asked if they'd like another. Both said yes.

"That is something else," Pete observed in a non-specific sort of way. "It almost makes you feel sorry for Old Green Eyes," he lied.

"Oh, I wouldn't feel too sorry for him. I think if he really wanted to leave, he could. And for that matter, I doubt there are too many kin left around here anyway. The one guy, his family went back up north. And the other one... what was his name? Started with a 'B.' "

"Boynton," Pete said a bit too readily.

"Boynton, yeah. That's not a name you hear around here much, is it? Not like the other old families, what've got their names on every other building downtown. I bet they died out years ago."

"I bet they didn't," Pete said under his breath, but then he wished he hadn't.

"What're you getting at?" Orin suddenly demanded, his curiosity stoked. "What're you wondering about, that you'd come all the way out here to hear it from me?"

Pete thought hard before he answered, and since thinking hard wasn't his area of expertise, it took him longer than might have been considered mannerly. Maybe an accomplice wasn't the worst of all possible ideas. Maybe it was too ambitious to try to do everything himself. "Two heads are better than one," his mother'd always said. And in the case of the Bufords, that second head usually needed to belong to an outsider.

He didn't know Orin very well, but he knew he was a local boy who was partly full of shit, but partly knew his shit too. Orin wasn't entitled to anything, not like Pete was. But having all of nothing wasn't doing Pete any good. Maybe he ought to aim more modestly, for something like half of a whole lot.

So Pete set his beer down and leaned his body against the bar. "It's like this," he said, looking the other man straight in the eye. "I could use a hand with something big."

"This is a bad idea," Pete said aloud.

"It's the *only* idea," Orin corrected him. "I thought you wanted this."

"I do."

"Then this is the only way."

Pete knew he was right. He'd been thinking himself in circles trying to come up with something else, but the only other "something else" he'd been able to scare up involved facing down Green Eyes again, and he frankly lacked the intestinal fortitude.

"He's only a kid."

"We're not going to hurt him," Orin reminded him. "We've just got to make him leave."

"He'll be leaving at the end of next year, anyway. When he graduates he'll go off to school someplace else."

"You want to wait another year and a half?"

"No." Pete sulked. Orin was right. After making a few discreet phone calls, Orin had learned that Ryan Boynton had been orphaned as a youngster and fostered through middle school, when good grades, exceptional test scores, and a knack for football had landed him at McCallie, an expensive, exclusive boys' school. So he was alone, and so far as Pete and Orin could tell, the last of his kind.

They just needed to put the fear of God into the kid, and Orin had a plan for that. Pete wasn't happy about it, but kept reminding himself that this was exactly why he'd brought Orin on board in the first place: because Pete's plans were usually rotten, and he needed someone else to help him think.

He wasn't morally averse to the idea of scaring some kid into another county; he didn't mind that part at all. If anything, it almost sounded like fun. But it definitely sounded risky, especially since they were using real guns and real ammunition.

"It's safer that way," Orin had said. Pete knew what he meant, but it still sounded wrong. "Safer for us, anyway," Orin clarified. "The kid's a football player, and what? Maybe sixteen? He's gonna be a fast, slippery bruiser of a thing, and we don't want to take a chance that he'll get away. We probably won't get a second chance." So Pete carried his .357, and Orin had brought a sawed-off shotgun because he thought it looked meaner than a handgun.

And they weren't going to kill him or anything. No way. Too risky, and unnecessary. All they had to do, if they understood the folklore correctly, was make him leave. Though, as Orin had pointed out, if merely making him leave didn't work, there were always options. There were always alternatives.

Pete chose not to think about them yet.

He chose instead to focus on the fact that he was sitting in the cab of his uncle's car while armed to the teeth and wearing a black ski mask that practically screamed "criminal" at thirty paces.

The kid would be heading back to his dorm from practice at any moment. He would be driving pretty fast so as not to miss curfew. He probably would not notice the tree lying down across his shortcut until he was right on top of it. At least that's what Orin figured, which was why his dad's still-warm chainsaw was lying in the trunk of Pete's uncle's car.

Headlights crawled quickly around the bend. They held

their breaths. They were cutting this close, and they had only hope and prayer to prevent the vehicle from belonging to some other poor driver.

It had to be the kid. It *had* to be.

Orin had enjoyed playing mastermind so much that he'd planned every small detail. They'd almost been caught while they were taking down the tree, and they'd almost let it drop right on top of an innocent bypasser's car, but luck had been with them so far.

But Christ, it was dark.

They'd turned off the dome light and sat in the blackness, listening to each other try not to breathe. This next vehicle, it had to be the one. It had to be the small red pickup truck.

And it was.

Ryan hit the brake pedal and swerved, nearly managing to stop, but losing control instead. He slid sideways into the trunk, brakes squealing all the way. The driver's side door crumpled, and all around the cab glass shattered in a spray of blue crystals. One headlight went out, but one stayed on.

Rock 105 didn't miss a beat, and with all the windows busted out, Pete and Rudy could hear the hard rock tune loudly enough to bother them both.

"We've got to turn that off," Pete observed, sliding his hands into the gloves he'd brought.

"I don't see why," Orin said. "If nobody heard that crash, nobody's going to give a damn about the radio music."

In the cab, the driver's head wobbled loosely on his neck, side to side. In his disorientation, he hadn't noticed the tree holding his door closed, so he tried it and found himself pinned from the left. He fumbled with his seat belt and released it.

Pete opened his own door, and Orin did the same. They tugged their masks down over their ears and checked their weapons.

Orin reached the passenger door first, yanking it open and pointing his shotgun inside. "Get out of there, boy," he ordered.

Ryan was crawling forward along the seat. His head might've been the thing that broke the window, for the left side of his face was bloody, and one of his eyes looked like it was glued shut. "I'm trying," he said, not seeing the gun or not registering it well enough to understand. "Did you see what happened? Can you call the cops?"

"We're not calling nobody. You're getting out and—"

"Shit," the kid said, seeing the rough, circular edges of the weapon pointing down at his nose.

"Get out," Pete backed Orin up. "Hurry up."

Ryan's hand lost its grip on the vinyl seat, and he pitched forward. "I need help, man. What are you doing? What do you want?"

Orin reached in and grabbed his shoulder, pulling him forward—though only by a few inches.

He wasn't a huge kid, but he was solid and scared. He put his hands out to brace himself—to make himself as big as possible so as not to be dragged out of the cab. One leg thrust up behind him, and he snared his foot around the steering wheel.

"Goddamn it, come out now!" Orin commanded, but the kid wasn't having any of it.

Ryan peeled Orin's hand off his shoulder and jammed his own fist into the other man's face. It wasn't a punch, exactly, but the closed-fingered shove hurt enough to make Orin mad.

Pete stood aside while they wrestled, the wounded boy getting enough adrenaline to put up a decent fight against Orin, who was trying to juggle the shotgun and his own agenda. Years ago, Pete had watched his mother try to shove a large, violently reluctant puppy into a small carrier to go to the vet. This looked just like that, but in reverse.

He might've laughed if he weren't getting worried.

The kid in the truck didn't seem too impressed by the gun, and he was fighting like it wasn't even there in the cab. It could've been that he was still in shock from the wreck, but Pete thought he looked beefy, like a boy who'd spent a lot of time outside. If he was the kind of kid who was used to being around guns, the sight of one wouldn't have intimidated him into complacency.

"Pete, you son of a bitch," Orin swore.

Pete wanted to bash the other man's head in for using his name, but he answered, "What?" anyway and took a step or two closer.

"Help me out here, man. Or are you just going to stand there?"

Ryan had not noticed the second man until Pete spoke, and the sudden knowledge that he was outnumbered made him more desperate. He flailed harder, and righted himself so that his legs and arms both were facing out, kicking and swinging.

"Help!" he yelled. "Somebody help me!"

Orin yelled back, "Shut up!" as if it made any difference.

The radio was blaring still, turned up way too loud and way too hard on a station that played nothing but music Pete hated to hear.

The kid was thrashing like a hooked bass, and Orin was on the verge of losing the gun in the fray or of having it go off in his face—Pete wasn't sure which was more likely. Either way, another car could be along any minute, someone may have heard the wreck and called the cops already, and the kid knew Pete's first name.

This was turning out to be a *very* bad idea—right up there with running cars to Canada.

"Orin"—he used the name for retribution's sake—"this is

bad. Forget it, we'll think of something else."

"What're you doing... using my name for, you fucker? You think he can't hear you or something?" He got another grip on Ryan's shoulder and was forced to drop the gun in order to keep it. The fat-barreled thing clattered to the ground beneath them, but didn't fire. "Cover me, you useless bastard, cover me!"

Orin had a pair of good handholds then, one on each of Ryan's shoulders. All it would take was one good backwards heave and the kid would be successfully birthed from the vehicle.

The DJ came on as a song ended, and he chatted merrily about concert tickets while the struggle raged. Pete wished to God the kid's hip or knee would knock the radio in and shut it off.

"Get him out, man. Get him out and hurry *up*."

"I'm working on it!" Orin bellowed, and Ryan shouted over them both for help from anyone within hearing distance.

"This is gone bad, Orin. It's gone bad. If you can't get him out, let him go, for Christ's sake!"

The suggestion enraged Orin and invigorated the bleeding kid, who wrenched himself back into the cab and kicked against everything that appeared in the passenger's side door space.

Orin blasphemed something unintelligible and snared one whipping ankle. He braced one of his legs against the seat and the other against the truck's frame and lunged back for all he was worth, which was maybe two hundred pounds—which was enough to get him halfway to where he wanted to be.

Ryan's legs and most of his ass came sliding out, but he still hung on to the gear shift, to the window frame, to the seat belt—to anything he could hold.

"You've almost got him!" Pete said, but wasn't sure whether or not to be happy about it.

Especially not when he saw the kid's slipping hand reach for the glove compartment. He jabbed at it until it popped open, and inside Pete saw something he didn't want to see. It was black, and about palm-sized, and it gleamed under the dome light.

"No way," he said, and he brought his own revolver up. "Don't do it, kid, don't you fucking do it! Or I'll shoot!"

But Ryan didn't hear or didn't listen, or he didn't care. He pushed his fingers into the glove box.

So Pete fired.

The kick surprised him. He hadn't fired a gun since before he went into the joint, and the little leap moved his wrist, sending the shot wild. He'd been aiming for the boy's hand, or the box itself—anything inside it.

What he hit instead was the side of Orin's neck.

Orin reeled back, releasing Ryan's feet and clutching at the bloody spray that gushed from beneath his ear.

"Holy fuck!" the kid in the truck exclaimed, and he sounded more panicked than before, when he was only hurt from the wreck. "Holy fuck!" he said again, like he couldn't believe whatever he was seeing.

"Stay there!" Pete insisted, pointing the gun at the kid but keeping his distance.

He approached Orin, who dropped himself down against the fender, then the tire, until his rear hit the pavement and he was forced to stop his descent. Orin was panting, and holding his neck so tight he was choking himself with the effort.

Pete didn't even know a body could hold so much blood, much less lose it in such a quantity and at such a speed. Orin's clothes were saturated; he could've wrung them out and filled a bucket. Pete pulled off the hurt man's mask and used it to try to wipe the spot. But the spot was everywhere.

Orin gagged, and sighed, and his grip on himself loosened.

"Holy fuck," Ryan said again.

He'd removed himself from the cab by then, and was hobbling backwards away from the pair. In his hand the boy held a cell phone, which was surely what he'd been reaching for in the glove box.

Pete swung the gun around, and in the dim light of the overhead cab bulb, he saw that the kid was bleeding from the thigh. Pete had only fired once, but what had grazed Orin in the wrong spot must've kept going and landed in Ryan.

"You stay right there," he commanded.

The kid hesitated. He checked to see how far he was from cover, and from his truck. He glanced down at the phone in his hand.

"Hold it right there!"

Pete was frantic with rage and fear. The gun wasn't holding steady, and the DJ on the too-loud radio had a voice like a jackhammer. Orin was dead, or if he wasn't, he would be. Everything had unraveled. Everything had come undone. So much for Pete and his ideas. So much for getting help. So much for his first accomplice.

"Don't you try it! I said, don't you try it!"

Ryan tried it.

SIXTEEN

THE RECOVERY

"We'd better do it quick," Dana said. "I've got to head back to Greensboro tomorrow afternoon. With or without Tripp there are contractual obligations to be met and work to be done."

We all got quiet, because anything else seemed disrespectful. None of us knew how to respond, but she tried not to keep us on the spot about it.

"Look, stop looking so morose every time I bring him up. This isn't your problem, your grief. Don't feel like you need to share it with me. You're not going to make it better." She pulled her hands up to her face and breathed into them for a minute, collecting herself or simply hiding from us temporarily.

"Okay then," I said, mostly to break up the awkwardness. "This afternoon. We'll go out to the Bend and see if we can find him."

Jamie was dubious. "Shouldn't we wait until tonight? Doesn't all this spooky stuff have to go down after sundown?"

Benny butted in so I didn't need to. "I don't see why. Didn't the ghosts that started all this—I mean, the ones that came out on

Decoration Day—didn't they appear in the middle of the day?"

"Correct, my friend," I told him.

"And you don't think Green Eyes will be any different?"

"Why would he be? If anything, he's something more substantial than a spirit. I think he might be easier to spot in daylight than one of the battlefield pointers."

"Allow me to note"—Jamie flipped a thumb towards the window—"that we've only got a few more hours of daylight anyway." He was right. The sun had hit that sharp, yellow slant that means the day is closer to ending than beginning.

I lifted an eyebrow. "Wow. I didn't realize we'd been here so long. But there's time. Is everybody in?"

I knew Dana was, so I didn't even give her a glance. The boys looked less sure of the project.

"I have to work," Benny complained.

"I don't have to work," Jamie admitted. "But I don't know about this."

Benny looked horrified by the thought that someone he called a friend might think that this wasn't a great idea. "Why not? I'm already composing an excuse to get out of work. Do I look sick to you? Here—look down my throat. Does it look red?"

"Ew."

"Good. I might be coming down with strep throat. I can't possibly drive a cab with strep throat. Eden, can I see your cell phone? I've got a call to make."

My purse was on the floor beside me. I picked it up with my foot and retrieved my phone from inside it. "Here you go." I tossed it to him. "Jamie, that leaves you. Except…" Something dawned on me. I knew for a fact that he wasn't too chicken to come ghost-hunting with us, and that left only one obvious reason that he wouldn't want to. "You've got a date, don't you?"

"I do."

"You're joking." Benny rolled his eyes. "You'd give up the chance to shake hands with one of the most famous spooks in the South for the prospect of a little action?"

"You wouldn't?"

"No, he wouldn't," I answered for him. "Probably. But if you don't want to come, you don't have to."

"Thanks, I know. But if things end early, or if she's game for adventure, I'll give you a call. You'll leave your phone on?"

"Yeah," I said out of reflex, then realized I didn't mean it. If we ended up out on the battlefield in the dark again, he could forget it. "Give us a call if your night gets boring. But the rest of us are going to hit the Bend. Right?"

Dana and Benny both signified agreement, and we reached for our respective belongings.

"Drop me off at the 'Friar's?" Jamie was polite enough to ask, and not assume.

I said sure, and we packed ourselves back into my car. The Nugget's backseat isn't the most spacious in the world, but the boys sucked it up and didn't fight over "shotgun" out of deference to Dana. I didn't think they would do as much for me, were the shoe on some other foot, but that was all right. I appreciated the fact they were going out of their way to be nice to her.

After leaving Jamie at the door of our favorite coffeehouse, Benny wanted to stop for drinks and I needed gas anyway, so we ran by a Favorite Market and filled up all around. Then we stopped in at the hotel where Dana was staying and loaded up enough electronic equipment to stuff a U-Haul. I wasn't entirely sure it would all fit, but we got the bulk of it into my trunk.

Finally, we rolled down the windows and drove out to Moccasin Bend.

By the time we got there it was after six. As I'd noticed during my midnight run to pick up Malachi, there weren't any places to turn off or park anywhere past the entry sign, and there was a big stretch of road between the entrance and the tip of the peninsula.

We had no idea where to begin looking, so we idled beside the same sign where I'd hunted for my brother not long before.

"We can't park here," Dana observed. I agreed with her wholeheartedly, but I didn't know where else to take us.

Benny squeezed himself forward between the bucket seats up front. "We could pretend we have car trouble. Throw on the hazard lights and pull over."

"That's not a bad idea," I said. "But what if someone comes along and tries to help, and we've wandered off?"

"Could we leave a note?"

Dana reached for her bag and pulled out a notebook. "We could leave a note. It could say something about how we've walked out to the nearest gas station. We passed one back... back a while ago. Maybe a mile ago."

"But if anyone stopped to read the note and then tried to help us, they'd double back and notice that we weren't walking towards the gas station."

"Oh, *seriously*," I said. "What are the odds that someone would go to all that trouble? Southern hospitality has its limits, you know. Let's leave the thing with the hazards on, and walk it."

I pulled off to the side of the road, well into the grass—but not so far that we'd have trouble pulling out again. I turned on the hazard lights, and we climbed out.

"We should split up," Dana suggested.

Benny looked at her like she'd just suggested we go skinny dipping. "Are you serious? Have you ever seen a horror movie in your life?"

"Benny—" I tried to head him off.

"I mean, we're about to go hunting down one of the most famous and fearsome paranormal entities south of the Mason-Dixon, and you think we should split up? That's crazy talk!"

"No, sweetheart," she corrected him. "That's fantasy, and *this* is three people who have a lot of territory to cover before it gets dark. We're on the lookout for an entity that has never displayed any violence towards anyone so far as we know, and the clock is ticking."

"Don't care. I'm staying with… with one of you, at least."

"Then you're staying with Eden."

"That's fine, because *I'm* staying with *her*." I indicated Dana with my head.

She threw her hands up and rolled her eyes. "Oh, for God's sake. What's wrong with you two? We've only got an hour, or two hours tops before it gets dark. What good exactly do you think it would do to stay with me, anyway?"

"You're the professional here," Benny said, reaching into my trunk and lifting out a satchel filled with equipment. "And you're going to need a caddie for all this shit, aren't you?"

"We aren't bringing all of it. Just some of it. Here—hand me that one there. The black one with the Velcro and the zippers."

"This one?"

"The one that looks like the Bat-belt on a strap?"

She stepped past me and lifted the latch. "Very funny. Very fucking funny. Open the doors again. I'll need that one."

"What is it?" I wondered.

"A high-resolution digital video recorder. It's got a night-shot mode for low light, which we might want here before long. And the other bag, the one beside it there, yeah—that one."

"What's this one?" Benny asked as he handed it to her.

"Um… let's call it a multimeter, and I won't bother to explain all the bells and whistles. It was custom-ordered from a Japanese company."

Benny again looked astounded. "Not the one that makes cheesy 'ghost detectors,' is it? Oh, *please* tell me those don't really work."

"No, they don't work. They're useless. This isn't one of those. This is a custom engineering device. The base unit is designed to detect electrical leaks and assorted magnetic fields in commercial and residential properties. It is very, *very* sensitive. So sensitive that I have to calibrate it to account for my body's own fields before I can use it. Sometimes it's easier to set it down and walk away than carry it around. It's also expensive. Be careful with it, would you?"

"Yes ma'am."

"Good boy. Give it here."

He handed it over and reached for the last large bag in the trunk. "Do we need anything else?"

She thought about it, and weighed what she was already holding. "No, probably not. Leave it for now—unless there's anything in there that either one of you wants to take."

The sentence hadn't left her mouth before Benny had opened up the bag and started rummaging. In the end, he found a great number of toys that he didn't know what to do with, but opted to go with his standby of a flashlight and a tape recorder.

I'd already nabbed my mini metal flashlight from my glove

320

box, and I couldn't see needing anything else. I wasn't looking to record Old Green Eyes, just track him down and chase him back to the battlefield. And I didn't think weapons would do me any good, aside from a small knife that I kept in my boot in case of an accidental and incapacitating tangle in tree roots, rope, or anything comparable. In case of monsters, I might be in trouble, but I tried not to look at it that way. Old Green Eyes hadn't made any threatening moves towards me during our first meeting, and unless he had some aggressive reaction to being talked to, I ought to be quite safe.

Dana obviously operated that way too: I didn't see anything remotely violence-capable in her luggage, except possibly a set of small screwdrivers, if the wielder really used her imagination. Satisfied that my companions also meant only to find and not to catch him, I pushed my little flashlight into my back jeans pocket and asked if they were ready to begin.

They were.

As a compromise between splitting up and sticking together, we opted to stay together at least at first; and if we had no luck within thirty minutes, we'd spread out. So, leaving the car with the hazard lights blinking, we set off along the road onto the peninsula of Moccasin Bend.

We stuck to the paved strip at first, because the way onto the main body is narrow and we didn't have much choice. But then we were out in the open. Above us, the sky was a darkening blue, and only a few clouds fluttered past the sun for shade. Around us were strips of open grass that terminated sharply into the tree line.

"We can't hang out here, where everyone can see us. You can bet Green Eyes isn't," Dana said. "Where did you see him last,

Eden? Take us to where you ran into him. We can start there."

"Sure. If I can find it."

"How hard could it be?" Benny asked, keeping pace with us even as he lugged the bulk of the baggage.

"I don't know. Let's see—it was the middle of the night, there weren't any lights, and I was distracted and shaken from my recent automobile accident. What do I look like to you, a homing pigeon?"

I led them at a diagonal angle, across the street and towards the far side of the woods. Wherever the wreck had taken place, I knew that it was, at least, on that side of the road. Our feet made simultaneous swishes in the grass, kicking up rocks and sticks as we went. None of us were being too quiet—partly because we didn't need to, and partly because there was no one to hear us anyway. Though the occasional car passed us on the way out to the hospital, we could hardly see the facilities off in the distance, and there were no other hikers or explorers that we saw.

Long tree shadows stretched themselves out, reaching for us with the coming darkness. Lookout Mountain cast its pall over our group as well, since we were sitting at its foot.

"Technically, we have another hour at least before sunset," Dana observed, but her analysis didn't prevent the Bend from being a prematurely gloomy place.

"Technically," Benny offered a weak agreement. "But with the mountains and ridges, when the sun falls behind them, it's, you know, darker than you expect."

"Don't worry about it. We can see to keep going, can't we?" I asked.

Neither of them replied.

We stayed together past the prearranged thirty minutes,

322

though. Once the light really started to leave us, no one wanted to go at it alone.

We didn't talk much. I guess we were all working on exactly what we were going to say if we found him. I wondered how much it mattered, except insomuch as we were distracting Dana by giving her something to do.

How would we begin a conversation with something so inhuman? After all, the prospect of company may not have been necessarily welcome to him, but I had to assume it didn't intimidate him much either. I'd run into Green Eyes after a very loud wreck and a lot of swearing; on that occasion I would've been easy to avoid, but he didn't bother.

I don't know what thoughts kept my companions silent, but I could safely bet that Dana's impression of the place wasn't terribly different from mine. She might have been preoccupied with her grief, but no one with an ounce of psychic sensitivity could fail to notice the oppressive feel that weighed down on us.

It wasn't like the battlefield, with its benignly frustrated ghosts. It wasn't like the old Pine Breeze location either, where the bashful dead were nebulous, and distant.

"You feel it too?" I ventured, even though I didn't need to.

Dana nodded.

"What?" Benny asked.

"Malice. Confusion," she answered.

"Not malice exactly, I don't think. More like aggression. Anger without a focus." If I had the words, I would've argued further. Sometimes I think that there are things people deliberately fail to name, as if refusing to label them can make them any less real. "There's sadness, too," I concluded.

"Sure," Dana said, but she didn't look at me, and I couldn't tell if she was agreeing with me or just being nice.

"I don't feel anything, except sticky. This sucks. I want to be psychic."

"No you don't," Dana and I said in perfect time. My amazing psychic powers told me he didn't believe us.

"Your car," Dana said abruptly. "I saw it was damaged. You did that here?"

"I did that here."

"Against a tree?"

"Against a tree."

"So if we find a tree that looks like it had a high-velocity date with your fender, we're in the ballpark, right?"

"Sounds good to me. Sure, yeah. That'd be a good starting point."

"It's getting dark," Benny whined.

I nudged him with my shoulder and started keeping my eyes on the tree line. "It's been *getting* dark for an hour, but it's not dark yet. It's just the mountain's shadow, and the trees. It's fine."

"I wouldn't call it 'fine,' but it'll do for now. Get the lights handy, though. We're going to need them soon. Weren't we going to split up?"

It was Benny's turn to join my chorus. "No."

Mine was as ready as it was going to get, there in my back pocket; Benny took her suggestion, though, and fished his flashlight free of the bag he carried.

"Eden, is that your tree?" Dana pointed at a likely candidate a few yards ahead.

I squinted at it, and tried to picture everything as it had happened. "No, I don't think so. It's farther down. I was closer to the hospital than this when I hit. I remember because I was looking for—" And at that moment I realized that I'd not told Benny the whole truth, and I wasn't sure I was interested in laying it all out now. I wrapped it up short. "It's a long story."

"You wrecked out here? I know you said you went out this way, but I thought you said it was a skunk you almost hit?"

"That's correct. Incomplete, but correct. Look, I'll fill you in later. I didn't want Dave and Lu to worry, so I told them it happened on the mountain. That's the version you heard, right?"

"Right. And now I feel all left out."

"Don't," I assured him. "It was complicated and weird. I didn't tell *anyone*, so don't get pouty on me."

Up ahead, I spotted a more suitable candidate for the tree-victim, and I called their attention to it. "Maybe there. That looks about right; I think I see something on the ground, too. That must be it."

As one, we broke into a jog until we reached the spot where the tree had been violently skinned right around fender level. Benny confirmed the site by holding up a red plastic piece of my blinker light.

"Okay. Now where did you go from here?"

"I went… this way, through the trees. I didn't have a crowbar or a tire iron or anything, so I went looking for a good stiff branch to pry the car's wheel-well away from the tire. It was bent in sharp—I was afraid it was going to blow the tire if I tried to drive it away like that."

"Right. Lead the way." She prompted me forward, and I reluctantly led.

"I went along like this," I narrated as I went. I didn't want to stop talking, or the eerie, harsh atmosphere would get too good a foothold. "It was dark though, pitch dark, and my light was—no, I didn't have a light." I'd left it with Malachi, so I could find my way back to him.

"Don't you always keep that little one right there in your car?" Benny asked, and I wanted to kick him in the shin for being so observant.

"The batteries were dead. I left it. Anyway, I followed the sound of the river. Listen. You can hear the river from here, but you've got to be quiet." I quit talking then. My companions didn't.

"Are we that close to the water? I don't hear anything," Benny said.

Dana frowned. "Me either."

I closed my eyes. "Right. Okay, no. That's why. I've got it now—I didn't hear the river. I *thought* I was hearing the river. But I wasn't. It was *him*."

"He sounds like the river?"

"When he was near, I heard a funny noise. Or, I didn't hear it, I… felt it in my ears. It's hard to explain. Like radio static or electricity, but not quite. You'll know it if you run into it. You may not know what it is at first, but you'll figure it out."

The humidity pulled close around us, and I wiped my forehead with the back of my hand. Again I felt the pull of something negative and restless. Every time I wasn't specifically concentrating on something else, like talking, the creeping grudge closed in.

Dana didn't comment on it, and I knew she must have been aware of it; so maybe she wanted it near. Maybe, in her grief, she enjoyed its almost fierce unhappiness.

Benny was blissfully oblivious, or if he wasn't, he had me fooled.

"Just keep your ears open," I told them both. "Listen for it.

You'll hear it in your head, and in the pit of your stomach. It's not bad, but it's strange."

I thought of Kitty, less than a mile away and locked in her clean white room. She might be able to tell us something more specific, or then again, she might not; if the Hairy Man hadn't been underneath her windowsill recently, she probably wouldn't have much to tell us. I wondered how she was doing. I wondered if she was okay.

I looked over at Dana, and directed my attention to her instead. "I know he hangs around the hospital sometimes," I said.

"How do you know that?" Dana asked, and, as was becoming a habit, I fudged the answer rather than give away my brother's involvement.

"I know some people who work there. He's been spotted by patients on the first floor—not that anyone believes them. Inmates in an asylum don't have reams of credibility, I'm afraid." *Not as much as television personalities,* I thought. I didn't say it, though.

"Are you sure they're talking about the same guy?"

"Pretty sure, yes. What are the odds that they're not? How many hair-covered paranormal beasts can a few acres hold, anyway?"

She scowled, pulling her eyebrows close together until there was a sharp vertical wrinkle above her nose. "I ask, because the way you talked about him he was interesting, strange, and possibly confused; and that's not what I'm getting here. This whole area feels... it feels..."

"Mean," I answered for her. It wasn't exactly what I meant, but the words at my disposal were limited and inadequate. "Whatever's here, it doesn't like us. It doesn't want us here. But I think that this is something different from Green Eyes. I think it was that way before he came here."

"What? What are you guys talking about?" Benny wanted to know. I didn't blame him, but I couldn't make him understand, either.

Dana stopped, and we stopped with her, turning to face her. "It's kind of like…" she began, hesitated, and started again. "It feels like a child, or an animal that's been hurt by someone—but it's not sure who, or why. And it doesn't know what to do about it. But it wants restitution all the same. And I'm sorry, kid, but that's the best I can do."

"Nice. Your best is better than mine," I congratulated her. "Good call."

"Thanks."

Inertia kept us in place, and something more primal kept us close together. Even if Benny couldn't consciously detect the malaise that hunkered over the Bend, some subconscious demand for self-preservation smelled it all the same and didn't like it.

You didn't have to have any special abilities to pick it up, anyway. The danger was in the way the birds never sang, and the way there was no wind coming off the wide band of water that surrounds the place. It was there in the absence of everything else—in the failure of small animals to scuttle, and in the stiffness of the trees.

There's a special fear that God, or evolution, or Mother Nature builds into slow, fleshy, unclawed bipeds. It's a hypersensitivity to ambience, and it keeps us alive, even when we don't know it when we feel it.

Benny was feeling it hardcore. I could see it by the way he hung close between Dana and me, where at the beginning of the quest he was our intrepid leader. His eyes were dilated wide like a nervous cat's.

He was sweating, too, but we were all sweating, even though the lateness of the hour meant a slight and blessed cooling. "Spring has sprung, fall has fell, summer's here, it's hot as hell," as the naughty fourth-grade jump-rope rhyme goes. July means sauna, and it probably wouldn't drop below eighty degrees before nine o'clock. Some people never get used to it. Others never get used to anything else.

We pushed our way through the unyielding trees and between them. Beneath the canopy it was almost too dark to see, but it was that funny sort of mid-light that a flashlight doesn't help much.

Benny turned his on anyway. I waited.

Dana tugged at the satchel on Benny's arm and pulled out the multimeter.

"Do you hear something?"

"I can't tell," she replied. "Maybe, I'd be more confident if I could see something, though. Give me a minute."

The device she held was about the size of a paperback novel, with a screen and a whole lot of buttons. She slid her thumb around the side and pressed a power switch, made some adjustments, and ordered us both behind her. "You two. Over here. And hold very, very still."

I'd never seen anything like it. "You're not suggesting we could affect the—"

"That's exactly what I'm suggesting. This isn't a toy. Shit."

"What?"

"I can't hold it steady enough; it's reading funny."

"I'll hold it," Benny offered.

"No, that's okay. There's a rock there big enough to hold it. I'm going to set it down. We'll get a better read that way anyhow." She set a dial the way she wanted it and carefully set the meter down on the rock. If my sense of direction served me, she aimed it at the river.

She stepped away, backwards, towards us. She held her arms out as if she were holding us back or telling us to wait for something; and when the lighted LCD on the meter began to flicker with data, she twitched her wrists as if she were conducting the information with a baton.

"Yes," she breathed. "Yes, yes, yes. Pick it up. Where is it?"

"Where's what?" Benny wanted to know, but even as he asked the question I was just beginning to hear it myself.

Oh so faint. Oh so light. Barely within my range of hearing. There it was.

"Listen, Benny," I said, my voice roughly as quiet as Dana's. "Close your eyes and listen. Do you hear the river now?"

He did as I told him. "Yes? I think I hear it. The river—it's a rushing, a quiet hissing. Is that what that sound is, the river?"

"No," I murmured. "It's not."

Dana raised one arm and pointed at the meter, which flickered with numbers that were meaningless to me.

"What does it say?" I asked. "Is it getting closer?"

"No," she said.

"Where is he?" Benny raised the more direct question.

"I don't know. But if he's the thing making that sound, he's stranger than anything I've ever met."

Strange. That's what everyone who'd seen him said. Of course, most people claimed he was evil, too, but I didn't buy it. I was willing to buy strange, but the dismal pall that the Bend played host to was not of Green Eyes's making. I wondered what it was, though.

I'd heard people talk about the way it felt to stand at the Bend, and the sense of wrongness the place held. An old friend of mine who'd done an internship there while she was getting her psych degree had said it felt like something was unfinished, and that the Bend had become impatient, and frustrated. I hadn't known what she meant before. Not when I'd been out there with Malachi the first time; and the second time, when I'd gone to see Kitty, it had not been so strong. "It's growing," I said, not about the signal the meter registered, but to conclude my thoughts.

Benny was getting nervous, much more nervous now. "What is?"

"Hush," I said.

"Green Eyes?"

"No. The rest of it. It knows him."

"Now you're just talking crazy talk," he said, trying to infuse the words with some levity. It came out strained instead.

"Look at the meter." Dana moved close to it again, and stared down at it without touching it. "This is wild."

"We can see it fine, but we don't know what it means," I said, for Benny and myself. "What do those numbers mean?"

"They mean energy. Lots of it. Electrical energy, to be more precise. We're not too close to its source yet, but it's moving around. It's moving, but not coming for us or anything. It's like watching a tiger pacing, if that tiger were made of liquid. My God, what *is* this thing?"

"A guardian." Another word popped into my head, inserted by my subconscious or by some instinct I didn't recognize. I said it out loud. "A sentry."

"Eden? Eden, what did you just say? Benny, darling, move your flashlight. Don't shine it right on the meter, I can't see what it says when you do that."

"Sorry."

"Eden, what you just said. Say it again."

I obeyed, because I knew that it meant something important. I said it louder, with a touch more volume than a normal speaking voice. "He's a sentry. And he heard me, didn't he?"

"You've definitely got his attention."

"What?" Benny was beyond more complex questions, which was fine, because I had no complex answers for him, and neither did Dana.

"It stopped moving," she said. "For a few seconds."

"*He* stopped moving for a few seconds. And now he's coming towards us, isn't he?"

"Something is. Or someone, if you like it better that way."

She didn't need to say it. We could all sense it by the way the static hummed harder in our ears. It came before him, like a force around him, pouring itself through the trunks and along the winding riverbank. We could feel him. Even Benny could feel him coming for us.

"Sentry." I used the word because it drew him. When I said it, the static swelled, a pulse or a wave answering me.

"Eden," Dana said, but whether she was warning me or asking what I was doing, I couldn't tell.

The last rays of daylight slid behind the mountain, and we passed the point of almost dark. Benny and Dana held their lights aloft, and they beamed them left and right, trying to pin down the source of the sound. I left mine in my pocket still. I think I forgot about it. I think I didn't care.

I am coming.

He spoke, and we heard the words before we saw him. They had a timbre not terribly different from the EVP we collected.

It wasn't terribly like the EVP either, but there was so little to compare it to that nothing else was even close.

I am coming.

"He's coming," Benny said, and it was the closest thing to a sob I'd ever heard him make.

Dana kept the coolest head; she snared her camcorder and slid her right hand under the strap to hold it anchored against her palm. "Shit," she grumbled. "Shit," she said again, because it refused to switch on. "He's doing this. For God's sake, turn *on*," she ordered, but it failed her.

And he came to us, as promised. Through the trees, and into our personal space he oozed, or glided, or manifested. We hadn't made it to a clearing, or to any kind of open space at all. We were surrounded on all sides by the trunks, and by this brilliant-eyed creature who towered over us all.

"Hello," I whispered.

Up close, he was even more remarkable than I remembered. He must have been nearly eight feet tall, and even with this estimate I got the impression he was crouching slightly to better meet our level. His shoulders were drawn in, and his hands hung long at his sides. The things at the tips of his fingers were not claws, exactly; but they were long nails, and they were yellowed and dirty, a filthy amber. He could've stood up straight and still scratched his knees with those thick, long-nailed fingers. A dense curtain of brownish hair fell vertically over his apelike arms; the ends trailed down around his hips.

When first I'd seen him, I hadn't gotten close enough to catch his face, or I hadn't seen it clearly beyond the tart-bright eyes. But here he stood and he stared down at me, as if he were awaiting some order—because I was the one who had said his name.

The face that gazed from such a height was a construct of fantasy nightmares.

Beneath the famously gleaming eyes, a flattened nose with wide nostrils hunched. He had no upper lip to speak of, but a wide mouth all the same; and from each corner two huge, bony fangs curled up from his heavy lower jaw to protrude and crease his cheeks.

"Whoa." From the corner of my eye I saw Benny, his own smaller jaw hanging open. Dana did not speak, but I saw her hand moving slowly in her pocket. When she pulled her hand out again, it held the tape recorder.

"Sentry," I addressed him, because it was a sound he recognized and claimed.

He nodded, and like every other gesture of his, the movement looked massive.

I am here.

"Thank you. Thank you for coming. We hoped…" I looked over at my friends, and they were staring too hard to speak. "We wanted to talk to you."

His mouth—that fearsome straight line punctuated with teeth at either end—moved and constricted, as if he meant to smile or grimace, but lacked the facial muscles for either. I couldn't tell if he was glad or if he found us annoying.

"Please," I said, since talking kept him at a polite distance. "Are you the Sentry of the battlefield—the one that's south of here?"

His enormous, hair-draped head dipped again, but he offered no further information on the matter.

Introductions seemed in order, so I offered them. "I'm Eden. This is Ben, and Dana. Is there, um, some name you prefer? I don't know what to call you except by that title."

Sentry.

"Okay. Sentry it is."

He didn't move when he spoke, though his mouth made the appearance of writhing slightly. Whatever sound his words made they did not come from his wall-like chest. My eyes were beginning to water; from pure distraction, I'd forgotten to blink.

I seemed to be face-level with his chest, but as dense as he appeared, there was a sense of fluidity about him too. It confused me and preoccupied me, the way a being so seemingly solid could also look ready to evaporate at a moment's notice.

Maybe I waited too long to speak. He turned his attention to Dana and Benny, who still stood all-but-petrified beside me.

It is a name your people gave me.

He looked back at me and I understood. "The settlers? The white people?"

The old warriors, he corrected me.

That one took me a second. "The generals. There were two of them, Boynton and Van Derveer. That's what they called you, a sentry?"

Yes. I guard them.

"The dead?"

He turned away then, and I thought at first that I'd offended him somehow. His shifting looked like a ship changing course—slow, and ponderous.

I left them.

"We know. They said the pact was up. You had a pact with the two old generals." He nodded, though his back was facing me now, so I only saw his shoulders bob. "You only had to stay until the last child of the generals was gone. And now there's a boy who's missing."

Dead.

Benny found his voice. "I knew it."

Killed not in war. Not to be eaten.

"We call it murder these days," Dana chimed in. "Do you know where he is? Do you know who did it?"

I could answer the first question, and I did. "He's buried in Dyer's field, isn't he? Back behind the house there. That's what the ghosts have been trying to tell us."

Yes. Ghosts? He faced me again, or rather he loomed above me once more. I saw something like eagerness in that inhuman visage.

"The dead. They've awakened. They walk the fields, trying to communicate. They said you were gone. They told us you left them. And they tried to tell us about the body someone buried in Dyer's field."

Bodies.

"Bodies?"

Two men. Both killed. Same man dug the hole for them both. He paused. *The dead. They walk?*

"They walk," I confirmed, but I tried to steer him back to his first point. "You said there were two? We only know about the one—the Boynton boy. There was another, too?"

Yes. One more. The dead should sleep. I have failed them.

"They're okay," I said, because surely it was more or less true. "They're okay. They're just worried. They want to know where you are, and what happened to you. They don't understand."

They understood well enough to tell us about the pact, but I figured that knowing why and understanding why weren't the same thing. "I know you fulfilled your agreement," I told him. "I know you were doing what you thought was right. No one is angry with you. But they sure would love it if you'd come back."

I stayed. I honored the agreement. The last one died, and I can leave.

Benny broached the next question softly. "But you can stay if you want, too. Can't you?"

The Sentry didn't answer. Maybe it simply hadn't occurred to him. I didn't know why it wouldn't, but there was much about this creature I did not comprehend. "Was there anything in the… in the agreement you made—was there anything that said you had to leave?"

Those lizard-hued orbs narrowed, and glanced away from me, as if he was thinking. I felt an almost tangible pressure lift when his gaze was removed.

A sentry follows orders.

"Is that what they told you? Is that why they gave you this name?" I asked, and then I did the dumbest thing I'd ever done in my life. I took a step towards him, even though every instinct in my body told me not to. Every primal nerve ending screamed at me to stay away, but something more modern made me press on. I didn't touch him; I couldn't offer him a gesture that human. But I inserted myself beneath his averted gaze.

"You know," I continued, barely able to breathe for how intimidated I was, "sentries—the soldiers they named you for— they don't follow orders forever. They sign a contract, an agreement like yours, and then when the contract is up, they choose their paths for themselves. They can go away if they like. Or…"

Or they can stay?

"Or they can stay. They can do whatever they want. What do you want to do?"

He met my eyes, and again I felt the weight of his stare. It pressed down into me, pushing on my face as if to warn me away from something more dangerous than I had ever touched before.

I want… he began, though the assertion sounded strange. He seemed to find it strange too. He was not accustomed to the freedom to want.

I want orders to follow.

Dana was most surprised, I think. "What?" she said, or almost demanded. "What? He wants *what*? That doesn't make sense."

"Who cares?" I argued. "I want a car that flies, and that doesn't make sense either. He wants what he wants."

"He wants a purpose." Benny called it. I was suddenly proud of him, almost beyond speaking. He nailed it, with four words— what I'd been thinking my way around with hundreds.

I was summoned. Now those who gave the tasks are gone. And I do not know where I came from. I cannot return.

It was the longest he'd ever spoken, as if the need to explain himself called for more sentences than merely answering questions.

"You don't know where you came from, but do you know who summoned you first?" I asked.

He thought about it hard, turning and walking a pace or two, then returning his attention to me. His legs folded beneath him, sitting his immense bulk squarely in front of me, and putting us nearly on eye level. I still looked up at the underside of his chin.

I sat down too, crossing my legs.

A holy woman. I helped her people win a great war.

"When?" Dana asked. "It must have been a long time ago."

He didn't seem to know, but after considering the query he tried to answer it.

There were more trees then. And no people with yellow hair. As

338

he said this, he gave Dana a glimpse. *This was before they came. A long time before. Many, many seasons.*

With a swiftness that surprised me, I felt very, very sorry for him. I wondered if he wasn't projecting his sorrow to me, augmenting his attempts to communicate.

"But those people are gone now. They've been gone for hundreds of years. And after they were gone, there was another great war."

The light-haired men fought there. Many of them died. But they were not honored. The dead were left for the animals, and the black birds came to feed on their eyes.

The dead did not understand. They had no wings, and they stayed behind. They did not fly, and they did not sleep. Then the old men came, and they asked me to watch. I told them I would watch, until their last heir had passed. I would harm not the living, and I would tend the dead.

"And you did. For over a hundred years, you watched them well. I know your bargain is over," I said, "but there's no reason for you to leave if you don't want to. You are welcome there. You have a home there."

"You're missed there," Benny added. "They need you." I thought maybe he wanted to say more, but he bit it back, whatever it was.

Dana put her camcorder and her tape recorder down on the ground, and came to stand behind me. She was a small woman, even when she stood above me. I was acutely aware of her size, and her vulnerability, and… her grief. Even though I couldn't see her, she was larger than life, and unnaturally complete.

I saw her from all sides.

And I saw Benny too, my old acquaintance and newer friend

who once rolled on a battered skateboard through parts of town that have since been paved and refurbished into blandness. I was proud of him for holding his ground and not running, when other, saner people might have made for the hills. I was deeply glad that I had a friend like this, one who did not know, but who believed enough to trust.

I couldn't explain the experience, the peculiar opening of my mind or tapping of my senses. But all three of them there with me—I felt like I knew them all and knew them thoroughly.

It overwhelmed me, and I couldn't think of anything else to say, or to ask. I didn't think I could remember how to stand.

Dana leaned down to murmur in my ear. "Stay with me, kid. You're opening too far. You're not used to this. Get a grip on it. Hold it down, or it'll sweep you away."

Then she returned her attention to the beast seated before us. "Come home. You are tied to that land, not to this place. This is a place that was lost years ago. It will drive you mad if you stay here. It will break your heart. Go back to those who need you. They are lost without you. They are being dishonored without you."

The man with the spade. The man who killed the last heir.

"Yes." I gathered my wits enough to spit out the answer. I felt Dana's hand on my shoulder, and it was strong. "He's looking for something on the fields. He won't quit until he finds it. He'll tear up the hills and run his shovel through the remains of the dead until he's stopped. Will you let him do this?"

I should not.

"Will you stop him?"

Can I?

"You can," I assured him. "You can. Please—please go help them."

340

"We tried," Benny said.

"We failed," Dana added. "We've added another dead to your number. This is what it's come to without you."

The last heir is dead. There is no more contract.

He said it slowly, turning the words over in his head or in his mouth.

A light went on in my own head, and the words that rattled there came tumbling out. "Then there are no rules anymore. You don't have to stay, and you don't have to abide by anyone's terms but your own. Don't you want to hurt the man who treated your"—I used his word, then—"your *children* with such disrespect?"

"Eden," Dana said, and this time it was definitely a warning.

I did want to hurt him. But I could not.

"Because of the pact. But now there's no pact. And there's nothing to stop you from going after him."

"Eden!"

I could hurt him if I wanted.

"You sure could. And maybe you should. He's hurting people, Sentry. He's killing people because he wants something and he'll do anything to get it. We tried to stop him, but we couldn't. We weren't strong enough."

I could hurt him.

He sounded far away now. I liked it. He was thinking.

"Nothing's stopping you. You can protect them. You can help them. You can stop the man who's doing this. Please—they need you. *We* need you. Will you go back to Chickamauga? Will you go and take care of them?"

I... I do not know. Do you command me?

"No."

But you are like the holy woman who first called me. You see with the same eyes. You could command me. There is no one else to do so.

"No. You're missing the point. Command your own damn self for once."

He rose to his feet then, in a movement that was shockingly fast for a monster so large. His hair sprawled and waved like a hula skirt, settling over his shoulders and grazing his belly.

And without a word, he vanished.

SEVENTEEN

INVITED

"I think that went pretty well," I said. I was lying on my back where I'd dropped to the ground in the dark, in the woods, at the Bend. Dana and Benny were standing over me, shining flashlights down on me in such a fashion that there was no way I could see either of them.

"You're an idiot," Dana told me, and it made me smile.

"Thanks."

"You really don't get it, do you? You turned him loose, Eden. You told him to do his own thing, and his own thing may well involve killing people. How do you feel about that?"

I winced against the light she now directed straight into my eyes. "If by 'people' you mean 'that guy who shot your husband' what, forty-eight hours ago now? Then I've got to say I feel pretty good about it. Why don't *you*?"

"Because there's a bigger picture at stake here, dumbass. Say he decides—and we still don't know what he's decided, by the way—that he's going to go back to the battlefield and keep watch.

But now he's not bound by any of his prior restrictions. Now he's a homicidal maniac the size of an oak tree, and it's not like he's a vampire and we can just chuck a vial of holy water at him."

"I bet that wouldn't work," Benny said.

"I'm going to write this off to hyperbole," I grumbled, pulling myself back up to a sitting position.

"You're crazy. You are fucking crazy!"

"He's not an animal!" I yelled back at her. "He's not an animal, and he's not a homicidal maniac! He's… he's lost. And he's looking for meaning. People in a philosophical crisis do not go on killing sprees, Dana."

"He's not *people,* honey. You were sitting pretty close to him; I would've thought you'd figured that out. He isn't 'people,' and he's operating right now with no moral compass. He's angry, he's scared, and he wants revenge."

"What about you?" Benny asked her before I could. "Aren't you angry? Aren't you scared? Don't you want—"

"I want justice! It's not the same thing."

"Since when?"

"I am *not* having this conversation." She cut us both off. She threw her hands to her face and squeezed, massaging her temples and rubbing her eyes. "Fine. I'm angry. Is that what you want to hear?"

"It's a start," I said, prying my flashlight out of my back pocket and turning it on.

"Okay, I'm angry, and I'm scared. I'm so angry, and I'm so scared, that I can hardly stand to stand here right now without killing the pair of you with my bare hands from pure rage and horror and grief and a thousand other things that neither of you can relate to!"

Contrite, we both held our tongues.

"You can't! I know you can't!"

I thought she was about to cry, but she held it together enough to continue screaming at us—and she *was* screaming. I knew we were far away from the hospital yet, but I couldn't help but wonder if anyone heard her.

"Tripp is dead—he's dead, and he's not coming back—and that means that my life is going to change a lot, and I'm *horrified* by it. I can't imagine where it's going to go from here—I can't imagine doing our work, or living in our house, or feeding our cats, because everything is ours. Not mine, *ours*. Only now it's *not* anymore. It's mine."

She must have heard herself, and what an explosion the outburst had sounded like, because she lowered her voice—even though it meant she had a harder time controlling it. "I don't want everything to be mine. I liked it when everything was *ours*. And that's *my* problem—not anyone else's. But this? What you're pulling here? You could be making a very big problem for a lot of other people. You are turning something loose that you can't control—that no one can control. And you think that's not a problem?"

"It has the potential to be a problem," I admitted, using my best calm-the-hell-down voice. "But right now, it also has the potential to be a very good thing—don't you see?"

"He can fix this," Benny said.

"So *you* think."

"So I think, too." I put an arm out to her, and at first I think she was afraid I was going to hug her, because she recoiled out of reach. I was only trying to steer her out of the woods, but I withdrew the gesture anyway.

"Think of it. He can flush out your husband's murderer. He can put all the ghosts back to bed. You're a scientist, aren't you? You could study him. Interview him. This thing—this creature— he could answer questions that could make your career, or enrich your philosophy."

"He's been given permission to destroy."

"He's been given permission to *live*."

Just then my phone began to buzz heartily against my hip bone. I popped it off its plastic clip and pressed a light on the side, revealing my caller's number. I didn't recognize the digits. "Let's start walking back to the road, while I see who this is."

I flipped the lid and held it up to my face, assuming the rear of our short train as we began to push our way back towards open ground.

"Hello?"

"There you are. Don't you ever answer this thing?"

I held the phone away from my face and glanced at the display. This was his third attempt. I'd never noticed the first two.

"Sorry. We've been busy over here. How's the date going?"

"It went fine. She's here now. Say 'hi,' Becca."

In the background, someone gave me a disinterested "hi."

"Yeah. Um. Why are you calling me? Where are you?"

"I'm at the battlefield."

"What? Why? Why did you take your date to the battlefield, you creep?"

He laughed. "Because it was profitable."

"Oh, *do* explain." Ahead of me, Benny pushed aside a tree branch and it snapped back into my face. I caught it on my wrist and pushed ahead, following the bobbing lights. "It's Jamie," I told them.

346

"I'd gathered," Benny said, not looking back. "Watch out for this one. Is this the way we came?"

"I think so. Got it, thanks. We should be almost back to the road."

"Where are you?"

"We're at the Bend still. Why did you take your date to the battlefield?"

"Because I'm being paid to. We went to Tony's for supper—"

"Ooh, good pick," I interrupted.

"I thought so, yeah. Anyway, we were there and this guy sneaks up behind me. It's that reporter—the one who was looking for us yesterday. He offered me fifty bucks if I'd come out to the battlefield and let him interview me for an exclusive. This is his phone, by the way, in case you were wondering about the number."

"I was, thanks. So you agreed to go back out there for fifty bucks? What are you, crazy?"

"No. I held out for three hundred."

"Three hundred?"

"He was paying out of his own pocket, man. That was all he had in his wallet after paying for supper."

"Good of you to leave him that much."

"I do what I can."

A creeping discomfort worked its way into my head as I dodged a stump and ducked another leafy branch. "Jamie, I don't think you should be there. I've got a bad feeling about it."

"We're not—" He stopped, and it sounded like he was answering a question asked by someone else. "We're not anywhere close to where we were, the other night. We're not out by the house or anything. We're over by the Tower again. There's a news SUV here, and a cameraman, and that Nate guy."

"Nick, wasn't it?"

"Nick, that's right."

Somewhere on his end, I heard a faint retort: "You can call me whatever you want as long as you smile for the camera."

"I remember him," I said. "But look, can't you do this anywhere else? The front of the park, in front of the sign? At the visitors' center? Someplace else?"

"He said that the station has a strict on-site policy."

"The visitors' center *is* on-site."

"The visitors' center isn't as *cool,* though. He wanted to get as close to the scene of the murder as possible."

"And he let you stop at the Tower?"

"Yes. I'm sitting on one of the benches right now."

He was lying. I *knew* he was lying. "You're not lying to me, are you?"

"No. Why would I?"

Because he needed the money, and three hundred dollars would probably cover the repairs his car so desperately needed, though he was too proud to admit it; or it would cover his rent and maybe the water bill too. He might go to greater lengths than he'd say—lengths that would get him bitched at by me.

"Shit, Jamie. You'd better not be lying."

Benny craned his neck around. "What's he doing?"

"He's on the battlefield," I answered. "Lying."

"Why?"

"Long story. Jamie, get out of there. Bad things are afoot. Please? Do me a favor here. Tell him you've got to piss or something, and you need to go to the visitors' center."

"I'm in the woods, darling. Pissing requires no plumbing."

"So you're *not* at the Tower? The woods aren't that close to the Tower, Jamie, you jackass. Leave. Get out. Now."

"No. What? What is it?" After the first word, he wasn't talking to me. It was someone else, Nick or Becca.

"I don't like it, Jamie. Look, would you do me a favor?"

"What?"

"Would you wait? Give us thirty minutes, and we'll be out there."

"What?" Dana had heard me, and was objecting. She'd just burst free of the woods and was stepping across the trimmed grass.

"The battlefield," I told her. "Jamie's out there."

"He's *where*?"

"The battlefield. Jamie, get out of there. Big things are coming your way."

"Big things?"

"Big things with glowing green eyes. At least I hope so."

I was distracted by the woods, but Dana pulled me out as she said, "Oh, great. Green Eyes isn't dangerous, but you're going to warn your friends about him. *You're* all consistent."

"Dana," I started to scold her, then returned to Jamie instead. "Jamie, what's going on out there?"

"Nothing, why?" But behind him, I heard commotion. Not violent commotion; it wasn't loud commotion, even. Just... commotion. And a popping noise that made my stomach turn.

Maybe he dropped the phone, or maybe he was holding it against his chest for a second. "I've got to go," he said abruptly. "I've got to go. Did you say you were coming out here?"

I stopped in my tracks. "We're on our way. Jamie? Jamie?"

I stepped into open air, with no trees above me. It was invigorating—like a blanket had been lifted off my head.

"What's he doing?" Benny asked, curious and a touch concerned.

"God knows. He hung up on me."

"On purpose? Or did your phone just drop the call?"

"I don't know."

We stood together, there beside the road, aiming flashlights at each other's chests.

"We've got to get out of here, don't we? We've got to get to the battlefield."

I nodded. "I think so, yeah. Something's going on there. Something's… "

"Something's gone to shit," Dana finished it. "Jesus, they never learn, do they?"

We started running.

The woods began to sing around us, croaking and chirping and thrashing with all the small things that had held silent while we were in the forest. Once free of the trees we sprinted, and it felt like they were cheering us on.

The car was farther away than I'd remembered. It was farther than I could easily dash in one headlong charge; but Dana and Benny either kept up or outpaced me, so I didn't slow down.

No one passed us. No cars came from either direction.

For some reason, this added a sense of urgency to it all—like we were the only people in the world, and in the dark, and the ridges and the river were conspiring against us. The rocky shape of Lookout Mountain loomed above us, stretching itself to cloak us in its shadow. It's a place covered with rock gardens, and tourist traps, and gift shops. Never before had I felt that it was ominous, or that it had something to say to me, personally.

Now I felt like it was pushing us on. I looked up at its

overwhelming profile, silhouetted against the purple-black clouds. I heard the river, and all its residents swimming or flowing.

Faster.

We were all starting to pant, but we weren't spent yet, and we held ourselves and our clattering equipment together until we reached the Death Nugget. Benny flattened himself across its hood with exhaustion and happiness. He sat the satchel he carried on the dented fender and waved at me to open the door.

"Sure," I answered his unspoken plea. "Just a second." I jammed my fingers into my pocket and pulled out my keys, plugging the right one into the lock and flinging the door open.

Everyone piled inside.

I threw the Nugget into gear and almost peeled out swinging it around. Grass and mud sprayed behind us as we slid onto the road. I pulled a U-turn on the spot, and within seconds we were headed back to the interstate.

"Benny, what do you think the fastest way to the battlefield is from here? Freeway? Back roads? Rossville? It's night, and there won't be much traffic. Should we stay on the main road?"

"Rossville, probably. We'll have to keep our eyes peeled for cops."

I took his suggestion and exited at 27 South, zipping down the exit to the right and towards Georgia. I knew Benny was right about the cops, but I forgot and was speeding through the lights anyway when I saw blue lights behind me.

"Eden." Dana said it casually, with a hint of "you ought to know better."

"Shit. Shit. I see him." My stomach and all its contents sank, and I felt myself flush with anger that seethed in every direction. I slowed down and pulled over to the right lane, preparing to take the shoulder or the nearest parking lot.

But the flashing cruiser ignored me, flying around to my left and charging forward. Behind us, a second and third came up and did likewise. I held my pace for a few moments, hardly breathing, waiting for one of my passengers to speak first. Benny was the one to break the silence.

"You don't think they're headed for the battlefield, do you?"

Dana said, "Let's not think that way yet. We're still miles away from the battlefield. They could be headed for… for a car wreck. Or a fire."

"I don't see any fire trucks," I replied, my teeth clenching around the words.

I upshifted back to fifth gear and hightailed it after them.

We arrived at the battlefield about ten minutes later, and found it sealed off by news crews, police cars, and an ambulance. I kicked at the brakes and stopped in front of the nearest news truck.

Dana was out of the car before I was, and she was quickly recognized. "What's going on here?" she asked the first reporter who knew her name—a red-haired girl who looked barely old enough to be out of college. "What's happened?"

"Mrs. Marshall, would you like to make a statement about tonight's events?"

Dana snatched the microphone out of her hand and threw it on the ground, pulling the taller woman close by one handful of her sweater. "I would like for you to tell me what the fuck is going on, and talk quick because these days my attention span isn't what it used to be."

"There's… there's…"

"Talk faster, sweetheart."

"A hostage situation." She jerked herself away from Dana, who was drawing a small crowd. At least one man with a camera aimed it her way.

"A hostage situation?" I walked around my car and came to stand beside her, between her and the enclosing crowd. "Someone tell us what's going on." I stopped. A familiar face was pushing its way close to us.

"Alders," I growled.

"Call me Nick!" he reminded us, squeezing between two microphone-wielding reporters and forcing his way through until he was on perfect eye level with me. "And don't worry. They're making it sound worse than it is."

"You'd better not be saying so just because my knee's about a foot away from your crotch."

He backed up. "No. I'm not. It's not... Look—it was his girlfriend."

"She's not his girlfriend."

"The girl he was with, then. The dumb bitch ran off into the woods. Said she saw something."

I took him by the arm then and dragged him off back towards my car, flashing a glare over my shoulder that dared anyone to follow us. "Keep talking. I'm listening."

"And—and she ran. He went after her, and then there was some shooting, and some screaming. The girl came staggering back—they took her off in one of the ambulances. She got hit in the side; it went right through. But then the shooter, he said he had a hostage and not to follow him. He's holed up back in the Tower. At the top of the tower."

"Jamie was telling the truth. I thought he was lying about that part."

"No, no way. We stayed over at the Tower. I thought it'd be safe. I thought it would be no big—" A police officer approached us then, undeterred by my warning glare.

"Mr. Alders? A word, please?" Nick looked positively delighted to get away from me, despite the uniform and the implication that the cop wasn't very happy with him.

"Officer." I chased after them. "Officer, what's going on? There's a hostage? Is it Jamie Hammond?"

He paused, one hand still on Nick's arm. "Ma'am, we don't have all the details yet. Are you a friend of the hostage?"

"Yes. And I want to know what's going on."

"What are you doing here?" he asked. "Did this guy call you?"

"No. No, Jamie called. He called and said for us to come here and get him." It wasn't perfectly true, but it was close enough. "I told him we were on our way. That was, um, that was…"

"About half an hour ago," Benny offered.

"Okay. We're going to want to talk to you too, then. Do us a favor and don't leave, okay, miss? Okay?"

"Okay," I agreed. "When you're through with him, we can talk." But even as I said it, I was feeling around in the crowd for Benny and Dana.

I found Benny first, and then Dana behind him. "The Tower," I said to them both, as if it explained everything.

"We can get there around back, like before," Benny said, putting a hand on my shoulder and steering me towards my car.

I nodded. "You're right. They've shut off the front way; we'll never get past the crews."

"Everybody back in," Dana said, but I pushed her away.

"No, no, you two stay here. Distract them, or something. I'll go."

"Don't be batty. I'm coming too."

"*We* are coming too."

Neither of them looked prepared to take no for an answer, so I shrugged and grabbed the driver's side door handle. Everything was still unlocked, so Dana and Benny got in as well.

But our window of opportunity was smaller than I thought.

Another police cruiser pulled up behind and beside my car, effectively blocking us into our improvised parking spot. He exited the cruiser and left the door hanging open behind him.

"Hey!" I cried out after him, but if he noticed, he didn't care. He stomped off in the direction of the reporters and left us pinned.

"Mother*fucker*," Dana said. "You think we can back around him?"

I almost told her, "Sure," but another ambulance came wailing around the turn to park beside the cruiser. "I guess not."

"Guys," Benny said, staring off into the park. "This place isn't fenced in or anything, is it?"

I shook my head. "No, of course not."

He pointed at the trees, and at the big stretch of field beyond the clot of emergency vehicles. Red, yellow, orange, and blue lights swiveled, beamed, and bounced off every surface. But beyond the knotted crowd of cars and officials, the way was open and more or less clear—except for the filmy white mist that was settling between the old stone markers.

"Benny, this car wasn't made for off-roading."

"Then we can hoof it."

I thought hard about running with Dana, from Dyer's cabin to the visitors' center. It had seemed like forever; it had felt like miles and years. But it couldn't have been that far, really. Nick had said it was only a couple of miles. Assuming we could get past the police, and the reporters, and the medical personnel… assuming we could make it to the trees, or deep enough into the gathering fog, or far enough into the thigh-deep grass in the middle of the first big field… assuming all this, we could maybe do it.

"Wait." I crawled into my car. My tiny but mighty purple flashlight had wound up on the floor at Dana's feet. I picked it up with one hand and popped the trunk with the other.

"Benny? You still got that army flashlight?"

"Yes ma'am," he said, diving into the trunk and excavating the ugly green torch from his bag.

"Put the red lens on it."

"I'm way ahead of you."

While he worked on that, I wiggled my way back through the crowd to Nick Alders, who looked a little afraid to see me. The cop who'd been talking to him was now working on one of the EMTs, leaving Nick to sit on the back bumper of the ambulance.

I sat down beside him and talked low, into his ear. "It goes like this," I began. "You distract these people for about thirty seconds, and I promise not to kill you later on."

"Dis—distract them?"

"Yes. I don't care how, but get them *not* looking into the park. If everything goes well, you've got a scoop."

He caught on quick, and his eyes went big. "You guys can't go in there. You'll get killed. I think I'm in enough trouble already here."

"Wasn't your last investigative piece for Channel 3 something about fainting goats? Wouldn't you rather report on something important for once? And hey, if nothing works and we all wind up dead, it's not on your head—and then you *definitely* don't have to worry about me coming around to beat you senseless for dragging Jamie into this. So help us out here and redeem yourself."

Nick looked out into the darkness beyond the flashing lights and intermittent buzz of police radios. He looked back at me, and whatever he saw in my face, he believed. With something like resolve, he picked up his microphone and turned his head hard to the left, then hard to the right. I heard a small cracking noise.

He shifted his shoulders. He fixed his eyes on a spot on the other side of the street. "You need distracting bullshit? All right. Watch *this*."

Nick raised the microphone like a banner and yelled, "Bobby! Bobby! Holy shit, Bobby, check that out!"

Bobby must have been his camera guy tonight, because an overburdened fellow carrying a camera the size of a small suitcase lurched to attention.

"This way!" Nick shouted, and took off running towards nothing in particular. "Hey you! Stop right there!"

What followed looked like the media version of the Charge of the Light Brigade. Every information-greedy reporter—horrified at the prospect of being second to the story—immediately leapt into a gallop, tearing after Nick, who was following his microphone as if it were a divining rod.

All the police paused what they were doing and stared; then a few began to make an uncertain chase.

Through the chaos, I sought out Benny and Dana. Our eyes connected. We weren't going to get a better chance. So we took it.

Off past the cars, and around the nearest ambulance, and into the grass we charged—finally meeting up together in the midst of the first open field. Behind us a couple of people called out, but whether they were talking about us or whatever Nick was doing, I didn't know and I didn't look to find out.

"How do we get back to the Tower from here?" Benny panted,

fumbling for his flashlight switch as he ran. We were getting far enough from the headlights and flashing siren lights that we were starting to have a hard time seeing.

"Where's the road?" Dana asked.

"We should hit it at any minute," I said, hoping I remembered correctly. "If we follow the road, there'll be, um, there'll be a turn-off to the right. But not for a while."

The fog was rising around us, coming in close up against us. It was not the perfect dense blanket it had been during our last rampage through the park, but there was no guarantee that it wouldn't be blinding within an hour. Since Benny had the least-detectable light, Dana and I let him take the lead. We fell into a flight pattern behind him, slowing to a jog as we all began to wear out.

The grass whipped at our legs, and sometimes our thighs, and occasionally it slapped us around the middle. It was too tall to even wade through—it felt like swimming through a tide of reeds or a very dry swamp.

"Slow down." Dana was the first to suggest it. "Jesus, slow down. I can't keep this up. I can't, I can't." Her sentiment petered out, but we got the gist anyway. I knew she hadn't been sleeping, and she was older than us besides.

"Right," Benny agreed, but then he abruptly went face-down and hands-down with a cracking clatter.

"Benny!" I tripped over him, but caught myself before I stepped on his hands. He'd fallen over the edge of the road, at the startling hard place where the pavement strip began and the ocean of grass ended.

"I'm okay! I'm okay!"

"What was that sound? What the hell did you break?" Dana

asked, dropping to her knees beside him out of concern or exhaustion.

"Nothing—it was the light. It's okay though." He retrieved it and knocked it against the road. "See? Army surplus, remember? You could run over this thing with a truck. Ow. My hands."

"Let me see," I said, taking the one that wasn't holding the light. "Let me look."

I flipped on my own light and aimed it at his hands, where raw, red scrapes marred the bottom of his palms and one set of knuckles.

"Ow," he complained, pulling away from me and wiping the ooze on his pants. "It's okay. I'm okay. A little Bactine and I'll be good as new. And hey, look—I found the road."

"That you did, my lad. Well done."

"How far do you think it is to the Tower from here?"

"Not far," I mumbled. It had to be the better part of a mile still, if not farther. "But I bet we can use the regular light for a while. I don't think we're within shouting distance of it yet."

Dana didn't say anything to contradict me, though she must have known better. "Does it strike anyone as strange how quiet it is?"

I helped Benny up, and the three of us stood together on the road, looking back towards the front of the park. Every few seconds, a siren would burp to life, and then be cut off. It looked very far away. "Maybe. Shouldn't those guys be over by the Tower? Why camp out at the entrance? That's not where the action is."

"That's the idea," Dana said. "The cops wouldn't let the news crews get any closer than that. There must be more cops around back. Even if we could've gotten the car out, we never would've gotten much closer anyway. That's not what I meant by 'quiet,' though. This place was crawling with ghosts just the other night. There were more dead people wandering around than you could shake a stick at. Where are they now?"

"We can talk about this and walk at the same time," Benny griped. "One of those reporters said the hostage situation was contained. They said he was holed up in the Tower. And you said we're not within shouting distance. So come on. Let's *go* already."

He was right, so we started off along the road.

Dana didn't let the subject drop, though. "Do you think it's Green Eyes? Do you think he came back already? How long would it take him to get here? And how would he get here—would he walk? Teleport? Something like that?"

"I doubt he hitchhiked," I said, following the bouncing light of my metallic purple torch. "But you're right; it's awfully quiet. Maybe he beat us back."

"How?" Benny asked.

"Who knows? How does he do *anything*?"

"Magic," Dana grumbled.

"Well, at least the fog's not as bad as it was the other night," I said, trying to pretend there was a bright side. "We must have visibility of… of at least a quarter of a mile."

"Yeah, that's great. Once we get within a quarter mile of the Tower, we'll be in good shape." Dana was the only one without a light, so she held back behind us.

Benny unscrewed the lens from his light, giving us a big white source of illumination, at least for the time being. He stuck the lens into his back pocket. "How do you think it happened? Do you think Jamie's okay? I mean, if he wasn't, they couldn't call it a hostage situation, right? If he was dead, they'd just call it a stand-off."

"That sounds good to me," I replied, trying not to worry about everyone at once. Benny, and his bleeding hands. Dana, and her soft gasping that leaked out with every step. Jamie, and some homicidal maniac with a gun.

Sometimes Jamie drove me up a wall, but he could be a pretty good friend when he wanted to, too. I was the one who'd gotten him into this whole thing, and it was my responsibility to get him out. If I hadn't talked him into coming out with me the first time, that jackass Nick Alders would never have offered him three hundred bucks to revisit the scene.

If anything happened to Jamie, it was all my fault.

Or mostly my fault. It would be Nick's fault too, a little—that smarmy, tidy-haired bastard with the unnaturally white smile and the foul mouth when the camera was turned off. Even if we all survived this, I might renege on that promise not to kick the crap out of him.

Or maybe I'd only promised not to *kill* him?

I found it hard to think out on the battlefield. I knew that there were ley lines crossing to and fro all over it; and even though I didn't know what that meant, exactly, I knew it had something to do with energy, or vibes, or something like that. But the whole place was distracting. The fields seemed to swallow things up, and the woods around them promised secrets, and baited themselves like traps.

"It feels different now," I said, clomping along beside Benny and in front of Dana. "It wasn't always like this."

"Like what?" Dana asked, but I thought maybe she was only making conversation. The world was so silent, and so dark, and so hard to see through the fog caulked in the spaces between us. It was better to talk, and pretend that all was normal and well.

"Like… when I was a kid, when I came here, I thought it was boring. It didn't feel like anything—just a park. It was just some nice place that got mowed from time to time, and where old people came to have picnics. Thousands and thousands of people died here, but it was quiet."

"It was, once?" Dana shuffled along, her shoes kicking gravel at my ankles. "By the time I got here, it was crawling with unhappiness. It was restless, and uncomfortable."

"By the time you got here, Green Eyes had left. But listen." And that wasn't the right verb command, but it was as close as I could do. "Do you sense that? It's different now. It isn't restless. It isn't uncomfortable, like it wants help or assistance, or understanding. But it's something."

"It's awake." Benny breathed it out before Dana or I could, and I was impressed—but unnerved. If even *he* was picking up on the psychic ambience, it must be damn near overwhelming. "But where—where is everyone? Where did all the ghosts go?"

No one knew, and no one responded.

I got distracted by a fork in the road and used it to change the subject. "We turn off here, don't we?"

"No, not yet." Dana flipped a couple of fingers up and forward. "It's the next one. We're not even up to the Dyer's place yet."

At the very distant edge of my hearing, I caught a short, sweet buzz. It fluttered and faded, in and out, like the sound of a fly throwing itself against a window. I knew that sound. And even though Dana and Benny didn't appear to have noticed it, I reacted to it.

I stopped. I turned myself in a circle, sweeping the fields with my light. Dana and Benny hesitated when they saw they'd lost me.

"Sentry?"

"What are you doing?" Benny wanted to know, and he swung his light around to follow mine, even though it wasn't showing anything but endless curtains of patchy white fog.

"Sentry?" I called again. "He's here. I hear him. That noise. You know—the static sound. I hear it. He's nearby. Sentry!"

"Stop yelling, he'll hear us!" Benny begged, but I moved away from him, still searching the fields and the trees with my limited fistful of light.

"I *want* him to hear us."

"What about the guy who's got Jamie? You want him to hear you too? Or do you think we're still out of shouting distance?" He looked so worried that I let my wrist droop and quit calling.

"He might help us. He might—" But I couldn't think of a good way to end the thought, so I quit talking. Besides, the fizzing air was drawing itself close up around us, and if my companions couldn't hear it yet, they would hear it soon enough.

The mist around us was quickening too, as if it also heard the approaching and familiar hum, and it gathered itself up to meet the source. It did not congeal so hard that we couldn't see through it, though, or around it. It appeared to be flowing, and not hardening into something so impenetrable that we couldn't pass through.

A wind kicked up, steady and pulsing, helping to push the pale tendrils of damp air along.

"What's going on?" It was a useless question, but Benny asked it anyway. We were all wondering. We were all speculating. And we were all going to find out, one way or another. "What's happening? Do you see any ghosts yet? Is that what this is?"

"No," I told him. I saw no shapes, no personalities, no movement that could not be accounted for by the swirl of the low, damp cloud.

But I could hear that noise, and it kept me on guard. It kept me looking, even when squinting showed me nothing at all.

"Where are you?" I asked, but no one answered me.

"Hey, look," Dana said, and she meant that we should look at the fields and the road, back the way we came. "Does that look weird to you at all? The way it's so clear? It was hazy when we went through it not ten minutes ago."

She was right. The fog that billowed and burst past us in fleeting ribbons was not merely gathering, it was slipping. Pouring. It emptied itself from the distant stretches of grass and woods, and it charged on towards the back of the park. It was as if someone had released a sink plug and the fog was being drawn down the drain. It leaked past us in a fluffy gray gushing that parted around us as though we were rocks in a stream.

"It's going towards the Tower, isn't it?" I watched it bleed away, into a tighter cloud as its collective density increased. "We've got to follow it."

So we did.

We began to run again, directly into the maelstrom; and the less we could see, the more we tried to tell ourselves that we were headed the right way. And the whiter the night became, the louder the static became—until even Dana and Benny could no longer pretend it didn't reach their ears.

Our feet skidded off the edge of the road back into gravel and grass, and we almost tumbled over each other trying to stop. The déjà vu was nearly painful; we were back into the near-perfect blindness that had held us prisoner before.

It made us stiff, and nervous. It made us afraid.

But we were in the literal thick of it, and there was nothing we could do. We couldn't see to move forward, and there could be no retreat. We drew close together. Dana reached for my hand. I took hers and squeezed it, and with my other—the one that held the light, too—I took Benny's free hand.

"What do we do now?" he asked.

"Listen," I told him. And I snapped off my light.

He did the same. We stood in the pale black spot beside the road, and we clung to one another. And then, we were not alone.

Here. And there. And to our left. To the right.

Behind us, and past us. The night became sentient, and it began to move. Shadows were rising up, out of the ground. They were moving out from behind trees. They were falling into step, into patterns, into rows, and into waves. The dead came up in a tide of determined faces, and they marched.

"Sentry," I said, "you're doing this, aren't you?"

Bring it, bring it all. It will cover us.

He wasn't talking to me. He was talking to them. And they brought it—every tendril, and every white breath. The fog came with them, every bit of it. They wore it like clothing, they pulled it along, they drew it out, and they dragged it after themselves deeper into the park.

Some of the shades still wore their uniforms, and here and there I saw the larger shape of a horse. One came very close to me; it stomped and stepped past, its eyes flashing a strange silver light as it glanced down to look at me.

Follow.

I didn't know who said it, if it was Green Eyes or if it was one of the ghosts, but the word was perfect, and I understood every letter.

Follow. It will hide you, too.

Dana heard it also, and she tugged at my hand. I couldn't tell if Benny could see or hear anything at all, but he didn't fight when

I began to tow him after me. In this way, blind but attentive, afraid but resolute, we joined the stoic ranks of the walking dead.

Every one of them stared straight ahead, and every one stepped in flawless time. We fell into step too, only later noticing the drums. At least two, or more—maybe three or four. The acoustics on the fields were broken, and the echoes were cast back by the trees; but there were definitely drums.

We are coming.

"Hang in there, Jamie," Benny whispered, and again the spirit army reassured me, *We are coming.*

The ghosts led us back onto the paved road, and guided us up to the turn that would take us to the Tower. Before long we began to see the first flickering glints of blue and red lights, and we heard a man with a megaphone speaking with a tinny timbre, directing his voice up, up to the top of Wilder Tower.

Soon we could make out headlights, too—and darkly uniformed shapes walking back and forth, detectable only by their motion on the other side of the cloud.

It will cover us, a chorus of breathless voices believed, and the voices were right.

The fog settled hard over the Tower and the clearing that surrounded it. It smothered the stone benches, and draped itself across the trash cans, the historical markers, and maps that talked when their buttons were pressed.

A carefully contained panic settled just as thoroughly over the police, parked in the lot down by the foot of the Tower. I knew they were only there to help. I knew they were struggling to protect my friend. But I wanted them to leave. This conflict was not theirs.

They withdrew when the fog hit them; they grew confused

and nervous when it doused them with air that was visually as thick as paint. Everyone knows about the fog, but not everyone has been gulped down by it. Not everyone has been caught in it, and knows how suffocating the air becomes when it fills your mouth and clogs your ears.

We came closer—close enough to hear a muffled commotion coming from somewhere above us. I thought I caught Jamie's voice, unintelligible, but complaining. A lower, slower one argued back.

"That's him." Benny confirmed my suspicion.

"What the hell is that weird noise?" someone down by the parking lot asked, and then I knew that Green Eyes must be close, if even the cops were hearing the signature sign of his presence.

A crunching implosion of metal slammed through the pseudo-silence, and the piercing wail of a siren screamed out. A flat popping coughed out too, and then a second one. At first I didn't know what the second set of noises were, but then I heard a grating squeal and knew that they were blown tires.

"What's going on over there, anyway?" Dana demanded under her breath, but it was impossible to tell.

Around us the posthumous militia massed, side by side—some in the remains of battered blue, or grungy gray. I saw several women in bulky skirts, and four black men standing in a row. And the harder I looked, the more I saw. There were dozens. No, hundreds.

I turned around, looking behind us.

Thousands.

All eyes were on the Tower.

Down in the parking lot, havoc was coming to a boil. Another thunderous crash and a second agitated siren joined the first. Glass and plastic cracked and caved. Headlights that appeared as small white orbs went dim.

"I don't know what you're doing down there, but you stop it! You stop it or I'll kill him!"

This was the first time I'd ever distinctly heard him speak, the lumbering shooter who'd terrorized us twice—the man who had killed poor Tripp, and who had wounded several others. His voice was heavy, like it came from a big man; and it was sticky with over-pronounced vowels.

I closed my eyes because it made little difference in the fog, except that I heard things better, or I thought I did. From those two sentences I extracted everything I could—I discerned that he was white, and a middle-aged adult. He was a local guy too, that much was obvious; but the twang on his letters didn't have the smoothness of a city's polish.

In the parking lot, three sirens chimed and at least that many sets of blue and white lights churned their beams through the fog. I could see them, but just barely—they were weak pulses of light and color pounding against the air, like punches thrown underwater.

Someone was calling out, "Hold your fire!" over and over again, calming the officers with force of will. It was a frightened voice, but one that commanded desperate authority.

"Hold your fire!"

They obeyed, even as they retreated to regroup.

Then the white air parted—curling and recoiling as if it were expelling something violently in a cough. It expelled the Sentry.

He strode forward through the gap, impossibly tall and unnervingly wide. His eyes blazed with fury and aggression, and more than that too—though I wouldn't have known what to call it.

I think he saw us, though he didn't care and didn't acknowledge us.

To my left was Benny, openmouthed and staring. He saw them, all the ghosts. He must have. He was breathing them.

To my right Dana was immobile too; but she was watching Green Eyes, and her own eyes gleamed. I couldn't tell if she was angry, or horrified, or frightened; but the longer I looked at her, the more I thought she must be happy. It was a dismal sort of happiness, more of a vengeful satisfaction than joy. For all her talk of me being irresponsible to cut him loose, she was wishing him on more fervently than I ever could.

He didn't need any unspoken encouragement from us. He stalked up to the Tower, pushing a trash can over and knocking a stone bench onto its side with the merest brush of his knee.

A locked iron gate barred the Tower entrance, but not for long. The shooter must have pulled it closed behind himself. It was a useless gesture, and it wouldn't help him any.

Green Eyes planted two massive fists through the metal latticework and yanked the entire structure clear of the stone— hinges, locks, mounts, and all. He cast it aside and disappeared into the flawless blackness that filled the interior.

I ran after him. I left Dana and Benny where they were, though after a few seconds they opted to follow me. I heard them running through the grass behind me. One of them tripped over the removed gate, or part of a broken bench.

I didn't wait. I didn't glance over my shoulder. I wouldn't have been able to see them anyway.

I followed the big black shape and his illuminated eyes through the portal and into the tall stone coil of the Tower interior. I tripped over the first step, which surprised me with its immediacy, but I recovered myself and stumbled up the stairs. Above me I heard the heavy stomping footsteps of the Sentry, who needed no light.

I most definitely did need a light, but when I reached for my flashlight I fumbled it and it clattered onto the ground and down a stair or two. I gasped and dropped to one knee and one hand, but upon feeling around with the other set of fingers I couldn't find it.

"Eden?" I heard Dana ask from outside. But I didn't want to wait for her and I didn't want to slow down, so I left the light and charged on up, knocking my shins on every third sharp stair edge.

I bruised my palms as I dragged them along the infinite spiral of the Tower wall, its lumpy and rough-hewn surface beating my knuckles, or my wrists, or the occasional stray knee that collided with it. I had no other means of finding my way.

Every second cycle of circles, a small rectangular window with bars would provide a dim semblance of light.

It wasn't enough. I fell anyway, battering my elbow, hip, and shoulder. A second fall, close behind, landed me collarbone-down on something sharp and hard—another stair. They came so close together. I couldn't get a rhythm down to climb them; the corkscrew stylings of the Tower's guts made it impossible to climb them blind without banging myself up.

"Sentry!" I cried, though whether it was to slow him down or ask his help, I hadn't decided. Either way, he didn't answer.

I clambered on, taking the bruises as they came and soldiering forward even as my thighs started to burn from the effort. I had no idea how tall the Tower was; from the outside it was only another phallic monument. From within it seemed to be taller than life.

On I climbed.

There were hundreds of stairs. My legs were aching in earnest. I slowed, catching my breath. Whoever was behind me—whether it was Dana or Benny, I didn't know—slowed too. I didn't hear any footsteps behind me.

Up again. Higher. More. How tall could it be?

I heard them talking before I could understand what they were saying. It wasn't until I was nearly to the top that any of it made any sense at all. Then my head cleared the final hurdle and I could breathe, and I could see. The air above the battlefield was clear, and the sky above was absolutely empty of clouds. The moon was out in half, and it was enough.

I saw them clearly, all three of them.

Jamie was on the ground, clutching his shoulder and backing himself as far against the barricade wall as he could. He was moving slow, and his left arm hung at a funny angle. Back, and back, he scooted—like he was trying to crawl into the wall itself. He saw me, but didn't say anything.

He tried not to look at me.

Green Eyes was walking the circle, slow and steady, treading his way around the parapet. His flowing hair was caught and teased by the cross breeze that gusted against us all.

And then there was the shooter. He was so much less than I imagined, so much more human than I'd feared. He looked every bit as scared as I would be if I were on the cusp of being trampled by something like the Sentry.

He scooted too, backwards like Jamie had, around the Tower's deck and towards the stairs.

"You were supposed to leave!" he complained. "This isn't your place anymore!"

It doesn't have to be that way, Green Eyes corrected him.

The man cowered—literally, and completely, ducking away and back. He hoisted the gun and put it into the Sentry's face. It quivered there. "The bargain is up." The words were barely a breath in the clear, starlit air.

Yes. It is. I am not here because I have to be.

"Then why?"

Because I want to be.

"Back off!" he squealed, shrill and pathetic.

No.

In the course of the man's retreat he tripped over Jamie, who curled himself as tightly into a ball as he could. *That's it,* I thought. *Stay down, Jamie.* When the man fell over Jamie, he picked himself up and kept moving—back, back, as far away as he could get from the unrelenting sentry.

"I have a right to be here. My people fought here. My people died here too. You can't keep me away." And then, when Green Eyes took one long step close, he gasped the rest. "You can't hurt me! You're not allowed to. You can't harm the living, even to guard the dead."

This gave Green Eyes pause.

While he mulled it over, I crawled up to the very top of the stairs so that my shoulders were exposed to the night air. I stretched out my arm to Jamie, who was fetal a couple of feet away. His head jerked up when I grasped his ankle; but he knew it was me, and he'd never looked so happy to see me. The feeling was mutual. I put my finger up over my lips so he would hush.

He nodded, and slipped down low—offering his good arm out. I took it and pulled, gently but firmly. I drew him towards me, and he let me do it.

Inch by inch, I tugged him across the stone floor. Quietly, I reeled him towards the stairs. I hooked my foot on the topmost step and used it to anchor myself as I leveraged him into the stairway. "I've got you," I breathed so gently he might not have heard me.

That was the bargain.

"Yes, that was the bargain!"

The Sentry looked back down at me, either for affirmation, or because he was seeing me there for the first time. *The bargain has ended. I do not owe you safety.*

The man's eyes followed the Sentry's. For a moment he wobbled and sent the barrel of the gun my way, but reason prevailed and he returned it to the greater threat. He snatched his glance away from us both, and dropped it over the edge of the Tower. Below, he must have seen the army amassed. He must have spied them through the pudding-deep mist, their upturned faces and antiquated clothes.

"You don't owe *them* anything, either! This ground holds something of mine, and I want it back—and you've got no right to interfere. You've got no *reason* to interfere. Why don't you just leave?"

Because I don't want to.

He lunged, faster than any cat, and the man fired his gun directly into the Sentry's bulk. He was too big a target to miss, but if Green Eyes felt the impact, it didn't bother him any.

Again, and again, and again, the man fired. He almost emptied the barrel against the huge, hairy creature—even as he was lifted into the air. He kicked, and he jerked. He pushed his foot against the Sentry's neck.

The shooter had one bullet left by my count, and he was running out of air.

Desperate, he flapped the hand forward and landed the last shot directly into one of those glowing green eyes, the only target that stood out in the dark.

The Sentry roared, though it sounded like no lion I'd ever

heard; there was a scream underneath it, something that could have belonged to human or animal, but was certainly neither.

He lifted one great arm to clutch his face, and the other—the clenched fist that held the murderer—flailed hard. He beat the man's body against the impassable stones of the Tower's parapet. He thrashed, pushing the man up over the edge and releasing him.

But the man dropped his empty gun and clutched the simian arm, clinging to the limb lest he fall. "No! No!" he shrieked, his voice swaying with the pendulum swing of his body.

Green Eyes ignored the pleas, though it might not have been from callousness. He withdrew the long, sturdy arm that held the man and brought it towards him—a gesture that smashed the man's head against the faux fortifications.

It might have knocked him out, or it might have only stunned him.

At any rate, he dropped like a stone.

I didn't hear him cry as he toppled the seven or eight stories down onto the packed earth below. He landed sooner than I expected; if you watch too many movies you expect a dramatic delay.

But no. He was there, clawing at the Sentry's arm.

Then he thudded on the ground, like a mallet hitting a wet tree.

And Jamie was there, not bleeding, but broken in some way I couldn't see yet. He was mad, though, which I considered a good sign. When he saw that the shooter had gone over the edge, he sat up and pulled his feet up underneath himself. "This hurts like *fuck*!" he swore, and the hang of his arm told me he was telling the truth.

And in a moment Dana was beside me, and Benny was behind her.

"What's happened? Where'd he go?" Dana demanded, but I didn't answer her. I pulled Jamie almost into my lap, then pushed him past me onto the two newcomers. I climbed up beyond the knot of bodies and went to Green Eyes, who was clutching his face and growling, or grumbling.

I touched the corner of his elbow, and he jerked it away from me; then he removed the fist from his wounded eye.

It shocked and pained me to see that it was dark, and he regarded me with only the one brilliant slit.

"Are you okay?" I asked him, unsure of how stupid a question it was.

Okay, he echoed, almost as if he wasn't sure what it meant.

"You're hurt," I tried to clarify. "Do you need help?"

Then I *did* feel silly. Whatever he was, he'd just absorbed or ignored a full barrel's worth of bullets, and the only damage done appeared to be a partial squint.

With a surprising gentleness, he pushed me away and turned to look over the side of the Tower. I joined him.

Below, the fog had consumed whatever fell through it, and the spirits were swarming over the spot where the man had landed. I couldn't see what they were doing, but it probably didn't matter. It was not the sort of fall that a man would survive.

Or that's what I hoped, even if it was wrong of me.

The Sentry looked up and past me then, and I wondered why until I heard the human voices rise. "They're coming," I said, but he already knew.

I will stay here.

"You don't have to if you don't want."

The dead are my children. I will watch over them, so they can rest. They will need no wings to the kingdom.

Over one shoulder, I saw Jamie being coddled by Benny and Dana. Over the other, the police were rallying—drawn by the shockingly loud sound of a body falling so many stories onto the rocky, grassy ground.

"Thank you," I said, because nothing else seemed appropriate.

I couldn't tell if he understood. I didn't know if he was replying in kind or only echoing me when he said, a moment before vanishing,

Thank you.

EIGHTEEN

WINDING DOWN

"I just have one question, then," Dave said, pulling his hands back behind his head and reclining against the couch.

"One?" Lu and I said it together.

Benny groaned, and rose from his seat beside Dave. "I've got dozens, but I don't think we're ever going to know the whole thing."

I had more answers than I probably deserved, but there were still holes that would likely never be patched. Mostly, all I had was a lot of speculation buttressed with a handful of facts. Together with Jamie, Dana, and some help from Pete Buford's confused and brokenhearted uncle the pieces had fallen into something like a whole.

Pete had broken his neck on the hard Georgia clay. So far as the authorities knew or cared, he'd toppled during a struggle with me and Dana. We'd pushed his arm up. He'd fired those rounds into the air, and we were not hurt.

Of my own group of friends, Jamie had gotten the worst of it:

he'd cracked his collarbone and dislocated his shoulder when he fell halfway down the stairs while he was being shoved up them by Pete. He'd thrown a fit about going in the ambulance. I'd almost had to sit on him to make him shut up and go.

He'd caught up to his date at the hospital. She'd received a few stitches and been turned loose, not having been hurt as badly as anyone feared; but she'd waited for him once she heard he was coming. I resigned myself to the idea that I might be forced to get to know her, as he seemed inclined to keep her around.

Or maybe that was just his painkillers talking.

Dana had collected her husband's body and returned to Carolina, but not before offering Benny and me jobs working with her crew. I had thought Benny was going to explode from sheer bliss at the prospect. Money for art supplies and a job in the paranormal—it was as if the mothership had called him home.

At first it had annoyed me, the fast and opportunistic way he leaped at the chance to flee the valley. Everyone here talks about wanting to leave Chattanooga. Everyone complains about how much it sucks, and how little opportunity there is; and everyone daydreams about going somewhere else. But few people do. It's a sucking vortex of a place.

When we argued about it, he told me I was being selfish, and that I didn't understand. He told me that it wasn't the same for people who didn't live on the mountain, and didn't have educations or trust funds.

I was shocked to hear the frantic delight in his words. I don't think I ever really grasped how trapped he'd felt all this time. I was also a little shocked at how disappointed I was to know he was going.

I told him that he'd be back. He said I was probably right, but he hoped I wasn't.

I, however, declined Dana's offer, using school as an excuse. I was thinking about going back and finishing up that history major, or maybe even going in for some psychology somewhere. There was a lot about the world I didn't understand—a lot about people, anyway.

I really was tempted to leave with Dana, but the time wasn't right yet—or perhaps I was a bigger coward than I liked to think. So I stayed. Just for the time being. I told her I'd keep it in mind, though, and that I was open to the idea of the occasional collaboration. She told me to take my time.

Speaking of understanding people, I tried to go back and visit Kitty, but the nurses and orderlies were reluctant to let me see her. They said she wasn't doing well. I thought that was odd. I'd figured that once Green Eyes had gone away, she'd return to whatever state of normal had suited her best all these years.

But that's not how it happened. They'd been medicating her a lot lately. She'd been temperamental and unpredictable.

I suggested to the nurse that maybe she just needed someone to talk to, but she wouldn't go against the doctor's recommendation of solitude. Give the meds time to work on her, and see if it brought her back around—that's what they told me.

I had a feeling it wouldn't work.

She was a Russian doll of isolation. She lived in Chattanooga, where social and economic stagnation is the norm; was imprisoned in an asylum on a peninsula; locked in a small room; and driven to distraction by the voices in her head.

No pill or injection on Earth could change that.

I'll keep trying to reach her, though. I have to. Harry and Dave and Lu were right—I need to know that there's someone else who understands and believes. And I need to remember what happens if I forget and go at it alone.

And I swore to keep an open mind. I didn't have any choice. Every time I think the universe is beginning to make sense, something crazy knocks it all down and I have to start over, reconstructing my worldview as I go.

If I can't stay flexible, I will surely crack.

"All right. What's your one question?" I asked, tossing a pillow at Dave and joining Benny in the kitchen, where he was collecting snack food, as had become downright traditional.

"It's this—that Pete guy was looking for Confederate gold, right? Well, if he'd been left alone, or at least not caught, do you think he would've found it?"

Lu shook her head, answering for me. "Darling, there is no way at all to know whether or not he'd have found what he was looking for out there."

"And even if it *was* there," I added. "Who knows if it would've led him to amazing riches? His uncle said he was looking for a watch that would lead him to someone's body in the hope that the body would also have a ledger that led to Confederate gold. But that's just a big fat rural legend."

"A rural legend?" Benny asked. He passed me a jar of guacamole from the fridge.

"As opposed to an urban legend, yes. There's no Confederate gold out there. I mean, come *on*. Someone would've found it by now. Someone would be sitting pretty in Mexico, or out in Texas where the war didn't do much damage. Pete was just a deluded old

380

redneck with the world's wackiest get-rich-quick scheme."

Benny shrugged. "Maybe. Or maybe he just lived here too long, and he wanted *out*."

No trace of the Sentry had ever been found. There was nothing to indicate he'd ever existed, or that he'd ever made a stand at the Wilder Tower. Within a week, the park reopened and visitors roamed with freshly morbid curiosity.

Dana was worried that he'd run amuck with too much freedom, and maybe she had a good reason to be concerned; but so far, so good. I haven't heard any reports of hair-covered humanoids trashing cars and knocking heads together, so I hope he's struck his own balance between discretion and duty.

The stories are leaking out again—not the gesticulating ghosts, but the older stories, the ones about a sentinel who watches, and waits, and does not sleep. The boogeyman has returned, and the dead are at peace.

And everywhere around the valley, parents tell warning tales about him again. They frighten their little ones by dropping their voices and waving their fingers as they talk about the giant monster who walks the fields at night.

If I had a child, I would tell her stories too.

But I would tell her about a tower and a knight covered in hair instead of shining armor. I would tell her how hard it is to run in the dark, and how tricky it is to climb hundreds of stairs up into the night. I would remind her that not all heroes are easy to understand, and that there are bigger reasons to rise to the occasion than the rescuing of princesses.

And if she's any kid of mine, I expect she'll understand.

* * *

I told myself that this stop would be easier in the morning, in the bright orange light before the sun got too high. I zipped down the mountain in my freshly repaired Death Nugget, and went out to the main drag of a north Chattanooga suburb.

I turned off Dayton Boulevard and drove down a winding two-lane road beside a cemetery. A pond full of ducks flapped to excited attention as I puttered past.

Off to the right, a narrow strip of pavement veered up a hill. I followed it. Even farther to the right, an even narrower band of half-paved road squeaked between fluffy arches of bright green foliage.

It seemed there was nowhere to go—the road was swallowed by the forest. I couldn't see beyond ten feet in front of my hood.

But I kept going, creeping slowly, with my foot off the gas, but off the brake too. My car crawled over the gravel, over the rocks, over the branches that had fallen or toppled or been blown over the path.

It had only been a year.

I simply couldn't believe the change. It was as if, when all the old buildings were bulldozed and carried away, the hill had swallowed the foundations whole.

Over here I saw an overgrown stone wall, and over there I picked out a leftover pile of bricks. Along the gravel strip, hanging over the edge of a ditch, there were stacks of old tires. I didn't know what the old tires were from, and I didn't know why there was a decrepit washing machine beside a big tree, so I was forced to conclude that people had started using the place for a dump.

I tried to remember how far up to go and what the rough layout of the place had been, but it wasn't until I reached the top of the hill that anything looked familiar. Where the incline leveled out, a set of foundations remained uncovered; these were the larger buildings—the gymnasium, the dormitories, and an administration building. Only rubble remained, but at least the field was relatively clear and the trees were taller, higher above and not dangling down to obscure my field of vision.

I parked there, wondering exactly how I was going to turn around and leave again, but not so worried this time that I might be spotted by the cops.

No one was going to spot anything up there now. Even if there was trouble, it was highly unlikely that a passer-by would come to my assistance. I didn't like the thought of it, but I'd made a stupid promise and I intended to keep it.

I turned off the car, and immediately felt the weight of the place. It felt heavy, and bleak, and wet—even though it hadn't rained in over a week. And it was deeply dark, despite the hour. Between the leaves, thin orange columns of light spilled to the forest floor; but the canopy was laced tight, and I felt like this could have been late afternoon instead of late morning.

I took a deep breath and climbed out of the vehicle.

My boots sounded loud on the knotted, gravelly ground beside my tires. I shuffled my feet a little just to make that noise, so I could hear it and not feel so alone. Except for my intrusion, the place was perfectly quiet. No birds, no leaf-scattering lizards or squirrels.

"It must be me. Or the car," I thought aloud. It must have been the sound of my engine that scattered the wildlife.

All around me, the slow, insistent growth of vines, the wheedling of roots, and the spreading of ferny branches marked the hill's progress in reclaiming the site. Without intervention, another two or three years ought to hide the human scarring of development altogether if someone didn't buy the property and build there.

I closed the car door and walked to the nearest overgrown slab of concrete. I couldn't remember if it was the foundation of the gymnasium or the main administration building, but either way I was mildly surprised by how small it appeared. Without the trappings of walls and ceilings, the naked under-flooring looked like it could not possibly have supported the three-story structure I remembered.

I stepped up onto it, that bare gray dance floor beneath the trees. I wasn't sure why. For some reason I felt the need to get off the ground, away from the carpet of nature. I didn't want to touch it. I didn't want to stand on it at all.

"Hello?"

I could've said it louder, but then I might have gotten an answer—and I didn't really want an answer. In my perfect world, in my perfect morning, I would stand there feeling stupid for a few minutes and then leave… with nothing eventful to report.

"Hello?" I asked again.

The sound of my voice was too loud, even though I was deliberately keeping it down. The silence was thorough and thick.

"Anyone?"

Around me the quiet air moved. It shifted in a mass, all at once. It drew closer to me and I retreated, back-stepping along the concrete slab until I stood nearly in the center.

I remembered the heartbeat—the angry, rhythmic pulse of syllables that had followed me once before. I remembered it, but I didn't hear it.

I remembered something else too, when the shadows began to come forward. I remembered that this place was once a hospital where people went to die. A figure popped into my head, a number I'd read a long time ago: *two thousand people.*

I didn't see anything solid, not even a shape I could definitely pick out as human. Along the encroaching tree line blackness shifted—not hard, not fast. Freeze-frame slow, and stilted. If I looked away and then back again, I couldn't swear I'd seen anything at all. But if I stared, and if I could keep from blinking, I saw it.

Them.

More than one, whatever they were, dragging themselves out from between the moss-covered trunks. Not close. They stayed back. Whether their caution was brought on by fear or weakness, I couldn't tell. But they stayed back, and I stayed barely on the mobile side of fright.

It wasn't about *them.* I wasn't afraid of them. Not very.

I was afraid that any moment I'd hear the heartbeat. But the heartbeat didn't come, and as the seconds passed and I remained unmolested, I relaxed just enough to try speaking again.

"I'm looking for Rachel," I told the long, lumpy shadow.

The shadow did not respond in any manner that I could discern.

"I think she was here. Before they tore everything down, I mean. There was something else here. Something… definitely not like you. Something fast, and mean. It followed me. It talked to me. Can you talk to me?"

Nothing answered—not with any cue that I could hear or see.

"Is there anyone here who can talk to me? Anyone who would like to? I can hear you, if you talk. I can listen. Christ, what *are* you?"

I closed my eyes for a count of ten, thinking maybe I could draw the presences out by showing some vulnerability. It didn't work. The line of tangible emptiness stayed where it was, at least at first. Then I saw that the mass was withdrawing in the same drawn-out, incremental fashion with which it had arrived.

Them, I thought again. *Not "it."*

Within a minute or two, they were all but gone. And in a minute more, I heard the first bird sing since I'd arrived. The feathered thing whistled high and sweet from a few feet into the woods, and at the edge of the dormitory foundation a pair of lizards chased one another into the grass.

Nothing.

I glanced around one last time for good measure. When I left, after some careful vehicular maneuvering, I was reasonably confident that the poltergeist of Pine Breeze had abandoned the place to its ruin.

Whether or not it had been Malachi's mother I might never know, but my suspicion was that the bitter shade could have been no one else. I toyed with the idea of feeding Malachi a line out of kindness. I could tell him that I'd seen other ghosts there.

Two thousand people, wasting away.

I could tell him that some other specter had told me his mother's name, and that she was gone. He'd believe me, as likely as not. It was true, as likely as not. It would be less a lie than an educated guess.

I went back to my car. My purse was on the passenger's seat. I fished my cell phone out of the inner pocket and dialed the church in St Augustine, but no one answered. An answering machine with a cheery greeting encouraged me to leave a message, so I did: a short and sweet one.

"Malachi, I went to Pine Breeze."

I looked out my window over the empty area where the

sanitarium had once stood, and I made a decision that I knew I might come to regret. But I couldn't tell him the truth, because the truth was only that there was nothing to know. It might not have been the right thing to do, but I was tired of hurting people. So I said, "Look, Malachi, I asked around up here at the old sanitarium. You don't need to worry about your mother. She's gone on."

Then I held my breath and whispered into the phone, "Come up to Tennessee if you want—you and Harry. We'll make a weekend of it. Maybe—maybe I'll even introduce you to Lu and Dave.

"Your mother's found her peace. And we should make ours."

AUTHOR'S NOTE

As with *Four and Twenty Blackbirds,* almost all of the places featured in *Wings to the Kingdom* are—or *were*—real, and are reproduced to the best of my ability. Businesses close, buildings are torn down, the river rises… and I have no control over these things. A great deal of urban renewal has been inflicted upon the city, and downtown Chattanooga has changed a lot since I first moved there in 1994. It has been suggested that I'm writing about the Chattanooga that existed in 1997, and this might be a fair accusation.

It is entirely possible that I'm too nostalgic for my own good.

But at any rate, I've worked hard to treat the city fairly. Likewise, the battlefield park at Chickamauga, Georgia, is more or less precisely how I've described it. I add the "more or less" disclaimer because I am by no means infallible, and in the course of my research I encountered many competing theories and statistics on the battles and history of the park offered by various respectable historians.

This much at least is true: in September of 1863, Union and

Confederate armies clashed at Chickamauga for the prize of nearby Chattanooga, which was a key Confederate transportation center. Chickamauga's preservation is owed largely to the efforts of General H. V. Boynton and Ferdinand Van Derveer, both of whom were veterans of the Army of the Cumberland. In 1888 these two men visited the area and saw the need to preserve it to commemorate the conflict there.

Between 1890 and 1899, Congress established the first four national military parks: Chickamauga and Chattanooga, Shiloh, Gettysburg, and Vicksburg. The first and largest of these was the park at Chickamauga and Chattanooga; and in 2003, Moccasin Bend was added to the territories protected under that designation.

But other than these things, in lieu of any expert consensus, I made up some historical people and places, and I tweaked others to better serve my nefarious purposes. Most readers probably will not notice the difference, but I know a few Civil War reenactors who will happily stitch-count me to Kingdom Come. Please don't. It's only fiction. So I wouldn't go citing my facts on any research papers, if I were you. Just in case.

For example, there is no longer any cabin at Dyer's field— at least, not one that I could find. There *is* a cabin at the corner of Dyer's field, on Dyer's Road, with a sign that says "Dyer's" something-or-another right next to it… but against all logic, this is the Brotherton cabin.

There are quite a few aspects of the park that I can vouch for firsthand, though. The fog at night is positively unreal, and the Wilder Tower is a dark, brutal climb even in the middle of the day. I've known people who lived at the edge of the battlefield—which sits up against residential neighborhoods—and they've often complained about hearing artillery fire and disembodied cries for help in their backyards.

And yes, everybody really does have an Old Green Eyes story.

Furthermore, in a fine example of truth being stranger than fiction, the Moccasin Bend Mental Health Center is really and truly built on a sacred Cherokee village and/or burial site.

I couldn't make that up if I tried.

ACKNOWLEDGMENTS

Additional thanks, accolades, and a fanatical devotion to my unstoppable, socks-rocking editor, Liz Gorinsky; and similar gratitude goes to Lantz Powell, and to Dot Lin and Fiona Lee at Tor. These are the folks who have answered my questions, patted my back, and kicked my butt into gear (as necessary). They are wonderful, and I owe them the world.

Further friendly acknowledgments go to Karl Epperson and Cowboy, for being so gracious as to put in an appearance; and also, thanks to Scottie Morgan—comic artist and all-around nice fellow—for letting me call him Benny. Likewise I must note and give thanks to Greg Wild-Smith for providing me with the gorgeous webpage and hosting, because heaven knows he didn't have to.

And, as always, I declare my permanent gratefulness and everlasting loyalty to Aric (a.k.a. "Jym"), who was crazy enough to marry me.

ABOUT THE AUTHOR

Cherie Priest is the award-winning author of several novels, including the Eden Moore series, *Bloodshot* and *Hellbent* and the steampunk pulp adventures in the Clockwork Century series. Her 2009 book *Boneshaker* was nominated for both the Hugo Award and the Nebula Award; it was a PNBA Award winner and winner of the Locus Award for Best Science Fiction Novel.